THE NIGHT
THE RICH
MEN BURNED

THE NIGHT
THE RICH
MEN BURNED

Malcolm Mackay

MULHOLLAND BOOKS

Little, Brown and Company
New York Boston London

Mulholland Books/Little, Brown and Company
Hachette Book Group
1290 Avenue of the Americas, New York, NY 10104
mulhollandbooks.com

First United States Edition, May 2016
Originally published in the United Kingdom by Mantle, an imprint of Pan Macmillan, a division of Macmillan Publishers Limited, August 2014

Mulholland Books is an imprint of Little, Brown and Company, a division of Hachette Book Group, Inc. The Mulholland Books name and logo are trademarks of Hachette Book Group, Inc.

The publisher is not responsible for websites (or their content) that are not owned by the publisher.

The Hachette Speakers Bureau provides a wide range of authors for speaking events. To find out more, go to hachettespeakersbureau.com or call (866) 376-6591.

ISBN 978-0-316-27176-9
Library of Congress Control Number 2015953465

10 9 8 7 6 5 4 3 2 1

RRD-C

Printed in the United States of America

CHARACTERS

Oliver Peterkinney—A young man ready to make his way in a world that seems determined to give him few options. He's smart enough to make his own.

Alex Glass—As unemployable as his best friend Oliver, but much more of a dreamer. There are chances out there for tough young men, he's sure of it.

Ella Fowler—They call her a party girl, but it's all about work for Ella. Work a horrible job to pay for what will one day be a good life.

Ronald "Potty" Cruickshank—Certainly the biggest, and probably the most unpleasant, debt collector in the business. People are money, and money is king.

Arnold Peterkinney—Has looked after his grandson Oliver for a few years now, still worried about what direction the boy's life might meander in.

Billy Patterson—Ruthless, efficient and tough. Don't let the rough exterior fool you though, he's more than smart enough to grow his debt collection business in a crowded market.

Marty Jones—Marty is a lot of things. Pimp and debt collector are two of them, and a lot of people find those things ugly. Marty makes money though, and everyone loves that.

Alan Bavidge—There's nobody Patterson trusts more than

Bavidge. Tough, yeah, and seemingly without emotion, he does his job as well as anyone in the city.

Jim Holmes — There are plenty of men like Jim. Big, brutal and inexplicably angry, he bounces from one employer to the next, wasting no time in making himself expendable.

Norah Faulkner — It's not easy building a life with a man like Jim Holmes, you have to make yourself at least as tough as he is. So she has.

Gary "Jazzy" Jefferson — Jazzy provides a public service, lending money to those who couldn't otherwise borrow. Charge creative interest rates and sell the debt on when they can't pay. Easy money.

PC Paul Greig — A cop, and to many, a criminal. He'll take money from criminals, slip them some info now and then, but it's all in the name of crime management, you understand.

Roy Bowles — Decades doing a steady trade in selling weapons to the criminal industry. A good, reliable, solid individual: who could be better to work for?

Jamie Stamford — Alex MacArthur's hard man of choice, therefore a man who doesn't often have to face consequences. But then, you gamble like he does, and consequences will catch you up.

Neil Fraser — A tough guy, sure, but not a smart guy. Doing a few menial jobs for John Young doesn't make you important, he doesn't seem to have realized that yet.

Alex MacArthur — His organization has been running at the top for decades now, but that makes him old, and illness has left him weak. Even he can sense the change coming.

Howard "Howie" Lawson — A man with connections and no money, looking to get a little by selling guns to the suppliers who desire them most.

Peter Jamieson — Runs one of the biggest organizations in the city, maybe the fastest-growing too. A lot of people, like Marty, are happy to be under his umbrella.

Ray Buller — People think of them as old men, maybe a little feeble, but you don't get to be Alex MacArthur's second in command without being as sharp and dangerous as a razor.

Ronald "Rolly" Cruickshank — He created the Cruickshank family business, collecting bad debts from weak people, and trained his delightful, beloved nephew to replace him.

Kevin Currie — Controls the counterfeit end of the Jamieson business, and controls it well. A man to be trusted, a man to listen to.

Angus Lafferty — The drug business is a constant battlefield, and Lafferty is the man importing the goods for the Jamieson army.

John Young — Peter Jamieson's right-hand man, has been since the start. Very little gets past him, so you'd better stick to whatever rules he gives you. Not much to ask, is it?

Don Park — He's the brightest star in the MacArthur organization, which, coincidentally, makes him the biggest threat to MacArthur's leadership.

Mark Garvey — A gun seller, not as cautious as some, not as desperate as others. Always on the lookout for a good connection.

Gordon Aird — Mr. Typical, when it comes to a debt collector's clients. A man who only knows the value of what goes into his arm and will pay for it any way he can.

Conn Griffiths — Ranks among the best muscle in the city. Like all the best, he's not just brutal, he's smart too. That's where the danger lies, and it's why Patterson hired him.

Mikey Summers — Got a reputation for brutality, and once he got it, the offers flooded in. Chooses to work alongside Conn for Patterson.

John Kilbanne — He used to be a legitimate bookkeeper with ambitions. Might not be legitimate anymore, but he's still occasionally ambitious.

Andy Leven — Businesses like Patterson's are built on men like Leven, at the bottom of the ladder, doing the dirty work for him.

Collette Duffy — She hasn't quite switched on to the real world yet. When she does she might just realize borrowing money to pay your previous debt isn't clever financial management.

Liam Duffy — He has a good job working for Chris Argyle, and a sister he constantly needs to keep an eye on. It can be a hard life.

Chris Argyle — Everyone's known for years that Argyle has a growing business as an importer. Always been good at keeping himself off bigger people's target lists.

Willie Caldwell — He was Uncle Rolly's moneyman for years, carried on working for Potty. Not much lately though, poor old sod hasn't been well.

Steven Wales — Potty's full-time moneyman, charged with making sure dirty money comes out of the accounts smelling of roses, or any similarly fragrant cliché.

Ewan Drummond — A pal of Oliver and Alex, a boy with the same problems and the same ambitions. Bigger than them, and maybe a little dumber. Not a great combination, really.

Adam Jones — He's Marty's twin brother, and runs a club that Marty uses for some private parties. Whether Adam knows it or not, he's in his brother's shadow for keeps.

Nate Colgan — In the conversation about hardest men in a hard city, Colgan often tops the list. A man who can scare the beasts out of nightmares.

Russell Conrad — Like many gunmen, he's a hard man to know, harder still to like. If he's looking for you, you have a problem.

Ian Allen — With his cousin Charlie, he runs an efficient drug business that makes an effort to stay out of the city itself. Why pick a big fight when you're winning all the little ones?

Charlie Allen — Yes, he does get fed up of people calling him and Ian brothers, but who really cares? More than cousins, they're a damned profitable business partnership.

Donall "Spikey" Tokely — Trying to elbow his way into the gun market, but he's mostly selling to the young and inexperienced right now. People like himself.

Robby Draper — He'll sell you a gun if you want one, whoever you are. In desperate times, anyone who'll buy is a good customer.

Stephen "Gully" Fitzgerald—An old-school hard man, taught the likes of Bavidge and Colgan a lot of lessons they've put into meaningful practice.

THE NIGHT
THE RICH
MEN BURNED

PROLOGUE

He ended up unconscious and broken on the floor of a warehouse, penniless and alone. He was two weeks in hospital, unemployable thereafter, but that didn't matter. What mattered was that, for a few weeks beforehand, he had money. Not just a little money, but enough to show off with, and that was the impression that stuck.

It had been a while since they'd seen him. Months, probably. They were heading back from the job center, having made a typically fruitless effort at sniffing out employment. They went in, they searched the touchscreen computer near the door, and they left. Two friends, officially unemployed since the day they left school together a year before, both willing to do unofficial work if that was available. They bumped into Ewan Drummond as they walked back up towards Peterkinney's grandfather's flat.

"All right, lads," Drummond said, grinning at them, "need a lift anywhere?" He was as big and gormless as ever, but the suggestion of transport was new.

"Lift? From you?" Glass asked.

"Yeah, me. Got myself a motor these days. Got to have one in my line of work, you know." He said it to provoke questions that would allow him to trot out boastful answers.

Glass and Peterkinney looked at each other before they looked at Drummond. There wasn't a lot of work among their circle of friends. The kind of work that let a man like Drummond make

3

enough money to buy a car was unheard of. They could guess what was involved in the work, but they wanted to hear it.

"Yeah, we'll take a lift," Peterkinney nodded.

They followed Drummond back down to where his car was parked. Turned out to be a very respectable-looking saloon, not some old banger or boy racer's toy.

"Well, yeah, got to keep up appearances, you see."

Glass dropped into the passenger seat, Peterkinney the back. They were in no hurry to get anywhere, but this was too intriguing to pass on.

"Come on then, big man," Glass said with a mischievous smile, "what's this big job you got?"

"Well, uh, I can't really tell you much. Shouldn't tell you much, I mean. Hush-hush, you know."

By this point Peterkinney was leaning over from the back seat, crowding Drummond, knowing he couldn't keep quiet for long. Drummond's mouth and brain had always been loosely acquainted, so things he shouldn't say frequently slipped out.

"I mean, I suppose I can tell you a bit, but you got to keep it quiet, right."

"Sure," they answered together.

"I'm working for Potty Cruickshank. I'm one of his boys." He said it with such pride, such force, that they both assumed it meant something. Then they thought about it.

"Who?" Glass asked.

"One of his boys? The hell does that mean?" Peterkinney asked warily.

"Nah, nothing like that. He's, like, a debt collector. I go round and pick up money that people owe him. It's all legit. Well, sort of, financial services, that sort of thing. Good money, real good money. You know how much I made last week alone?"

"Isn't that dangerous?" Peterkinney asked.

"Not really, no. Well, now and again, but you got to be tough to make a living these days, guys, that's how it is. How else you going to make good money?" Said with wisdom he presumed but didn't possess. "So come on, guess what I made last week." He was desperate to tell them by this point and unwilling to wait for a guess that might be accurate enough to take the wind out of his sails. "Six-fifty I made last week. Worked four days, couple of hours a day. Six-fifty. I'm telling you, it's the life."

They didn't say much more to Drummond; just let him rumble on about how much money he was making until he dropped them off. They walked up to the flat Peterkinney shared with his grandfather, a poky little place you would only invite a real friend back to. They went silently into Peterkinney's small bedroom, a cramped room with nothing in the way of luxuries. There was only one subject of conversation.

"Six-fifty a week he's making. Him," Glass said. "He's making ten times what we make on Job Seekers."

"Come on, it ain't six-fifty a week. It was six-fifty in one week, but that doesn't mean he'll get it every week. And look what he has to do for it. How long you think it's going to be before someone kicks the living shit out of him? His teeth will be down his throat and his money will be up the wall."

Glass sighed. "All right, yeah, fine, but look at the money. He's making good money. Even if it's short-term, right, it's still money. And he's got to do some shitty stuff for it, but come on, you think we're going to get a job that pays us that for non-shitty work?"

"I don't think we're going to get a job at all," Peterkinney sighed, and slumped back on his bed.

A sentence he was tired of uttering. Glass sat on the chair in the room and tilted his head back, thinking about Ewan Drummond. No smarter than either him or Peterkinney, probably less so. No tougher when push came to shove, although he was bigger than them, which helped. He was no better connected than they were, which was to say that he hadn't been connected to the criminal industry at all as far as Glass knew. Must have gotten his foot in the door without realizing where he was stepping. All of which suggested that employment in the business, and six hundred and fifty quid a week, was within their grasp.

Glass didn't say any of this to Peterkinney because he knew what the reaction would be. Peterkinney would pour scorn on it; tell him he needed to get real. Peterkinney was all about getting whatever job he could, no daydreaming attached. That was fine by Glass; how his best friend had always been. A realist. They left school under-qualified and stumbled together into a job market that had no room for them or interest in them. So they struggled along together, and were still struggling.

Glass couldn't stop thinking about it, and that was really the point. People like Ewan Drummond were useful both in the work they did and the people they encouraged. None too bright and loaded with cash. He was a walking billboard for employers like Potty Cruickshank. A debt collector like Potty had a high turnover of staff, so that positive PR was worth its weight. Glass saw Drummond and knew he was at least as capable. Six-fifty a week, four days a week, a couple of hours a day. Think about it. The money, the cars, the women, the parties. Him and Peterkinney, lounging around doing fuck-all, waiting for some godawful nine-to-five that would pay them buttons and last six months if they were lucky. No, what Drummond was doing, that was real work.

It wouldn't have mattered if Glass had known. Even if he'd seen Drummond lying on that warehouse floor two weeks later, it would have made no impact. He would have spent the previous two weeks thinking of nothing but the money Drummond was making, and working out how he and Peterkinney could do the same. Nothing, no matter how grim, was going to change his mind. That was the way to make good money. That was the best option.

"I'll ask the old man if he's heard of anything going," Peterkinney said quietly. "We can go back down the job center again in a couple of days." His grandfather was going to have a word with a friend at a packaging factory on their behalf sometime today, although that would lead nowhere as usual. Their names on a list for future reference.

"Yeah," Glass said. But he wasn't thinking about the job center. Wasn't thinking about any sort of work that was going to be advertised. He was thinking of the world Drummond now inhabited. He was thinking of the money. He was thinking of the life.

PART ONE

1

Start with a kick to the door. He got a crack out of it, and the plain door shuddered in the frame. Didn't open though. Still staring back at them. Try again. Not a boot this time. Give it a shoulder. A short run-up and a collision with the door. A bigger crack and the door caves in, buckled on the hinges and smashed around the lock. Alex Glass stumbles in with it.

"Shit." A mutter under his breath. Embarrassed by his ungainly entrance. Embarrassment pushed aside by an attempt at professionalism. He's taking the lead here. Older by six months. His accomplice, Oliver Peterkinney, is still only nineteen. Anyway, this is Glass's job. He set it up. He found the target.

They're searching downstairs, through the kitchen, through the living room. It's a small house, which helps. Tidy as well, everything where it should be. No rubbish for someone to leap out from behind. Flicking lights on and off as they check each room. No attempt at subtlety, not after that entrance. To the bottom of the stairs. If he's here, he's heard them by now. He's had time enough to get a weapon. They didn't plan for that. What if he keeps a weapon by his bed? Something else to put on the long list of things they didn't plan for.

A light comes on at the top of the stairs. Glass and Peterkinney look at each other. Never been here before. Never been in this situation. If they had to make a split-second decision, they would be too late. A man has emerged at the top of the stairs. Older than these two by ten years. Fatter by three stone. Wearing nothing but his boxer shorts. That makes up their minds for them.

They're looking up the stairs, necks craned. Suddenly feeling confident. The amateurs just got lucky, as all amateurs need to in this business. Peterkinney moves up one step.

"All right, Holmes," he's saying. Because it is Jim Holmes, the target. He doesn't need clothes to look like his picture. Big and broad, with a thick head of dark hair and a dimpled chin. "We can sort this out nice and quiet. No need for trouble." Peterkinney's smart enough to know how dumb that sounds. You smash your way into a guy's house and tell him there's no need for trouble. This isn't how Peterkinney would have played it.

Holmes had his hands in the air, but they're falling now. Who did he think he was going to find at the bottom of the stairs? Maybe the police. Probably the police. Would be about fucking time. He'd raise his hands to them; try to make a good impression. Could have been worse than the police. Could have been a real tough guy. He knows Marty Jones is looking for him. Wants to send a strong message. Marty's big on sending messages. Marty is under the protection of Peter Jamieson. That could get him the use of a man like Nate Colgan. Now there's a man you raise your hands to, no matter how tough you are. But these two? These are just kids. The one coming up the stairs doesn't even look like he's started shaving.

"The fuck are you pair?" Holmes is growling. Going for his best tough-guy voice, which is pretty good by general standards. He's had plenty of practice. Being a tough guy is his job. It's how he makes his living. Marty lends money to people. That money gathers interest at a mathematically improbable rate. Men like Holmes collect the debt. But Holmes got a little tired of handing all that nice money over to a smarmy prick like Marty. Holmes did the hard work, deserved more of the reward. So he started keeping a bigger share for himself. Took Marty an awful long time to work that out, for a guy who figures himself as sharp as a razor. But he was always going to work it out eventually. Marty's no mug.

"We're here for Marty," Glass is saying. Saying it like it means something.

Peterkinney, three steps up, is looking back at him. Scowling. Shouldn't have said Marty. Should have said Jamieson. That would have carried more weight. Common sense says you exaggerate the power you have behind you.

"Pft." A snort of derision. Not aimed at Marty. Holmes isn't stupid either; he knows how dangerous Marty can be. A well-connected guy with a big ego and a short temper? Those are always dangerous. "He sending kids to do his fighting for him now?" There's a smile in his eyes. Marty actually has sent kids. There are other debt collectors he could have sent. Tough guys. They'd have done it too, for the right price, even though they know Holmes. Plenty of general muscle he could have hired for the job. But Marty sent the cheap option. A couple of kids looking to make a good first impression.

"Look, we can sort this out," Glass is saying from the bottom of the stairs. Still trying to lure him down. Trying to fool a man who does this for a living. Still hoping this can be easy. It was never going to be that easy.

Peterkinney isn't waiting. Holmes won't be won round. Once he has it in his head that they're kids, he's going to treat them that way until they change his mind. Only way to change his mind is to do what they came here to do. And the clock is ticking. You don't think the neighbors heard them smash the door in? You don't think they'll be calling the police right now?

Glass is about to open his mouth to say something else when Peterkinney moves. Jumping two steps at a time, getting to Holmes and making a grab for him. So what if he's older? So what if he's tougher, has a reputation for bad things? He's nearly naked. There are two of them. They came here to send a message for Marty. They can't leave until they've tried and they need to leave soon. So you do something, don't you?

Holmes has seen him coming. Leaning his weight forwards on the balls of his feet. Shoulders down, ready. Peterkinney is two steps from the top and reaching out for a grab. It looks like a wild attempt. A throw of the arms in the general direction of the target. An amateur lunging at a pro. That's what Holmes thinks. It's what he thinks when he throws his weight directly at Peterkinney. He thinks he's going to knock the kid back down the way he came.

That's not what Peterkinney's thinking. He's thrown his arms out there, but he's not watching where he's throwing. He's watching Holmes's feet. Waiting for that reactive lurch forwards. And now it's coming, and Peterkinney's moving his feet, pushing himself backwards against the stair wall with a thud. Watching as Holmes goes sailing past. Holmes's shoulder catches him, but it's glancing, no impact. Holmes is falling onto the stairs, shouting something loud that doesn't involve words. But Holmes has experience of falling over at other people's insistence. This is standard for him. He's managed to push out and wedge himself in the stairs, three steps down from the top.

But that isn't enough to make him safe. Not nearly enough, and Holmes knows it. You can't be on your back in this situation. You're either on your feet or you're out of the fight. You can rely on them being kids, but you can't rely on them being stupid. Before Holmes can struggle to his feet, Peterkinney's got his first kick in.

Knocking Holmes down a couple of steps with the first kick. Holmes shouting, but this fight is over. All Holmes has left is noise. Peterkinney jumping downward, kicking into Holmes with both feet. Peterkinney's landing on his arse, it's jarring but worth it. Holmes is bouncing down the stairs now. Glass had been moving up the stairs to help, now jumping down the last three to get out of the way. A grunting ball of flesh crashing down after him. Holmes has rolled to the bottom. Lying there. Not moving. Groaning, but not moving.

Glass is watching, doing nothing. Standing beside Holmes, looking up at Peterkinney. As far as Glass is concerned, this is over. Peterkinney's quickly down the stairs, standing beside Glass now. Looking down at Holmes. Taking a step back and kicking him hard in his ample guts.

"Try and knock me down the fucking stairs," Peterkinney's saying. Speaking low, a little spit on his lips. "That's for Marty. You remember that. That's what happens." An intensity conjured from a place Glass didn't know his friend possessed.

Glass is pulling at Peterkinney's arm. The job is more than done, time to go. A second person has emerged at the top of the stairs. A thickset woman, glaring down at them. The woman who keeps this house organized and tidy.

"Get out," she's shouting at them. "Go on, get out." She's starting to march down the stairs towards them. Wrapped up in a thick dressing gown, hair tied back, slippers too big for her making an unsettling slapping noise as she walks. Scowling like she was born that way. Moving towards her partner at the bottom of the stairs. He's groaning on the floor, rolling slightly. Trying to twist into a position that relieves the pain. Trying to turn his back on them, so they can't kick him in the stomach again. Facing the striped wallpaper, hoping this is over. Peterkinney's given him one last kick in the small of the back, he and Glass turning for the door.

The woman's still shouting something, but it's unintelligible and entirely her own business. They're out into the night, across the small front garden with no fence and moving down the street. Trying not to run, but walking fast enough to draw attention. The neighbors will have heard the door being broken. They'll hear the shouting. People will be looking out of windows.

"We should have brought balaclavas," Glass is saying.

"We should have brought a lot of things." Peterkinney's thinking of all the things they did wrong in this job. More than he realizes. Their first job. Thrown into it by Marty Jones. Someone with experience, a professional, would have done it differently. They did the best that amateurs could.

"First thing I'm spending money on is a car," Glass is saying. They're still walking too fast, but they're putting distance between themselves and the house. Looking backwards half the time. Nobody following. But then, nobody would need to. You can see their guilt from a distance.

Peterkinney isn't saying anything. Glass wanted this. He's in charge, so let him do the talking. He's his best mate, and you don't puncture your best mate's balloon. But this has been a shambles. They didn't think about it beforehand. Marty gave Glass the job. Their first chance to make a good impression. They rushed out to do it, knowing the prize that will be waiting for them. Next time will be different. Next time they'll make an effort to plan it. Having a vehicle to get away in will be a good start. Neither of them owns a car. Peterkinney doesn't even have a license.

They've reached the bottom of the street, round the corner. A little relief. They're out of view of the scene of the crime. Walking faster, almost jogging. Anyone looks out a window and they see two guilty-looking young men running past. The kind of guilty young men you remember. Maybe mention to the police if they knock on your door looking for information.

"We did it though," Glass is saying. "We fucking did it."

"Yeah," Peterkinney's nodding, and he's smiling despite himself. "We fucking did."

2

He's tired. They say you shouldn't drive when you're tired. He's driving, and driving carefully. Got the call twenty minutes ago. Doesn't know why the hell he's bothering. Petty games, and they've lost this round. So what, just win the next one and move on. But Patterson insisted. Get round there, talk to the man. Try to keep him onside. So Alan Bavidge is nearly there. Nearly ready for his conversation with Jim Holmes. Nearly caring about it. But not quite.

He's pulling into the street and already there's a problem. There are people around Holmes's front door. Must be four or five of them, standing on the patch of grass that serves as a front garden. Neighbors, probably. Some of them are still in pajamas. Nosy bastards. Get a little dignity, for God's sake. Semi-detached houses in batches of two, tightly packed along either side of the street. A mix of former and current council housing, he's guessing. Bavidge is stopping the car at the side of the road. Switching the lights off. None of the neighbors have clocked him yet. He's waiting. Hoping they'll bugger off back home before he goes in. An unknown guy in his late twenties at the scene of the crime will instantly become a suspect.

One of the neighbors has turned round and is staring at the car. A middle-aged man, glaring right at him. Turning and saying something to the group, proud to be breaking news. Now they're all looking at him and murmuring. A broad woman in her mid-thirties pushing her way past them. Norah Faulkner. Holmes's girlfriend. Not the sort of woman you marry. Not if you can help it. A tough one, her. At least as tough as her man. Kind of woman you might have thought would do a better job keeping Holmes out of trouble.

Bavidge knows who she is; she doesn't know who he is. With another sigh, he's getting out of the car.

Across the patch of grass and walking towards her. Making a noticeable effort at ignoring the gawkers. Nodding, and hoping she's bright enough to let him speak before she gets abusive.

"Norah? I'm Alan, you were told to expect me." Speaking as quietly as possible. Trying to keep this between the two of them.

She's nodding now. Still scowling, but nodding. "Come in." She's turning and walking back to the door. Stopping suddenly enough that Bavidge almost crashes into the back of her. Turning to her neighbors. "All right, you had your wee nose about, now piss off." Some of them are shaking their heads, giving her looks, but not one of them will disobey. She's coarse, and they're all just a little bit scared of her. Sure, they all want her arguing their case when the housing association routinely lets them down on repairs. But even when she's on your side, you're scared of her. They're all turning and walking back to their houses.

Norah's inside, holding the door for Bavidge. Once he's inside, she's trying to push it shut. Isn't working. Won't hold shut, just leans open of its own accord. The top hinge is damaged, Bavidge can see.

"Buggers managed to smash this in the process," she's saying redundantly.

Bavidge doesn't care about the door. If his boss is serious about Holmes, then Bavidge will send someone round in the morning to put a new door in. He's concerned about what he's not seeing. He's not seeing Holmes. She told his boss, Billy Patterson, that Holmes was unconscious at the bottom of the stairs. There's nothing at the bottom of the stairs. Just a wet patch where Norah's been trying to wipe blood off her plain fitted carpet.

"Through here," she's saying. She has a more feminine voice than he expected. Especially now that she's calmed down. A broad face on broad shoulders, a hard look about her. No soft edges that Bavidge will ever see. But they're there. She cares about Holmes, and she looks after him. This is a better life than most people in

Holmes's profession get to live. She's leading Bavidge into the living room.

Holmes is sitting on the floor, back against the black leather couch. He's tilting his head back, holding something to his nose that used to be white and is now red. He's still in his boxer shorts. He's looking at Bavidge. A glare. They've never met. Bavidge can only hope his reputation goes before him. When it does, it buys him all the respect he needs.

"I'm Alan Bavidge," he's saying. "Billy sent me round."

"Uh-huh," Holmes is saying. Turning and staring back up at the ceiling, more interested in what's pouring from his nose.

"Who was it?" Bavidge is asking. Not here for polite conversation. Not here to make a new chum. Get this over and get out.

Holmes went to Patterson. Ran to him when Marty Jones found out he was skimming money off his collections. Wanted protection from Billy. Offered himself as an employee in exchange. It was a hell of a job application. I want to work for you because you can protect me from my old boss. By the way, my old boss hates me because I ripped him off. Yeah, that'll get you through the door. But Holmes did get through the door. Not because he offered to work for Patterson. He got through because everyone knows he worked for Marty. He was one of Marty's boys for a few years. Throwing his weight around, trying to make a name for himself. Suddenly he starts working for Patterson, and people think Patterson is taking employees away from Marty. A cheap way of making a rival look vulnerable. So Patterson took him on. Just wasn't able to offer him protection in time.

"Them," Holmes is mumbling. "There was two of them."

"Who?" There's impatience in Bavidge's voice now. Doesn't care if Holmes hears it. Holmes is a thug. The sort of guy who goes round picking fights with drug addicts and hopeless cases. That's the difference between a tough guy like Holmes and a tough guy like Bavidge. The reason Bavidge has a reputation and Holmes doesn't. The standard of person they have to intimidate.

"Kids. I don't know who they were. Kids, working for Marty. Some shitty little bastards he picked up from somewhere. I can handle them."

"Uh-huh," Bavidge is saying now.

Holmes doesn't want to talk about it. Probably wouldn't have told Patterson at all if it wasn't for Norah. Doesn't want to admit that he got battered by a couple of kids. The big bad bastard, bloodied and beaten. It wounds his pride. A lot of thugs live off their pride because they have nothing else. Proud and stupid. He's a hell of a new employee to have on board. There's a few seconds of silence, before Norah decides to stamp on it.

"Smashed their way in through the front door. The *front* door. Jim challenged them. One of them came up the stairs, got into a fight with him. Threw Jim down the stairs. Top to bottom. Then they started laying into him. Vicious, like animals."

Holmes is glaring across at her, saying nothing. He doesn't want her causing trouble. He knows the position he's in. Screwed over one boss, already bothering another. Patterson doesn't need to stand by Holmes. Could just as easy leave him out in the rain. Holmes needs to be useful, and this isn't a good start.

Bavidge is looking round at Norah. Surprised by her disgust at the violence of the kids. She knows what her man does for a living. She's not daft. She must know that Holmes behaves like those very same animals on a near daily basis. The only talent he's known to have. Yet she seems repulsed by them.

"Billy Patterson said he would protect us," Norah is saying. "Said we'd be looked after. Well, a fine fucking job he did of that, uh? Where were you?"

"Norah," Holmes is saying loudly, then groaning and tipping his head back again.

"Well, where were you? Where were you when Jim was bouncing down the stairs? When I was confronted by those kids in my dressing gown? They could have killed us. We could be dead now. What sort of protection is that?"

Bavidge is waiting a second. Let her vent. Let her have her moment, she's not at fault here. Then tell her the truth. "You will get protection. What you won't get is a fucking babysitter. You're not important enough. You're not in enough danger. You got to earn that sort of protection. All your man has done for us so far is wake me up. When he's done something more useful, you'll get more in return from us. Until then, the best we can do is make sure there's punishment. Did either of you see them?"

Holmes knows enough about the business to know that Bavidge is close to Patterson. Not just some muscle, but a senior man. Right-hand man, maybe. You piss off Bavidge and you piss off Patterson. That's the way it works. Tell him what he wants to know.

"I saw them. Couple of kids," Holmes is saying quietly. "They didn't even cover their faces. No weapon. Didn't even have a car, Norah reckons."

Norah's nodding. "They walked to the bottom of the street. If they had a car, it was round the corner." She's talking quietly now too. Catching Holmes's mood. Bavidge's authority has subdued them both.

"Couple of first-timers, I reckon," Holmes is saying. "One of them was tall, over six feet. Skinny-looking, sort of light-brown, blond hair. Looked about twelve in the face, but he'd be a teenager, early twenties. That's the one that threw me down the stairs. Other one was shorter, darker hair. Never seen either of them before. They weren't working for Marty a week ago, I know that. Probably not in the business. New blood."

Bavidge is nodding. It's as much of a description as Holmes can give. Seems like he spent most of their visit rolling down the stairs. Should be grateful he can manage this much. Just need to find a couple of kids that have recently started working for Marty. Not impossible, but he does hire and fire a lot. All the kids go to him first. He has the recruitment tool of throwing parties with whores and drugs. It works.

"You going to be okay?" he's asking Holmes.

Holmes is nodding very slowly. "Don't think anything's broken. Nose is burst. Sore guts. That's where they kicked me. I'll live."

Bavidge is nodding. He hates these situations. People looking to him for leadership, just because he's close to the boss. He's not a leader. Doesn't want to be, anyway. "We'll find out who it was. We'll do something about it. Billy will be in touch soon about work. We'll try and sort this out so that Marty isn't a problem anymore."

A grunt from Holmes, nothing from his woman. Bavidge is leaving the house, happy to get out. One of those disgruntled neighbors might have phoned the police the minute they got back in the house. Doubtful. Wouldn't risk the wrath of Norah Faulkner. Just glad to be out of that atmosphere of stupidity and entitlement. Back into the car and driving away.

There's a feeling he gets. Like a weight, pushing him down. Like it's all basically pointless, and it's all going to end badly anyway.

3

Out the front it's all locked up. You wouldn't think a soul was alive in the place. Glass is starting to have his doubts. The Heavenly night-club. A large front entrance, shabby trying to look grand. Its dim name in lights. Glass and Peterkinney are walking past. They were told to go in a side door by Marty. They were told that side door would be open. Glass is leading the way round the corner and onto a narrow street where the side door is waiting. Hopefully unlocked.

"Hey," Peterkinney's saying. "Take off that jumper; we'll put them in the bin there. Come on."

Glass is staring at him, watching Peterkinney pull his sweater over his head. "Chuck them? The hell would I chuck this for? Cost me forty quid, this. It's a good top."

"People saw us. We were wearing these tops. The police will be looking for them. It's what people will remember about us. We need to get rid of them. If we go in there wearing the same clothes we used at the scene of a crime, what's Marty going to say? Us leading the police right to him?"

Glass is nodding. He suspects, wrongly, that Marty wouldn't say a word. Wouldn't much care. He suspects that if it didn't occur to him, it wouldn't occur to Marty. But it's a good point, so he's look-ing around to make sure no one can see him, and he's taking the top off. Something else to mention to Marty. How they sacrificed de-cent clothing to do a decent job. That might impress. Might even get them a little more money. Now that is naive.

Peterkinney was wearing a dark-green shirt underneath his top. Glass was wearing a black T-shirt, which is hardly appropriate attire for the company they hope to keep tonight. If Marty has a problem with it he'll just have to find a spare shirt. He was the one who sent them on the job. Promised them an invite to the private party in the club as a reward for a job well done. The job was done and done well. Now the reward.

Once the tops are stuffed into the black wheelie bin on the street, Peterkinney's dropping back. Let Glass lead the way. He's the one that this matters to. He knows Marty, or thinks he does. He's the one with dreams of working for the man. Glass is pushing open the side door, stopping and turning as it opens. Looking at Peterkinney with a smile. They can both hear the music. Not too loud, but a thumping background beat. The welcoming sound of a waiting party.

"You hear that," Glass is saying. "That's our reward, man, that's what it was all for." Giddy excitement in his voice. The reward he's always imagined but never seen.

Glass is walking in. Standing in the corridor as Peterkinney pulls the door shut behind them. Glass is itching to get to the party, but business first. Doesn't matter how good the reward is, business first. Glass is leading the way along the corridor, clapping his hands together. All kinds of adrenaline at work. Peterkinney behind him, sauntering along with hands in pockets. No need to feel giddy when it's not your ambition being realized.

Glass stopping outside the door of the manager's office. Knocking twice. Thinking there's no guarantee that Marty will be in there. He might be on the dance floor like any sensible person. Peterkinney is guessing different. This won't be a party to Marty. This will be work, and work will keep him in the office.

"In." A loud shout, making itself heard over the music.

Glass opens the door, steps inside. It's a small office. A grotty little place, in fact. It was painted once, but only once. There are scuff marks on the wall, little blobs of Blu-Tack that once held up posters. At a glance, Peterkinney can see little holes where something was once screwed into the wall. Probably a shelf that was removed for daring to take up so much space in this dingy little office.

A small desk under a small window, facing the door. Adam Jones is sitting behind the desk, staring back at them. Manager of the club, twin brother of Marty. He lacks Marty's charisma, Marty's ability to spot a good opportunity. Adam ain't dumb, he just ain't Marty. Marty, prone though he is to occasional misguided outbursts of ambition and emotion, is sharp. Not well educated. Not book smart. Just the kind of sharp you have to be to make it in this business. This revenge attack on Holmes would fall into the emotional category.

Marty's sitting on the only other chair in the room, to the right of his brother's desk. There's a relaxed smile on his face that his brother hasn't thought to replicate. Sharp, you see. Pretending that all is well and nothing can ever go wrong. It spreads confidence to these kids. The smile is false. Three girls didn't turn up for the party, which has left him short-staffed. This Holmes thing has the potential to be trouble if Billy Patterson can show off that he's gotten the better of Marty. There's a lot to hide behind that cocky grin.

"Fellows," Marty's saying, looking to disguise the fact that he can't remember their names. So many young men come and go. You use them; you throw them away when you're done. Bad idea to keep them on too long. Not unless they're specialists. You keep muscle because you need men that have a reputation to do your collecting. Kids like these, doing menial stuff? Nah. Use them once or twice, then chuck them before they get complacent. Bring in the next bunch of enthusiastic young whelps that'll do whatever you demand of them. Gratitude gives you an opportunity to exploit. It can be the difference between profit and loss.

"So how did it go?" The smile on Marty's face suggests he already knows. Both of them have walked back in here without a scratch and the short one's smiling proudly. They could walk in without a scratch if they hadn't bothered doing the job, but there would be no smiles. Not unless they were good actors, and Marty's seen too many of them over the years to be fooled.

"Went well, Marty," Glass is saying, and wondering if he should call him Mr. Jones. But there's two Mr. Joneses in the room. Better to differentiate. "He was at the house, like you said. We had to smash the door to get in, but we got in. Then we delivered the message." Saying it with an enthusiastic nod. Trying to sound casually tough.

Marty seems pleased, but there's more he needs to know. You hang around with big players like Peter Jamieson and you learn that detail is king. Marty doesn't know that Glass has skimped on the detail because he'd be embarrassed to tell about Holmes being in his boxers. Doesn't seem like a fair fight, when you tell the story that way. Almost makes Holmes sound harmless. Like he was the victim here. Marty doesn't care. Wouldn't care if Holmes was chained upside down to a wall when they got there, naked as the day he was born. He wants to know that the message was properly delivered.

"Tell me what happened. Details, boys, details." Marty's sitting back in his chair, looking up at them with that plastic grin. His brother looks depressed, but that seems to be a default setting. The look of the spare wheel.

"We had to smash the door in, like I said," Glass is saying with a nod. "Searched downstairs but he wasn't there. Then he came to the top of the stairs. Oliver went up the stairs. Holmes threw himself at Oliver, Oliver dodged. Holmes fell over. Oliver kicked him down the stairs. Bounced right down. We gave him a couple of kicks at the bottom. Told him it was from you. Made sure he knew that we were delivering your message, Marty. He knows. He won't forget."

Marty's nodding. Sounds like it went well. According to the general plan, anyway. They're probably putting some gloss on it, but they're entitled. "Anyone see you?"

Glass is shrugging. "Holmes, maybe his wife."

"Girlfriend," Marty's interrupting.

"Girlfriend, yeah. Don't think anyone else did. No one else in the house, no one out on the street when we left. We ditched the tops we were wearing as well, so . . ." he's saying, trailing off.

Marty's nodding. All sounds good. Sounds like they took the right precautions. He's assuming they wore balaclavas, because common sense says they did. He's assuming they drove away from the scene, common sense tripping him up and laughing behind his back again. If nobody outside of the Holmes house saw them, they'll be fine. Nobody inside the house is going to get the police involved.

"Sounds like you did well," Marty's saying. "Why don't you both go out there and enjoy the party. It's a good one." A pause, thinking of a little test. Play games with the dumb kids. "What do you think of the club?" His brother's giving him a dirty look. Adam knows what Marty thinks of the club, and it's not an opinion he would put on a poster.

"It's great, Marty, yeah," Glass is saying quickly. "Great club, great party, can't wait."

Marty's nodding, still smiling the patented Marty smile. "What about you, Silent Bob?" he's asking Peterkinney. "What do you think of this place?"

Peterkinney, standing slightly behind Glass, is shrugging. "Club's a bit of a dive," he's saying. Quietly but casually, knowing he's right and not seeing why anyone would have a problem with his opinion. He's not important enough to care about, not wrong enough to argue with. Not here to suck up to this pair. "Party should be good though. Location doesn't matter if the party's good."

Adam Jones is frowning from behind his desk, shaking his head slightly. Who wants to hear that casual insult, even if you've heard it many times before? That's nothing compared to Glass. He's turned right round on the spot and is glaring at Peterkinney. If he gets them thrown out, by God, he won't be responsible. He won't. Peterkinney's this close to blowing it.

The only person not frowning is Marty. He's laughing. "Brilliant. This place is a shithole. Everyone knows that much. But you're right; the party is the main thing. People don't give a shit about location if the girls are good, the music's loud and the coke is free. Overwhelm the senses, obliterate reality," he's saying, sounding like he's said that before and is proud of it. There's a pause as Marty looks at the two of them. Judging them both. He fancies himself a good judge of people. One of his many skills. The shorter one at the front, so eager to please. He's the desperate one, trying to get into the business. A head full of dreams and nothing else. The one at the back is different. Yeah, the taller one is the sort of person you might just keep around. He doesn't care if he's a part of it or not. Having a little fun, seeing what happens. Honest, tough, willing to offend. Knocked Holmes down the stairs, then came here and insulted the club. "What's your name, kid?" Marty's asking.

"Oliver Peterkinney."

Marty's giving him a look. A what-the-hell-sort-of-name-is-that-for-a-Glaswegian look. He's not saying it though. "Okay. Good. You two go enjoy the party. When I have another job for either of you, I'll be in touch."

As soon as they're out in the corridor and the door's shut behind them, Glass is turning on Peterkinney. He's started to talk, but stopped, realizing how loud his voice was. They're moving up the corridor, away from the office. Towards the door that leads out to the main entrance. One left turn from the dance floor. The music's getting louder. They can feel the little thumps in the soles of their feet as they walk towards the door. That's relaxing Glass, but not enough.

"What the hell was that? You want to get us chucked out of here?"

"For what? For telling him what he already knows? They want you to be honest. Surely you know that. How many arse-lickers does a guy like Marty Jones see every day? And I ain't just talking about the hookers he employs." Saying it with a smile, cutting the anger from the conversation.

Glass is rolling his shoulders. It's a thing he does when he knows he's lost an argument but wants to pretend it's ended inconclusively. It would look like a dismissive shrug, if it wasn't so self-aware.

Out into the corridor at the front door. The doors to the dance floor are shut, just in case someone presses their nose to the glass of the front door and looks in. Big heavy things, Glass leaning against one to push it open. Both of them stepping through and stopping. Must be fifty people in the club. About half of them are men in suits, the other half are all young women. Everyone looks like they're enjoying themselves, but only the women are making an effort. The men are playing, the women are working. Some of the people are on the dance floor. The rest are sitting round large tables on the right-hand side of the room. The VIP area. Glass and Peterkinney look at each other with a smile, and head for the tables.

4

There are a few different kinds of people who end up in the money business. Moneylending, debt collection, that sort of thing. There are people like Marty Jones. Marty does it because he can. It's a way of making money, but it's not the only way he has. He's the consummate opportunist. He found his way into the criminal industry with women. A pimp, not to put too fine a point on it. Since then, he's always been on the lookout for a good opportunity. Raising more money, raising his profile. And he got into money because it was a chance at fast cash. Wouldn't have done it if he didn't have the protection of Peter Jamieson. The boss of one of the biggest criminal organizations in the city. With his protection, Marty's taking his chance to elbow into the collection business.

For Marty it's just another string to the bow. Something he'll do while he can make easy money from it. When the going gets tough, Marty will shrug and walk away. Money's only good for him if it's easy. For someone like Billy Patterson, it's an ambition. He'll tough it out, no matter the threats. Surround himself with people like Alan Bavidge. Go out there and specifically target the debt business. Billy wants to build something that'll last. This isn't just a short-term moneymaker; he's in it for the long haul. Focused only on the money business, all day every day.

Then there's the third kind. Not a short-term money-grabber, not an aggressive grower of his business. The kind who've always been around. The lifers. People like Ronald "Potty" Cruickshank. He's actually only forty-eight, but he looks older. A big unit, fat and broad. Bald on top, and recognizable. Everyone knows Potty. Everyone knew his uncle Rolly. Had the same proper name as Potty, and Potty followed him everywhere. Rolly is still remembered to this day as one of the biggest bastards to walk the streets of Glasgow. A memory he earned.

Rolly set up the debt collection business back in the late sixties. He was lawless. Had no concept of the rule of law. Seemed to genuinely assume that it didn't apply to him. Treated people like seven colors of shit. Except for Potty. He loved his little nephew. The boy was always hanging around the offices. Worshipped his uncle. Learned everything he knows from him, which is the problem.

Potty was working for the family business from the age of fourteen. When big fat Rolly dropped dead of the world's most predictable heart attack, young fat Potty just kept on running the business. Did everything exactly the same way his uncle had. Kept things rolling along. But times have changed. The market isn't the same as it was in the sixties and seventies. More competition, for a start. More awkward police. But there's always a market. There will always be a market for money.

So Potty goes through life looking to hold on to what he's got. Always strictly following the rules his uncle laid down. No lending. You don't give money away; you just go and collect it. Always know your employees. You don't have to like them, don't have to treat them well, but you do have to pay them properly. If they're getting a decent share of the money they see, you won't have a problem with them. And protect your reputation. It's the single most important thing you have. Nothing matters more when persuading a person to hand over money. You lose your reputation, you lose your business.

Protecting reputation isn't just about keeping up the standard of the work you do. It's also about making sure that nobody else grows to challenge you. People will accept your standards are the best if they have little to compare them to. Potty has the biggest debt collection service in the city. Nobody's ever been allowed to get close. Forty-five years of Cruickshank dominance. As soon as he spots a threat, Potty stamps on it with all his considerable weight.

That's why Potty's been thinking about Billy Patterson so much recently. He's aware of Marty. Doesn't care about him at all. Marty won't last. Fly-by-night. He has good protection in Jamieson, but that's not the point. Marty isn't committed to it. Doesn't understand how much hard work it takes to maintain credibility in this brutal part of the business. He'll go back to chasing easier money somewhere else. That's inevitable. Not Patterson. Patterson's a threat.

Potty's on the phone right now. Sitting in the large drawing room of the large house that other people's violence has bought him. Potty, like his uncle, never lifted a finger. You hire dumb muscle for that. You do the organizing. You set up deals with moneylenders who aren't getting their money back. Buy the debt from them, and then collect it in your own way.

"I get that, Gary. I do, I get it," Potty's saying. He doesn't hide his impatience well. He's always either been indulged or in charge. When he has to deal with defiance, deal with people with a mind of their own…Well, it's not easy. It's why his two marriages ended violently. It's why he sees so little of his two teenage kids, both from the first marriage.

"Gary, listen to me." Said with more force than he realizes. Trying to be persuasive, but wandering off into vicious. "You sell debts to Billy Patterson at that percentage, and a few months down the road he'll be biting you for it. He'll have to make all that money back somehow. The money you save now, you lose later. You know the business, Gary. You know how it works. Really, Gary, I'm surprised at you. He can't buy those debts at ninety and turn a profit. When he needs that money back, he'll take it from you. Mark my words, Gary. Six months from now, you'll be lucky to break 50 percent from him."

Gary is Gary Jefferson. Everyone calls him Jazzy, but not to his face. Gary, like Potty, has a strict understanding of professional respect. Unlike Potty, Gary Jefferson can see the benefit of Billy Patterson. Potty buys debts at 75 to 80 percent of their supposed value on a safe debt. It varies, of course. Some debts are less likely to be paid than others. Some can be collected, but will cost more in manpower to recover. But Potty's always been a good buyer. He'll take on the bad debts as well as the good, just to keep his sellers happy.

"I know it's late, Gary. I appreciate that it's late. I can see the time as well as you can. I have a watch on my wrist. What you do not seem to appreciate is just how important this is. This could have a serious effect on your business, Gary. A serious effect on our professional relationship. I don't want that, and I really don't think you do either."

That was much more of a threat than intended. But it's true. Say what you want, history suggests Potty is right. Doesn't change Gary Jefferson's point of view. He can sell 70 percent of a debt to Potty or he can sell 90 percent of a debt to Patterson. People like Marty aren't in this equation. A jack of all trades, lending and collecting. A specialist lender like Jefferson wants a long-term, specialist collector. And he wants the one that will give him the most of his money back.

"That's all good and well, Gary, but you're not looking at the bigger picture." A pause. "Yes, I do know it's late. You have already pointed that out, thank you. Fine, I will speak to you tomorrow." He's pressed the button on the phone to hang up. Pausing with the phone in his hand, bouncing it slowly up and down. Now throwing it across the room. Not with much force, not at anything in particular. It's clattering against the wall and falling to the thick carpet. It'll be fine. It's made that journey before.

Not easy to get up. He's meant to lose weight for years, but there's so much else to do. He's busy. That's his excuse. Too busy to avoid eating badly. Too busy to exercise. Getting up in stages from the low cushioned chair. His second wife furnished the house. She picked what was attractive to her, rather than convenient for him. Potty's walking in a small circle. Doesn't know where to go. Doesn't know what to do next.

Target Patterson. That goes without saying. Doesn't need you to tell him that. But what do you use? How do you get at him? There have been others in the past. People who were brutal and ambitious, same as Patterson. Something's changed. Maybe Patterson is different from the others. More ruthless. Certainly done a good job of surrounding himself exclusively with hard nuts. Hard to remember a collection service run by such a collection of tough guys. No weak links near the top of that business. Or maybe it's Potty that's changed. Second divorce. No kids from that marriage. No relationship in his life like the one he had with his uncle. Nobody looking up to him. Nobody to pass it all on to.

He's growling loudly at himself and walking with what little pace he has. Through to the kitchen. To the fridge. For a bottle this time, as a matter of fact. A beer, and sitting at the large kitchen table. Sitting proudly at the head of a long table that only he ever uses. Tapping the bottle on the top of the table, and thinking. Plan every move. Better to be meticulous and dull than sloppy and dead. Another lesson passed down from Rolly Cruickshank.

There's a grim expression across his face as he makes his way to bed ten minutes later. A bedroom with flowery wallpaper and an oversized bed for his second wife to hide from him in. All the different strategies that have served him well have been considered and discarded. The go-to options that require nothing more than instinct these days. Patterson doesn't have the weak spots needed. He's been allowed to grow for too long. Growing in the shadows, nobody stepping in to slap him down. Well, whose fault's that? There's no worse anger than the one pointing towards you. Now that Potty needs to stamp on Patterson, he can't think of a way. Get help from someone else? Done it before. Use someone who isn't a threat to you. Nobody who could benefit from stabbing you in the back. But who? That's a tough one. Who?

5

The house is in darkness. Bavidge is ringing the doorbell anyway. It takes less than ten seconds for the door to open. Billy Patterson looking back at him. Short, skinny, shaven head. There are a lot of things you think when you first look at Patterson. Clever and ruthless are not necessarily two of them. That's part of his success. He's built a reputation as being relatively harmless. A tough wee fellow, a stereotype of the little hard man with lots of anger and little brains. Nothing the big movers need to worry about. Persuading people not to worry about you is quite a trick to pull.

Nobody would believe he cultivated that image for himself. None of the established collectors could believe that anyone would deliberately play themselves down. It's invariably the other way round. People come into the business, exaggerate their power. It's a way of attracting business. You convince people that you're bigger than they are. Convince them you're big enough to fear. Patterson was too smart for that. Why draw attention to yourself? Why invite rivalry? Let people think you're small and they leave you alone. While they leave you alone, you contact their debt sellers and do some deals. That's Patterson's genius, the ability to grow in shadow.

He's stepping aside to let Bavidge in. Walking through to the back of the house. A dim little lamp on in a spare room at the back of the house. The curtains shut, keeping the little light in. There's a small round table in the middle of the room for card games, a couple of seats around it. This is where Patterson has his business conversations.

"So?" Patterson's asking.

"They kicked the fat guy down the stairs. His girlfriend scared them off. No bloody wonder. Just about scared me off too. Beast of a woman. It was for Marty Jones. They named him. Couple of kids. Just need to find out what suckers he has working for him now. They come and go though, so…" All said in the sighing tone of a man who couldn't give a shit.

Patterson's nodding. He knows Bavidge doesn't see a lot of potential in Holmes. There isn't a lot, to be fair. But there's some, and you have to take the little opportunities as well as the big ones. Ten little ones can add up to stronger business than one big one.

"What was his reaction to being kicked down the stairs?"

"Got a little pissy about a lack of protection. Well, the girlfriend did. He didn't want to rock the boat. I don't know, I don't think they'll say anything about it. Never know."

Patterson's nodding again. Mulling over his next step. He could go down the tit-for-tat route that Bavidge is suggesting. Find out who these kids were and give them a kicking. It's what people would expect him to do. It's what Marty will be expecting. That's probably why he used the kids, because he doesn't care if they get battered senseless. They're not important enough to care about. So it would be no punishment to Marty if they went down that road, just PR for Patterson. And Patterson has never been about PR. Growing in the dark. Never predictable in his responses.

"What do you think we should do next, Alan?" he's asking. A slight smile, because he knows what the reaction is going to be.

Patterson does this all the time. He asks you a question he's already decided the answer to. Sometimes it's to buy himself time to think of a way of explaining it to you. Sometimes it's a test to see if you agree with him or not. With those he doesn't know, it's a test of their judgment. With Bavidge, who he knows so well, it's a game. Let him whine about how he doesn't care and how he'll do whatever Patterson wants him to do. Let him get all that out of his system before they talk about what's actually going to happen. What they've both known for some time was going to happen.

"I think if you go after the kids, this just keeps happening. I think I'm fed up of chasing little arseholes around the city, just to give them a kicking. I'm not kidding, Billy, I'm sick of it. I can find these kids if you want me to. I can kick the shit out of them if you want me to. I can kill them if you really want me to. But where does that put us? Marty Jones still has a queue of spotty-faced, snot-nosed little pricks banging at his door. You'll never scare them away from the life he's offering them. You knock two over, another two spring up. We need to do something decisive. We need to make bigger moves."

Patterson's leaning back in his chair. The ferocity of the answer has surprised him. It shouldn't; he's known Bavidge has felt this way for a long time. Just didn't expect it to all come pouring out like that. That concern he has about his friend is being washed away though, replaced with contentment. Bavidge sees it too. Sees the pettiness of moving against these kids. They need to do something bigger. Now Patterson's nodding, and smiling. Now he can share the answer he already had to the question he asked.

"You're right about the kids. There's nothing to gain from going after them. Not if we can go after a bigger target."

"Marty?"

"Maybe not Marty. Not if he still has protection from Jamieson. We're not ready to go up against that. Jamieson would crush us, if he could be bothered. Actually, I don't think Marty's even the right target for us, protection or not. We go after him, after those kids, what difference does it make? Amounts to nothing. As long as we keep chipping away at Marty, he'll get bored and go back to his hookers."

Bavidge is grimacing. "How sure are you of that? Everyone thinks he's flaky, but he didn't make money out of his women by being soft. Don't underestimate him, is all I'm saying."

"I don't," Patterson's saying. A little quieter. A rare warning has quieted him. "I don't underestimate that he's tough and smart. And I don't underestimate what Jamieson could do. I just don't see him as the right target."

"So?"

"So we need to look somewhere else."

"This is Potty Cruickshank again, isn't it?" Said with another grimace. Not necessarily arguing, but obviously not a cheerleader for the idea either. Potty still seems like too big a target to Bavidge. His history, his strength in this business, doesn't get wiped out quickly. It wouldn't be a battle to defeat him, it would be a war. They'd be smarter growing their business more before they turn their aim towards that sort of competition.

"Yes. Potty Cruickshank. We need to move against him, because he's going to move against us."

"I've seen no sign of that. His people haven't made any move against us…"

"I got a call just before you got here," Patterson's saying, raising his hand. "Jazzy Jefferson. Seems like Potty found out about my offer. Someone's been telling stories. Probably someone working for Jazzy. Potty tried to talk him out of it. Did a piss-poor job by the sound of things. Jazzy's still up for the deal, seemed a bit pissed off at Potty, but he needs reassurance. Needs to see we can handle Potty if things get nasty. I told him yeah, course we can. You leave that to me. I'll put Potty in his place."

Bavidge is leaning back in his chair. He doesn't like the sound of this. This sounds horribly like the start of a war a lot of people won't survive until the end of. The very war Bavidge has been hoping to avoid. The key to their success has been picking their fights carefully. This is throwing caution to the wind. The start of a new era.

"This is the way of it, Alan, we both know that. Can't keep creeping around forever. This stuff with Holmes and Marty. That's baby stuff. We both know that. You can't live off that forever. Eventually you got to step it up. It's either that or stay as we are now. Well, we're going to step it up, because I don't want to stand still. I'm not saying we go after Potty personally. He's still too strong for that. But we weaken him around the edges. Do the sorts of jobs that make Potty vulnerable. If we take him down, we have the whole industry in our pocket. I'm telling you, Alan, we take down a Cruickshank and we're it."

Bavidge is nodding. Nodding because it's true, and because it is ultimately what he wants. But all he can see ahead are the pitfalls. The risks. The fact that they're woefully untested at this sort of thing. There's a comfort in knowing you're good at what you do. Knowing that you will be successful. They're about to shed that comfort. Take a walk down a dark path where they can't see what lies ahead. It's easy to see that Patterson's excited by that. Not Bavidge. Patterson lives this life because he enjoys it. Bavidge does this job because he's reluctantly good at it.

"Look, Alan, go home, get some sleep. You're working too hard anyway. Forget about Holmes, I'll get someone else to handle him. He's not worth this much of your attention. Sure as shit not worth as much of mine."

Bavidge is nodding, getting up from the little table. Can't argue with any of that. "Let me know about Cruickshank. We don't want to hurl ourselves into this until we're ready."

"Course I will."

Bavidge is up and walking out of the room. Patterson's sitting back, watching him go. There's a creeping feeling he gets, watching his friend. Only known Bavidge for about three years. In that time he's become the person he trusts the most. An honest man, for this business. Intelligent way beyond his years and experience. And willing to do whatever it takes, no matter how much he hates doing it. But there's something about him. A feeling Patterson always gets when he's in Bavidge's company. The feeling that Bavidge is a man doomed.

6

Oh, it's a party all right. This is what they thought it would be like. What they hoped it would be like. Girls, basically. Let's not pretend they were looking for anything else here. The drugs they can get anywhere. The club is a dive. The music is one long headache with a faint hint of rhythm. Most of the other men at the club are in the industry in some capacity. All of them are more senior than Glass and Peterkinney. None of them are paying the young men any attention at all. Which is fine. Better to be ignored than looked down on, which is the other option.

Glass thinks he recognized a footballer at one of the tables, but he's not sure. Might have been. Only two kinds of celebrities stay in this city: gangsters and footballers. The former always happy to get their claws into the latter. They've ignored that table and sat at a quieter one. More sense than to impose themselves on others. Not really knowing what to do next.

Everyone else seems like they know the rules. Know how all this works. They feel like the only two first-timers. They're not, as it happens, but that's how it feels. Not that it matters. This is exactly what they pictured. Girls everywhere, and willing. Not exactly enthusiastic, but they're doing their jobs. If they want to get paid, they have to keep all the men at the party happy. That now includes Glass and Peterkinney. Being in a world where others exist to satisfy you is intoxicating.

This is where natural ebullience begins to pay off. They took a seat at a table that only had two other men at it. They were both at the other end of the table, on the other side, with two young women. Older guys, don't recognize either of them. Took about four seconds for Glass to start looking for women. He doesn't have a lot of experience with them. Neither of them has much. No experience at all with the kind of experienced women here. But that's what should make it fun. You're in a room full of women whose job it is to say yes.

Took him about five minutes to spot two alone. Went over and talked to them. Talked them back to the table. They're not pretending to be thrilled about being there. That's because they've done these parties before. They know the kind of person you should go for. First off, you want someone very drunk. Someone so drunk you're almost certainly not going to have to do any work that night. As long as you keep them happy, you get paid. There's no guideline on what you have to do to make them happy. Happy is all that matters. A drunk guy can be happy with his clothes on, because he's too drunk to get them off. Glass and Peterkinney are not drunk. They're also young, which is bad. The inexperienced ones are the worst. They think they can do whatever they please. Live out any gangster fantasy they have. They have less understanding of manners.

The girls have sat next to each other, the more talkative of them sitting next to Glass. Peterkinney now has two bodies between him and the girl he's guessing is supposed to be his. He's the patient type. He'll let Glass spin whatever yarn he's concocted first.

"I mean, okay, we don't have a lot of experience," Glass is saying to the girl, "but when you have a start like we've had, that doesn't matter. I mean, look at what we've done."

"What have you done?"

"Well, I can't tell you that, can I," Glass is grinning. "I hardly know you. Yet."

Peterkinney's wincing. Glass has always been terrible at talking to women. Pretty bad at talking to people generally when the pressure's on. Always comes over a little desperate, very rehearsed. In moments like that, Peterkinney's reminded that his friend just isn't that bright.

"How about we hit the dance floor," the girl is saying. "We can get to know each other better there." A smart way of saying, let's spend time together without you talking.

The yes that comes out of Glass's mouth is so filled with enthusiasm, Peterkinney laughs. Glass is getting up quickly from the table, but it's the girl who's leading the way down to the dance floor. She knows the routine. She knows that Glass doesn't. He's a dumb kid, trying too hard to impress. One of so many kids learning to be a gangster from bad movies. She's left her friend behind with Peterkinney, but neither of them is the talkative type. Or the dancing type, it seems. Sitting there, with two empty chairs between them. Peterkinney occasionally sneaking a glance, hoping the girl will be glancing back. She never is.

Must be the best part of ten minutes now since Glass went dancing. Still down there, putting all sorts of effort into looking cool for his girl. Truth is, most of the men are older than Glass, most of them are either pissed or off their face on something. He may just be the coolest dancer out there. All relative, obviously.

Peterkinney still hasn't spoken to the girl, and it looks like he never will. Another man has just walked past Peterkinney, over to the girl. Standing at the side of her, his back to Peterkinney. It's a big back, that's as much as Peterkinney can decipher. Tall fellow, broad shoulders, short hair. Sort of fellow you don't want to pick a fair fight with. You can guess his occupation from that, presumptuous as that might be.

The big fellow is pulling out the chair that Glass's dance partner was sitting in. He's leaning close to the silent girl and saying something to her. Too quiet to hear over the music. She's looking back at him. Peterkinney's just tall enough to see her face over the slouching man's shoulder. She looks unhappy. A little frightened perhaps. She looks like she doesn't want to be a part of anything the new arrival has brought to the table. She's saying something to him, nodding her head back towards Peterkinney.

Doesn't matter that she's sat there and ignored him since Glass and his girl went dancing. Doesn't matter that she has no more enthusiasm for him than she has for being set on fire. She's obviously scared of this guy. That makes Peterkinney take notice. Maybe not enough notice to help her, mind you. He might only be nineteen, but he's a smart nineteen. The kind that knows how to avoid trouble, by and large. But when the big guy turns round and looks at him with that ugly, beaten face of snorting contempt, it seals the deal. The damsel has herself a potential savior.

"You're with her?" the big guy's saying.

A slight pause. The big guy is too dumb, drunk, high and dumb a second time round to notice it. It's indecision. The girl recognizes it. There's a pleading look on her face. Yeah, she gets that look now. Where was that ten minutes ago? Anyway, he's helping. Helping because, smart as he is, he can be vicious too. That little streak that needs to be let out once in a while. Like now.

"Yeah, I'm with her."

Big guy's turn to pause. A nose that's been broken more than once. Lips that have been burst. The puffed and ugly look of a man who can't say no to a good fight. A slow smile spreading across his face. The smile he gets when he's thought of something clever. A smile he doesn't get often.

"So why are there two chairs between you then, huh? Two fucking chairs. What for?"

"Our friends were sitting there," Peterkinney's saying. His voice is loud, has to be over the music. But it's steady, and his expression is calm. He feels calm, as a matter of fact. Dancing with danger, and he's not nervous. He has the moves to keep up. "Now they're dancing."

But the big guy is still grinning. Sitting between the aspiring couple, turning in the chair to leer at Peterkinney. "I been watching since your mates went down there," he's saying. Slurring his words and nodding his head down the three steps to the dance floor. "You ain't said a fucking word since then. Neither of you has."

"You ever been in the sort of relationship where you don't need to talk all the time? Where you can just be happy to be together?" Peterkinney is asking. There's smugness in the tone, even when shouting. "Course you haven't, a guy like you. I feel sorry for you."

The big guy's not going to sit there and take that. You're a big guy, and you work as muscle. The only thing you have is reputation. You let people make fun of you and get away with it, what have you got left then? You're soft muscle, and nobody's going to pay good money for that. So he's standing up and he's glaring at Peterkinney. Ready to make this a fight. His first instinct, every time.

"Come on, get up," the big guy's shouting. "Come on." Shouting so loud people are looking. Loud enough to be more than a regular shout.

Peterkinney's looking up at him. Smiling. Not planning on getting up. He wants to sit where he is, try and force the big guy to back down. But it's not up to Peterkinney.

The big guy is lurching forwards. A big boot crashing into the side of Peterkinney's chair, a hand shoving him on the shoulder. Tipping him and the chair sideways. The big guy stumbling with the effort, but getting what he wanted. Peterkinney sprawled on the floor. It's embarrassing, but it's no more than that. Getting caught out by the big guy. Being face down on the floor, everyone looking. It's a humiliation, not a hurt. Humiliation doesn't keep you down.

Peterkinney's getting to his feet. The big guy is turning to look at the girl, grinning at her. She's stony faced. No change there then. She thinks her rescuer has lost the fight already. Peterkinney's getting to his feet, slowly. Considering his options before he picks the right one. Another new situation. You can handle it any number of ways. Laugh it off. The girl is nothing to him. Why should he take a risk on her behalf? But then it happens again and again. People see you as a guy that can easily be tipped off his chair. A guy that can be pushed around. No, don't want to be one of those. Seen what happens to them. That's not a life Peterkinney's going to accept for himself. Won't get him where he wants to go. You could try and bluff it. Talk the talk, play it out and hope it never turns nasty. Nah, any smart person will know you're a fraud, and it's the smart people you need to impress. You have to take the fight. Accept it, win it.

So now, in the second split second since he stood up, Peterkinney is thinking strategy. How do you win a fight you shouldn't win? This guy's bigger. Tougher. Definitely more experienced. If this is a fair fight, Peterkinney loses. So it can't be a fair fight, obviously. That means a weapon. None to hand. Create one. Only option. Might not be popular in a place like this, but anything's better than being humiliated by this moron.

Peterkinney's turned to face the big guy. Smiling slightly at him. Keeping it smug. Let him think that Peterkinney isn't nervous in the least. He is a little nervous now, but knows he should be more nervous. This could go very wrong, but that's okay, because he's decided it's still the right thing to do. He's standing beside the table, taking a casual glance at it. Picking up a champagne glass. Not his. Someone must have been at the table drinking it before they got there. Holding it casually in his hand for about half a second, then slowly bringing it down against the edge of the table. When it breaks, more of the glass falls away than he expected. Enough left to constitute a weapon. Enough left to intimidate.

The big guy is looking at him. Still grinning, but it's an uncertain effort now. The silent girl's eyes have gone wider. There's noticeably less movement around the club. People are watching. The people nearest them turning first, then the rest turning to see what everyone else is looking at. The key, having smashed the glass, is to not take any more initiative. Make sure people think you're using it only in defense. Otherwise you look like a nutter, and people blame you instead of the big guy.

"Why don't you fuck off," Big Guy is saying. Still smiling, still uncertain. This moved out of his control real quick. Not used to someone else escalating matters like this. Smashing the glass was his kind of move.

Peterkinney's about to say something when a figure moves between him and the big guy. It's Glass. Pushing out his chest, standing on his tiptoes and still only reaching Big Guy's chin.

"Why don't you fuck off instead," he's saying. Sounds childish. The little guy trying to be the big hero, but there's more to it. Looking to throw himself in the middle of the fight, sure. Also looking to stop Peterkinney from using that broken glass. Protecting his friend from himself, as much as this big lump.

"You're a pair of fucking idiots," the big guy is saying, emphasizing *pair*. Already looking for a way out. Trying to make it clear to everyone in earshot that it's two against one. That a man of his standing shouldn't have to bother with this sort of thing. Trying to make a withdrawal look like a victory.

"They'd have to go some to be as big an idiot as you are, Fraser," a voice is interrupting.

Peterkinney and Glass turning. Looking at the middle-aged man at the other end of the table. Standing up, watching the conflict. He looks angry. He looks important. That's enough to silence all of them. Balding on top, a middle-aged spread. Short fellow, good suit, takes more care of his hair than he should. Nothing much to look at, frankly. But there's a look on his face that straddles the border between angry and bored. The look of a man who doesn't like his night out being interrupted by those less important. A look that says he's used to people doing just exactly what he tells them. He's telling Fraser to back off.

Fraser, obviously the big guy, is looking at him too. Just staring back. Not saying anything. Leaving it too long. Anything he said now would sound too considered. Taking a step back. Trying to stare down the more important man, but not willing to open his mouth. Now turning and stepping down to the dance floor. Peterkinney and Glass are watching him go, walking along the edge of the floor to the exit.

As soon as he's gone, Peterkinney is turning to Glass. Nodding a thank you, getting a nod back.

"Find a bin for that," Glass is saying. Sooner the mess is cleared up, sooner everyone chooses to forget about what they saw. If there's no evidence, no consequence, there's no need to let it spoil a good night.

Peterkinney is gathering up the bigger bits of glass he can find. Glass is leading his girl back to the table, exaggerating his gentlemanly performance. Hoping he's scored a few macho points. The silent girl is moving seat, dropping into Glass's seat before he can take it. Making sure she's next to Peterkinney now. He's standing up with the glass in his hands. Smiling at the girl, who's now smiling back. That's a step forwards.

Now he's turning to look at the middle-aged man who stepped in to help. Too late. He's already sitting back down, whispering something to the girl next to him. She looks like a teenager. A pretty teenager. Not one of the bottle-blonde, orange-skin brigade. There's a few of them here, but not many. Marty's more discerning than that. He knows his clients look for something better. Something that gives the appearance of being a higher class, even when it's not. The aura of unattainability; nothing sells better. No point interrupting. That wouldn't be any kind of a thank you.

There was a bin over by the doorway. He tipped the broken glass into it. On the way over and the way back, three people patted him on the back. A couple of others gave him a smile and a nod. Men and women. People here to party, and people here to work. Obviously Fraser was not a popular partygoer. Back at the table, sitting in his seat. Someone's tipped it back the right way. On the tabletop there are white lines ready. Silent Girl is passing him a note and smiling. It suits her. The party's starting.

7

Had a couple of drinks, which was a couple more than he intended. Now going to visit a friend of his. Well, friend's the wrong word. Old associate. They knew each other a long time ago. Back when they both had hair and good health. Been a while since Arnie Peterkinney had either of those. At least as long for Roy Bowles. Roy's a few years older than Arnie, mind you. Roy is sixty-six, Arnie three years younger.

Been a while since they had any kind of a conversation. Shouldn't be an issue. You go a long time without talking to people, but they don't forget who you are. They sure as hell don't forget what you've done. Not if they're any kind of smart. And Roy Bowles is all kinds of smart. That's why he's lasted so long in this business. So long since the police even looked twice at him. He knows what he's doing, and always has done. That's why he's the right man to talk to.

There's a reason why it's been a long time since Arnie spoke to Roy Bowles. Since he spoke to anyone in the business. Arnie takes no pride in some of the things he did to make money back in the day. Nothing too extreme. He avoided the worst of what could be done, but he made some extra money doing things decent people should frown upon. He always thought he was decent. Always wanted to be. Spent most of his life doing legitimate jobs, working hard. But no great training, no great brain at work and no great luck. So he lost jobs. Never his own fault, but shit happens. Had to find some way of making money. On a few occasions he helped out old friends he shouldn't have been friends with.

One of those old friends was Roy Bowles. Roy was always sneaky. The quiet guy. You never quite knew what he did for a living. You knew it was illegal, and you didn't ask more than that. Arnie knew. It was guns. Always was. Bowles has been handling them for the best part of forty years now. Selling them to all kinds of scum. Doesn't care about the consequences, because the consequences have nothing to do with him.

Arnie didn't sell them for Roy, he collected them. When someone was selling a gun to Bowles, Bowles wanted a layer of protection. An employee who could go and pick the gun up from the seller. Someone smart enough to handle a nervous seller and tough enough to handle a dishonest one. There was never rough stuff for Arnie. Willing seller, willing buyer. But Bowles was a wary soul. So Arnie worked for him a couple of times over the years. Never for longer than he had to. Always glad to leave. You don't get a slap on the wrist for handling guns.

Now he's going back. Not for himself. He's approaching Roy's house to scrounge a job for someone else. Ringing the doorbell. Good Lord, it's late. Should not have stayed in the pub. Needed to steel himself for this. It's going to be awkward. Begging. Never mind, one thing he learned about Roy is that Roy is not a fan of sleep.

Door's opening. A look of surprise from Roy.

"Arnie." A pause. "Good to see you." Sounded almost like a question, the unconvincing way he said it.

"Roy. Too late in the day to have a quick conversation?"

They're in Roy's living room. He's insisted on making a cup of tea for them. Not what Arnie's bladder needed. They're sitting, talking a little about old times. Small talk. Tiny, in fact. Neither one of them cares at all about the conversation.

"So what brings you here in the dead of night?" Roy's asking.

"I knew you'd be up," Arnie's shrugging. "That never changes." Roy used to be up all night, even when he was married. Even when he was married with a kid. Arnie would get phone calls from him at two o'clock in the bloody morning. That was the nature of his business. Not many people want to buy or sell guns in the middle of the day. It was a nighttime pursuit, and Roy lived accordingly. "I need to ask you a favor."

Roy's frowning a little. Not easy to spot the frown on that lined face with the beady little eyes, but it's there. That was how Arnie used to start the conversations when he was looking for work. Roy remembers those reluctant conversations. Arnie hating the job but needing the money. Roy uncomfortable at having such an unhappy employee. He has a good memory. Another part of what makes him good at his work.

"Don't worry," Arnie's saying with a knowing smile, "it's not for me." He remembers those conversations too. Arnie knows he's too old and too long out of the business to work for Roy now. Things have changed since he last did a job for Roy. Must be close to twenty years. Close to ten since they had more than a passing word to say to each other. Now he turns up looking for a favor. Yeah, he knows how that looks. "It's for my grandson."

Roy's nodding a little. Noncommittal. He doesn't know anything about Arnie's grandson. Didn't know the boy was old enough to work. Better hear it out. You never know. Sometimes you end up unearthing a gem from these kinds of conversations. Rarely, but sometimes. "Go on."

"He's nineteen. He's a good kid. Sharp as they come. Needs to find some work though. You know how it is out there. There's nothing at all. The boy's living with me. It's not where he wants to be. He's desperate to get out into the world and do something, but…"

That's half the story. The half that Roy Bowles needs to know about. He doesn't need to know that Arnie's worried about the boy. Hanging around with halfwits like Alex Glass. Half-witted friends are no big deal. Where they lead you can become a big deal. As soon as Arnie heard mention of Marty Jones, he knew he had to do something. So here he is, doing something. Finding an alternative. Not a big leap up from Marty, but better. If Oliver insists on working for someone that isn't above board, it might as well be someone reliable. Someone who isn't going to end up inside, with Oliver in the next cell. Marty is a disaster waiting to happen.

"So he's looking for work. What's he done?"

This is where it starts to get awkward. Having to admit that Oliver's in no way the best person for the job. Times like this, so many people looking for work, Roy could have his pick. "Not a lot so far. Like I said, he's a kid. But he's a smart kid. A good judge of a situation. Sharp, you know. Clean record. I know I'm his grandfather so you'd expect me to say this, but he's a kid who's worth a chance."

Arnie's opinion was always solid, but that's not worth anything now. Arnie doesn't know the business now. And he can't be a proper judge of his own grandchild.

"Does the kid know you're here?" Roy's asking.

"No, he doesn't."

"So how do you know that he wants to work for me?"

"He's desperate to make a start," Arnie's saying. Thinking of him, hanging around people like Marty Jones. Sure, Arnie hasn't been around the business much these last twenty years. Doesn't mean he doesn't know about Marty and his kind. A fucking pimp. That's not the worst of it. A bloody debt collector too. Preying on the weak and vulnerable. Snaring them in a money trap and bleeding them dry. Ruining their lives. Anything is better than that. "The boy will be thrilled with a job with you, Roy, I know it. He'll take the chance if you give him it. He's a good long-term option." Throwing in the reference to long-term, because he knows Roy will like that.

Roy's pausing, thinking about it. His is a small operation, always has been. There are some who try to go industrial, but that doesn't work in a marketplace this size. You work in a city with just over a million people in it. That means the number of people who would ever buy from a man like Roy is relatively small. They want something cozy, trustworthy, long-lasting. Industrial doesn't reassure them. Only way you can sustain industrial is to be national, and Roy's never wanted that. He'll stick to his territory. Besides, you go industrial, and you get noticed fast. So he's always stayed small and that's always worked for him. One or two people helping him at any one time. No more than that. Right now, only one employee. Could do with a second.

"You know how it works, Arnie. I can't promise him regular work. Little stuff, now and again. I'll pay reasonable, I always do. Tell him to come round and see me tomorrow. I'll talk to him then. If that goes well, if I think he's up to it, I'll have something for him. Nothing regular to start, but we'll see."

"Thanks, Roy. I do appreciate this."

"You were lucky with your timing. I've only had one fellow helping for the last couple of months. I don't like using him as much as I do. I'd rather split the workload, safer that way. Draws less attention to each one. Still, I'm not guaranteeing anything until I've spoken to him."

Arnie's out of the house. Walking down the street, wishing he had enough money for a car. His poverty embarrasses him. He's always been a grafter, but he's had health problems. Lack of circulation in the legs making them painful and bloated. Angina. Damaged lungs too, apparently, you can throw that one onto the list. Lifestyle. That's what the doctor said. Hard living, Mr. Peterkinney, he said smugly. Bastard. He was right, but still a bastard.

Sixty-three years old and what does he have for all that living? A dead wife, a feckless son and a dependent grandson. No money, no job and no prospects. A small, damp flat, no car and a long walk home on his bad legs. He won't let this happen to Oliver. His son he did nothing for. But then, his son did fuck-all for himself. Ran off, left his wife and kid. Then the wife ditches Oliver with Arnie when the kid was thirteen. Good kid, but not what Arnie wanted in his life.

Now trying to do right by the boy. Find him work. Is this doing right by him? Setting him up with Roy Bowles? It's the last resort. Arnie spent months trying to find Oliver a legit job. Anything legit. The boy did his fair share of looking too. Just nothing out there. So it's this or Marty Jones. That's the only reason Arnie can justify this. The devil or the deep blue sea. Time to send Oliver swimming.

It was a long walk. Tiring and sore. He's grumpy by the time he puts the key in the flat door and steps inside. Cold inside. Always bloody cold inside. Switching on a light, and standing outside Oliver's bedroom door. These walls and doors are paper-thin. No privacy. Another good reason to get the boy out of the house. No sound from inside the room. Knocking and opening the door. Switching on the light. Little more than a box room. Not home. Okay, well, he's a young fellow, can't tie him to the flat. Out with his mate Glass, no doubt. Having a bit of fun. Fine. Lucky him. Arnie will give him the good news in the morning. For now, he's going for a long-awaited piss. Narrow little bathroom at the end of the corridor. Then bed. His bedroom larger than Oliver's, but small, damp and basically furnished. Struggling to sleep. Hoping Oliver isn't doing anything stupid.

8

Didn't sleep a lot last night. Doesn't sleep a lot most nights. Too much to think about. Plenty of work to do today. Bavidge has a small house, in a good area. Tidy, plain, predictable. The sort of house that hardly looks lived in. A house whose occupant has no interest in creating a home. He's a quiet neighbor, polite and well-mannered to all he meets. Occasional relationships. Never anything that lasts. He has too much sense to try to create a long-term relationship. Not with his work. With his lifestyle. That's just asking for trouble.

Does get lonely though. One of the reasons he doesn't much like being at home. Always alone there. He resents the loneliness that closes in on him here. No photos on the walls or mantelpiece. No hints of a hobby. No character. Just emptiness. Better to be out working. Day and night. On the streets, getting the job done. Make the money. Gain the security that comes with success. Then you settle down. Always persuading himself that that's the plan. That he'll see it through, and one day settle down with someone. Trying to persuade himself that that's possible for a person like him. It's a hard argument to keep having with himself. Cynical reality stamping on hopeless naïveté.

A quick breakfast, and out of the house. Consumed by work. Into the car and deciding on his first port of call. Not Jim Holmes. Someone else can deal with that hopeless bastard. Patterson will get someone to fix his door. Patterson will call him and reassure him that they're doing all they can. Might calm his girlfriend a bit, hearing from the boss direct. The plan to ignore the kids and focus on bigger things won't be shared with Holmes. He's probably still sitting on his arse in front of his couch, doing what his girlfriend tells him.

His first job is to drive past the house of Potty Cruickshank. Not exactly a job. A hobby, until there's a plan. Big place. Old town house, where old money lives. Gardens too well maintained to be looked after by their owners. Estate cars and four-by-fours. Bavidge has no intention of doing anything to Potty yet. Leave him alone until Patterson decides otherwise. When that time comes, Bavidge will have to be ready.

For now he's getting an idea of the man. He's seen him around. Watched him waddle from the door of a shop to his car one time. Didn't look intimidating, but Bavidge knew better. The ones who look intimidating aren't often the ones you should be most afraid of. Big tough muscular guys are not the best fighters. They rely on their muscle. They fight with the confidence of superior size. It's the little ones, the smart ones. The ones that don't have limits. The ones that don't have size to depend on. People like Bavidge. And it's the ones that come with consequences. Like Potty.

Bavidge has heard all the stories that get told. As with most people in the business in this city, most of the stories are bullshit. The fantastic criminal tapestry of myth, half-truth and possibilities. A lot of the bullshit is spread by Potty and his people. They know how to build and maintain a reputation. But some of the stories are true. Enough are true to make Potty a very scary man. Enough to make him an exceptionally dangerous target. Patterson didn't say it, but they both know it. If you're going to take down Potty Cruickshank, then you have to kill him. Leave nothing standing.

Won't be here though. Too many big houses. Too many people walking their dogs and bossing around their gardeners. Too many people wary of threats and on the lookout for strangers. Big front gardens. Long driveway up to the garage. Potty isn't daft. He'll have all sorts of security at the house. Every inch down to the road will be covered. That makes the drive past worthwhile.

Knowing that if they have to move in a hurry, this isn't the place you hurry to.

Turning at the bottom of the street and heading towards the west end. Work to do. There's a difficult collection that Bavidge knows hasn't been done yet. Other people are avoiding it. They have tough men collecting for them, but this one has been left simmering on the books too long. Has to be done. If he has to be the person that does it, so be it. Never bothered him much, the difficult work. If the job turns nasty, he turns nasty. If it's awkward, it's awkward. So what? You can't expect to work in this business and have no trouble. Accept that whatever is going to happen will happen, and face it. You either survive or you don't, and Bavidge isn't too concerned either way right now.

The guy's name is Jamie Stamford. Tough son of a bitch. Works as muscle for Alex MacArthur, which is reason enough to be cautious. Stamford's young and nasty. Thirty years old. Chucked twenty grand down a hole gambling on anything that moved and a lot of stuff that didn't. Patterson bought the debt for 50 percent. Nobody else would touch something that poisonous, which is why it was going cheap. Hell, the two bookies he bought it from were delighted with 50 percent. Just getting that much made Patterson their new best friend.

Finding Stamford isn't hard. One of Patterson's men knows the gym he goes to pretty much every day. Wait for him outside. Have a conversation. Got to find the bloody place first. Bavidge isn't one for gyms. His one impressive feat of agility was body-swerving the whole health and fitness movement. Not that he's unhealthy. He's trim because he works a lot and doesn't eat too much. But the gym? Watching yourself sweat and pant in a big mirror while running on a treadmill like a fucking madman? Running to nowhere. No thanks. More of a metaphor than he wants to stare at all day.

Took him a while to find the gym, but he did. Stamford's car is still in the car park. Swanky-looking gym, swanky-looking car. Gym membership won't be cheap. Neither is the car. For a guy with a twenty-grand debt, he seems to know how to spend money. How to waste it. That's because he thinks he can get away with it.

Stamford's been doing it for years. Gambling like a moron, throwing his money away. Getting into debt, and then hiding behind MacArthur's skirts. Being MacArthur's favorite muscle has gotten him off the hook on all sorts of debt. And every time, the debt gets bigger. This twenty-grand debt is the biggest yet. Addiction running further and further out of control. Nobody else wanted to buy it. Nobody else wanted to piss off MacArthur. Patterson basically bought it to make a good impression on the two bookies. But he figures it's worth trying to pick up.

Bavidge agrees. You let one thug get away with it and they all think they can. A free run for the stupidity collective. Stamford is an example the collection industry can't afford to set. So you go and get the money. You make an example of him. If he can't get off the hook, no one can; that sort of example. If MacArthur decides to get pissy about it, you ask him what he would have done. Shit, if the old man's dumb enough to have someone like Stamford close to him, that's his problem. MacArthur knows how it works round here. If you owe money, you bloody well pay it.

A few people have come and gone from the gym. All looking bronzed and vacant. All getting into their little mid-range sports cars or gaudy four-by-fours. Then Stamford. A bag slung over his shoulder. Wearing shirt and trousers, looking semiformal. Always a guy that likes to dress well. Those clothes won't have come cheap either.

Bavidge is out of his car and walking across to Stamford. Intercepting him before he reaches the safety of his car. Black Nissan GT-R, polished to a mirrored shine. Stamford's seen him coming. Been muscle long enough to know trouble when he sees it. But he's bigger than Bavidge. Taller, broader, firmer and with a longer reach. All the things he thinks matter. He doesn't know who Alan Bavidge is. Doesn't know what he's done in his life. And his financial management shows that he's a complacent prick with the judgment of a lemming. So Bavidge isn't worrying too much.

"Jamie. Good workout?"

Stamford's looking at him. Sneering, but with way too much effort to look anything other than dumb. "What are you, cop?"

And Bavidge is laughing. A genuine laugh too. Not just doing it to piss Stamford off. Bavidge looks so much younger when he laughs. He can look so happy. It is hilarious that Stamford thinks Bavidge is a cop. Coming to question or arrest Stamford on his own? Yeah, right. He really is dumb muscle if he can't tell the difference between a collector and a cop.

"No, I'm not a cop. I just wanted to have a wee chat about some money you owe."

"I don't owe any money," Stamford's saying, moving to push past Bavidge to his car. Confident and dismissive and happy that this isn't a conversation he needs to worry about.

Lay down a marker. You let him push past you once and he keeps trying to push past you. You let him walk away from this conversation and you never get him back. The key to being a good collector is setting the tone. Do it early. Make sure the person knows who controls this. Make sure they know it's never going to be them.

So Bavidge is shoving hard against Stamford. Shoulder to shoulder. Stamford is bigger, but he's not expecting it. People don't shove back against him. So when Bavidge does, Stamford stumbles. And now he's looking at Bavidge. A little bit of disbelief. A lot of anger. Ready to lash out, which is why Bavidge is acting first. He's done this sort of thing before, you will have gathered.

"You throw a punch and this gets out of control fast," Bavidge is saying with a snarl. "I'm here to let you know how it's going to be. You owe exactly twenty thousand, one hundred and forty-two pounds. You are going to pay exactly twenty thousand, one hundred and forty-two pounds. No discounts. No deals. No getting off the hook. No hiding behind your boss like a pussy. We have your debt and we are going to collect. Other people might not collect on you, Stamford, but I will. You're fuck-all to me. No hiding. However far I have to go to get that money, I will go."

Almost doesn't matter what you say. Chances are Stamford's heard some variation of this before, and it meant nothing to him then. He's wriggled off so many similar hooks, the words don't matter anymore. It's all about tone. You have to sound threatening. You have to sound confident. You can't afford to sound like you're out of control. And you can't afford to sound like you're trying your hardest. He has to believe that you have several more gears of the tough-bastard routine to go through.

Stamford's taking a step back, which is good. Everything he says beyond this point means nothing. Point is, he stepped back. He's not trying to push through. He's accepted that Bavidge is controlling this conversation. It ends when Bavidge says it does.

"You don't know who you're fucking with, pal."

"Not a pal. And I do know. Jamie Stamford. Slack-jawed piss ant for Alex MacArthur. Problem gambler. Using his boss to get off the hook. Not anymore. This is a big debt and a big problem, Jamie. Twenty grand. You need to pay that money, before it buries you."

Can't make it clearer than that. But with some people, you can never make it clear enough. Stamford is starting to laugh. Not the nervous laugh of someone trying to look strong in a weak position. The complacent laugh of someone who knows their boss is bigger than any collector in the city. Who knows he has enough standing with the boss to expect yet another bailout.

Kill that complacency. Fast. A punch in the stomach and Stamford is stepping backward. Not a great punch, but he wasn't expecting it, so it had impact. The second one's better. Side of the mouth. It'll definitely bruise, might even loosen a tooth or two. Always leave them something to remember you by. Always leave them with a mark they have to explain to others. Keeps reminding them how serious you are. It'll bruise Bavidge's knuckles as well, but he has no one to have to explain that to. Stamford still isn't down. He's set his feet well, ready to counter. But this is one of those rare occasions where Stamford is not the more experienced fighter. Bavidge is charging him. Catching him hard with his shoulder, right in the chest. Stamford is down. On his back, instinctively trying to get back to his feet quickly. Ignoring the pain in the back of his head where it hit the concrete to try and get vertical. Always stay on your feet. Golden rule. But Bavidge is on him. He didn't go down in the charge. That was the point. Now he's kneeling down. Putting his knee, and all his weight, on the side of Stamford's neck.

"You want to go running to MacArthur? Fine, you go running to him. I'll let you up and you can mince off to him now. You can cry into his fucking lap. Tell him what I did to you. Every time you go to him, he thinks less of you. You do get that, don't you? You understand that every time he has to rescue you, he hates you a wee bit more? The more he has to help, the less he wants to. That's rule number one. Never beg from your boss. You've been doing that a lot, haven't you, Jamie?"

"Get off me. You're fucking dead."

"Sooner or later," Bavidge is saying, leaning in closer and lowering his voice, "you're going to have to clean up your own shit. Start with this one. Impress the world by doing your own dirty work for once. Get my twenty grand. If I don't have it inside a fortnight, I'm coming back for you."

Bavidge is getting up now. Two people have come out of the gym. They're standing close to the glass door, watching. Both dressed the same, so they must be staff. Must have seen it on the security camera. Bavidge is turning and walking back towards his car. He can hear the scuff of Stamford getting quickly to his feet. Waiting for the idiot to make a charge at him.

"Is everything okay?" one of the staff is shouting across.

Bavidge is ignoring them. So is Stamford. Bavidge is at his car. Dropping into the driver's seat, facing Stamford. He's beside his car now, angrily throwing his bag into the passenger seat. Watching Bavidge as he drives away. Didn't go brilliantly. Didn't go badly. Probably won't get the money, which is why he's going to have to pay Stamford another visit. Something else he won't bother looking forward to.

9

There are memories. They're vague, but they're definitely there. Some of them might be imaginary. Romanticized, at least. But Oliver Peterkinney can remember a few things about the night before. He remembers them as soon as he wakes up on the floor of Alex Glass's living room. Yeah, that was a good night. He's blinking heavily, and then looking around. Nobody there. Just him.

Ah, that's what that bang was. The front door. Someone leaving the flat. Who was it? Probably the silent girl. She didn't say a lot last night, even after the four of them came back to the flat. She seemed happy, at least. Sure as hell relaxed. And they had a good time. He thinks.

There was more alcohol. There was sex. There, the memories get a little confused. They were in the living room. Glass and his girl went into the only bedroom in the flat. Then there's another memory. On top of the silent girl. The other girl sitting on the floor behind him. His leg rubbing against the thigh of the other girl while she sat there. Did that happen? Maybe not. Probably not. He remembers the feeling of skin. That's about it.

He's wondering what the silent girl thought of him as he finds the pile of his clothes on the couch. Why was he on the floor and the clothes on the couch? No idea. Never mind. What did she think? Not a lot, probably. He doesn't remember much about his own performance. Did he speak well? Was he intelligent and funny? Did he seduce her and perform manfully? Not bloody likely. He was drunk and high and has little experience with either state. That won't have helped. And she's a hooker, after all. How much experience of better men does she have? Ah well, she's gone anyway. He can make any assumption he wants, and she isn't here to contradict.

Into the bathroom. Grubby little bathroom. When he gets a place of his own, he'll keep it cleaner than this. His grandfather's flat is tiny too, but at least it's clean. A lot of cold water on his face. He's nearly woken up now. Feels like he needs a shower. Smells like he needs a shower. Not this shower. He'll get one when he goes home. Stand in the bath, then wrap himself in a towel and go sit on the radiator in his bedroom in the search for heat. For now, he just needs to be awake.

He's in the kitchen now, trying to find some coffee. Scruffy kitchen. Not dirty, just everything scratched and scuffed and poorly maintained. The cooker and toaster and kettle all old, on their last legs. The best Glass could afford, but the best isn't much. Peterkinney's thinking about Jim Holmes. Jesus, what a mess they made of that. Okay, they got away with it on the night, but come on. What a fucking joke performance. They made enough mistakes to fill a book with. He's shaking his head. You learn by doing. Learn by making mistakes. Last night they learned a lot.

And he's thinking about Marty Jones. Slimy bastard. Asking them questions in his brother's office. Trying to play the king of the castle. He's well connected though. Everyone knows that. Connected to Peter Jamieson. Everyone knows that much because Marty makes a point of telling them. That's his protection. People need to know how protected he is. The money he makes from parties like last night's is one of the reasons he has that protection. He might be slimy and an arsehole, but he always knows how to make good money. That's a trick worth knowing. A trick to be envied.

They were the victims of the sharp man's trick last night. Played them like the kids they are. He could have sent anyone to handle that Holmes job. Sent someone more experienced, who would have handled it better. But he didn't. He chose kids because he wanted someone he didn't care about. Someone that didn't matter. If Holmes had battered them. If the cops had caught them. Doesn't matter. Message is still delivered. Holmes knows that Marty's willing to try and get him. The quality of the job didn't matter, just the message. So he sent the kids.

Peterkinney's filling his mug when Glass wanders in. In boxers and a T-shirt. Grinning like a child at Christmas. Now he's stopping, looking around.

"Where's your girl?"

"Think she left," Peterkinney's saying with a shrug.

"Ah," Glass is saying, and tilting his head with exaggerated sympathy. "Well, it's harder to keep them than get them. Some of us have that gift, some of us do not. Mine's still lying in bed, happy and waiting for a cup of that stuff."

Just a little too smug to go unchallenged. "Of course they're harder to keep than to get. They're prostitutes. That's the point. You're not supposed to keep them."

"Hey, it's not like that," Glass is saying. A little angry now. Peterkinney can be caustic when he wants. Has a habit of knocking down other people's good moments. Putting Glass on the defensive, because he knows he's smart enough to keep him there. "Me and Ella were just talking about it."

"Ella?"

"Her. The girl."

"The prostitute?"

"Fuck off. We were talking about it. Look, it's not the way you think it is. They're not like hookers or anything. They go to parties. That's it. They go to parties and dance along with the guys. Keep them happy. That's it. It's not as bad as you're making it out. It's not."

"That's not what you were saying yesterday," Peterkinney's arguing. Keeping his voice down so the girl doesn't hear. He's incredulous at his friend, but he still has some manners. "When Marty said we could go to the party after the job, you said we were on a promise. You said it was guaranteed. You said the girls had to. That's their job."

"I said, I said, I said. The hell are you listening to me for all of a sudden, Captain Snarky. I said that yesterday when I didn't know. I was just going on the rumors and shit. Now I know. I've spoken to Ella and I know."

Peterkinney isn't saying anything. Getting out of Glass's way so he can make another two cups of coffee. Seems pretty obvious that Glass knew better before the party. He said it was guaranteed and he turned out to be right. Apparently evidence isn't worth as much as a naked girl's point of view.

By the time Glass has finished making the coffee, she's come into the kitchen looking for him. She's four years older than Glass, but she looks and acts younger. Peterkinney can see the difference between her and the silent girl straight away. The silent girl was mature enough to see the misery in what she was doing. To see how it will all end if she keeps doing it. Not this girl. Not Ella. She only sees the potential upsides. Blind optimism.

"Here you go," Glass is saying, passing her the cup.

She's wearing what she was wearing last night. Last night a short skirt and tight shirt open three buttons down was appropriate. Worked well in the club. Here it looks ridiculous. She's taking the mug and sipping from it.

"What are you guys doing today?" she's asking Glass. Glancing at Peterkinney to politely include him, but focusing on Glass. Talking sweetly to her new favorite person in the whole wide world.

"Uh, don't know really. Probably go see Marty," Glass is shrugging, looking at Peterkinney. "See if he has any work needs doing. You know, make ourselves useful, get some cash in our pockets."

"So you work for Marty?" she's asking. She seems impressed by this. What's so impressive about it, Peterkinney can't guess.

"Yeah, we do," Glass is saying. There's pride in his voice.

Peterkinney is looking at him, but not saying anything. If these two want to be so impressed by Marty, let them. Their mistake. They're all being used by that snake, only Peterkinney can see it. It's depressing to think that the other two aren't smart enough to see that. Fine, whatever, let them circle the drain hand in hand.

"I work for him too," she's saying. Said with an enthusiasm she doesn't get to use often regarding work. Smiling at Glass, at this thing they have in common. The bond of working for the same guy, and not telling people what they do. The secret of success. Like working for Marty is a ticket to wealth, health and happiness that only they know about.

Where the hell is this pride coming from? What's to be proud of? Peterkinney's draining the last of his mug in one scalding gulp. Marty Jones is scum. Even Marty Jones knows that. The entire population of the world that doesn't know it is now concentrated entirely within this kitchen. A place Peterkinney doesn't much want to be anymore.

"It was nice to meet you, Ella," he's saying. "I'd better head home. I'll call you later," he's saying to Glass.

Ella smiled politely and nodded to him, but she could see he was faking the smile he gave back. He didn't like her, but he was leaving. Now she's turning to smile at Glass instead, because his smile is real. Glass is shouting to make sure he does call as Peterkinney pulls the front door shut behind him. He doesn't always call. There isn't always a reason to call. No guarantee that last night will change that. They did a bad job well enough. They got Marty what he wanted. Doesn't mean that Marty has any intention of using them again.

10

Arnie is sitting in the kitchen when he hears the key in the front door. He's sitting and waiting. Don't rush the boy. Don't start pelting him with questions. He doesn't like it. Always been thin-skinned and bloody-minded. Doesn't like being asked a question he doesn't want to answer. Never afraid to show you that he doesn't like it.

He's closed the door, coming along the corridor. Where he goes first is usually a good indicator of his mood. Into his bedroom and he's in no mood to talk. Nope. Past his bedroom door and along the narrow corridor to the kitchen.

"Hey Grandpa," he's saying, giving an ironic twang to the word "Grandpa." Knowing Arnie isn't thrilled about feeling his age.

"Funny hour of the morning to be coming home at night," Arnie's saying.

"Yeah, good one. I stayed over at Alex's."

He's getting a chocolate biscuit from a cupboard. That's breakfast out of the way. Now he's making his way out of the kitchen. There's hardly enough room for the two of them in here anyway. The old yellow cupboards dominate the space. There's a fridge-freezer, a cooker and a little table that's been there for over twenty years, always folded. You can sit a person on either side of the table when it's folded like that. Just enough. Arnie always sits on the far side, where he has a view of the door out to the corridor. Where he's sitting now. And that's it. That's all the furniture the kitchen can hold, and it still leaves not quite enough floor space for two people to avoid elbowing each other.

"I have some news," Arnie's saying, calling him back. Not looking at him, because Oliver won't be thrilled about his grandfather sticking his nose into his business. Got that from his father. He had no business worth sticking your nose into, but he protected it jealously. Too bad, it's for Oliver's own good. "I spoke to a friend of mine last night. Said he might have some work for a smart young man. If a smart young man is interested."

"He is." Peterkinney junior is standing in the doorway, looking down at his grandfather. Wary of what crappy job might be available to him. But enthusiastic, because a job is a job. A job is money, and money is a place of his own. A car. A life. Money is the one thing he's never had in his life, and has always wanted. Strange tone in the old man's voice. He hardly sounds thrilled with his achievement. "Who's the friend?"

"Man named Roy Bowles. You ever heard of Roy Bowles?"

"Don't think so, no."

"No. Well, that's because he's too smart to be known. Roy is . . . Well, Roy's not a good person. I used to work for him, so I know. I've seen it all with my own eyes, what becomes of it. Listen to me, Oliver. If you go work for him, I want you to promise me something. I want you to promise that you won't stop looking for a proper job. Something you don't have to hide from people. What Roy does is rotten. Rotten from end to end."

"Jesus, what have you set me up with?" Said as a joke, but the smile isn't entirely light-hearted.

"He buys and sells guns. Not legally, obviously. The stuff he'll want you to do, well, he'll want you to do donkey work. Go pick things up for him, that sort of thing. You'll have to be smart. And discreet. Very discreet. It'll only be now and again he uses you, so you ain't getting rich off this. You'll make something, and that's a start. But not riches. Hopefully, that'll keep you looking for something else."

"Okay," Oliver's nodding. Actually sounds like it could be useful. Occasional work, but the pay won't be bad. Something like that, there has to be decent money around. Come on, guns shift for good money. Could be little work with decent pay. "When do I go see him?"

"Today. Afternoon. I'll write down his address for you. And the first thing you're going to do with any money you make is get driving lessons. You'll need a car to be taken seriously with something like this. You don't want people thinking you're just some kid."

Watching his grandson leave the room. That felt wrong. It felt like he just kicked the boy into a hole. But what else could he do? What's the other option? Let him wander round the streets with Alex Glass, trying to impress people like Marty Jones? No fucking way. Not a chance. This is better than that. Has to be.

A shower. Struggling to get dry in a flat damper than he is. Finding some decent clothes to wear to go visit Roy Bowles. This is a chance. Then the phone's ringing out in the hallway. Arnie's out. Gone to the shops, as he often does. Goes out and gets a handful of things. Never just buys the week's needs in one go. He says it's about saving money. Oliver thinks it's about having an excuse to get out of the flat more often. Can't blame him. Picking up the phone.

"Hello."

"Is this Oliver Peterkinney?" There's a slightly mocking tone in the voice, like the name is just too funny to say normally.

"Speaking."

"This is Marty Jones. We should talk. Come round to the club, be here at twelve." And he's hung up. Presumptuous bastard. Calling it the club, like he owns it. His brother is the manager, that's it. Neither of them owns that dive.

A look at his watch. He can make it for midday and still have plenty of time to go see Roy Bowles. He's out of the flat and running. Drenched in sweat is not the best way to turn up at the club, but he doesn't have time for a stroll. Marty obviously thinks Peterkinney has transport. That he can get to the club at the drop of a hat. Thinks he can even afford a bus fare, which he can't. Not without thinking long and hard about the other things he needs the money for. Oh boy, this amateurism is going to have to change.

He's got to the club before midday. Taking a few minutes outside to catch his breath. Let the panting stop. Hoping he looks halfway presentable. Then stopping. Chastising himself. Wasn't he just pissed off with Alex and Ella for fawning over Marty like he was a somebody? How is this different? Fine, this could be important. Could be a warning about last night. Could be something he really needs to hear. But the difference between five minutes early and five minutes late should be fuck-all to him. Get your head together. Remember who this is. Remember how little you care.

Into the club. Through the foyer and marching past the door to the dance floor. He knows where the office is.

"I help you?" someone's shouting from behind him. Gruff and deliberately unfriendly. It's a where-the-hell-are-you-going-without-my-permission offer of help.

"I'm here to see Marty. He's expecting me. Oliver Peterkinney." Talking to some guy sticking his head round the door from the dance floor.

"Fine. Go on." His tone making it clear that he doesn't care much either way. If you're here to help Marty, good luck to you. If you're here to stick a knife in him, hey, good luck to you too.

Through the heavy door and down the corridor. Knocking on the door. Hearing a shout to enter. Going in to find Marty sitting behind the desk. His brother nowhere to be seen. Marty looking at him and leaning back in the chair.

"Close the door, kid," he's saying. Kid. Marty's thirty-three years old. He calls people kid because he heard it in a movie and thought it sounded cool. Made him feel senior to talk down to people. Starting to wonder why the really senior people don't talk that way. Starting to think that maybe he shouldn't. But it's a habit now, and habits are hard to break.

Peterkinney's closed the door. Standing in front of the desk, looking down at Marty. Quite happy to stay standing. Hoping this is going to be a short conversation. Thinking of his interview with Roy Bowles. Quite enjoying looking down on Marty.

"Jesus, take over a seat, man," Marty's saying. "Standing there like a fucking schoolboy."

Peterkinney's giving him the kind of look Marty doesn't get often. A look that tells him he shouldn't be talking that way to the person in front of him. Peterkinney doesn't even know he's doing it. More a glance than a look. Instinctive and unrecognized by Peterkinney. Spotted by Marty though. Recognized as something rare and valuable. Peterkinney's going across and getting the chair, putting it down in front of the desk and sitting. Looking at Marty. Straight at him, holding eye contact. Keeping a cold expression.

"So you and your mate want to do more work for me?"

"If the work is right, yeah," Peterkinney's saying. Shouldn't be putting in conditions, but he has that Bowles interview coming up. And he doesn't like Marty. And he's still pissed with himself for running to get here. There's a lot of reasons for the contempt that dripped off that sentence. Trying to establish some authority of his own is another, although that's subconscious. He's not thinking about authority over someone he doesn't want to work for.

"That's big of you," Marty's saying. Saying it with a smile though, because he likes this. Doesn't hear it often enough. It's amusing. "How would you feel about doing work alone?"

"Without Alex? This was all his big plan. He's the one that wants to work for you. If you're only looking for one guy, he's the guy you're looking for. He'll do whatever work you want done."

"And you?"

"And I'm a little fussier." Making it clear that he considers himself more discerning. Maybe too discerning to work for someone like Marty.

Marty's nodding. Impressed by the balls on this one. Talking to Marty like he's his equal. Hell, talking to him the way people in charge talk to him. That cold tone. People like Peter Jamieson and his right-hand man John Young use it all the time. Like they don't want to be in his company, but they'll suffer it. Stuck-up bastards. They'll take his money though. Oh yeah, you can bet on that. Real quick to take their cut, but don't want to hang around with him. Don't want to give him the opportunities to step up to bigger things that he's earned.

"Sounds like you handled Holmes well. And I heard about your wee confrontation with Neil Fraser last night. That wasn't too clever. Fraser's good muscle. John Young uses him. Not their favorite, but he's got a reputation. If you get the chance, you should thank Angus Lafferty for stepping in and saving you. Fraser's a nutter; he'd have stuck you, right there in front of everyone. But you had the balls to stand up to him. I like that." Talking with the casual certainty of a man who knows. He knows who these people are, knows what they're capable of, knows how to handle them. The sharpness that makes Marty rich shining through.

"Okay." A one-word response with no emotion. Can't think of anything else to say. Hearing a lot of names he only vaguely recognizes. Being told to do things he knows he won't do.

"I looked up your number, called you personally. That's because I want you to come and do a few jobs for me. What do you say to that?"

Peterkinney's shrugging. "Depends on the work. Depends on the reward."

Marty's smiling. "Listen, kid. I called you up. I know where you live. I know you live with your grandfather, for fuck's sake. I know those flats. Small spaces, ain't they? You don't want to be there forever, do you? I know you probably had to take the fucking bus to get here. Riding along with the plebs. You enjoy that? There's good money in what I do. For a guy your age, life-changing money. I think you're the sort of person who can help me with it. I think you can handle it. I'm giving you the chance to move up in the world here, kiddo. Don't throw that back in my face. You might not get another chance."

Said it like he was offering him the world. Sitting in the shittiest little office Peterkinney's ever seen in his life, and Marty thinks he can sound impressive. But it's not about the surroundings, they both know that. It's about the rewards.

"If the money's right, and if there's work for Alex too."

"Your wee mate? I can find some work for him. Won't be much. You'll be getting the better stuff. I think you're cut out for the good stuff. Kind of things I have to be careful about. Takes brain, as well as brawn. And there will be real money. Money, parties, women. All of it. Think about that, huh. Last night? That was bullshit. I throw better parties than that every fucking week. You could be in that life."

"Fine," Peterkinney's saying with a reluctant nod. "I'll do a few jobs for you, see how it goes. Can't promise anything, but we'll play it by ear. You know how to get in touch with me, obviously."

"Excellent," Marty's saying. Getting up and shaking him by the hand. As Peterkinney's walking out of the office, Marty's wondering how the hell that just happened. It was like he had to twist the kid's arm. In the end, it was like the kid was doing him a favor. Wrong way round, that was. Bloody hell. Got to keep an eye on this kid.

Peterkinney's out the front door and looking at his watch. Plenty of time to get across to the address his grandfather gave him. Could have two jobs by the end of the day. Two jobs, real money. This could be the start of a little something. A flat of his own. Lounging in the living room, watching the TV he wants to watch. Taking his time in the bathroom, because there's nobody grumbling outside the door waiting to get in. Privacy. Peace. A leap towards the life he craves. Now he's smiling.

PART TWO

1

Peterkinney knows the routine by now. He's done this four times in the last two and a half months. First time he did a job for Roy Bowles it was nerve-racking. Creeping around, terrified of being caught with a gun on you. Convinced that everyone knew what you were carrying as you returned the gun from the supplier. Not anymore. You relax, when you know what's going to happen. You understand the routine. You understand how little the rest of the world cares about what you're carrying.

Bowles called him this morning, told him to get round to the house. That's much easier done now. He's got himself a little car. Doesn't have a license, but he has a car. Cost him four hundred quid. Little blue Peugeot. Peterkinney should get along with it, because they're not far off being the same age. Mostly held together by bloody-mindedness, but it's faster than walking, just about. And he'll get that license when he has time. No, really, he will. Next thing is a flat of his own. Gathering savings to pay for the essentials he'll need for that. Then a driving license. It's all planned, and the plans are getting bigger.

He's been a busy boy, these last couple of months. Used to have no job at all. Now he has two. And people say the economy's circling the drain. Marty keeps him busy. That's dirty work. Doing shitty collection jobs. Doing them well, but not enjoying it. Gets reasonable money, but smarty Marty's always trying to screw you. Always trying to persuade you to take anything other than money. Take some girls. Take some drugs. Take anything other than the money you earned. Marty understands the value of cash, understands that nothing matters more. That's why he hangs on to every damn penny. Peterkinney understands the value of paper money too. Always insists on cash. That's why he and Marty don't always get along.

Bowles is different. He has a different sort of business, a different way of handling it. Give your people the money they earn, keep your head down and your mouth shut. His is a business of silence. In many ways, he's the anti-Marty. Doesn't make him a good person, mind you. Don't make that mistake. Does make him dependable. Right now, dependable is attractive. Every job is well paid. Usually about a hundred and fifty quid for a couple of hours of easy work. The money reflects the risk, and buys silence.

Pulling up along the street from the house. Taking precautions, because that's what common sense tells him to do. Look around, play it careful. Not a lot of people know what Bowles does. He's smart and careful. But some people know. That makes working for him a risk. The police could find out. They follow you on a job, pick you up after you've collected the gun. Automatic jail term. Years inside. You don't want your name connected with him.

Through the side gate and round to the back garden. Glancing across at the little wooden shed, wondering if there's a gun in there. That's where they're returned, when people are finished with them and don't want to keep them. See, most people, most professionals, only want a gun for a short time. Then, after using it the one time they want it, they're stuck with something incriminating. Why chuck it in the river and lose all your investment? It still has value, just not to the person who's used it. Take it back to Bowles, dropped inside the loose panel on the side of the shed. A few days later, you'll get some of your money back. Not all of it. Bowles still has to make a living. No charity in this industry, you'll find. But it becomes a rental fee, rather than a purchase. If you don't return the gun, Bowles keeps all the money.

Knocking on the back door and waiting. You do not go into his house without permission. You do not go into his shed at all. You do not ever deal with the people he sells to. You do not recommend him to anyone. You do not mention that you've ever even heard of the man. Keeping your gob shut is the key to being a good employee. He finds his own clients, develops relationships with them over time. Any verbal element to a job belongs solely to Bowles.

Door's opening. Bowles looking back at him, nodding for him to come in. This is all familiar. First time Bowles called Peterkinney to come and do a job for him, Peterkinney thought it was going to happen there and then. That's how it works with Marty. Marty calls you up. Tells you what he wants done. You go and do it straight away. Not Bowles. Bowles always gives him at least a day's warning, sometimes more. Different business, different set of rules. No set of rules is right or wrong. Frankly, Peterkinney thinks they could each learn something from the other.

They're into the living room, sitting in familiar seats. Bowles always does it the same way. Every single time, no matter the job. Continuity.

"There's a pick-up tomorrow," Bowles is saying. Always speaks slowly. Always feels like he thinks you're an idiot, the way he talks to you. Just his way. Keeps everything slow and simple, making sure there's never a misunderstanding. Those are very dangerous. More dangerous than talking down to a tough guy. Besides, if he thought Peterkinney was stupid he wouldn't have him working for him. "New fellow, a little twitchy. I'm not convinced by him, but he has good connections. I'm sure he can deliver the piece, but I worry. I want you to be cautious."

"Anything specific?"

"No," Bowles is saying, shaking his head. "Just a feeling I got from him. I spoke to him on the telephone. He was unconvincing. Granted, as I said, he has the connections. He can get his hands on the piece. I have no doubt of that. He just didn't sound reliable. I don't like people who aren't reliable."

Peterkinney's nodding. "Where's the meet?"

"Tomorrow at two. I have an address. It's not residential. This is another problem I have with it. It's an old garage, terribly rough area. Industrial, no housing. I suspect he wants to meet you outside."

"In the open?"

"That's what he suggested. Said he'd be waiting outside. I doubt this fellow has a key to get in. He's down on his luck, as they say. As though luck is the reason he's down. Desperate for the money, so I don't doubt he'll be there."

Bowles researches people. Checks up on anyone he's going to buy from. Makes sure that they meet his definition of reliable. Not like him to even consider someone he doesn't fully trust. Having a piece to sell isn't enough to persuade a man like Bowles. All those years avoiding detection, he won't take a risk now. Yet this guy doesn't sound reliable at all. Must have very good contacts. Probably ex-military. A lot of them are. Or maybe someone with connections across the water in Northern Ireland. He's obviously convinced Bowles that he can deliver something worthwhile.

Bowles has gotten up to go and get the money, which means he has no intention of going into any further detail. If Peterkinney wants to work out why this guy's unreliable, then it's up to him to do so. Bowles wouldn't tell him just because of a feeling, though. That's not him. Feelings intrude very rarely. He must know something that leaves him so worried. Keeping it to himself, for now.

Back in with the cash. A thick wad of used notes in a small white envelope. Passing it carefully, almost respectfully, to Peterkinney. Watching Peterkinney slip it into the inside pocket of his coat. Always have a pocket with a zip when you come visit Bowles for a job. He's going to give you money, and he's going to demand that the money be put in a pocket with a zip. Demanded it on the first visit, made it clear that he expected Peterkinney to remember that demand.

"His name's Howard Lawson. Apparently everyone calls him Howie. He's forty, skinny fellow, rather scraggly. Well, he should be the only one there, so you shouldn't have trouble picking him out." A pause, thinking. "Any sign of trouble, get out of there, Oliver. If he's not alone, leave, immediately. I specifically told him to be alone. He swore he would be. If you hear or see anything untoward, leave immediately. And of course, my name never comes up."

That's always the cue to leave. The reminder that his name never makes it into a conversation, even with the person you're getting the gun from. It's always the last words he wants in your ears when he sends you out the door.

But the words that came before are what Peterkinney remembers. Warning. But also, trusting. Trusting Peterkinney to make his own judgment on the deal. If he sees anything untoward, he must walk away. Up to him to decide what constitutes untoward. Not just Bowles playing careful, although he always does that. It's also a sign of trust. He considers Peterkinney smart enough to handle this job, to make this judgment.

Peterkinney's in his car. He'll go back to the flat first, stash the money. Would be nice to find out a little more about this Howie Lawson before he does the job tomorrow. No chance. Peterkinney doesn't know enough people in the business that he could ask. Not yet. Only been involved for a couple of months, mind you. He's learning fast and learning well. He has a few contacts of his own already, and he's picking up more as he goes along. He has the intelligence, and he has the attitude.

Would be nice to hang out with Glass for a while, but what's the point? He'll be with little Ella Fowler. Always with Ella these days. Living the life, is what Alex calls it. She practically lives with him now. Going out to parties all the time. She works a lot of parties. Glass goes along and has fun, apparently. Peterkinney still hasn't gotten his head round that. She's a very sweet girl, in a girly sort of a way. But she does get on his fucking nerves. All sweetness and light, giggles and mumbles. Glass has fallen for her big time. Fair enough, she's pretty, and she's obviously into him. Or some idea of him. A hooker and a jobless thug, trying to play happy families. Trying to pretend that they've got something unique going on. That's what gets on Peterkinney's nerves. They can't see how hard you have to work to get anything good in this business. He sees it. He's doing it.

Fine. Let her take Glass to her parties. Let them get hammered every night. Let them wallow in their childish idea of a loving relationship. Whatever keeps them happy. Not like he doesn't have other things to be getting along with now. Marty's given Glass a few jobs, but it's real garbage stuff, and it's only now and again. He always has something for Peterkinney, as long as Peterkinney's willing. Today, he is.

2

Last night was a good night. Lots of drink. Some coke that was given out free. Got home about two. Ella got back around six. Glass doesn't know where she went. Hasn't asked. Won't ask. She makes more money than he does. She seems to like it. She seems happy with her life. He isn't going to do anything to rock that boat. Why would he? This is what he wanted. What he always thought was the perfect life. Parties most nights. Drinking every night. Out with his girl. A pretty girl. A girl who loves him back. That's what it's all about.

Been like this for a couple of months. Honestly, he's pretty exhausted. And it ain't cheap. All the drink, all the drugs. That costs money. Sure, some parties have freebies. The big parties. Most don't. It's an expensive life. Money he doesn't have, going up his nose or down the toilet. Wouldn't be a problem if he could get more work from Marty. Marty isn't helping him out as much as he should.

This is another thing that pisses him off. Why is Marty giving Peterkinney all the work, and hardly any to Glass? That doesn't make sense. It was Glass that set up the job on Holmes. It was Glass who led the job. They did a good job. Must have, because Marty's using them both still. But he uses Peterkinney all the time. Glass hardly at all. Occasional jobs that don't pay much. Not much use. Just doesn't seem fair.

He'd mention it to Peterkinney, if he ever saw Peterkinney. Hardly ever comes round these days. Seems like he's working hard to keep his distance. Obviously doesn't like Ella. Or doesn't like the fact that Glass has a girl and he doesn't. Or maybe just doesn't like

the life that Glass and Ella are living now. A couple. A proper relationship. Hard to tell what his problem is. Probably because he
doesn't like Ella, which is another thing to piss him off. Peterkinney
could always be a bit snobby. Not much to be snobby about, but
that's the way he was. Looking down his nose at people like Ella.

Ella's out of the bathroom now. Slept until afternoon. Hasn't spoken to her since some time last night. Can't remember anything
they said since before they left the flat last night. There are a lot
of episodes like that in his life now. Vague conversations. Lost
evenings. Failed memories. Still, as long as she's a part of it, this is
what he wants.

"Morning. How you feeling?" he's asking. He knows how to work
the tone now. Took him a little time to realize that what you say is
less important than how you say it. With Ella, anyway. Say it with a
smile, a little charm. Don't let it sound anywhere close to an accu-
sation. No judgment allowed.

"Little tired. Little sore," she's saying with a weary smile.

She has a small cut on the top of her shoulder. He saw that when
he was getting up in the morning. Wasn't there last night. He won't
mention it. It's happened a few times. She's arrived home hours after him. She's had a bruise or a cut or something like that. And he
says nothing because she doesn't want to talk about it. Upsets her to
talk. It's a separate part of her life, she said the first time. Work and
home, they stay apart. One doesn't talk to the other. So he doesn't
mention these things, because they're work and he's home.

"Got anything on today?" he's asking. Trying to make it sound
hopeful, like he wants to spend time with her. That'll keep her
happy.

"I got to go see someone," she's saying. "But I'm not doing anything tonight. We should go out. I know a guy who can get us in at
Fourteen. You been there before? It's a great club. Real classy. We
should go."

How does he say no? They've been together a couple of months.
Long enough for him to know that she's out of his league. Long

enough to know that he has to work very hard to keep a hold of her. You don't say no. That's the first rule. He's worked that one out for himself. No trial and error required. He knows. He has to say yes.

"Sure, that sounds great. I haven't been."

"Oh, you'll love it," she's saying. All casual and happy now. Her chirpy, flirty self. Going across to the fridge to see if there's anything that could pretend to be breakfast in there. "I've been there a couple of times before. Great parties. But even without a party, it's a great night."

"Sure. Great." He's nodding. Happy to make her happy. Working hard to make this work. Oblivious to the fact that what she loves most about him is the chance of normality. The chance of a proper relationship and regular life. The parties, the nights out, they're just what she's used to. Part of the routine.

Thinking about the cost. Fourteen is a swanky kind of place. An expensive kind of a place. If it was just him, he would never have thought of it. Not his kind of hangout. Not the sort of club him and Peterkinney used to hit for a night out. Ella can only know it through her work. It's the sort of place those sorts of men go. The kind of men who can show her luxury Glass can't afford.

While she's making her breakfast at lunchtime, he's thinking about Marty. Needs to get in touch with him. Call him up, see if there's anything to do. Must be, surely. Could do with a little extra money. Actually, scratch the word "extra." He needs money. Right now his wallet contains a video rental card he hasn't used in two years. That's it.

He's left her to it, walking through to the living room. She likes to be alone when she's making food. A little bit obsessive about it. Started baking as well, the other afternoon. Made a banana loaf. It was okay. She loves that, cooking and baking. Likes to drag him round the supermarket, picking out ingredients.

He has a number for Marty, but Marty's fussy about answering. He made it very clear that he doesn't want to be called all the time. Doesn't want every little nobody calling him every time they're short of cash. Well, Glass has been careful. He's only called once before, and Marty didn't seem to mind. So he's got his phone in his hand and he's tapping on Marty's name. Holding it up to his ear and worrying that he's pushing his luck. But he isn't. Truth is, Marty loves it when people call him up. Loves it because he gets to feel important. Tell people that he has work for them. Or tell them that he doesn't, and listen to them deflate.

"Hi, Marty, it's Alex Glass. Is now a good time to talk? Good, cool. Listen, do you have any work needs doing? I'm happy to do whatever, you know, anything at all." Now he's standing there and he's listening. You wouldn't need to hear what Marty's saying to know that it isn't good news. You can read the expression on Glass's face. "Okay. Yeah, that's fine. You know, whenever you need any work, I'll be around. You know I...Sure, I'll let you go. Bye, Marty."

He's dropped his phone onto the couch and he's standing in the middle of the room. He can hear Ella moving around in the kitchen. She expects to go out to Fourteen. She wants to be there, and if he can't take her, someone else will. He can see how tenuous this is. He needs to keep impressing her. So he'll get the money. Hook or crook, he'll get it.

Ella's out of the kitchen with a poor excuse for a sandwich in one hand and a mug in the other. Not much effort went into that, but she's tired. Dropping into the chair that happens to have the TV remote on the arm of it. Looking up at Glass and smiling. He's standing there in the middle of the room, for no obvious reason. He smiles back and nods.

"Just going to head out for a wee while. Bit of work, maybe," he's saying.

She looks disappointed. Always does when he does anything to compromise the domestic bliss. She hoped they'd have an hour together before she went to work. It's always nice to spend time with Glass. He's always nice. Always considerate. Always different from all the others.

"Right, sure. I'll be away in an hour. So, I don't know, I'll see you later."

"Yeah," he's smiling, and leaning down for a kiss. She likes that. Proper couples kiss goodbye.

He's getting his coat and his phone and he's out of the flat. Got to think about this. Think, man. Think of an alternative. There isn't one. He knows what he has to do; something he doesn't want to do. Got to make sure he gets this just right. Make the wrong judgment here and he's under the thumb for years.

3

You can make all the plans you want. Doesn't matter. Not a damn bit. Potty spent the thick end of two months trying to come up with a clever way of getting to Patterson. All through those two months, Patterson was growing and growing. Getting stronger, taking more clients away from him. All the time, Potty stewed. Trying to come up with some ingenious route to the heart of Patterson's business. Trying to find a weak spot and the silver bullet to exploit it. Two months wasted.

Then it fell right into his fat lap. Straight out of nowhere. A rumor that one of his muscle heard and passed on to him. Muscle didn't even know that it might be important. Dickhead. Even muscle should have the basic sense to keep their ear to the ground. To know what matters and what doesn't. Hardly brain surgery, is it? But some people...

Potty would have found out eventually. Everyone found out eventually. Not the sort of thing that could be hidden. Jamie Stamford ends up in hospital and the city gets to hear about it. Now, Stamford was the first one to try and cover the whole thing up. Didn't reflect well on him. Premier muscle, beaten to a pulp. But details leak out. People find out. They have to, otherwise the message Patterson was sending isn't heard. It was in Patterson's interest to make sure the story got out. But that was always going to piss important people off. Impressed some important people, no doubt, but pissed a whole bunch of other ones off.

So Patterson had sent one of his boys to smash up Stamford. Punishment for not paying a debt Patterson had bought. Potty was offered that debt. Turned away the two bookies that had come to-gether to try and sell it. No way Potty was going looking for trouble with Alex MacArthur. Everyone knows MacArthur likes Stamford. One of the muscle he keeps close. He trusts. So you ignore his many debts.

Patterson made the mistake of buying it. Of thinking he could act without consequence. All men are equal, and all that. Nope. Not true. You don't treat everyone the same. You're never in your own little bubble. People won't accept your behavior just because you're right. Being right means very little in this business.

Potty knew all that when he made the phone call to Alex MacArthur. He knew MacArthur would talk to him. The Cruick-shank name still carries a lot of weight in this city. In the right circles, at least. And MacArthur is the master of his circle. Just about the biggest criminal network in the city. One of the big three. Not a man a little shit like Billy Patterson should be picking a fight with. Potty chatted to MacArthur. Mentioned Patterson's name just the once. Casual, in passing. The mention of a mutual problem. That got him an invite to one of MacArthur's offices.

A good office. You can tell a lot about what he thinks of you by the office you meet him in. He has a lot to choose from. Clubs and pubs, shops and companies. You name it, he's either got it or got access to it. He's been in the business so long. A fixture. One of those people you don't want to see leave. Not that anyone really likes him. Rasp-ing, chainsmoking old egomaniac. But what replaces him? He's one of the few big old sharks that know how to keep order. If that goes, you don't know what'll step in to fill the gap he leaves. Nothing de-serves greater fear than the unknown. Stick with this old devil, he's familiar.

Potty's being driven to the office block where the meeting will take place. Have a driver, have an expensive car. Make sure MacArthur can see that the Cruickshanks are still in the money business. The office block is nothing special to look at, but it con-tains the heart of MacArthur's operation. His office on the top floor is one of his favorite offices. Probably makes him feel legitimate. Potty knows that a meeting here is a sign of respect. It's MacArthur acknowledging that Potty is a man worthy of respect. Two big beasts of the old guard, meeting on equal terms. Up in the lift, and being shown through to the office straight away by a young secretary. More respect. It's a good start to the meeting.

"Ronald, good to see you," MacArthur's saying. Standing up from behind the desk in the office. There's always a desk for the boss to sit behind. Doesn't matter if he needs it. Doesn't matter if he never uses it. Sitting behind it makes him feel important. Makes him feel like he's in charge, the rest of the room facing him. Potty understands that. Does it himself. He does appreciate that they've put a large cushioned chair in front of the desk for him. Making an effort. MacArthur's domain, but Potty's welcome.

"Alex. How are you keeping, sir?"

"I'm a decrepit old bastard, Ronald. Can't say more than that." Said with a smile, but nobody's going to argue with the truth of it. That smile is sad and knowing, not funny. Been rumors about his health recently. Smoking God knows how many a day will do that.

As will eating too much, Potty is thinking to himself. MacArthur's a skinny little fellow. Always looked weak, now looking frail. A little wisp of a man, aware that he's survived all the dangers just long enough to kill himself with his own lifestyle. Something Potty's doing, just at a faster rate. Should have taken up smoking instead of eating.

Ray Buller is in the room too, but he's sitting off behind them at a small table. Buller has been one of MacArthur's senior men for decades. If MacArthur's age and health are worrying, Buller won't make you feel any better. At sixty-four, he's two years older than MacArthur. His health is better, sure, but better is relative. Better doesn't mean healthy. He's not a replacement. That's probably why MacArthur keeps him so close. Nobody wants the man standing next to them to be eyeing up their seat.

It's quite the office. Paintings on the walls, furniture designed to look expensive. Good views, if you want to spend your time looking out the window. Even got a TV up in the corner of the room. Supposed to give a more casual feel to the place. A thin computer monitor and keyboard on the desk, no sign of the hard drive. No filing cabinets or stacks of paper; that would cheapen the place. This is an office in which you reflect on your success. There are other, more functional offices where you go to earn the money to pay for this.

"I hope I'm not intruding with this wee problem I have," Potty's saying. Careful to call it his problem, not theirs. You never imply that MacArthur has a problem, not unless he brings it up. Not some bullshit "you must respect the boss" routine. Just good manners. Uncle Rolly always stressed the value of good manners around the wealthy and respectable.

"Never an intrusion. I've been interested in this Patterson kid for a while. Little shit's been running round without anyone slowing him down. Thinking he has the run of the place." And that's as much of a mention as Jamie Stamford will get. MacArthur likes the boy. He's not going to embarrass him by discussing this in front of an outsider. Potty knows, and MacArthur knows. That'll do for detail.

"Well, I've been looking to do something about him for months," Potty is saying with a shrug. Trying to sound casual, but he knows he's leaving himself open to criticism here. "Haven't had a chance. The lad has some mean bastards around him. Toughest crew I've seen coming up in a long time. He's been careful putting it together. I intend to do something about him, but I think it will take some support to wipe him out."

MacArthur's nodding. He likes that Potty is talking about wiping this boy out. Not holding him down or setting him back. Getting rid. Clean out the filth; don't just shove it out of the way. Never mind that Stamford's always been a good boy. Never mind the personal insult delivered. The real issue is that people know Patterson had one of MacArthur's men put in hospital. Gave him a real kicking. MacArthur has to be seen to do something about it. If he lets this pass, everyone thinks they can get away with it. Come up with some flimsy excuse and start kicking lumps out of people working for him. Be seen to be weak once, and vultures will circle. Besides, whose fault is all this? Not Stamford's, that's for damn sure. It's the bookies' fault. If you have a guy with big debts, you refuse to let him keep gambling. Common sense. If they were too scared to refuse Stamford, whose fault is that? Theirs again, you'll find. MacArthur won't pay a price for another man's cowardice.

"What's the plan?" MacArthur's asking.

"Well, he has a group of guys around him that are tough. Take them away and there's nothing left. I want to pick off the most important ones. Not all of them need to be attacked. One or two will be bought. If I'm sure of anything, I'm sure that there are always one or two that can be bought."

MacArthur's smiling. Here's a man that shares his vision of the business, his understanding. Buy the people you can. Remove the ones you can't. There have been so many times in the past when that strategy has worked. Almost none when it hasn't. You just have to pick the right targets for each option. The key is making sure you don't miss anyone out. Either buy or remove them all.

"I want to start working on them right away. Pick away at it until he's good and exposed. Then I can get rid of him," Potty's saying.

"You know I'd be more than happy to help you with that, Ronald. All the manpower you need."

That's what Potty came here to hear. This was never about funding. Potty will have to pay for anything that costs money. But manpower is another matter. MacArthur has far more of that than Potty. He has people better equipped to do the kind of work that needs to be done. This is a union. An agreement that they will now work together to destroy Billy Patterson.

Potty is smiling by the time he gets back into his car. The rest of the conversation with MacArthur was small talk. Bullshit. Two men of experience, chewing the cud. Remembering a few old stories about the good old days. This is a good day too. This is a day when he can start to stamp on Billy Patterson. Reinforce his position at the top of the collecting tree. A sloppy mistake. Thinking that they could target Stamford like that. Real sloppy. The kind of mistake that costs you your business.

4

They haven't had a happy conversation since the Stamford incident. Patterson thinks Bavidge went too far. He's right, of course. Bavidge knows it. He wasn't going to go that far. Stamford was actually trying. He was failing, but he was trying. He hadn't gone running to MacArthur this time. He was trying to put some money together. Working hard to solve his own problem. Trying to pay the debt, or at least some of it.

But Stamford's an addict. Can't stop gambling. He called Bavidge up, told him he had seven grand to put towards the debt. Bavidge was positive. Made it clear he still wanted the other thirteen, but seven was a decent start. Tried to sound encouraging. Said they would meet the following day. A handover. They met. Stamford had three grand. He'd gone gambling with the seven he'd accumulated. Thought he could double it, maybe more. Thought he could cover the twenty grand with a bit of luck. Lost four. Bavidge called him on it, told him what a moron he was. The meeting turned brutal. Two nasty men and a poisonous atmosphere made for an inevitable conclusion. Stamford learned how nasty Bavidge is capable of being.

Stupid thing is, if Stamford had called and said he had three grand, Bavidge would have settled for that. He doesn't expect a moron like Stamford to come up with every penny in one go. He should be getting it faster than he is, but he was trying. That was as much as Bavidge ever expected. It was the sheer stupidity of it. Throwing good money down the hole that sucked your wallet dry last time. That's what made him lose his temper.

He's into the little poker room, Patterson sitting at the table.

Bavidge sitting opposite him. These have been awkward conversations lately. Patterson trying not to imply that Bavidge has gotten them into a shitload of trouble, when they both know he has.

"We've got a problem," Patterson's saying as an opener.

Bavidge is grimacing, because he thinks this is going to be about Stamford. Patterson's smiling a little in response to the grimace. This isn't about Bavidge's mistake. This is about Patterson's.

"Jim Holmes," he's saying. Sitting back and waiting for the reaction.

"Already?" Bavidge is leaning back in his chair. Not going to make any more of an issue of it than that. The boss makes a mistake, you don't rub his nose in it. Even if you saw the mistake coming. Besides, Patterson's been determinedly gentle with him over the Stamford beating. He's earned the right to the occasional mistake of his own.

"Already. Spent last night going through a few figures. He's been skimming a few percent for a few weeks. In the last two weeks he's gone from about 5 percent to around 20. He must know I'm going to spot it."

"Does he have protection?" Meaning has he already organized to go work for someone else? Is this sabotage rather than stupidity?

"None that I've been able to spot. If he's gone to someone, then he's keeping quiet about it."

"Doubt it," Bavidge is saying quietly. "Who would take the bastard?"

"Exactly. Which makes me think he might be about to do a runner. I don't think working for me has turned out to be everything he thought it would. Thought he could come here and be some big shot. I haven't let him have any important jobs. Gutter work. I think he might be ready to bolt. I mean, he ain't going to jump to skimming 20 percent of my money without me knowing. Even he has to see that. He must have a foot out the door already."

Bavidge is nodding. This is something that has to be done fast. "Can we get the money back?"

"If it's in the house, great," Patterson's saying with a shrug. "Doesn't matter too much. He was taking 20 percent of small jobs. Only took about a grand and a half. I'm not going to turn the city upside down looking for it. But I want a message sent. A real message."

Patterson's messages are dark. Even by the standards of the inky-black collection industry. Might just be the most brutal part of the criminal industry, and he might just be the most brutal person in it. The most brutal person of influence, anyway. There are plenty of dickheads setting up shitty little operations, going too far and being shut down inside a few months. They don't count. Short term. Of the people that count, Patterson goes closest to the edge with his punishments. Bavidge is his favored means of delivering those messages.

"It'll need to be done tonight," Bavidge is saying. Then grimacing.

"Something wrong?"

"I have a date tonight. Shit, forgot about her."

"Serious?" Asked with a hint of hope in Patterson's voice.

"Nah," Bavidge is saying, shaking his head. "Not really. She's shacked up with some driver for Peter Jamieson. Nice, though."

Patterson's nodding. It's good that Bavidge has someone in his life, but it doesn't seem to be cheering him up much. Never does. He only ever goes in for relationships that he knows won't work. Never wants something that might matter to him. Depressing is what it is. Making his own life more miserable than it needs to be. He's never going to stop being a man to worry about.

Time might come, Patterson's thinking, when he'll need to interfere. Get involved in his friend's private affairs. If this girl is worth the effort, he might just have a word with the driver. After all, couldn't be hard to chase a driver away. Nah, works for Jamieson. Fine, set Bavidge up with someone else. Someone that can settle him down, make him happy. Not sure that's possible.

"Can you let her down gently?"

Bavidge is shrugging. "I can let her down. I think she's getting used to it. I'll get this done tonight, before he has a chance to get out. I'll make sure it's very clear. He still at the same address?"

"He is."

"Okay. Anything else?"

"No, that's it."

A brief shake of the hand, and Patterson's watching Bavidge leave. He will do something about him. Has to. Wouldn't be much of a friend if he didn't. He needs to get away from his work. Patterson won't sack him. Too good to be sacked. Force him to take a holiday. That might be a start. Probably wouldn't work. A holiday wouldn't be enough to make him happy-go-lucky. Often thought about having a conversation about him, but how weird would that be? You don't sit down with a guy like Alan Bavidge and talk about feelings. Talk about the fact that he seems to be a bit depressed. If he doesn't laugh in your face, he'd punch you in it. He'd be right to, as well. If someone started that conversation with Patterson, it would be a short conversation.

5

Treading carefully, because he doesn't know this guy. Heard about him, never met him. Glass found out where his little office was, dropped by. Seems like a decent enough guy. They all do though, don't they. They want you to borrow money from them. They're selling, not you. There are plenty of people you can borrow money from, so they all have to be nice until they have their claws into you. That's when the reassuring smile fades.

Jefferson's looking across the desk at him. Another man trying to feel big behind his desk. Or trying to make the other person feel small. That might be it. Trying to make Glass feel that he's dealing with someone so much bigger than himself. Impress him. Make him more agreeable to the terms he's about to be offered.

But it's not the office that makes people feel small. The office isn't capable. Basic, would be the word. Small room, small desk. Everything a little scuffed and worn. Stacks of paper, an old computer monitor on the side of the desk. Gloomy, too. There's a window, but the dirty glass seems to be more than the sunlight can cope with.

Jefferson isn't intimidating either. But then, we've already established that he's not trying to be. A man in his early forties, casually dressed. Smiling at Glass and treating him with exaggerated respect. He's not intimidating, but he knows what is. He knows that there's nothing so terrifying as money. Being without it is scary. Trying to find ways of acquiring it is demoralizing. And Jefferson has it. Sitting there behind his cheap desk, in his unimpressive office. He has what they want, and that intimidates them all.

"I really don't need much," Glass is saying. He's been trying for nonchalant since he got here. Like this whole thing is all rather beneath him. Just because you haven't done it before doesn't make it beneath you. "Don't need it for long either. A few days."

"You sound like the perfect customer," Jefferson's smiling. Jocular, false. Doesn't mean it. The perfect customer is one who can't pay back in the short term. Then you get them long term. Build up the debt. But you say the right thing. Let them think this is only going to last days. "How much are you looking for, Alex?" First names. Always first names. Try and make it sound like you're already their mate.

"Five hundred," Glass is saying with a shrug. Still going for nonchalant. It comes across as a little bit dumb this time. You should know with certainty how much you need to borrow. If you've arrived at a point in your life where you need to use someone like Jefferson then you should know exactly.

"Five hundred then," Jefferson's nodding. "How long will you need to pay it back?"

This time the shrug is genuinely uncertain. Glass is trying to work out how long he can ask for. How long it would take him to come up with that kind of money. How long would it normally take to put together five hundred quid? Not long if you're Peterkinney. Much longer if you're Glass.

"A month. Maybe two." Did he make five hundred quid in the last month? Just about. Five hundred with the interest rate he'll pay here? Nope, not quite.

Jefferson's looking at him with raised eyebrows. "Shall we split it and call it six weeks?"

"Yeah, yeah, six weeks."

"Do you have a job? A source of income, so that I can be sure you'll be able to repay?"

"Oh yeah, I have a job," Glass is saying. Confident this time. He does have a job. A sort of job. He's thinking about his work for Marty. Occasional, and becoming more occasional as time passes. The more he thinks about it, the less of a job it feels. "It's not always reliable, you know. Sometimes loads of work, sometimes hardly any. That's why I've been caught short."

Jefferson's nodding. "Sure. Not a problem. Cash flow, I understand. Just reassuring to know you have a source of income. I'm not prying." Always so reasonable. "Now the interest rate may seem rather high," he's saying. Try to work out how smart the person borrowing is. If they're sharp, they know your rates are a fucking disgrace to decency. They will hate you for charging such an amount and they will become difficult. They'll justify their failure to repay because of it. If they're not too bright, you can convince them it's the best deal they'll ever get. They'll take it, be thankful and make every effort to repay. This boy's been around. Might not be too clever, but knows enough about the business to know he's not getting a great deal. "It's about as good as you'll get from someone like me. And you have to remember, the 6,000 percent is annual. You don't need to worry about annual. You're only borrowing for six weeks."

Glass is nodding. He knows he'll get screwed on the deal. He knows he'll end up paying back more than he should. Or working it off somehow. But that's six weeks away. This is now, and now is Ella. Now is a night out at her favorite club. Now is proving to her that he can give her what she wants.

She'll be out of the flat by now. Off with some guy, probably. Getting her own money. She always manages to get some. She's always very careful to make sure that she doesn't mention clients. That she doesn't let him hear anything that would upset him. But she goes to these parties and he knows what happens there. And some afternoons she goes out. Doesn't say where she's going. Comes back with money. He knows.

Jefferson's unlocking a drawer in his desk. Taking out a small wad of cash. Counting off fifties. As he peels them from the wad, Glass is thinking about Ella. Thinking about that first morning. The first morning, when Peterkinney was there. Never saw his girl again. The silent one. Ella knows her, but Peterkinney had no interest in seeing her again. He called Ella a prostitute. Glass argued. Said she was just a girl who went to parties. Worked them. No big deal. Not the same as being a hooker. He still tries to believe that.

Jefferson's sliding the cash across the desk. "I want you to sign this contract," Jefferson's saying. Contract means almost nothing. A piece of paper with no legal weight whatsoever. But it gets Glass's signature in Jefferson's office. Makes it feel official, which adds to the intimidation factor. Means Glass can't deny that he borrowed money from Jefferson. But that amounts to very little as well. If this comes to an argument, it's unlikely it'll be settled by the presence of that signature. They both know what happens if you refuse to pay. It's not the sort of thing a contract has any role in.

Glass is signing. Not reading it, just signing. The money's on the desk in front of him. He wants it in his pocket. He wants to get out of this office. Phone Ella. Tell her he has plenty of money for the both of them. Maybe she hasn't left the flat yet.

Jefferson's taking the piece of paper back, slipping it into the drawer. "It's been good doing business with you, Alex. I hope the money serves you well. I'll put you down in the book. Let's say six weeks from today as the deadline. If you have the money for me before then, obviously, drop in. Sooner the better," he's saying with a smile, and reaching out a hand. Sooner the better is bullshit. Alex knows that. They both know that. Sooner is the worst option. Keep the money, build up the debt. The longer it builds, the more the lender benefits. He can't lose.

They're both thinking the same thing as they shake hands. If this debt isn't repaid inside a week or two, it's going to become a millstone. Jefferson knows it and he likes it. He's not like a bookie. If a bookie lets you run a tab you can't pay back, the bookie loses that value. They need that value back, every penny. That's their legit profit. With a moneylender it's different. Your final debt is guaranteed to be a lot higher than your initial borrow. The lender can sell the debt to a collector, and as long as he gets more than his original outlay back, he's up on the deal. A five-hundred-pound lend becomes a three-grand debt. He sells the debt to a collector for a grand and a half. Triples his money without doing a damn thing. And he'll usually sell for more than 50 percent.

Glass is thinking about that as he walks out of the little office. He needs this money for tonight. Try and spend as little of it as possible. If he can keep a hold of some of it, get a few jobs from Marty in quick succession. It could happen. He could have enough to pay it off inside three or four weeks. He'll have to pay three or four times what he borrowed. When was the last time he made two grand in a month? Never has.

Getting his phone out of his pocket. Scrolling to Ella's name and tapping to dial. One hand holding the phone, the other holding the notes in his pocket. Come on, where are you? Pick up. Through to voicemail. Shit. Hide your disappointment.

"Ella, it's Alex. Listen, I just came into a bit of money. Got enough for a good night out. Couple of good nights out, you know. So, yeah, I thought I'd let you know. Give me a call, whatever. See you later."

Hanging up, dialing again. Through to voicemail again. Hanging up. Phone's back in his pocket. Walking along the street, instinctively heading home. Ella will be gone. Peterkinney. He might be around. Phone out of his pocket. Trying Peterkinney's number. This person's phone is switched off. Shit. Might be a good idea to spend some time with Peterkinney in the next few weeks. Money seems to be gravitating towards him.

6

Getting dark. Good. That's what Peterkinney's been waiting for. Marty had a job for him. Go find Gordon Aird. He owes eight hundred quid. Tell him he owes a grand and knock him around a bit until he pays. Aird borrowed a couple of hundred, and has zero chance of even paying that back. Aird is a user. He borrows money, injects it, borrows from another lender to pay off the first debt. Always going round in one big depressing circle. Not even trying to solve his problem.

Marty doesn't expect any money to come back to him. He didn't say that to Peterkinney; you always cross your fingers and hope. But a couple of months is enough time for Peterkinney to know how this works. Marty likes to use people like Aird. If they can pay up then that's great. But people like Aird rarely can. And a guy like Marty knows that when he takes the debt. Aird is such a mess; he'll do whatever's asked of him to get through another day. All about survival. Marty likes that. He can use that. But first you have to soften them up. Make sure they know you're serious. That's where Peterkinney comes in.

Marty hasn't told Peterkinney that he's his best muscle these days. Peterkinney worked that out for himself. Being given increasingly awkward jobs. Getting more frequent work than most other muscle. It all adds up to Peterkinney being the best. Fine, whatever. He doesn't much care. This is short term for him. Make some money then walk away, best or not.

Working for Roy Bowles might be more long term, but it's not frequent enough. If Bowles came up with the work often enough,

Peterkinney would settle for it. Ditch Marty and his shitty, scum-of-the-earth work. But that's not an option. Need the regular income. Bowles is so careful, keeps his workload down. The work is carefully plotted, reassuring. But there's so little of it. Peterkinney has to earn more than Bowles provides. He wants to get a place of his own. Needs to. Starting to climb the walls in that damp little flat of his grandfather's. The flat's no worse than it ever was, nor is his grandfather. But the more money he saves, the more he wants. The closer he comes to escaping the flat, the more desperate he gets.

Anyway, he's been waiting for the darkness to come. Shouldn't need to. Aird isn't going to make an issue of this. You get to his point in life and you don't make an issue of anything. Aird's living on the edge. He won't fight back. He won't argue. He'll take whatever's dished out to him. He'll be grateful for anything that stops short of pushing him over the edge. The challenge for Peterkinney is to make sure he doesn't go too far.

A guy like Aird is easy to misjudge. You knock him around, maybe he panics. Maybe he turns up at Marty's office with the money. Marty doesn't want that. Can't use a man who pays his debts. Can't misuse him. Intimidate him, but don't send him running to another lender. Intimidate him enough to put him under pressure. Then, when a favor is requested, he'll be only too happy to oblige.

Peterkinney doesn't ask about the favors. Marty needs something done, he sends someone round to Aird to request a favor. Tells a man who owes a grand that he can have three hundred dropped if he does something useful. What constitutes useful in Marty's world is Marty's business. Peterkinney doesn't care. He can guess. Go rob a house owned by a rival. This car will be parked in this location. Go trash it. Use expendable, desperate losers to annoy and intimidate your rivals. That sort of thing. He's hardly going to give them important work, is he? Just risky, trashy, low-grade stuff that he couldn't persuade anyone else to do. If it's a woman who owes the money? That's different.

Aird lives in a shitty little flat in a rough part of town. According to Marty there might be a couple of other people living there with him. Might be. Marty doesn't know. Rumor has it that Aird doesn't live alone. Needs other people to help him pay the rent. But Marty can't be sure, because Marty can't ever seem to be fucking sure. It's always vague information and a demand for the job to be done as soon as possible. Not that Marty couldn't find out. He could, if he could be bothered. He just doesn't care about the risks his staff take.

Peterkinney's learned how sloppy Marty is at what he does by working with Bowles. Bowles is good. He knows how to handle these things. He understands the value of information. Understands the need for preparation. It's not just because Bowles has more experience. And it's not because what he does carries more risk. He does have more experience and gunrunning does carry more risk. But that's not it. Bowles cares about people working for him getting into trouble. Entirely selfish. He doesn't want them arrested, hospitalized or killed. That would raise awkward questions. But he also wants to make sure that good employees stick around. Marty doesn't care. Everyone's expendable to Marty. If Marty cared to make an effort, he could match Bowles for detail. Even exceed him. Marty has connections Bowles can't get. But Marty's only thinking about Marty. Not even taking the collection business all that seriously, it seems to Peterkinney. Too lazy, too distracted by the other strings to his bow.

That's why Peterkinney's already looking for a way out. Not desperately. He'll keep working for Marty until an opportunity comes along. But he won't settle for this. This won't be the rest of his life. No way working for someone like Marty can last. Too unpleasant. Sitting in his car, outside this block of flats. A street of four-story blocks. Watching lights come on as daylight runs away. He has the address for the flat. Might as well get this out of the way.

He's not wearing a balaclava, although he has purchased one. One of the first things he did when he knew he was going to be working for Marty. Bought a balaclava and a pair of gloves. Ditched the gloves. They were a stupid idea. As seen on TV. Wearing a pair of actual gloves makes every part of the job harder. Some thug working for Marty tipped him off to thin surgical gloves. Sort of thing cleaners wear. You can buy them by the boxful in the supermarket. But he's not going to wear them either. Not tonight.

Tonight isn't a job that needs any sort of protection. Tonight is a job where faces can be seen and fingerprints left. There's nothing that Peterkinney could do to Aird that would make Aird go to the police. Not a thing in the world. Could torture the boy, he still wouldn't go to the cops. See, a boy like Aird lives in greater fear of the cops than Peterkinney does. Aird has a habit that will get him into trouble. He has probably resorted to paying for that habit by doing things he shouldn't. He won't want the police getting his fingerprints on file, comparing them to those found at the scenes of robberies and muggings. No, the police have no role to play in tonight's criminality.

Through the door of the building and along to the front door of the flat. Ground floor, which helps. Something else Peterkinney has learned. You don't know how fast you'll have to get away. Look, Aird should be soft. People like him almost always are. But there could be other people there, Marty said. One of them might decide that the best way out of debt is to kill the collector. Attack him at least. People react stupidly, violently. You have to know the way out. Need to have a clean run to the exit. That's easier if you don't have a dark stairwell to negotiate.

Knocking on the door. No need to kick your way in. That was a mistake Peterkinney only made once. Made it when him and Glass went after that Jim Holmes character. That was a fuck-up. A lucky fuck-up, but that doesn't make it any less of a fuck-up. Kicking down the door? Behaving like the bloody A-Team. You don't kick down doors. You knock on them. Even people who know they're in trouble answer the door. Even people in trouble know other people who might come visit. As long as you're not too late in the night, there's nothing suspicious about a knock on the door. You just have to know how to make the work easy.

The door's opening slowly. Looks like the description of Aird. Mop of thick black hair. Broad-shouldered but skinny round the waist. Brown bags under his eyes. Befuddled look. Doesn't cope well with the unexpected. Not a lot of people knock on his door. Someone new turns up, and it's likely to upset him.

"You Gordon?"

"Uh, yeah." Had to think about that one.

"Good. I'll come in then." Take the initiative. Never give them the chance to pull the strings of the conversation. Once they get used to the sound of their own voice, they'll try and fill the room with it. Make sure yours gets there first and takes all the space available.

Peterkinney's pushed his way inside. It's small, narrow, almost empty in here. Furniture is a luxury for people with the spare cash. Aird has something else to spend his money on. Smells like a small place, never cleaned and always occupied. Bloody freezing as well. Too bad. Aird has his life, Peterkinney has his. When this is done, Peterkinney will go home to his grandfather's flat. He won't give Aird and his little hovel another thought.

"You know that you owe money, Gordon." Peterkinney standing in the gloomy corridor. Nothing on the walls but flaky white paint and damp. There's no bulb or shade on the light above them. The only light reaching the corridor is coming from the open door to the empty living room. Peterkinney stopping in the corridor. Good a place as any. Less space for Aird to wriggle out of a punch. "Been a long time since you made any effort to pay."

"Ah, shit, yeah." Early enough in the evening for Gordon to know what he's in trouble for. That helps. You occasionally get people who are too far gone to remember who they owe money to. You knock them around. Following morning they wake up with cuts and bruises and no memory of how they got them. And still no memory that they owe anyone cash. They're not faking it. It comes as a shock to them to find out they owe anything at all. Almost no chance of gaining anything from those ones.

"So it's time to pay up. You owe a thousand pounds, Gordon."

"A thousand. Do I owe a thousand? Shit. Thousand pounds is a lot of money, you know. I don't think I owe that. Do I?"

"You do. And you need to pay it, before it gets any bigger. Need to pay it now." Putting a harsh tone into his voice. Don't let the junkie run the conversation round in circles. Confusion can be infectious. "So are you going to pay?"

Aird is making a startled noise. The idea that he would have a thousand pounds on him is pretty startling. "I don't have that cash. I don't. But I'll get it. I mean, I can. I can get it."

No point hanging around here. Doesn't seem to be anybody else in the flat. Time to give the boy a fright and leave. Peterkinney's reached the end of the corridor, able to see into almost every room. There's nobody there, no chance of this spinning out of his control. As long as it's just him and Aird, it's under control. Turning back, and quickly punching Aird in the stomach. No warning. No pulling back of the arm. Quick little rabbit punch. Catch him off guard.

Thing is, a guy like Aird can't take a punch. He's young and he's broad-shouldered, but that counts for nothing. He's spent nearly a decade wrecking his body. He lives in terrible conditions. He is basically unhealthy. Undernourished, rotten teeth, broken fingernails. Pick a body part, and it's not in the condition evolution intended. One punch and he's dropped down onto his knees. That makes this more difficult. Peterkinney has to really scare him. One punch isn't enough for that. One punch won't even be memorable. Not when you've taken as many as Aird.

Now that Aird's down, he's awkward to hit. Peterkinney's shuffling to get his footing right. Leaning slightly. Swinging a second punch. Better backswing this time. Looking to hit him on the side of the jaw. Avoid the top of the head unless you want to know what broken knuckles feel like. You don't want to know what broken knuckles feel like. Neither does Peterkinney. It's an awkward punch. Not going to do a lot of harm. But it has shock value. Aird thought being down would protect him. It's sending him sideways, into the wall in this narrow corridor. It'll bruise. It'll make talking and eating uncomfortable for a few days. Nothing broken though. Wasn't able to hit him hard enough for that. Not in this stupid crouching position. But it'll remind him about the money he owes, every time he feels the pain of it.

Peterkinney's straightening up. "You listen to me, Gordon. You have a week. One week from today. You pay up one week from today or there's going to be serious trouble. You understand me?"

"Uh-huh. Uh-huh."

Peterkinney's stepping over Aird. Walking to the front door and out of the flat. No colder outside than in. Aird probably doesn't even know what day it is. He won't remember that he has seven days to pay. But he will remember that he has to pay. He might even try and do something about it. But before he has any chance to find the money, someone will come pay him a visit. Another one of Marty's men. Always a different one from the attacker. The attacker is the angry face you must fear. The man offering work will be the friendly face, helping you out of a hole. They'll tell him they've got an idea to help him. Do this little favor, and some of the problems will go away. And he'll be so desperate to help. So pathetic.

7

A different kind of job. A punishment. Bavidge is letting the clock tick a little further. Get closer to midnight. He's been seen in this area before. The neighbors gawked at him last time he was here. Couple of months ago. Long enough that most of them won't remember. Not going to take any risks though. A person with an empty life will remember the few interesting faces that pop up. He's borrowed a car. Patterson has a couple of them that he keeps spare. Rotate between them; use them on jobs like this. Bavidge is dressed plainly. He has a pair of thin gloves and a black cap on. Not a bala-clava, that shouldn't be necessary.

He's parked near the bottom of the street. Watching the street ahead. Looking for any sign of action. If Holmes is running then he might have people helping him. There might be a bunch of them at the house. Packing up, and helping him run. No sign of it. Just a few cars parked on the street. None right outside the house. A deep breath. Doesn't matter how many times you've done this, a deep breath always helps. Starting the car.

He's parking right outside the house. The shortest escape route. Looking up and down the street. Trying to work out if it's worth the risk or not. No, take the keys with you. If he thought he could get away with it, he would leave the keys in the ignition. Gain a few po-tentially precious seconds. Not this time. Shouldn't need that extra time, but hell, you should never need it. In this area, you don't gam-ble with your transport. Protect your escape route. Take the keys in with you.

This job requires all the thought you can give it. Not a normal job. A normal job is an attack on someone with only a basic idea of how to defend themselves. Of how to attack back. Not Holmes. He knows the business. Been doing this longer than Bavidge has. Not better, but longer. Long enough to learn the lessons. Long enough to make this a handle-with-care job.

Pulling the cap down a little and getting out of the car. Locking it. Looking at the house. There's a light on downstairs. Front window was the living room, if he remembers right. That means the thief and his woman are in there. Still up and about. Maybe packing up their stuff, if they have any idea of what's good for them. Amazing that they haven't run already. Stupid of them, and stupidity carries a price. Bavidge is walking quickly up the path. Ringing the door-bell. Be interesting to see how long they take to answer. A glance at his watch. Ten to midnight. Should take enough time for question-ing looks and a reluctant walk to the door. If there's a rush to the door, then they might be expecting someone else. Someone to help them run.

Ten seconds. Twenty seconds. Finally the sound of the door be-ing unlocked. Then opened. Hope to God it's not on one of those wee chains. Then you have to try and talk your way in. Bavidge can do it. Holmes knows him now. Knows they both work for Patterson. Bavidge could bluff his way in with that. And if the bluff fails, you have to kick it in, and the job's gone to hell before you've crossed the threshold. But he doesn't have to. The door's opening wide and Norah Faulkner is staring back at him. That same rough expres-sion. The same dressing gown as two months ago, although Bavidge doesn't recognize that. Hair tied back, no make-up. Ready for bed. So not running tonight.

"Norah. Alan Bavidge, Jim home?"

She's relaxing. More than she should. More than he thinks she would if she knew Jim was skimming 20 percent from his boss. Now that is interesting. She's nodding, and waving a hand for him to come in. Looking out the door behind him to make sure that none of the nosy neighbors are around and watching.

"Something the matter?" she's asking. Leading him through to the living room. "Is it that Marty Jones again?"

"No, Norah, it isn't," Bavidge is saying.

Holmes is in the living room. He was sitting in his chair watching TV, but he's getting to his feet. The look on his face started out intrigued, but that's been knocked out of the way by panic. Bavidge can see it. Holmes is scared. More likely to do something stupid. More likely that this is about to turn nasty.

Bavidge is moving fast. Has to, because of that look. Because Holmes knows why he's there. And because of Norah. He's one against two. She might not know what's going on, but she's going to work it out. She's going to back her man. Probably. And she's as tough as buggery, is Norah Faulkner. Dismiss her as the wife if you want, but a wife with a weapon is more dangerous than a man without. So Bavidge already has his hand in his pocket. Pulling out the Stanley knife. Clicking the blade up a single notch. Keep it short and manageable. Makes it much less likely to snap, which these blades are prone to doing. Moving round the side of the chair and closer to Holmes, before Holmes has half a chance to react.

Bavidge just doesn't get nervous. This is his life. Day in, day out. Dealing with people like Jim Holmes. Getting into violent and dangerous situations. You do it often enough, and you lose the fear of it. Bavidge lost that fear years ago. Only thirty-two, but he's been around this life long enough not to worry about it. Not to fear the danger he's putting himself in. Not to fear the pain that he might suffer if it goes wrong. Pain and suffering are part of the job. He'll think about it afterwards. Sometimes he'll even worry about it afterwards. But not at the time. Never at the time.

So the knife is in his hand. Slashing out. If you didn't know what to look for, you might think it was a wild swing of the arm. It wasn't. He was aiming for the left cheek, and he got it. Not just got it, but caught it near the ear and is running the blade swiftly down towards the mouth. Not casual. Fast and certain. Finding the target with one swing. In the first couple of seconds afterwards, there's very little of anything. Not a lot of blood. Just a thin red line welling up on Holmes's face. Not a lot of reaction. Holmes has stumbled backwards a step, raising a hand towards his face but not touching the wound. He can feel the sting, but hasn't realized how serious it is. Staring ahead at Bavidge. Norah is still standing by the living-room door. Watching.

Now the reaction. Bavidge should have moved quicker after the slash. That was a mistake. Can't afford two of those in one night. Holmes is lurching forwards. Shouting something that only made sense in his head. Loud and big and throwing himself at Bavidge. Trying to use size to intimidate and overwhelm. Worked for him many times before. Bavidge is ducking sideways. Holding the knife outward, hoping for a glancing blow. But Holmes is past him, and stumbling towards the couch. Not looking to tackle Bavidge, just looking to get past him. Stumbling towards the drinks cabinet behind the couch.

Still shouting sentences constructed entirely of vowels. Like his fury is something the world deserves to hear about. And Norah joining in now. Screaming baffling words. A choir of panic. Bavidge is across to Holmes. Kicking the back of his leg and leaning in after the kick. Holmes going down beside the drinks cabinet. Hard on his knee, ignoring the pain. Still trying to reach for the little handle of the cabinet. There's something in there. A weapon he wants to go for. Something he knows would turn the tide of this fight. Not today. Should have had it closer to hand. That was his mistake. Bavidge is down beside him. On his knees. Grabbing Holmes's mouth in one hand and squeezing until the lips part. He saw a guy do this once. Years ago now: "Gully" Fitzgerald. Tough bastard, had a lot of little tricks up his sleeve. Taught Bavidge this one. A good way to shut someone up and panic them. You get a man panicked, and the fight is yours. Quickly slashing the tip of the blade along the upper gum. Got a lot of tooth, but enough gum. Enough blood. As an injury, it's little more than nuisance value. But it's a scary nuisance for the first few minutes. A wound you can't see, but can taste.

Holmes is panicking. Thrashing around with both hands up to his mouth. The more he moves, the more the blood from the wound on his cheek spreads and spills. Now Norah's screaming something they can all understand.

"What did you do to him? What did you do to him?"

Bavidge is beginning to lift himself up from his kneeling position. Something hits him in the back. Something big and solid. Jesus, Norah, you're heavier than you look. Bavidge is taking a couple of steps backward. Straightening up and throwing her off. He's not strong, but she doesn't have much of a grip. No grip of anything at this point, to be fair. Bavidge needs to end this quickly before he totally loses control. Lost some, but has more than anyone else. Norah charging at him now. Bavidge pushes her back with his left hand, keeping the knife away from her. She isn't a part of this. Don't spread punishment any further than it needs to go. Basic rule. She's stumbled backward. Crashing into the big TV and the little stand it's on. The TV's back against the wall, so it only tips over slightly. Nothing broken. Norah pausing, wheezing, and preparing her next attack. Bavidge has to stop her.

"He was skimming money again," Bavidge is saying. Loud enough to break through the cacophony of stupidity from the other two. Surprised by the edge in his voice. It almost sounds nervous. Definitely sounded angry.

Holmes is on his knees. Hands to his mouth. Ignoring everything and everyone. Forgetting about the old handgun he paid four hundred quid for and hid in the cabinet. Too late for that to do any good now. He's rumbled. It's been said. Norah's on her backside, one arm back against the slanting TV. Looking at Bavidge and shaking her head.

"No," she's saying. "I warned him. It wasn't him, it couldn't have been. I warned him." She had no idea. Desperate for Bavidge to be wrong. Sure that he's right. It's broken them, silenced them.

"It was him," Bavidge is saying. Quiet now. No need for raised voices. "Five percent to start with. In the last couple of weeks he's kicked it up to twenty. He knew we would notice. He had to know, but he did it anyway. He's been preparing to run. Must have it all planned out."

He was not planning to take Norah with him. She's shaking her head. Looking past Bavidge at Holmes. He's still on his knees. Hands to his mouth. Blood through the fingers. Looking across at Norah. Ignoring Bavidge. He's done all the damage he came to do. Delivered the message. One that will be seen and heard. The slash on the cheek lets everyone see the price of fucking with Billy Patterson. Holmes is looking at Norah. Norah's looking back. It's not a good way to end a relationship.

Bavidge has clicked the blade back down inside the plastic handle and slipped the knife into his pocket. He's pulling the dislodged cap back down over his head and walking out of the house. Leaving behind the mess of other people's lives. Whatever happens with these two is their business. None of his. He just wants out. Away. The neighbors will have heard that racket. How could they not? Even if they're scared of sticking their noses into Norah's business, one of them will call the cops. Bavidge is into the car, and relieved to be driving away.

Too late to call up his girlfriend. He'd already canceled the date. Been doing that a lot lately. He'll go home instead. Home alone. A small house, in a good part of town. Quiet and simple, devoid of any good reason to want to spend time there. It's a house that's only ever been occupied by a single man. A man with no idea how to create something that even he would be happy in. He's parked outside, gone in. Standing in the kitchen. Remembering Holmes's house. Not the fight, not the screaming. The decoration and the effort. Norah, you could tell, made that house what it was. Nice and comforting. Homely. Bavidge is shaking his head. Of all the things to be jealous of. Have a couple of drinks and try to get some sleep. There'll be more of this to come. Plenty more. It's getting late.

8

It is late. Glass has been thinking about going home for a while now. Ella was right about this place. It is a nice club. There is a good quality of clientele. It is expensive. One of the reasons it isn't his sort of place. It feels more buttoned up. The music isn't so loud. The people are all a little richer than he's used to hanging around. He feels out of place. He assumes everyone else has noticed that he's out of place. These are smart people, they can tell. Ella hasn't noticed. She's having the time of her life.

She was delighted when she got back to the flat and found that he had some money. She had some too. She had as much as she had been planning on spending that night. When she saw his five hundred, she suddenly planned to spend more. That's why she's having the time of her life. This is an escape for her. The chance to come to a place like this with her boyfriend, and her money. Not work, just play. The amount of fun she has seems to be directly linked to the amount she spends. The same is not true of Glass.

His five hundred is shrinking fast. He should have borrowed less. He realizes that, now that it's too late. No matter how much he borrowed, she would have spent the lot. She's enjoying showing people that she has money to spend. He could have gotten away with a couple of hundred. Cursing himself for that. It's spoiling his evening, watching the money disappear. Knowing that he'll have to find it all over again.

Ah, fuck it. Just forget about the money. Concentrate on Ella. Concentrate on the good time she's having. See how happy she is. She's having that great time with Glass. Being happy with him. Nobody else there. Nobody else impressing her with their largesse, just Glass. They feel like a couple. A proper couple, you know. Not just two young people who spend a lot of time together. Not friends with benefits. It feels like they're together. Like they're the sort of couple that will stay together. These are the first blocks in building a life together. That's a good feeling. One worth paying for.

After midnight, memories start to get a little hazy. He'd been drinking. They'd done a line or two. They were dancing. There have been a lot of nights like that in the last couple of months. Drink, drugs, dancing and little detail. But this one was different. This was his night out as much as hers. This was something he was able to pay for. On this night, his night, he realized how humiliating it was to tag along when she was working. Never noticed it before. Never felt it. There were embarrassing moments, sure. But this was different. This was the night that made him understand that he wants Ella to stop what she does for a living. Made him understand that to be his, she couldn't be anyone else's.

He stayed way past the point that he was enjoying himself. He paid for this night. He was damned if she wasn't going home with him. This wasn't a work night. He can't remember going home. It was late. Later than it should have been. Club stayed open past time. He remembers walking along the street with Ella. The pair of them needed every inch of that pavement. They were both long gone, weaving all over the place. But everything was funny. They had their arms round each other, laughing at things that usually seemed so boring. It was nice.

They got home. Not sure how, but they got back to Glass's flat. He remembers what a great mood she was in. She wasn't tired. She wasn't moody. She does a good line in both of those when it's late at night and she's just gotten home. Nope, she was happy. He was happy. They had a happy half hour before they fell asleep.

It's morning. Well, technically it isn't. Technically it's five past twelve in the afternoon, but Glass has just woken up so let's call it morning. Anyway, Ella is still asleep. She always sleeps late. That's her habit, whether she's working or not. So he's in the shower. Then into the kitchen. Making a cup of coffee. While he's waiting for the kettle, he's walking through to the bedroom. Silently sliding his wallet out of the pocket of the trousers he wore last night. Tiptoeing back into the kitchen.

There's one hundred and ninety quid left. Where did the other three hundred and ten go? No fucking clue. Might as well have thrown it into the air, for all he remembers. Yeah, he had a great time with it. But three hundred and ten quid of great time? Shit. That was more expensive than it should have been. Probably got ripped off by someone. Too late to care now. Last night is gone, and now he's looking down the barrel of the future. Now he has to worry about getting some money together. Get that debt paid.

Calling Marty. Can't think of any other source of money, so it's back to Marty. Aware that this phone call counts as haranguing. Turning himself into a boring nuisance, because he can feel the desperation creeping up behind him. Doesn't matter how long he has to pay the debt. He has to start collecting the money. As in, right now. It's ringing, taking a while to answer. Glass is filling his cup with boiling water, hearing the phone being answered. Hearing an annoyed voice on the other end.

"Yes?"

"Marty, this is Alex Glass. Listen, any chance of some work? Anything you need done, I'm there. Doesn't matter the work, I'm up for it." Couldn't sound a great deal more desperate than that. Knowing it, and accepting it. Desperation might persuade Marty to fob him off with some garbage job he has lying around. Anything for money. Anything.

There's a grumble on the other end of the phone. Marty pretending that he's fed up of people calling him for favors. He gets plenty calls from people looking for work, but that's always been part of the job. Used to it, not concerned about it. Be more worried if people weren't calling. It's a measure of how well he's doing. Reassuring, and important. Important to know that when you need people, they'll be ready and willing. Sometimes desperate.

Nobody else is as desperate as this boy. That usually means it's time to stop employing them. The desperate ones are the worst. They take risks. They get pushy. They screw things up for other people. You want someone who wants to do the job but doesn't really need to. Marty had no intention of hiring this kid anyway. He was always a little too enthusiastic. It was the other one he wanted. Glass's mate Peterkinney. He's worked out well. Did another fine job yesterday on that junkie. Stuck-up kid, but smart and tough. Little too smart and assertive for his own good, but profitable. Not this one. No profit from desperation.

"I don't really have any work for you right now, kid," Marty's saying. That's not true. Once this call is done, he's going to call up one of his other boys. Got a couple of collections need doing. Needs three guys to work as drivers for a party on Friday, another two or three to work security. None of them will be Glass. This loser at a big party? Nah, wouldn't know how to handle it.

"I'll do anything that needs doing, Marty?"

Oh God, he's pleading. "Listen, I don't have time for this," Marty's saying. Putting an edge on his voice. Make him understand. "I got things to do. I already told you, I have no work for you. Look around. Find someone else that needs some work done. You don't just have to work for me. This was never exclusive. I don't mind if you find work somewhere else, long as you don't step on my toes. Okay?"

Could not have made it any clearer. He doesn't care if Glass goes and works for someone else. He doesn't care if Glass never works for him again. He wants rid of Glass. This is a sacking. Glass knows it. Shit. Shouldn't have called him. That only pissed him off. Glass is hanging up about half a second after Marty's already done so. Drinking that cup of coffee.

Fine, so Marty doesn't want him. There are plenty of other people he can go work for. Plenty of other ways to make money. He's resourceful. He's willing. He'll go and do whatever needs to be done.

Hell, there's plenty jobs for a guy who's willing to work. He hasn't managed to find one before, sure. There aren't a lot of people hiring, the way things are. But there are jobs if you know how to do them. Look at Peterkinney. He's got two of the bloody things. One for Marty. Another one he doesn't talk about. Secrets and money, got plenty of both. Got enough money to go buy a car. Looking to get out of his grandfather's flat. Moving on to bigger things. Yeah, and leaving the rest of them behind.

Glass has his phone out, about to call Peterkinney, when Ella plods into the kitchen. Wearing a T-shirt and nothing else. Her hair tied back and messy. Looking tired. Looking for a coffee.

"Morning," Glass is saying with a smile.

"Morning, you. Last night was excellent," she's saying, drawing out the word "excellent" for no apparent reason. A happy little sigh and an impish smile. Last night was a great treat to her. Not something she expects or even wants every night. Just nice to have once in a while. Not a treat if you have it every day, is it?

"Yeah. It was. Listen, Ella. I was thinking, we should have more nights like last night."

She's smiling, and shaking her head. "It was good, Alex, but those places are expensive. We need to be careful. We got things to save up for. I want to decorate the bathroom. And we should get a new carpet for the living room, that one's full of holes and snags."

"Yeah, sure. But I mean nights where it's just you and me. Having fun and all that, but just you and me."

"It's always just you and me," she's saying. Trying to keep her tone playful, but she can see where this is going. She's had this conversation before. Doesn't want this to become an argument. Doesn't want this flat to fill with memories of battles between her and Alex. Keep it happy. Keep it a home.

"No, I mean, nights where . . . Nights where it's you and me and no work, you know. We should have a lot more of those. Lot less of, uh, other nights."

She's stopped and she's looking down at the worktop in front of her. She isn't frowning exactly. She's gone from happy to no expression, which feels like a frown. "So you want me to stop working?"

He's opened his mouth, but he's closed it again. It's a harder question to answer than it should be. The ice didn't look this thin when he thought about this. Seemed so simple. Not with the tone she's taken. He doesn't want arguments in here either. He fears that one argument could be enough for him to lose his grip on this relationship. Just doesn't realize how firm that grip is. Doesn't realize how simple it is to keep hold. Don't be a layabout and don't mention work. That's it. Everything else is happy.

"I think it would be nice if you worked less. I think we could be together more. I think, you know, we should both be looking for other work. You know, like work that'll last long term. That sort of thing. That's all I meant. Build for the future."

She's shaking her head. "I knew it would start eventually. You can't handle what I do. I make money. You're not bringing any in. I make money. We need that. We can't build for the future without it. Listen, Alex, we have to be realistic. I want us to get other things. I want us to have all the things you want us to have. The long-term jobs, all that. But…we don't have that. I don't know how to get that. I know how to do what I do. If you can find other jobs, then great. Until you do, I have to keep working." Made every effort to stay calm throughout that. Kept her voice down, kept it away from argumentative. But there's an argument in there. Feels like there needs to be. Something to drag Alex towards reality. "Unless you've come up with some way of making money…" she's saying. Trailing off and making it a question.

"No." A little bit sheepish. Looking down at the floor. This has gotten away from him. He just wants it to end.

"No. So I have to keep working. Keep earning money. We don't have a choice, for now. You get that, don't you, Alex?" Stepping towards him, and putting her hands on his sides.

"Yeah. For now. But I'll look for something else. Look for better opportunities."

"Yeah," she's saying with a smile, "better opportunities. They'll come, but we have to be patient. They'll come."

She's gone back to making her coffee. He's gone back to finishing his. Wishing he hadn't started that particular conversation. He can try again, but not yet. He can only try again when he's in a position of strength. When he's making some money. Then he can pull her round to his way of thinking. He needs to find work. Finishing off the last of the coffee.

"I'm heading out, I shouldn't be too long." He's reaching across and kissing her on the side of the head.

He doesn't see the look. The concern on her face. He's always running off somewhere or phoning someone these days. Trying to find something. A job. A way of making money. Running round all over the place and making nothing of himself. He's capable of better, if he would get real. You don't get rich quick, and there's no easy money.

Glass is out the door and walking. Go see Peterkinney. They've been best friends since they were in school. Since they were fourteen years old. Peterkinney has work. Has money coming in. Good money, probably. If anyone's going to help him out, it's going to be Peterkinney. Has to be.

9

Peterkinney's driven round the area a couple of times. That's standard, but Bowles's warning is still ringing in his ears. Something was making Howie Lawson nervous. It made Bowles nervous. Nervous enough to mention it, anyway. That's made Peterkinney nervous. So Peterkinney's driving a little more slowly, looking a little more closely.

It's an industrial area. Or was. Not much industry now. All warehouses and old buildings. Large buildings with nothing in there. Big wide doors on rusty hinges and broken windows. Most of the buildings have front yards for delivery, so they're not up against the wall. Makes it harder to see anyone peeking out a window or door at him as he drives past. Plenty hiding places. Doesn't like that. Better to do a handover of a single piece somewhere less isolated. Hiding in plain sight.

This is the sort of place you just know will be redeveloped soon. It'll be on the list. Especially this close to the river. Old grimy square buildings replaced by shiny angular ones. A place with potential, the redevelopers will say. The sort of place Peterkinney won't be frequenting anymore.

Nobody out of place. Not that he can see. That's the first thing. Nobody lurking around on the street, looking like they're waiting for him. Nobody around at all. Unless of course they're doing a very good job of it. Can't see into the buildings, obviously. Have to guess what is or isn't in there. Some of them are still in use, but none have activity around them. Big doors shut, nobody loading up or dropping off stock. So he's finding a place to park. Lawson wants to meet round the back of the large warehouse on the left. The dark-gray building with a row of broken windows close to the roof. No vehicles in front of it. Grass growing out of the concrete around the fence at the front. Looks like it hasn't been used in years.

This would be better if he didn't have to get out of the car. If he could drive it round the back of the building. No opening for a car. Even if there was, he doesn't want to be seen driving round there. Raises eyebrows, if anyone's watching. The only car in years to go round the back of that building. Do nothing that draws attention. So he's parking on the street and getting out. The street curves in the middle, so he can't actually see the end of it from here. Can see enough to reassure him. Nothing moving. Nothing grabbing his attention.

He has the money in his pocket. Tapping the pocket again, just to make sure. Feeling the shape of the envelope. Bowles has to be careful. He has to make sure that every penny finds its way to the seller. If he doesn't pay, he loses a seller. Worse, word might get round that he doesn't pay the agreed price. Then nobody sells to him. The seller has to trust the buyer as well, you know.

Peterkinney's found a gate that leads round to the back of the building. Seems to be on the property next door. Might have to find a way over the fence between the two. Along the fence and, yes, he is in the wrong place. Bloody hell. Fence is high, but it's easy to climb. Over it and dropping down into the yard behind the warehouse. Little jarring on the ankles, but not bad. Huh, weird layout. Big yard for lorries to collect stuff, but no way for them to get in or out. Obviously the land the fence is on used to be a part of this yard. People next door must have bought the strip of land from the warehouse owners. Or just taken it. Who really gives a shit?

He can see Lawson. There's a short wall running along the other side of the yard and Lawson's sitting on it. Wearing a dark hoodie, hood pulled up. That's a great way to look conspicuous, genius. A dry day and you're wrapped up like there's a snowstorm. When you're doing the pick-up on a gun, you need the seller to take the same precautions you do. You need them to have the same sense you do. To have some fucking sense, at least. Meeting outdoors at an unused location is not sensible. Sitting on the wall with your hood up in good weather is not sensible. At least he's alone.

Peterkinney's walking across to Lawson. Still keeping his eyes open. Don't get complacent. Not until the gun has been in Bowles's possession for at least eight hours. Then you can stop worrying about it. Then there's no chance of someone in a uniform knocking on your door. Well, not no chance. Less chance. There's never no chance. Not in this business.

"Howie?" Peterkinney's asking. He knows the answer already. Stopping four feet in front of Lawson. Far enough away to make sure Lawson doesn't do anything stupid. Because you never know that either. It was one of the first things Bowles taught him. With any new seller, you keep well back until you see the gun. They might be luring you there to take the money. Even after you see the gun, take nothing for granted. They might be planning to use it to take the money. Now Peterkinney's starting to understand why Bowles was so nervous about this.

"Yeah. You got the money?"

"You got the gun?"

Lawson's reaching under his top. Taking out a blue plastic bag. The bag is wrapped so tightly round the gun you can pretty much make out the outline of it. Not subtle. Lawson still has a lot to learn. Nervous, and making mistakes. He'll get better. He has connections so he can get the weapons. If he keeps delivering, Bowles will make sure he gets plenty of practice. Practice makes perfect.

"The money," Lawson's saying.

Peterkinney's taking the envelope from his pocket. That nervous moment when you have to swap. Money for gun. Who lets go first? Lawson at least has the sense to see that the seller lets go first. He's handing the bag over. Peterkinney taking it in his left hand, now passing the envelope with his right. Pulling open the top of the bag and looking inside. He could tell from the weight already, but you check. A handgun, as advertised.

Now things are happening fast. Peterkinney's about to look up and tell Lawson he's done well, when he hears scuffing. Boots on the ground. Lawson is looking behind him. Suddenly he's spinning over the wall and running. Off in the other direction. The direction of the single uniformed cop running towards them. Idiot. Trying to get out the way he came in, no matter the obstacles. Peterkinney's thinking about the car. His escape. Turning and sprinting for the high fence.

But it's harder this time. Struggling to get the footholds, but struggling more with his hands. The damn gun. Can't drop it. Need to get out and need to get the gun out too. Can't come away empty-handed. Can't leave the gun for the cops to play with. But it's slowing him. He's looking behind him as he's swinging his leg over the top of the fence. No cop. He must have gotten Lawson. That's Lawson's problem. He'll only talk if he's dead from the neck up. Even someone desperate and stupid knows that you don't name the buyer. So the cop has Lawson to play with. Good, gives Peterkinney a better chance.

Peterkinney's dropping to the other side of the fence. Jarring his ankles again. This time worse, but in a hurry. Ignore it and move. Something else Bowles told him. A uniformed cop is never alone. Always in pairs. And if they know there's a gun involved, there will be at least one detective as well. So there could be two more, and they could be close. Could be at his car. Play this careful.

But careful just took a jump out the broken window. There's a cop stepping inside the gate. Closing it behind him. Moving casually. Peterkinney's stopped. Back the way he came? Maybe run round the other side of this building and see how his luck holds. No idea what's there, but it's still an option. But he's not moving. He's standing, watching the cop come towards him. The cop's smiling.

"Well, young man, what have you got there?"

So smug. Happy as a pig in shit, as they say. And Peterkinney knows him. Learned this little lesson from one of Marty's boys. A guy he once did a collection job with pointed this cop out in a pub they went to. PC Paul Greig. Bent, the fellow told him. A fucking nightmare though. So bent he takes your money and still arrests you. You just can't rely on him at all. But bent. That's the important thing to remember here. It's Peterkinney, a gun and a bent copper. Now his mind's racing. Coming up with a new option.

Things are starting to make sense. Lawson was nervous about it. Bowles was worried that it might be a set-up. One cop came running after them. One, on his own. A situation with a gun, and only one cop came round the other way. Now Greig turns up. Nah, that doesn't add up to an honest situation. This is a stitch-up. Lawson probably in on it. They set up the sale to catch Peterkinney. Or any employee of Bowles. But that's not how they do things. Not when they're honest. One cop confronting Peterkinney, all on his own. Doesn't need to worry about the gun, the cop knows more about it than Peterkinney does. The cop will know there are no bullets to fear. But he shouldn't be here alone.

So Peterkinney's starting to talk. He's not going to fight his way out of this. Whatever Greig is, he's still a cop. Can't run. Doesn't know for sure what he's up against, although he's willing to bet now that there are only the two cops. Greig wouldn't be on his own if there were more. Best way out is talking.

"Can I help you, officer?" Pausing as Greig smiles a little. "I'm sure I can do something to help you."

Greig walking a little closer, standing a few feet away. "You think so, huh? I think if I opened that bag you're carrying I'd find a gun. I think I could arrest you. Get you locked up for a few years. Very serious crime, carrying a gun."

"You could do that. But what's the point? Another gun will replace it. Someone else will replace me. I'm sure you and me can come to a better arrangement than that. One that'll last. One that we can all benefit from." His heart's beating fast. This, talking to a cop, is far more nerve-racking than collecting a gun or money. But his mind is still sharp. It's the good kind of nerves. Inspiring.

Greig's looking at him. "So, what? You and me set up some scheme, huh? You and me take a cut of money away from the seller, that sort of thing? That your big idea?" Looking sharply at Peterkinney. Speaking sharp too.

This is where you pick your words carefully. What do you know about Greig? How do you judge what he just said? "That sort of set-up wouldn't work," Peterkinney's saying honestly. "People would never sell to my boss if they heard people were being ripped off. But there could be another way. My boss would pay for protection. He would pay for…"

"Please," Greig is saying, waving a dismissive hand. This isn't what he wants to hear. He needs to hear something convincing, and this ain't it. Roy Bowles will not pay a uniformed officer good money for limited protection.

Peterkinney's thinking. Remembering that conversation he had with one of Marty's boys. Greig still arrests you. He still does his job. He's still a cop who acts like one. That's why you don't trust him, apparently. But if you know he's still a proper cop, you can use that. Use it to get yourself out of this situation. Not like Greig's told him to shut up. They've both essentially accepted that a deal can happen. Now they're just negotiating.

"You keep the money from this sale, fine," Peterkinney is saying. "Maybe there's a way of sorting out other payments, maybe not. I'm sure we can come up with something. But look at it this way. You know there are much worse people than my boss moving guns in this city. Much worse. Much less careful. People like Mark Garvey. People like Robby Draper. You heard about this new kid Spikey?"

"I heard. So what?"

"So you know how my boss does his work. He's strict. He only sells to people in the business. Everything he sells is for use in the industry. None end up in civilian cases. You know that. Can't say that for the rest of them. Garvey will sell to anyone. Draper's been getting desperate. Losing business and selling to anyone who'll pay. This Spikey is a kid, selling to other kids. Street gangs. You want to keep these guns away from civilians, you need someone like my boss controlling the flow. Can't wipe out the trade, you know that. That's naive. If you can't wipe it out, next best thing is controlling it. There might be money in it for you, but what I'm talking about is worth more than that. I'm talking about taking charge of who does and who doesn't get guns in this city."

Damn, that sounded good to Peterkinney. Can't believe how easily it all spilled out. Almost casual. The nerves are dropping too, because he knows he's right. Knows he sounds convincing. Knows that this is what Greig wants to hear.

Greig is looking at him. Not saying no, which is a start. Looking back towards the gate. Looking thoughtful. "What's your name, kid?"

"Peterkinney. Oliver Peterkinney."

"Huh. Well, Peterkinney, you may have stumbled onto something worthwhile. Your boss doesn't get a free ride. He steps out of line and I'll be on him. And I'll be watching you too. We'll be having regular meetings. You and me are going to get to know each other, you understand?"

Peterkinney's nodding. He means that Peterkinney's going to have to pay him regularly. The control thing might matter most, but don't forget the money. "I'm sure it'll be a profitable relationship," Peterkinney's saying.

Greig's nodding. Nice to meet a kid who gets it. Who understands the ways of the industry. He'll do okay, this one. Greig's nodding for the kid to leave. Watching him walk to the gate and out. Walking comfortable. Not running, not stiff. Walking like he's just done a perfectly normal thing.

10

Arnie's never quick to answer the door these days. More often than not bad news. Why rush? Just be someone he doesn't want to talk to. So the person is knocking a second time when he opens it. A young fellow. Takes him a couple of seconds to recognize. It's Alex Glass. Oliver's wee mate. Or he was. Don't see nearly so much of him round here anymore. Which is a good thing, in Arnie's book.

"Hi, is Oliver about?"

The kid looks a mess. He was always a rogue, but at least he was a well-turned-out rogue. Now he looks tired. Looks like he hasn't had a shower after a long night. Looks nervy.

"No, he's out. You want to leave a message or something?" Kids these days. Don't need to leave messages. They got about a hundred different ways of getting in touch with each other. If you can't get through to someone it's because they don't want you to.

"No, no," Glass is saying. Doesn't sound convinced though. Still standing there. Seems like a boy with something to say.

Arnie's about to close the door when the kid pipes up. "Actually yeah, I do. Look, tell him to call me, yeah. Home or mobile, whatever. I really need to talk to him about work. It's important."

That's got Arnie pausing. "What work?" he's asking. The only work Arnie knows Oliver does is for Roy Bowles. Roy would not hire this unreliable moron. And he would not be happy to hear that one of his men has been passing work on to him. Or even talking about it, for that matter. This could be a sackable offense.

Glass is nodding, because he thinks he understands. Peterkinney has two jobs, and his grandfather wants to know which one he's talking about. The old man might be able to put in a good word for him. This could be a chance. "Working for Marty, I mean. I know Oliver's been getting loads of work from him. I haven't been getting any. It's a struggle, you know. Trying to make ends meet. I was hoping he might be able to help me out, get some work."

Arnie's nodding. His face has gone hard, but Glass is too wrapped up in his own problems to notice. "Why don't you come in and wait," Arnie's saying. "Have a cup of tea. He's only gone out for a wee while. He won't be long."

Glass has nowhere else to go, so he's stepping inside. Into the cramped kitchen. Taking a seat and a cup. Arnie sitting opposite him. Wanting to know about this Marty business, but not wanting to push it. He knows Glass will clam up if he thinks he's dropping his mate in it. So he has to pretend that he already knows. Pretend that Oliver doesn't mind him knowing. Even though Oliver's obviously been keeping it from him for a while. If he's been working for Marty since the first time Arnie heard mention of Marty's name then this has been going on for months. The boy lying to him.

"You not getting a lot of work then, Alex?" he's asking. Being friendlier than he's ever been to the worthless kid before. That should be enough to put the boy on high alert, but apparently not. He's just delighted to have someone show an interest.

"Nah. I think Marty's done with me. Says he doesn't have any work for me, but he's got plenty for Oliver. Plenty for everyone else. I was hoping me and Oliver could sort something out. You know, he takes a job from Marty, I do it for him. We split the cash. That sort of thing. Helps him take more work, helps me make some money. You know," he's saying, then trailing off. Aware that he's been talking for a while, and feeling uncomfortable. He always had the impression that Arnie didn't like him much, and that memory has suddenly come back to him.

"You struggling for cash?" Arnie's surprising himself. He actually cares.

"Little bit, yeah," Glass is saying, and shrugging. Looking down at the table. Looking awkward. Not the sort of thing he wants to admit. He's always been independent. Left home when he was eighteen. Always managed to keep his nose above the waterline. Been close a few times, but he's always been able to look after himself. Found work, earned money. Did a better job of looking after himself than his parents ever did of looking after him. Now he needs help.

A suspicion. Arnie frowning and looking at the boy. "You in trouble here, lad?"

Glass breathing out heavily. The truth is tempting. And maybe the old man can put pressure on Oliver to help. Getting to the point where humiliating yourself in front of this old man is the only choice he's got. "I...borrowed some money. Shouldn't have, but I needed it. So now I'm in a hole. I just need some work, that's all. Just a bit to get started, you know. I didn't borrow a lot, so I just need a little work to cover it. It's okay. Just a bit. Oliver can sort me out. He's well in with Marty."

"I didn't know he was doing so well," Arnie's saying, making it sound casual. Making it sound like he knew his grandson was working for that piece of shit, just didn't realize how successfully.

"Oh yeah, Oliver's doing great." Thinking he's doing his mate a favor by talking him up. Looking Arnie in the eye, across the little table. They can't both put their arms on the table; their hands would meet in the middle. So Glass has his hands in his lap, feeling uncomfortable and looking childish. "He gets a hell of a lot more work than me. Actually, I think he gets more than anyone. Marty likes him. I don't think Oliver likes Marty much," Glass is saying with a shrug. "Doesn't go in for the lifestyle or anything like that, you know. But he gets the work, so..."

One thing to be relieved about. But it's a small thing. He might not live the life, but he works the job. That's bad enough on its own. "Was it going in for the lifestyle that got you into a hole?" Arnie's asking.

Glass is smiling. He doesn't think about Ella as being part of the lifestyle. She's part of his life. "Sort of," he's saying reluctantly. Because he only met her through her work. Can't deny that. And her work is part of the lifestyle. Doesn't matter how much he wishes otherwise, it is and it will continue to be.

Arnie's about to pursue the point when he hears a key in the door. Oliver home. Hears him walking along the corridor and opening the door to his bedroom.

"Oliver, kitchen," Arnie's shouting.

Oliver sticks his head round the door. Sees his friend and his grandfather. A slight frown that he manages to kill before it gives his mood away. He was happy coming in the door. Came out of that meeting with Greig about as well as he could have. The adrenaline may be fading, but he's still a little high. The thrill, the confidence that he handled a treacherous situation well. Can't beat that feeling. It's going to cost him. He's the one who'll have to pay the cop, because he isn't going to tell Bowles about it. Not yet, anyway. You don't tell the boss that you got cornered by a bent copper. You pay the cost yourself. You see if there's any way you can make it work for you. A guy like Greig could be very useful. A guy like Glass, not so much.

"Alex. Good to see you, man. Come through." Nodding for his friend to follow him through to the bedroom where they can talk in private. Away from Arnie. Away from any conversation that reveals more than it should. Too late for that.

Arnie is still sitting in the kitchen. Waiting for Glass to leave and Oliver to come talk to him. Which he will, because he has to explain this Marty thing. Glass isn't smart enough to lie about what he told Arnie. They've been in there ten minutes now. At one point there was a raised voice. Oliver's, certainly. Harsh, it sounded. Almost mocking in tone. Now the bedroom door is opening. Now the front door, and someone's gone. Glass moved along that corridor quickly, leaving in a hurry and a huff.

Oliver's coming into the kitchen. Nodding to his grandfather. Looks grumpy, looks like he's ready for an argument. Arnie knows the look. Oliver gets it when he's annoyed with something, but he knows it better from Oliver's father. There was a fellow who never let a potential fight walk casually by. Always spoiling for trouble. Always in a howler. Had to handle him carefully, just like you do his son.

"I think that boy's in trouble," Arnie's saying. Open with agreement. Something obvious. Something that Oliver can't possibly object to.

"I think so too."

"Silly thing, to borrow money. Drags you down, that sort of thing. Never ends well. That boy needs a friend to help him out. Why don't you give him the work Marty Jones is giving you? You can concentrate on getting the hell away from Marty Jones, like you were going to."

A sigh for an answer. Oliver standing with his back to the worktop, looking down at the table where Arnie's sitting. A grim look, already on the defensive and ready to defend with aggression. "I've been doing a few jobs for Marty, yeah. Just a few. Now and again. I don't make enough money from Roy Bowles. You know how unreliable that work is. You know I don't make enough there. So I need something else. But it's temporary."

"And how long has it been temporary?"

"Fine. You're right. I know you are. Marty Jones is poison. You don't have to tell me that. You really don't. Listen, right. I'll make you a promise: I will be out from Marty's business within the month, okay? I'll be gone in a month. I'm looking at another opportunity. Something better. I've been thinking about it for a while. I did a job for Roy today. Made me realize a few things. Seriously, within a month. That enough to make you happy?"

Arnie's looking at him. Ignoring the snarky tone. The superior tone that's crept into a lot of what Oliver says these days. This time he meant it, but he doesn't always. There's been a tendency lately for him to speak down to his grandfather. Presumably because he's working and Arnie isn't. Gets on Arnie's nerves, sure, but he doesn't say anything. Why bother?

He wants to believe Oliver will get out from under Marty. He also wants to believe that when Oliver stops working for Marty, it will be for something better. Something legitimate. Wants to believe, but doesn't. If he has plans of his own then it'll be within the industry. What else does he know? But anything is better than Marty.

"Fine. You get away from Marty Jones; I'll say no more about it."

PART THREE

1

This hasn't gone as quickly as he would have liked. Not as quickly as MacArthur would like either. But Cruickshank can see it for what it is. Cracking a tough little nut. Once you get inside, it'll be soft. Break through and things happen quickly. But Patterson has surrounded his business with a wall of tough employees. Loyal and hard. Also very private. Done an amazing job of keeping mouths shut, not giving away any detail they don't want people to know. That's a hard challenge, even with loyal employees. People speak, but not the people working for Patterson. Been difficult for both Potty and MacArthur to work out who's who in the Patterson organization. They've done so well in protecting themselves. Today will change some of that. Today Potty has a meeting with a lowlife scumbag with a big mouth.

Best part of three months since Patterson got rid of Jim Holmes. Sent someone round to slash him. Left a mark for all the world to see. Lets people know that Holmes is not a man to be trusted. Which is a good thing to tell people. Helpful. Appreciated. But that doesn't stop Holmes from being useful. At least, Holmes better hope it doesn't. Today, he needs to be useful.

They're meeting in the back of a pub that Potty has a share of. Little place. Reasonably upmarket, as these places go. Potty doesn't much like pubs. Never visits. But he has to have places like this. Lots of little businesses where his money washes itself clean. Can't justify all of the returns that his "finance company" makes. Pubs are an easy sort of business to pick up these days, easy to work the books.

Holmes was early. Was here before Potty, and hit the bar while he waited. He was on his third pint when Potty's driver dropped him off. The landlord showed Potty through to the back, made sure he had everything he needed. A big, well-lit room with a small table. A large, cushioned seat for Potty, a small chair for the other guy. They have little events in here, put out a few tables. Just the one table for this meeting. The landlord showed Potty to his seat, asked if he wanted anything to eat or drink. Then went and got the waiting Holmes from his happy place at the bar.

Sitting opposite each other. Each thinking the same of the other. What a bastard. Everyone thinks Potty's a bastard. Principally because he is, and makes little effort to hide it. Potty thinks Holmes is a bastard for a couple of reasons. Both are that he's a little thief. Thieved from Marty Jones. Got caught. Thieved from Billy Patterson. Got caught. Three months go by, and now he's running to Potty, looking for help.

Potty's had Holmes's background looked into. Found out what he's been up to for the last three months. Struggling, is what. Split with his woman. Left his house. Tried to run, but couldn't make life work anywhere else. Came back to the city looking for work. Couldn't find it. Now begging at Potty's door. Saying he has info about Patterson that could help. The shaggy-haired, bearded, overweight prick better, because he's on thin ice. Three strikes and you're out. Got away with thieving from Marty. Was lucky to get away from Patterson with scarring. Piss off Potty Cruickshank and it goes further.

Don't show your distaste. Fellow looks like he could use a wash. Hair is a little too long, beard that's probably only there to hide scars. Clothes look scruffy, but Potty's seen a good deal worse. You think he's pathetic and disgusting. You think he's the sort of person you shouldn't have to lower yourself to meeting. But you do. Information can come from anywhere, and sometimes you just have to hold your nose to get a hold of it.

"So, Mr. Holmes, I'm led to believe that you have information you think I would find useful." Said in a tone that makes it clear Potty doesn't believe him. That makes it clear he better deliver fast. Keep this conversation short.

"I do. I know all about Patterson. Worked for him for a couple of months. I can name everyone working for him. Everyone close to him. The lot of them."

They know a few names already. They've taken action against a couple so far. A couple isn't enough. Not in three months. Especially when they're not at the top of the tree. You have to be seen to make a sustained attack. Less than one a month is not sustained. At times, it's felt like they shouldn't have bothered. Should have waited until they had three or four names and gone after them all in a week. You drip-feed it like this and you're the one who looks weak. Attacked the first guy. Beat him and set his house on fire. A little showy, but it sent out the message. Sent him scurrying off out of the business. Bought off the second guy. He was reluctant and expensive, but he took the money in the end.

"And what makes you think I would care about that?" Potty is saying. Throwing in the question because you have to pretend that you don't care. Make the bottom feeders think you have a thousand plates spinning. Make them think Patterson is no big deal to you. You don't want the likes of Holmes knowing your business, or even thinking he knows.

Holmes is watching him, mouth slightly open. Picking his answer from the short list of options running through his mind. Holmes is no fool. Been around the business too long for that. He knows that Potty doesn't want to hear that he's at war with Billy Patterson. You don't say that sort of thing out loud. Not to the guy in charge. Especially when the guy in charge isn't clearly winning the war.

"I thought it would be useful for you to know. Always good to know what a rival's got around him. Information, you know. Even if he ain't much of a rival, I mean." Said with a shrug. Grasping for the right tone.

Potty's smiling. He's even more unpleasant when he smiles, but isn't that often the way. "You have been around this business a long time, haven't you, Mr. Holmes. Yes, that might be useful. And what would you want in return?"

Pick this one carefully as well. Don't trip yourself up here. A shrug to begin with. Get the tone just right before you throw the options back at Potty. And you do give Potty the options. He has to be the one that decides the reward. You don't demand anything, because you don't have the right to choose.

"I'd be happy with work. Happy with payment. Whatever it's worth, Mr. Cruickshank, whatever it's worth."

Potty's nodding. Holmes doesn't expect work. Maybe doesn't even want it. Happy to take money, bonus money. Go sit at the bar with it. He must know work's never going to come his way from a man like Potty. You skim from one guy, you still have a chance of finding work. You skim from two and you can forget about it. Two is a pattern. Two is the end of your career. Two is the last time anyone credible looks at you as anything other than filth. And Holmes knows it, because Holmes has indeed been around the business for a long time. He was skimming from Patterson because he was going to run. Never planned to come back. But here he is. Back, desperate, and looking for money.

"I would be willing to pay you," Potty is saying. "Information is a valuable commodity, and I'm a generous man. But it has to be the right information."

"I know the people around him. I made a point of finding out. He keeps some things close, does Patterson. But you can always find out when you're in the company. They have to tell you something."

"The key men?"

"He has it, like, I guess you would say a pyramid. It's all very carefully put together, know what I mean. Conn Griffiths and Mikey Summers. Those two are high up the chain of command. Very high. They oversee a lot of stuff. Organizers. Collectors as well, but they're more than that. They collect to make it look like they're not that important. Tough guys, too, so they can do it. Real tough, actually. But they're a lot more than collectors. Those two are important day-to-day. They're who you go to if you have a problem. Who you go to if you need to find something out about a job, or to find out what the job is. People would notice if they weren't there anymore."

Potty can sense the sting in the tail. Very clear from his tone that Holmes is building to something bigger, but that he wants Potty to ask him about it. Makes Holmes feel clever. Fine, we shall play the game, just this once. Only because these are good names. Griffiths was a name one of MacArthur's boys brought them, but only as a collector. They didn't know he was important. Summers is interesting. Potty remembers the name. Used to have a reputation as brutal muscle, one of the toughest in the city. Lot of people wanted to employ that boy, and then he went off the radar. Now he knows why. Anyway, back to the game.

"So these are the two I should be concerning myself with, are they?" Asked with an almost bored tone. Almost, but not quite. Don't put Holmes off before he's had the chance to show how clever and useful he is.

"They're important," Holmes is saying, "but they're not the most important. If you want to get to Patterson, the man you want is Alan Bavidge. He's the one guy with full access to Patterson. The one guy Patterson trusts with all his biggest stuff. That's who he goes to, every time."

Potty's frowning a little. See, Potty had a good look at Holmes's background. He knows who attacked Holmes that night three months ago. Cut his face. Cut his mouth. Norah Faulkner dropped the name of Alan Bavidge. Young Mr. Bavidge has quite a reputation for being a ruthless bastard. Rather a good reputation to have in this business. A man that a lot of people, Holmes included, have good reason to hate.

"I do hope you're not giving me this name in some attempt at revenge," Potty is saying.

Holmes is frowning. Obviously didn't expect Potty to know who cut him. His right hand starts to make its way up to his face to touch the scar. A long ugly line, barely perceptible to the touch but very visible. The beard covers it, but imperfectly. He's realized what his hand is doing and he's bringing it back down to his lap. "No. Not revenge. It's the truth. Patterson doesn't have a right-hand man. Not in the usual way. But Bavidge is the closest thing to it that he has. Bavidge still collects. Still goes out and does the shitty jobs. That's a cover. He's the one. He attacked Jamie Stamford because Bavidge is the key guy. He attacked me because of it. He's the one Patterson uses on every big job. Just the big jobs. Takes his advice on every big move. All Patterson's men know that. You get rid of Bavidge and Patterson's weak."

It's not like this is the first time they've heard the name Alan Bavidge. They knew he attacked Holmes. There were suspicions he was the one who attacked Jamie Stamford. Stamford didn't confirm it, said he wasn't sure. Trying to cover his embarrassment. It was Bavidge. And now Potty's hearing that Bavidge is the most important person in Patterson's organization. He believes Holmes. Holmes has to be telling the truth, because he knows the price of a lie.

"Okay, Mr. Holmes," Potty is saying, and nodding. "I can accept that as a start. I want your contact details. I may be in touch with you again. I'll pay for this. Half up, half when I know you've been honest with me."

Holmes is pausing, but not for long. A man like Potty will pay. He might not be walking out of here with money, but he'll get something. Potty will pay the upfront money in the next couple of days. The rest will come when Potty sees how much damage he can do Patterson with the info. Doesn't serve Potty's interests to stiff someone on a deal. Even someone like Holmes. So Holmes is shaking Potty's fat hand and walking out to the front of the pub. Another drink or two before he leaves.

Potty's watching him go. Desperate. Maybe they both are, but Potty's hiding it better. This is what he was waiting for. Three names, all confirmed as senior movers. But it's Bavidge he'll go for. That's the star prize. A man close enough to Patterson to make an impact on the whole organization. And a man Alex MacArthur will be very happy to see the back of. There'll be no attempt to buy Bavidge. They will remove him instead.

2

He was in a hole. So he dug. Glass isn't proud of himself. Isn't proud of the situation he's found himself in. When he borrowed that money from Jefferson, he had every intention of paying it back. Pay it. Pay the interest. Cut the rope that the collector would hang you with. Never go back. But you have to have work. He could raise some money, but never fast enough. He paid and paid, but there was always more interest than he could keep up with. And all the time he was worried about losing Ella.

She never demanded that he bring in more money. It was never like that. That makes her sound like she was pushing him into it. It wasn't that. But there was a life she wanted for them both. Improvements to the flat. Even talking about finding a house. All these things that she wanted them to have, and she was the only one earning money to pay for them. She never pointed that out, but Glass knew, and it hurt. And he wanted to give her the lifestyle too. Parties, drink, drugs, fun. These things cost money, and he wanted her to have them. To have whatever made her happy. It was either that or lose her to someone who could pay for the life. See, she's pretty and popular. She knows a lot of men. Some of whom would give her that lifestyle. Glass was convinced that she wanted all that. Convinced that he had to help pay for it. So he borrowed more.

He was paying just enough back for Jefferson to lend him more. So he borrowed more, and the interest climbed higher. But he was able to get the things Ella wanted. They got a tumble dryer. They got a new carpet for the living room. And they went out a few times. Couple of times to a club, which is what Glass thought she wanted.

Then the third time he suggested it, she said they should go to a restaurant instead. That was even better. The money was to make her happy. To make sure that, at the end of the night, she went home with Glass. And it worked, for a while.

Money runs dry. If you don't have work, it runs dry fast. So he couldn't pay for the life. Ella had worked less when he had the money. The money went, so she started working more. They didn't talk about it. She didn't say anything, because she didn't want to upset him. But she was working more, and he knew it. Glass begged for work but got none. So he borrowed a little more. But that was his last borrow. Hasn't paid a penny back to Jefferson in over a month now. Jefferson, understandably, is not happy.

No point looking to Marty for work. He wasn't interested before, and he sure as hell isn't now. Being a friend of Peterkinney has suddenly made Glass's name poison with Marty. That little falling-out makes Marty a no-go area for Glass. Peterkinney stabbing Marty in the back cost Glass work. So Glass looked to Peterkinney. But Peterkinney has bigger fish to fry now. Doesn't need Glass anymore. Oh no, no time at all for his friends. All Glass did was introduce him to the industry. Get him started with Marty. Set him off on the road he's on now. Only has what he has because of Glass. You would think that would mean something. You would think being a friend meant something. Does it fuck. Not in Peterkinney's new world. Nah, Glass is yesterday's news. He tried getting in touch. Did everything he could to reach out to Peterkinney. Didn't matter how often he called or went round to Peterkinney's office though. He got nowhere.

So now he's going to see Jefferson. Jefferson called the flat about eleven this morning. Ella was still crashed out in bed. She worked last night. Arrived home five hours after Glass. Collapsed silently into bed and fell asleep in her clothes. She's been doing that more lately. Glass knows. He remembers that first night. Shit, that was more than five months ago. Feels like years to him. It was thrilling. It was fucking brilliant. Now other men are having their first night with Ella. Doesn't matter that she always comes home to him.

He never told Ella that he'd borrowed money. She would only get pissed off about it. Say that he wasn't earning proper money. She would start saying that he was making matters worse when she was working to make them better. It would push her away. So he didn't tell her where he was going. Just went into the bedroom and told her he was going out. She grumbled something inaudible. Her mind was still lost in the mists of last night. It'll take a good hour after waking to get her head together.

So he's walking to Jefferson's place, because he still doesn't have a car. Couldn't hope to get the cash for one of those. Couldn't buy one, couldn't fill it with petrol even if he could. Not going to spend the money for a bus fare when he's not in a hurry. Takes him the best part of half an hour to get there. Not long enough. Hasn't thought of anything to say. He needs to buy time, but he has nothing to buy with. Only way to buy time is to pay some money to Jefferson. Money Glass doesn't have. Hasn't had in an age. All he has is words. The poor man's currency.

Through to the back office, sitting opposite Jefferson. Same as it was when he borrowed the first time. And the second, and third. Same as when he paid back. Plain little office, Jefferson behind the desk. This time the mood is different. Gone from friendly, to understanding, to weary, to angry. Jefferson looking across the desk at him, shaking his head before he says a word.

"I'm hoping you're here with money, Alex, but I doubt it."

Glass is smiling a little bit. It's an unconvincing attempt at charm. "Listen, thing is, I ran out of work. But I'm confident. I am, real confident. I have something lined up. Shouldn't need more than a couple of weeks and I'll be able to come up with something for you. Something substantial, you know. Not just pennies this time."

Jefferson's frowning. "Not the first time you've told me that. Said that last time and it turned out to be baloney. I don't see why I should trust you this time. Do you even know how much you owe me, Alex?" Asking just to put the pressure on. They never know. Not unless they have a head for figures and the fiscal discipline to work out their interest payments. People with a head for figures and fiscal discipline don't borrow from Gary Jefferson. They never know, and Glass won't either.

"I know that I owe you a lot. I know..."

"Do you know that you owe me six thousand two hundred pounds?"

A frown. But no arguments. He's borrowed over a grand from Jefferson. Makes sense that it would be up to over six thousand. Actually, he thought it might be higher than that. He has paid back about eight hundred, but not fast enough. Yes, it's a rip-off. He knew it would be when he came here the first time. Knew it would get worse with each visit. So six thousand isn't a surprise.

"Okay. I owe you six thousand two hundred. And I will pay you every penny of that. You know I will."

"Excuse me, I do not know that. You are a client who's never paid a debt in full. Bits and pieces, but never in full. I do not know that you are capable of paying this."

Another frown. This is moving into territory Glass is afraid of. The lender selling the debt to a collector. He has to make sure that doesn't happen. He couldn't cope with that. The beatings. The intimidation. The truth spilling out. It would ruin his relationship with Ella in a heartbeat. She'd be gone. They'd take everything from him. Just hang on to what you've got. This might be bad, but it's the best he can do for now.

"Listen, okay, listen. I have some things I can sell. I have a couple of favors I can call in. I swear to you. I will raise some money by the end of the week. Can you give me until the end of the week?" Pleading, and trying to sound like the most reasonable man in the world while he does it.

A reluctant sigh. "Listen to me, Alex. If you don't have at least five hundred by the end of the week, I run out of patience. I have a business to run here. This isn't a charity." How often has he spoken these words?

"Sure. I get that, I do. Trust me: I will have five hundred by the weekend. I swear on my life I will."

Glass is up and shaking Jefferson by the hand. So enthusiastic, just because he thinks he's bought himself a week. They all get like that. Thinking they've done something brilliant. The great negotiators. Thinking a week will be enough to pay off the debt they've been building for months. Always thinking that something will come along and rescue them.

By the time he gets back to the flat and Ella, Glass is feeling pretty good about things. He's got five days to put something together. To come up with some real money. Right now he has thirty quid to his name. That's everything he has in the world. Where to find work in five days. Where to find work that will pay him five hundred quid. Okay, that's a tough one. Begging to Peterkinney again. That has to be the first port of call. After that, he's out of options. Into desperation territory. Kind of territory where you don't earn money, you just take it.

"I'm going out tonight," Ella's saying, sitting down beside him on the couch. "Work." Neatly dressed, made-up. Always ready to make a good impression.

"I'll come with," Glass is saying optimistically.

"No, can't. I'm going to Heavenly. Adam told me you're not allowed. Marty's orders."

Well, that's just fucking brilliant. Ella going to a private party and Glass isn't even allowed in the door. And whose fault is that? Peterkinney's. So he bloody well owes him a favor. A little work isn't much to ask. Not with the money Peterkinney's making these days.

3

There's a pleasure waking up in your own place for the first time. Not his parents' house. Not his grandfather's flat. A flat of his own. Small, sure, but he's the only one here. He doesn't have to wait for someone else to get out of the bathroom, or rush because they're waiting for him. He doesn't have to shuffle sideways to get past his grandfather in the kitchen. It's small, but it's big enough for one. And his own. All his own. Oliver Peterkinney, with his own place. His own privacy. His own life, at last. That's because he has the money for it. Because he's raising the cash to pay for this. Moving up in the world costs.

Did one shitty job too many for Marty. Got bored of waiting for Bowles to come up with more work. He knew he could do better than Marty. He could see how Marty was running his business. See all the mistakes he was making. Mistakes born from greed and complacency. Marty was too distracted. Had too many other things he was trying to make money from. Collecting was down his list, and that meant he took his eye off the ball too often. Peterkinney could do better than that; he just needed to take the initiative. So he did.

He had the connections. Knew plenty guys at the bottom of the heap from the work he'd already done. Easy to find the other connections he needed. They came thick and fast as soon as he started looking. You start with Paul Greig. He was willing to help. He's a very well-connected man. So he gave Peterkinney a few names to help him get his business off the ground. After that, it was all about setting the right tone.

He'd thought Greig was going to be tricky. Not a bit of it. You just need to know what to say. Greig wants two things from any deal he does. He wants money, and he wants to feel like he's doing his duty. See, the money on its own isn't enough. Greig's bent, but he doesn't want to be reminded of it. That's what some people don't get. People like Marty, who Greig thinks is a monumental dickhead. You have to give Greig the sense that he's doing what's right as a cop. That was simple. Just repeat the trick he used with the guns.

They had a good thing going with the guns. Peterkinney paid Greig from his share, Greig kept Peterkinney safe. Even dropped the name of a new buyer in town. So Peterkinney went for two in a row. Told Greig he was looking to get into the collecting business. That he saw the mess a guy like Marty was making, and thought he could do it better. Do it cleaner. Do it in a way that contains it. A lot of talk about moneylending and debt collection these days. Economy in the gutter and all that. Greig liked the idea of containing that business. Didn't much believe in it, but he liked it enough to justify helping. To justify taking his cut.

Out of the flat and along to his new car. Nicer than the last one. Not much to ask. Not exactly top of the range, but one step at a time. Got a decent deal from a garage owner looking to cut a debt he owed. Peterkinney knows better than to be flash. It's smart to stay under the radar. He's already made an enemy of Marty, which he didn't want to do. Didn't want to make an enemy of anyone. Best way to make your way in this business is quietly. Grow without drawing attention until you're big enough to defend yourself. These early days are the riskiest. But he's been at this nearly two months and nobody's stamped on him. So far, he's in the clear.

He's got a little office. It was Greig that pushed him towards it. Peterkinney wasn't sure about the expense, but Greig made it clear. People want you to have an office. People expect you to have an office. If you want to look significant, you go get an office. You get a covering business. If people don't see those things, they think you're not serious. Nothing worse than people thinking you're some bumbling amateur. So Peterkinney has them, and the expense they bring. Can't argue with it though, people respect the property as much as the business. People like to see it. Peterkinney likes them to see it. Loves the feeling of power, of intimidation. Makes the job so much easier. Once you're behind the desk, on the proper side of the desk, you realize what it means. You see the power of the office. Of legitimacy. There's nothing more powerful than that. He loves it.

Used to belong to a van hire business. They had the little office and the big garage next door. They sold the garage to some storage company that hasn't started using it yet. The office they're renting to Peterkinney. They don't ask questions, they have more sense than that. They must know what he's doing. It's not a secret. Can't be if you want customers. They must know, and they turn a blind eye. As long as they're getting their money.

Peterkinney's not greedy. That's the key to his good start. He takes wafer-thin margins on the debts he buys. Sometimes he buys at a loss. A lot of his profit goes back out the door in buying loss-leaders. Doesn't matter. Let the profit go. It'll be back. And it'll bring friends. You get a reputation as a good buyer, and all the lenders get in touch. The first few months are defined not by the money you make, but by the impression you make.

But a good buyer needs to show that he can last. That's the second thing. See, the big lenders like to stick to one debt collector. Preferably for years. Common sense. Builds trust and reduces risks. So Peterkinney has to show that he's capable of sticking around. At least as capable as his competitors. Needs to work harder than anyone to prove that, given his age. That means having good people around you. Get a smooth start. No fuck-ups. Another tick on that one. Didn't get every employee he wanted. A few were out of his reach. A few that would have made a difference. Still needs to prove himself to get the very best. But he got good people to work for him. The rest will come, he's sure.

The good employees he did get were attracted by the office too.

Here's a new guy, connected to Greig, setting up his own office. Still only twenty years old. The hot new thing. Something of a prodigy. Get one or two well-regarded employees, and the rest follow. Now he has a good little group around him. All busy, collecting. No mess made. They're tough with people, because they have to be. That's the job. He has to collect as much of the debt he buys as possible when his margins are walking on the edge like this. Needs every penny he can claw back. They're tough, but they've never crossed the line. Peterkinney made that very clear. First man crosses the line gets a dose of his own medicine. They respect that approach.

"Any news?" Peterkinney's asking John Kilbanne. Kilbanne works the office for him. Keeps the books. He's nearly twice Peterkinney's age, but that doesn't seem to be a problem. You just have to act mature, and people forget the age. You give them a reason to remember you're a kid, and you're in trouble.

"Nope. Few collections in. Three, actually. One of them paid in full. Other two are still on the hook, but they'll be good for it over time. Couple of jobs to do this afternoon. That's about it."

He sounds bored. Probably is. Excitement comes from being successful. Well, it does for Peterkinney. This isn't success for Kilbanne. A thirty-eight-year-old with a degree and ten years' work in accounting. Then a conviction for embezzlement. Then a year and a half inside. He did steal rather a lot of money. Stole it from a law firm, of all things. Then months of not being able to get a legit job. Then years of this kind of work. He doesn't like his work. He doesn't want to be doing this. But his name is poison, his reputation ruined, and this pays the bills.

Peterkinney understands that. It's one of his sharpest skills. He seems to have a knack for knowing what makes people tick. With Kilbanne, it's making sure he has a sense that there's something better on the horizon. Something befitting his old standards. He wants to kid himself that he can reclaim his credibility. So Peterkinney keeps feeding him lines about growing the business. About expanding into legitimate financial services. A wide variety of legitimate businesses that Kilbanne will run. And that keeps him happy. Bored, but happy.

The office is a small place. Room enough for a couple of desks and a filing cabinet. It gives the impression of being a busy place. Folders and sheets of paper on both desks and on top of the filing cabinet. The window's by the front door, a big whiteboard dominates one wall. Peterkinney's happy for people to think the whiteboard was his idea. Let them think they keep running tallies of debts there. They don't. It was here when they moved in and they've never used it. But he likes it. Likes that it makes the office feel like a working environment. Better a blank whiteboard than some smutty calendar.

There's a little toilet out back as well, but it's temperamental. Not worth the risk. Little corridor that leads out the back door to a small yard that now belongs to the storage company. Kilbanne goes out there for a smoke, but that's it. Peterkinney keeps the door to the corridor closed whenever there's a customer around. Let them think it leads somewhere bigger. Let them think there are more offices back there.

"Your grandfather called again this morning," Kilbanne is telling him. That's all he's saying. All he needs to say.

Peterkinney's dropping down into his chair. Looking across the small office at Kilbanne. He knows what Kilbanne thinks. Kilbanne thinks his dear old grandpa just wants to talk. Spend some quality time with his wee grandson. Kilbanne thinks that Peterkinney should call the old man back. Go round to see him. Spend some time with him. Arnie's been calling often, and Peterkinney hasn't called back once. Bad grandson. Naughty grandson.

But that isn't it. His grandfather doesn't want to spend more time with him. Living together was enough, thanks all the same. Arnie's about as glad as Oliver is that he's moved out. But Arnie still worries. And Arnie does not like Peterkinney's new venture one little bit. That's why he's calling. Took him a little time to find out what it was, but now he knows. Now that he knows, he's pissed off. He was pleased when Peterkinney told him he had quit working for Marty. The boy keeping a promise. A little relieved when he found out he wasn't working for Roy Bowles anymore. Thought the lad was going straight. Then he finds out he's set up his own collection agency. Well, that sent him off the deep end.

They had one argument about it. Only needed one. They've hardly spoken since. Won't either, if Peterkinney can help it. They're not living under each other's feet anymore. Easy to break contact. Let the old man get used to it, then get in touch. If he can't get used to it, then he loses a grandson. He doesn't want to lose his grandfather, but this is Peterkinney's choice. This is his life and his future. This, he knows, is what he's good at. He won't be held back by anyone. Can't be.

It's afternoon when the call comes into the office from another person that'll only hold him back. Alex Glass. Been a long time now since they spoke. He's still shacked up with that cheap hooker. Ella something or other. There's a pair of them. Total halfwits. Running round after Marty, looking for scraps from his table. Now looking to scrounge from Peterkinney.

Kilbanne's taken the call. Looking across at Peterkinney and getting a shake of the head.

"No, he's not in," Kilbanne's saying. "Can I take a message? Okay, I'll tell him when he gets back. Goodbye." Hanging up the phone and looking across at Peterkinney. "Wants you to call him. Says he has news."

Yeah, right. News. They always have news. Funny how quickly news turns into requests when people know you have money. Another one who needs to learn, before they can go back to being friends. He does care about Glass, but he won't be his safety net. He won't pay for Glass's mistakes. When Glass stops dreaming and gets rid of the girl, then they can talk. Peterkinney will find work for a friend, if the friend is mature. If the friend can help him.

4

He's been pacing around the office for the last ten minutes. You don't have to know him to know that the best thing to do right now is sit there and nod along. Don't say anything. For God's sake, don't open your mouth. Sit there. Nod when it feels like he's said something that requires agreement. Sit it out and wait for him to say something that requires an answer.

"I lifted him out of the gutter," Marty's saying. Well, shouting. Hissing, occasionally. They're sitting in the office above a gadget shop that Marty owns. Or leases. Like a lot of Marty's businesses, it's cloudy. Only Marty seems to really know, and he doesn't share info on his businesses.

He uses this office for his collection business. It's his favorite collection point. The muscle bring the money back to this office. Door out on the street that opens onto the staircase. Up the stairs and the door on your left. Unmarked. An office that doesn't advertise its financial service. Big enough place, airy and bright. A few desks, but nothing on any of them. It's not an office where office work gets done. Just a collection point. A place to give out a few orders and collect the returns. The real office work is done somewhere else. Somewhere the muscle don't get to see. No muscle coming in today. Today there are just the two of them in there.

Marty called Neil Fraser about an hour ago. Fraser arrived half an hour ago. All he's said so far was hello. That was ignored. Marty's on a rant. One that, even for him, is turning epic. Getting it out of his system, and there's a lot to get out. So Fraser's sitting on the comfy swivel chair at a desk, and he's dutifully nodding along in silence. Resisting the temptation to swivel back and forth while he listens.

"He was nothing. Nothing. Shit, wasn't even him I hired, it was his mate. That useless prick. What was his name? Doesn't matter. I hired him. I saw the potential. I gave him everything. Everything. Nobody in his life did more for him than I did. He was living with his grandfather in some shitty shoebox flat. I gave him everything he has. And he thanks me how? How? By fucking off and setting up in competition. Trying to cut me down. Then what does he do? Oh man. What does the bastard do? He grasses me to John Young. Me. The man who made him. And he's grassing me to Young."

It needn't have come to this. Peterkinney had no intention of picking a fight with Marty. He was going to walk away and hope Marty was smart enough to leave him alone. But Marty couldn't just let him be. Wounded pride. Bad PR. Marty wanted to be seen to bring down the man he had built up. Had to show the world that he took this sort of thing seriously. You let one bastard with big ideas set up against you, and the rest of these knuckleheads will try and do the same thing. They're impressionable. So he tried to take a few shots at Peterkinney. Undermine him with lenders. So Peterkinney decided to undermine Marty with the people that matter most.

Marty's position in the business is dependent upon the protection he gets from Peter Jamieson. We've established that. Marty couldn't get away with it all if he didn't have that protection. He can run his girls and his parties without Jamieson. He can run some of the other little businesses he has on the go as well. But collecting is different. Collecting is a business built on violence. Attack and defense. You need to be able to protect yourself, or have someone that'll protect you. Jamieson is the protection Marty hides behind.

Jamieson's right-hand man is John Young. Young handles the day-to-day stuff, including collecting their share of Marty's money. A reasonable cut for providing little-needed protection. The name — and reputation — Jamieson and his men carry is protection enough. But Peterkinney knew a little something. He knew that

Marty held his private parties at his brother's club instead of Jamieson's because it meant he could avoid paying Jamieson his cut. Thought he could keep a little more for himself. That was greedy, and very stupid. So Peterkinney made a phone call.

"That little bastard calling up John Young. Dropping me right into the shit. Thinking he was being clever. Thinking they would stop working with me because of it. Huh, little bastard doesn't know how this business works. Doesn't know a fucking thing. Now I'll have to spend the next few months sucking up to John fucking Young because of this. He's not getting away with it. Nobody gets away with treating me that way."

It's all clichéd ranting. In part, this is Marty trying to sound big and tough. Trying to reassure himself that he can sound big and tough. A brain-dead lump of wood like Fraser will believe it, and that boosts Marty's ego. But he also knows that nobody would grass a man they really feared. Nobody would grass Jamieson or Alex MacArthur. Nobody would grass men like Don Park or John Young. Even muscle like Nate Colgan and Mikey Summers would carry enough reputation to protect themselves from tattletales. But Peterkinney didn't fear Marty, and that worries Marty. People like Jamieson and Young see him as a profitable opportunist. People like Peterkinney see him as an unreliable party boy. None of them see him the way he sees himself. So he's going to have to persuade them. Prove that he's a man to fear. For that, he needs someone like Fraser.

Fraser's nodding along to every sentence. All this movie-mobster shouting sounds pretty good to his ears. This is the way a powerful person should talk, he thinks. This is a guy showing how tough he is. Fraser prefers this to the quiet, businesslike manner he sees in John Young.

"You know what we're going to do? You know what we're going to do about this?"

Fraser's opening his mouth, about to throw in what he thinks will be a convincing answer. Something he thinks will add to the conversation, if you can call it a conversation. But that wasn't a question that invited an answer. Fraser's only just gotten his mouth open when Marty starts talking again.

"We're going to send a message. You and me, we're going to send a message. A message to that shit Peterkinney. A message to everyone else as well. Let them see that you don't fuck with Marty Jones."

Now he's looking for a response. Looking to Neil Fraser, a man who's never been quick with his responses. Marty picked him carefully. Picked him because he knows Fraser loves this bullshit mouthing off. Loves going to Marty's parties. Loves playing at being the big tough guy. Slowthinking, but always willing to act. Willing to do what he's told, as long as the rewards are good. And Marty will make sure he gets a good reward for this. Parties, mostly. Drugs and women. That's what Fraser wants. A bit of money, sure, but it's more about the lifestyle.

Picked him for another reason, too. Marty remembers. Remembers who hates who. That's an important thing to remember in the industry. When you arrange parties, you get to meet a lot of people. Hear all the gossip. Marty knows how valuable that is. Fraser hates Peterkinney. It's been mentioned a few times. There was that scuffle between them. Was it a proper fight? No, hold on, Angus Lafferty broke it up before it turned physical. Another man people respect and fear. They do what he tells them, so the fight never really started. But Fraser was pissed off about it. Complained a few times. Made a few noises about what he would do if he saw Peterkinney again. Probably seen him again since. Did nothing. But now the opportunity is going to land right in his lap. He can't say no.

"Yeah," Fraser's saying. "We should go get him. We should make sure people know that he can't get away with it."

Marty's nodding. This is what he wants to hear. Fraser not only agreeing, but being enthusiastic about it. He wants to be a part of this. He wants to go out and hurt Peterkinney. He wants to deliver the message and get himself closer to Marty. No reluctance. Which is dumb, by the way. Marty knows how stupid Fraser is being here.

Fraser gets a lot of work from John Young. Young uses Fraser because Fraser is physically big and intimidating. As long as Fraser keeps his mouth shut and stays intimidating, Young's happy with it. But Fraser isn't happy. Fraser wants more, despite not being capable of handling more. He has ambitions he's not nearly smart enough to fulfill. Easy for Marty to exploit.

"Good," Marty's nodding. "Because I've got a plan. We're going to send him a real message. No fucking around, you know. Get the message out to him. Make sure everyone knows what a big deal it is to fuck with me, you know?"

"Yeah, sure."

Marty's nodding and smiling. This is the hard bit. See, Fraser's muscle. That's all he is. He's big dumb muscle, and he goes out and beats people up. Cheap and nasty. This is going to be something else. Marty wants to push Fraser a little further. Wants him to do more than just beat Peterkinney up. Peterkinney isn't some little bastard that didn't pay his debt. Beating him up doesn't send anything like enough of a message. He has to be seen to suffer more than a rogue client.

"I want you to send the message, Neil," Marty's saying. Standing in front of him. Fraser still sitting in the swivel chair, moving slightly back and forth. Marty trying to make a strong impression. "I want you to go and pay him a visit. I want you to send a message that can never be ignored. You with me on that?"

"Yeah, sure, I'll go pay him a visit." He still doesn't get it. He still doesn't see that this is more than just a beating. Marty's going to have to spell it out.

"You agree with me that it's not enough just to give the arrogant bastard a beating, right?"

"Yeah, okay. I do." Nodding along, but a little less enthusiastic now. Doesn't like the edge that's come into Marty's voice. Obvious that Marty's trying to push this a different way. This is going to move in a direction he hasn't gone before.

"We need to make sure that he's out of this. That people see that if you fuck with me, you're out of the business. You know? So it's not enough to beat him, right. We have to do more. I say we stick him. You go out, find him alone and stick him. That'll send the message. You and me, Neil, sending the message. Then you and me celebrating, you know."

Fraser's nodding. He wasn't nodding at the talk of stabbing Peterkinney. That's a little more than he's used to. But the talk of celebrating. That makes him happy. That's enough for him to start nodding along. He hasn't noticed that Marty kept using the word "we." It won't be we. It'll be Fraser going out and doing all the work. He will take all the risks. Do all the dirty work. The "we" will start when the job is done. Him and Marty celebrating. But it's the promise of the celebration that matters.

"Good," Marty's saying to the nod. Not letting Fraser talk about it. If he starts talking, he might start questioning. If he starts questioning, there might be a problem. "I'll get you a list of addresses. The place he lives, his office. You go find him. Get it done quick. Listen, I've got a huge party coming up this weekend. Big thing. You and me are going to make it a hell of a weekend."

And Fraser's bounding out the door. The big unit, happy as Larry. He's going to get the rewards. Marty's happy too. The rewards won't cost him anything, because he's throwing the party anyway. He'll let Fraser hang around. Could be useful. A guy close to Young could really help at a time like this. Marty's struggling to keep Jamieson's protection because of Peterkinney. He grassed him up to Young. Marty's in the bad books. He hasn't been kicked out yet. Jamieson hasn't abandoned him. Not yet. Marty's too profitable to be ditched for a first offense. But he's not going to be as well protected as he was. He's going to have to win them back around. Fraser might help with that. Sending a message. That always helps. Marty's sighing as the energy of the performance drains from him. He used to enjoy this sort of thing. Performing, fighting, striking back. Now it seems childish. Seems like it's getting in the way of bigger things.

5

Took the best part of an hour for Jefferson to pick up the phone and make a call. Glass won't get the money. Tough shit if he does. He's had more chances than he deserves. He won't, anyway. Jefferson's seen the like so many times. They buy a little time, and then turn up at the end of the week looking for more. Glass will be the same. He won't get the money. He'll come back begging for more time. Might as well get rid of the debt now and save a week of waiting.

So Jefferson made the phone call. That took more thought than you might imagine. Jefferson is a man with his ear to the ground. Every good lender is. It's not just knowing who you can lend to and who you can't. You need to know who to sell the debt to. He's been selling to Patterson for a while now. A few months, and it's been a good few months. Productive for both parties. Patterson bought some poor debts. Gave good percentage. But times are changing.

Jefferson listens. Jefferson understands. Potty Cruickshank is making moves against Billy Patterson. Potty Cruickshank has Alex MacArthur helping him. That means they're big moves. That means it's time to make sure that Potty isn't still pissed off with him. He needs to rebuild bridges. Not that he thinks Potty will definitely win. He and MacArthur are taking such a long time to make any impact on Patterson. That's a sign in Patterson's favor. But you cover your bases, don't you? Cruickshank and MacArthur together is one big fucking tag team.

So Jefferson called up Cruickshank. Let him know that he has a few debts he's looking to shift. See how Cruickshank took it. Potty's an old pro. Potty didn't make any fuss about Jefferson making sales to Patterson. Didn't even mention Patterson. And now Cruick-shank's car has pulled up outside the office. Making his way in. Fatter than ever, which is saying something. He's filling the doorway, looking out of breath already. Only taken a few paces from the car. Maybe it's the stress. A man like Potty isn't used to having to fight these battles. Not exactly in fighting condition.

"Gary, good to see you," he's saying, smiling. Waddling across to the desk. There's an extra-large and extra-comfortable chair in front of the desk to accommodate his fat arse. Jefferson had to borrow it from a neighboring office. Won't mention that, obviously. You don't mention the fact that you've had to take special measures to accommodate someone else's obesity. Potty's shaking hands with Jefferson and carefully lowering himself into the chair. The slow lowering of a man used to spilling over the sides. Used to straining the chair beneath him.

"Good to see you too. It only occurred to me this morning how long it's been since we did business."

Potty's smiling. Play the game. Create the convenient little lie. Pretend that they never really fell out. That they never really stopped doing business. Let's pretend and get on with it. But if Jefferson's stupid enough to think that Potty will forget, there could be a nasty surprise coming down the road. Potty doesn't forget. Let's not get melodramatic: he's not going to do anything about it. Not right now. Maybe not ever. He won't try to make something happen. But if an opportunity lands in his lap to punish Jefferson, he will take it. No more than that. Another lesson learned from his uncle. People will line up to cause trouble; don't join the queue. Keep people happy until the chance organically arises. It usually will. You only take direct action when you really need to. So Potty's playing the game, and waiting.

"It has been a while," Potty's nodding. "Time to put that right, I would say."

"Yes," Jefferson's saying. Not too enthusiastic. Not when Patterson's still in the game. Not when he's doing such a good job of standing up to Potty. This meeting still comes with the risk that Potty might not win this battle.

"Let's look at the book, shall we," Potty's saying. Leaning forwards to look at the debts that Jefferson's putting in front of him.

There are only a few debts on the book Jefferson's passing across the table. Keeping it soft. Mostly safe. Debts Potty can be sure of turning a profit on. Debts Jefferson's already made his profit on. He's put Alex Glass on that list. Right near the top. Right where Potty can see it. The ones at the top are the ones Jefferson wants rid of. The ones he hopes Potty will pick up, all in the name of rebuilding those collapsed bridges.

Potty's scanning them. Checking every name before he makes any sort of judgment. Another lesson from Uncle Rolly. Don't throw yourself at the first name on a list. When you're buying debt, you have to put yourself inside the head of the lender. There will always be debts he will want to sell you more than others. Of course, a lot of the time you'll just be negotiating for one particular debt. But when you're looking at the books, you look at the whole damn thing. Take in the detail. Spot the elephant traps, if you can.

Which is exactly what he's doing. Looking for names he recognizes. Ones he's dealt with before. Mercifully few of those. A few big debts here, a few small. Nothing to get wildly excited about. Occasionally you stumble across a debt that just blows you away. Impossible to understand how anyone could be so stupid as to get into that kind of trouble in the first place. Six figures, occasionally. That's usually gambling debts. People with a decent job and a house of their own who gamble more than they should. Keep getting credit extended because they've got that job and that house. In the end, they can't pay it back without selling the house. Won't sell the house. So Potty steps in and his boys persuade them. None of those today.

Eyes scanning back up towards the top of the list. Mid-range stuff. Again, all very ordinary. But these are the ones Jefferson wants to sell. So Potty will make the effort to be polite. He won't buy all of the names at the top. One or two out of the top three. Then a few from further down. Enough to make Jefferson happy. Enough to let him know that Potty has more generosity left in him if Jefferson behaves himself in the future.

"Anything I should know about any of these fellows?" he's asking. And they are all fellows, in case you're wondering. Not a woman on the list. Jefferson has women who owe him. Female debts to sell. But not to Potty. Other people will pay better to have a woman to collect from.

Potty wants to know if there's any good reason for him to avoid any of these names. If any of these men are connected to people that Potty would piss off by collecting on them. You don't want to be collecting from a Jamie Stamford without realizing it. Potty's smart, well connected. If any of these men were well connected he would know. But you always ask. Might be someone awkward, from lower down the chain. And if a problem turns up that Jefferson didn't warn him about, Jefferson's in trouble.

"Could be. I don't know how interesting it is to you. The boy Alex Glass, down for six thousand two hundred?"

"Uh-huh. What about him?"

"He used to be very tight with Oliver Peterkinney. You know the boy Peterkinney. Little kid, set up his own collection agency?"

"I know of him," Potty's saying. Of course he bloody does. Knows all about him. Keeping a close eye on that one. Got his fingers burnt with Patterson by not keeping a close eye on him. Won't make that mistake a second time. Keeping a close eye on the boy because he seems to know what he's doing. Everyone dismissing him as a kid. Like that matters. Doesn't matter how young he is, he's smart and tough. Smart and tough is worth watching. Managed to get some good people on board with him as well. Potty has a theory that there might be someone else in the background, pulling strings. Just a theory. Maybe Peterkinney isn't just the front man. Maybe he is the boss.

"Well, this kid Glass used to be his best pal. They ran together for years. Story is, it was Glass who got Peterkinney into the business. Got him a job with Marty Jones. Only in the last six months or so that they've grown apart. Glass doesn't work for him, so, I don't know. He doesn't work for him, needs to borrow money from me. Maybe they ain't that close anymore. But they were. Close as brothers for many years."

Potty's processing all that. Just sitting there, looking straight ahead. A slight smile on his face, but that's often there. Don't read too much into that. He's thinking. Thinking about Peterkinney, and about Alex MacArthur and Alan Bavidge and all the other pieces of the jigsaw scattered before him.

"So the boy Glass did work for Marty, did he?"

Jefferson's shrugging. "Did a bunch of scruff jobs for him. Low-end muscle work. Gofering. If he's doing anything for him now then it's not much. Certainly not enough to pay me off. His girlfriend works for Marty too," Jefferson's saying. A sneer at the word "girlfriend," turning quickly to a grin at the mention of working for Marty. Not hard to guess what a young woman working for Marty does. "She must be making money, but, I don't know, not enough. Or they don't share the finances. Whatever it is, I've not had a penny from him in nearly two months."

"So he doesn't have enough to live on?" Potty's saying. There's hope in that voice. The hope of a clever little plan. "Shame."

"I don't know about enough to live on. Not enough to live the life he wants to live. One of my boys saw him at a party. Told me all about it. One of those parties, if you know what I mean." Hoping Potty does, because Potty isn't the kind of guy you spell these things out to in gratuitous detail. "Expensive parties, those. I think the kid might be a user. But he was snorting his money away the night after he turns up here paying 6 percent of what he owed me. Six percent. So he's living the life all right. Or trying to."

A whore for a girlfriend. A party lifestyle. A past of working presumably violent jobs for Marty Jones. A childhood friend of the new kid on the block. Oh, this could work out nicely. Still has to play it the right way, but this could be the opportunity he's been waiting for.

Potty's buying up all three debts at the top of the list, because he's feeling a little happier about life. Buying a couple towards the bottom as well, just to round it off. They all seem reasonably safe. He'll turn a profit on every one of them, and rebuild his relationship with an important lender into the bargain. But that's just work. None of that is what makes him happy. What makes him happy is thinking of what Alex Glass will do for him. What he will have to do for him.

6

There's a different atmosphere when you're under attack. Not scared. Thrilled, a little bit. Nervy, sure, but that's not always a bad thing. If you're under attack and struggling, it feels bad. But that's not how Billy Patterson feels. He feels like he's doing rather well. That's where the thrill comes in. Someone's attacking you and you're standing up to it. Someone who considers themself a major player is failing to bring you down. Everyone can see it. Everyone knows. This could turn into the fight that confirms Billy Patterson as a serious force.

Potty's made moves against a couple of guys. Bought one. That was disappointing. Disappointing, but no more than that. People get bought in this industry. It happens. Patterson did a good job of keeping it quiet. Potty spread the word around, but it didn't seem to do a huge amount of damage. Truth is, it ended up being a relief. One man bought, nothing else happening. After the first attack, Patterson expected worse. Opening shot, followed by ever-increasing attacks. Didn't happen. Little while later they beat every ounce of snot out of Andy Leven and then set his house on fire. He was in hospital for a couple of weeks. No surprise that his wife decided for him that he wasn't going to work for Billy anymore. Patterson understood, made no issue of it. Last he heard, the Levens were packing up their kids and moving out of the city.

That one was a win for Potty. It scared a few people in Patterson's organization. He knew it. He and Alan Bavidge did a lot of work to reassure people. Worked extra hard to keep their heads down. Made sure they didn't give Potty any more targets. For a while, there was worry. Then it all calmed down. Potty didn't do anything. Potty didn't know who to aim for next. That was when Patterson realized that the attack on Leven was Potty throwing a hissy fit. Only having one target and throwing the kitchen sink at it. Leven wasn't important to Patterson. Potty got a win because he showed people how angry he was, how hard he could hit. Then, by doing nothing to follow it up, he lost all the impetus. A win, of sorts, for Patterson.

Yeah, it's a worry that Potty's hooked up with Alex MacArthur. MacArthur seems to have some hard-on for the boy Stamford. Going out of his way to hurt those who hurt Stamford. He should learn to accept that Stamford is just bad news. Cut him loose. Surprising that MacArthur isn't doing that. Never known for his sentimentality, should've ditched the kid to make a point. No surprise that Stamford's already back in debt somewhere else. No surprise that the new debt is causing all kinds of bother for MacArthur.

Word is Stamford's down eighty grand to the Allen brothers. Eighty fucking grand? The Allens, who are actually first cousins, were stupid to let it get that far, but they did. They let him run and run, lose and lose, and now there's an eighty-grand wedge between them and Alex MacArthur. The Allens are involved in the drug trade, mostly outside of the city. But it's causing friction. Big fall-out between them and MacArthur. MacArthur telling his suppliers to stop supplying the Allens, even though they don't compete for territory. All because MacArthur is willing to let Stamford get away with his bullshit. Makes you wonder if the old man is losing the plot.

Potty isn't losing the plot. Chance would be a fine thing. So Patterson's having a meeting with Alan Bavidge. There are things they need to do. Make alliances. Create more protection for themselves. My-enemy's-enemy-is-my-friend can work, but you have to be careful. Alliances cost money, and your enemy's enemy may turn out to be a greedy bastard. They may also have connections to another rival. Everyone's connected to someone. Peter Jamieson, for example. He would be a great option. Rival of MacArthur. But he's too close to Marty Jones. No deal there.

Bavidge is arriving, taking his seat. Looking tired. Looking ten years older than he is. Still hasn't taken a bloody holiday. Hasn't had a girlfriend for a while. The last one ended it with him. Needs a strong woman in his life. Someone to force him into relaxing. Patterson can't do it. Tried and failed. Given up trying, for now. Later, maybe, he'll try again. When the timing is better. Right now, he can't afford to tell Bavidge to take a week off. He needs him.

"What do you think of arranging a meeting with Charlie and Ian Allen?" Patterson's asking as Bavidge sits at the little round table.

Bavidge is shaking his head a little. "Don't see the gain. They can't give us anything. They won't come into the city to work with us. And we sure as shit don't need another Jamie Stamford debt on our books." Said with real distaste. Even Bavidge can see how badly he handled the last Stamford debt. Doesn't want any repeat of that embarrassment.

"Okay. But I want to start making moves. I want people backing us up. Not safe to go into this one alone."

"This one being?"

"I want to take down Potty Cruickshank."

"Take down or take out?"

"Whatever works."

Bavidge is leaning back in the chair. This is a bigger discussion. The right one to be having. Overdue, frankly, but still intimidatingly big. You don't just take out Potty Cruickshank. That's a move with a lot of loose ends. You have to remove the danger from all his connections and contacts. All the employees who think they're fit to step up and take his place. It's a dangerous move.

"You have a plan?" Bavidge is asking. Patterson wouldn't be mentioning the idea if there wasn't a plan to back it up. Something workable. Something he's confident they can put together.

"Lenders that crossed to us are starting to cross back to Potty. I know this. Not a lot, but they're selling to him again. Covering themselves in case we go to shit. If we don't do something, we could lose out a lot here. We have to be seen to do something."

"That something being?" Bavidge isn't entirely convinced. Needs to be won round. They aren't losing much business to Potty. Frankly, Potty's doing a piss-poor job of getting at them.

"That something being that we make a hit against Potty. Set someone else up for it. Jesus, there are plenty of candidates. But we get rid of him and let someone else take the blame. We move in and sweep up his best lenders. We try and get a few of his employees on board too. Try and take over. We won't get it all, but we'll get some. We won't be the big enemy. They'll blame someone else."

Bavidge is frowning. Sounds complicated, and complicated doesn't work as often as it should. "I take it you have a plan in mind. Someone you think will carry the can."

Patterson's smiling a little bit. "I do, as it happens. How would you feel about working for Marty Jones?"

"Not good, funnily enough."

"Fair enough. How would you feel about pretending to work for him?"

"A little better."

"Good. That's my plan. You're going to set up a meeting with someone. A gunman. I don't know who yet. I'll work that out in the next couple of days. Freelancer, obviously. You're going to make it clear that you're working for Marty. That the hit has Peter Jamieson's backing. The person we have to worry about most is MacArthur. His reaction is the big one. He'll be willing to believe that Jamieson was behind it. Making a move against him. People will be willing to believe that Marty would pull a stunt like that. Well, if he had Jamieson's backing."

It's not the worst plan he's ever heard. Sure, it has holes in it, but every plan does. It's bullshit to think you can work something like this and have it watertight. You always need a bit of luck. Even the big organizations have holes in a lot of their plans, and this isn't a big organization. This is a collection business with ambition.

"It could work," Bavidge is saying, nodding his head. Then thinking about the holes in the plan. Trying to convince people that Marty was behind it. Need to leave a lot more evidence than an easily misled gunman. "Could also go horribly wrong. Like, deadly wrong. Like Alex MacArthur sending all his boys round to drill holes in our heads wrong."

Patterson's nodding and smiling. "That's the fun of it, isn't it?"

Bavidge is smiling back, but it's a sad smile. He doesn't feel that sense of fun anymore. The thrill that used to be there. Patterson's telling him that he'll give him a call soon. Work out what gunman to use. Someone who can get at Potty and get away. It's not a great plan, but it's a plan.

"Look at it this way, Alan," Patterson's saying. "A week from now, this'll be done. Potty out of the way. Us taking up some of his best lenders. Some of his people. Not all, but some. We'll get through the messy aftermath. Then we'll be looking forwards." Sounded good to Patterson, but Bavidge is just nodding. Shaking hands and leaving. Patterson shaking his head. Best man he's got. Best muscle he's ever likely to have. And all the time he insists on looking all vulnerable, a man who needs saving.

7

Keep yourself busy. Don't spend all day sitting behind a desk. That's a good way to forget the things you need to remember. If you want to run a collection business then you need to be on the street. You need to know who's borrowing. You need to know what the lenders are doing. You need to see the business in action. Need to be seen by the people who owe you, the people who sell to you and the people who work for you. Peterkinney gets that. He's not going to become some fat bastard sitting behind a desk like Potty Cruickshank.

So Peterkinney's making a collection. He actually enjoys it now. Didn't think much of it when he was working for Marty. There was a difference. That money was going to Marty. Well, most of it. Peterkinney got his cut. Then Marty waltzed off with the rest. Sure, he had to kick a share up to Jamieson, but Marty was still getting more than he deserved. A man who never made a collection in his life. Spends his days hanging out with his dipshit brother. Picking up women for his other business. Coming up with ideas to make more money without working for it. Effort got in the way of Marty's work. Now the money is Peterkinney's, and that knowledge makes the experience of collecting it so much sweeter.

This should be an easy collection. That's another thing. Yeah, you're in charge, but you don't do the tough jobs. Your men don't like it if you do the tough jobs. Another lesson he learned from doing the muscle work himself. All the muscle want to do the biggest jobs. The toughest ones. The riskiest ones. They want to be able to say that they did the jobs that mattered. It's an ego thing. Their chance to prove themselves. Don't take that away from them.

But you do pick the job carefully. Don't just take something that doesn't matter to them. Take something that they don't want to do. Then they think you're a stand-up guy. So that's what he's doing. There are brutal jobs that the tough guys want to do. Makes them seem tough, on top of their game. The awkward stuff, the stuff that requires subtlety and brainpower, they prefer to avoid. That's why Peterkinney's here. Picking the most bloody awkward debt he has on the books, and going to collect. And he's still in a good mood.

Her name's Collette Duffy. Typical enough. Pretty young thing with a habit and a kid. No job, no prospect of one. Borrowing money with no hope of repaying. In the grand scheme of things, she's no big deal. Her debt isn't massive. She's easy to talk to. The problem is her brother. Her brother Liam is not a man you want to piss off. Does a lot of work for Chris Argyle, in what we will politely call the import business. Liam Duffy is not good people. Known to overreact to perceived slights. Known to protect his little sister and her kid. That's why lenders are scared to refuse her. It's why collectors are reluctant to buy her debt. That's why none of the muscle wants this collection.

Peterkinney bought the debt as a favor to a lender. He has almost no intention of collecting on it. Two grand he won't see again. Not necessarily two grand poorly spent. It's a connection. Peterkinney's going to be as nice as nice can be with Collette. He's going to leave her flat after making her a happy little girly. Make a good impression. She shares this good impression with her brother. Her brother shares it with the people he knows. Peterkinney gets a reputation in the industry as a man who knows how to treat other people in the industry. Reputation is worth paying for. Even if it doesn't work, he made a good impression on the lender just by buying the debt. Can't lose entirely.

He's found his way to her flat. Small place, but not a bad area. Better than a girl with no job and a habit would normally have. That'll be the brother's influence, Peterkinney's guessing. Up to her door and knocking. Waiting ten or twenty seconds. Not going to rush her. Not going to knock a second time. You get a lot of people who owe money who are allergic to answering doors. Understandable. Usually you knock and knock. Maybe you leave a note letting them know this isn't over. Eventually, you push your way in. Not today. Not ever with Collette.

Peterkinney's about to walk away when the door opens. A young woman looking back at him. Pretty, as it happens. You can see why her brother would feel the need to protect her from collectors. A girl like that, there are ways she could repay the debt. Ways people like Marty Jones would be real quick to exploit. Wouldn't stay pretty for long. She needs protecting.

"Hi, sorry, I was just giving my little one her tea." A giggly smile. She's nervous. A guy she doesn't recognize turns up at her door. That's worth worrying about when you're deep in debt.

"Oh, that's okay," he's saying with a friendly smile. This is where looking young and innocent helps Peterkinney. He's nonthreatening. People like Collette Duffy are willing to talk to him. "I don't know if you know me. My name's Oliver Peterkinney."

No flash of recognition. That's a good thing. If she knew him, it would almost certainly be because of negative things. She might have heard some stories that made her nervous. That scared her. Any collector has brutal stories to back up his work, his reputation. This way, he gets to introduce himself. He gets to set the tone of her perception of him. If the only profit from this deal is to enhance his reputation with people like Liam Duffy and Chris Argyle, then he needs to set the tone.

"I run a business that collects money," he's saying. Not using the term debt collector. Never use the term unless you want to frighten people. "I've picked up your debt from the man you borrowed from." Talking low, making sure no neighbor could overhear. "I'm not here to collect," he's saying quickly. Reassuring, friendly smile. "But I thought it would be good to have a chat about the debt. See what we can do about it. Make sure we can sort it out without any bother, you know? Is now a good time? I can come back some other time."

He's reassured her. He can already see it in her expression. He's said he's not here to collect money, which is a good start. She's seeing this as an opportunity. Here's a nice guy that's offering a chance to discuss her debt. This could be a chance for her to talk it downward. That's what she wants. She'll be glowing in her praise of him if that happens.

"I can talk," she's nodding. Holding the door open for him to come in. A collector welcomed into the home of the debtor. All because of the nice way he talked to her. That baby face of his, paying off again.

She's leading him through to the living room. He can hear a TV in another room. That'll be to entertain the kid through her dinner. The ever-present babysitter. Into the living room. The carpet's thin and stained. There's a couch and one chair that doesn't match, and both have seen far better days. But there's a big TV, a Sky box and a Wii in the corner. There's an iPad resting on the arm of the couch. Strange priorities. But she's a junkie, apparently. Her priorities are going to be all over the fucking place. Can't be that far off the deep end though, can she. Holding it together enough to keep a home, keep the child. Seen worse, that's for sure. Not Peterkinney's problem. He's sitting down.

"Thing is, Collette," he's saying, "I now own the debt. But I don't want to start making a big deal out of it. I know how it is. You borrow a little and the interest catches you out. It's a lousy system."

And she's nodding enthusiastically. Dark-brown hair bobbing up and down on her shoulders. Wearing a stripy vest and dark trousers. Shapely. Oh, the likes of Marty would have a field day with a client like this. Actually, Marty himself would be smart enough to keep away from Liam Duffy's little sister, but there would always be someone stupid enough not to.

"We need to work out a way that makes it easy for you to pay back. Something that doesn't stop you living your life. Something that doesn't get in the way of the other things you need to do."

"Yeah, yeah," she's saying, and nodding again. She has nothing else to say. She's hearing what she wants to hear and that's enough. Worried that anything she says might poison the well.

"So we need to look at how much you're earning. See what you can afford to pay. We'll do something about this interest, because that's not helping the situation. I also don't want you to think that there's any great urgency with this," he's saying. "I'm not in any great hurry about it. If we peg the interest, that'll give you breathing space."

She's smiling and nodding. Unaware that Peterkinney wants this to last because it gives more chance of spreading the word about what a good guy he is. What a good industry man he is. That's where the value is for him. A young man who understands how to treat the family of other insiders. She doesn't see that. Honestly, she doesn't care. The value for him is irrelevant to her. He's welcome to any kind of profit he can get. She's only concerned about her position.

"Do you lend?" she's asking.

Jesus Christ, this isn't going to be easy after all. She's looking to borrow more. Hasn't paid a penny of her original debt, and she's hoping he'll hand her more cash. That's going to make it more difficult. He sure as hell isn't going to go buying up an unlimited amount of her debt just to make a good impression. Reputation is worth paying for, but everything has a limit. Might actually work in his favor, he's musing, before he answers. If she borrows from someone. They sell her new debt to someone else. She then has someone else to compare him to. Someone else for her brother and mates to compare him to. That could help.

"No, I don't lend. I just collect. Listen, Collette. Don't go borrowing just to pay off other debts. That'll make it worse. That's how you end up with even more interest, and even more debt. You and me should try and come up with a plan to make sure that you can pay this back. Make sure that you don't even have to think about borrowing again."

She's nodding. She's uncertain, but she's not going to argue with him. He's here to help and she needs help. But she doesn't like the sound of not being able to borrow. Been a long time since she had an alternative money source. Borrow from lenders, get help from her brother. The lenders get rough and her brother sorts it out. That's the system that's kept her going for the best part of a year. Now Peterkinney's suggesting something else. But the other tactic that has served her well is nodding along with other people's ideas. She's just smart enough to realize that money doesn't flow from disagreement.

It's twenty minutes later when Peterkinney leaves the flat. Smiling and happy. He's gotten what he wanted. A payment plan that's so absurdly generous even she was surprised by it. All the time in the world to pay, interest suspended for the foreseeable future. She'll be very positive about this. Word will go around. It's a PR investment. She won't even meet the plan they've written out, but that's not the point either. Just gives him another opportunity to be all saintly when she fails to meet her obligations.

He's going back to the office. Put this on the file. Kilbanne will look at it and say nothing. He doesn't question. Too smart for questions. He'll look, he'll make a guess at the reasons for such an agreement, and he'll keep the conclusions to himself. And the business will get on with making money.

8

He has his coat on. Glass is ready to go. But he's scared. Properly scared, not just a little nervy. You get a telephone call straight from the mouth of Potty Cruickshank and you have a lot to be nervy about. A call from the blue. Telling him to come and visit Potty, right away. Giving him an address. A place Glass has heard of before. A little city center club. Not a nightclub, but a private club. At least that's what he's heard it called. Never been inside. Just heard people talk about it. Like it's an exclusive little casino or something. Not a place for the likes of him.

Potty didn't give details. Made it clear that Glass had better be there. That he won't stand for being stood up. Or kept waiting. That it was in Glass's best interests to be there. Tried to make it sound at least a little bit friendly. Slimy, more like. So Glass will be there. He hasn't been told why, but he can guess. Jefferson sold the debt. Sold it to Cruickshank. But that doesn't tell him why he's been called to a meeting with Cruickshank himself. How many debts does Potty buy in any week? How many of them are worth his private attention? None, on average. But Glass is getting a call on a six-grand bill. Something isn't right.

He's delayed as long as he could. Hoping that Ella might come home. She's been out all day. Hasn't come back and it's getting dark. Dark is her work hours. He might not see her until tomorrow. Shit. It would be nice to have someone to talk to about this. But could he talk to her? Admit that he's deep in debt trying to keep up with her aspirations? That's a stupid thing to think. It wasn't her fault. He made the choices. Blaming her for it's just cheap. Get yourself together, and get to that meeting. Stand up for yourself. Stand up to the world. Can't be that hard when so many other people do it.

As he walks to the bus stop, he's thinking about Peterkinney. Maybe that's why he gets a personal meeting. Not because of the amount. Six grand is chicken feed to Potty. Someone pointed out Potty's house to Glass once. Big place you could get lost in without a detailed map and a bit of luck. Yeah, six grand wouldn't buy you much of that place. So Potty's interested in something else. The six grand should get one of his grunts at the door with threats of limb removal. Not a call from the fat man himself.

Oliver Peterkinney. Glass is thinking of trying another call. For what? To get fobbed off again by one of his minions? Best friends for years. Hung out most days. Partied together. Glass got Peterkinney started in the business. Yeah, doesn't take long for the ambitious to forget their friends. Maybe Ella got in the way of the friendship a little. Maybe. But that wasn't deliberate. And it's no reason for Peterkinney to be acting the way he is now. Like he's too good to bother with Glass.

Here's the bus. He's getting on, paying. Thank Christ the club, if that's what's even behind that front door, is in the city center. Easy to get to. Closer he gets, the more he's starting to sweat. It's a cold evening, but temperature isn't a part of this. Potty Cruickshank. That'll be the biggest industry man Glass has ever met. Biggest in every sense, actually. But before now, Marty was the most important person Glass had come into contact with. Never got close to someone of Potty's stature. His reputation. Jesus, this has to be a step up.

As he's getting off the bus, he's trying to win himself round. Persuade himself that all is not lost. This might not be that bad. Walking towards the quiet street where the club is. Not so busy even in the busier areas. The brief time between shoppers shopping and drinkers drinking. But look at it this way. Potty wants to talk to Glass. Glass has that connection to Peterkinney. A guy like Potty knows that Peterkinney's in the collection business now. So he buys Glass's debt. Calls him along to a meeting. Maybe he has an offer. Maybe he wants Glass to be a go-between. Or he wants info. Could pay off a big chunk of the debt. Hell, maybe even all of it.

Back to being scared and miserable by the time he gets to the correct street. Back to reality. Info on Peterkinney. Talking to Peterkinney. That wouldn't be enough to pay off the debt. Info doesn't buy you freedom. Might cut the debt, but not by enough. If he has info, then Potty will want to keep him indebted. Keep him talking. Talking to Peterkinney wouldn't help either. If he's the messenger between the two, Potty will want him under his thumb. He'll keep the debt hanging over him. Use it. If Glass is any kind of useful, then it's common sense that Potty will want control of him.

By the time he's reached the door, he's just about terrified. This isn't his depth. Not even close. A big red door, no windows on it. A three-story, mid-terrace brown stone building. It looks like an expensive house. But that's the point, isn't it. What goes on behind closed doors. Knocking on the door a couple of times. Jesus, please don't answer. It would be so nice if he had an excuse not to go ahead with this. But it's opening.

The first little piece of his curiosity is stamped upon. The guy answering the door is muscle. Stereotypical muscle. Tall, a little overweight, shaven-headed. Looks like he'd break his granny's neck if the price was right. Not the sort of person that answers the door at a swanky private members' club. The muscle's nodding for him to come in.

Inside it looks like a nice house too. Not some special place the rich come to play. A corridor, doors closed on either side. A staircase on the right-hand side of the hallway. The muscle leading him along the corridor. Thin, cheap carpet. There's a big scratch on the wallpaper above the radiator. So not some private members' club after all. That's a disappointment. This isn't some special meeting place. Just a city-center location that a man like Potty has easy access to. Convenient, not special.

Places like this get their own mythology. A man like Potty is seen coming and going. It's a good location in the city center. It's the sort of property that could easily be used for something exclusive. Something exciting. So it gets a reputation as some special place. That's what people want to think. They want to think there's something clever and dangerous going on behind these doors. Something glamorous. Fascinating fantasy trumps tedious truth every time. Truth is it was a good piece of property that Potty managed to come by on the cheap. Owner owed some money. Gave Potty a big price cut on the deal. A good little investment. Property is a good way to clean money.

None of this matters to Glass now. He's following the muscle along the corridor. Getting more nervous as he goes. It's silent behind the closed doors. There's nobody else here. Just him and Potty and this thug. It suddenly feels dangerous. Ominous. It was intimidating before, but he was sure he would have a chance to pay off the debt somehow. Now it feels like a set-up. It feels like he's never going to get out of here.

The muscle's opening the door, nodding for Glass to go in. It's a large room, well lit, white walls. There's a sink over against one wall, but that's the only giveaway that this used to be a kitchen. All the units and features have been ripped out to leave the place almost empty. Looks like they started a conversion and ran out of interest. There's a table in what was the dining area. That's all the furniture. A long dining table, with Potty Cruickshank sitting at the head of it. The muscle who was sitting along from Potty is getting up, moving towards the sink.

That's Glass's cue to take a seat at the table, which he's doing. Looking behind him at the sound of the door closing. The muscle who led him in is standing just inside the now closed kitchen door. There's a closed window behind Potty, and no other way out. The other muscle is leaning back against the sink, looking casual. Both of them watching him. Not watching Potty. Just Glass. Potty's taking a sip from the glass on the table in front of him. Not offering Glass anything. The state of this place would suggest Potty did well to get anything for himself, never mind a guest.

"I'm glad you made it," Potty's saying. "You and I need to have a very serious discussion." His tone is somber. No messing around here. "We need to have a discussion that I don't think you're going to like. But you're a strong person, aren't you, Alex? A tough guy?" Little bit of mockery crept in there, just at the end. The little mouth curling up at the edges, ever-so-slightly creasing those big cheeks.

It could be an offer of work. Wanting an old friend of Peterkinney to be seen working for him. It could be something else. Either way, you agree with Potty. "I guess. Tough enough."

Potty's nodding. "Mm, good. Because what I have to offer you will require a tough person. It's an opportunity for you to pay off your debt to me in its entirety in one evening. The whole thing, gone. But it's tough work. Are you interested?"

It's not as if he can say no. Potty's just said that he owns the debt. He's giving him a chance to wipe it out. The man's offering a rare opportunity. A favor, it looks like. How often does Potty sit down with a man and offer one of those? Saying no is going to piss Potty off. Alone in a room with Potty and two of his muscle is not the time to piss him off.

"I guess, yeah. I'm interested."

Another nod. Potty hearing what he expected to hear, and knowing how worthless that can sometimes be. "Let me ask you, Alex. Do you know where your girlfriend is right now? Where Ella is?"

Glass is looking at Potty with alarm. His mouth is open, but his brain hasn't found a word ready to head out there yet. The fear turning to anger. He's about to get emotional when he remembers who the fat guy sitting in front of him is. Remembers the two thugs that are in the room with them. Watching him. And the fear returns. He's shaking his head. Not saying anything because he doesn't trust himself to speak. Just shaking his head.

"No," Potty's saying. "But you can guess. Don't take this as a threat. I just wanted to know if what I'd heard was true. What I'd heard about her occupation. So one of my boys tracked her down. Offered her money for her work. She agreed, of course. It's some money for you both, I suppose." Said with a smug shrug. "But what of you, Alex? Are you earning any money? Helping her out of this life she lives?"

Another shake of the head. If they were alone it would be different. If they were alone he would threaten and shout. He might even throw a punch. He's beaten people up. He knows how he would do it here. Charge all his weight at Potty. Knock him off the chair and onto the floor. Once you get a man that big onto the floor, it's easy to keep him there. But no. They're not alone. Potty's never going to let that happen. And Glass is never going to do anything. Just shaking his head until Potty starts talking.

"So she's the one bringing the money in. Doing all the work for the both of you. And here you are with a large debt. A debt you now owe to me. I'm going to offer you a chance to remove that. To wipe your slate clean. Isn't that what you want?" Talking quietly, confidently. Elbows on the table, chin resting on his folded hands.

Get him to agree to the job before he even knows what it is. It's a good tactic. Make it as hard as possible to back out. If he was thinking clearly, Glass would realize how big this is. Threatening Ella. Threatening him. Trying to force him to accept without details. It should tell him a lot about what's coming next. But he isn't thinking clearly. The threat to Ella made sure of that. All going to plan for Potty then.

"I do want that."

"Of course you do. Strong young man like you, you want to do the right thing for yourself and your partner," Potty's saying, and leaning forwards against the table. "I am going to give you an opportunity that can clear your debt. That could make you very popular with me. You do understand how valuable that could be, don't you, Alex? Being popular with me? It could serve you very well. Will you do it?"

"Yes."

"Good. One of my boys will give you a knife. You are going to go to this address. You are going to kill the man who lives there. Do you understand me? You are going to kill this man. You are going to do this."

There's a slight shake of the head. Watching as Potty passes a quarter of a page from a phone book. One name and address ringed in blue ink. Sliding it across the table. Potty saying nothing, just glaring back at Glass.

"I haven't...I don't know how. I couldn't."

Potty frowning. "Are you refusing to help me?" Asked quietly, with a sad expression. That's the nod for the guy by the sink to stop slouching and stand up straight. Take a noisy scuffed step towards the table. Let Glass know what pressure he's under.

"No, no," Glass is saying. "It's just, I haven't done this before. I don't know how. There must be someone better."

Potty's smiling and shaking his head. "First-night nerves. You'll get over it. You're the best person for the job. Tough lad like you, of course you are. You go there right now. You knock on the door. He answers and you do it. Then you get out of there. It's really rather simple. Don't overcomplicate it, Alex, that's where many people slip up. Do it quickly and keep it simple, and you'll be fine." Said with a quietly reassuring tone. Just about sounded like he cared. There's a pause. "You understand that I will be very happy with you if you do this well. I will be very angry if you don't."

Glass is looking at him. You can see that he means it. Potty Cruickshank doesn't have time for idle threats. Potty's never lived in a world of idle threats. Too busy issuing real ones. He's threatening Glass. Letting him know that he will be the one impaled on metal if he doesn't do the job. Probably be killed right after they do something to Ella.

"I know," Glass is saying. "I'll do it. Tonight."

"Good lad," Potty's saying, and smiling a smile so false it's an insult. "Show Alex out, would you," he's saying to the muscle at the door.

The muscle's walking Glass back along the corridor. Taking out a long thin knife from the inside pocket of his fleece. Passing it to Glass. Glass holding it and looking at it.

"Put it away," the muscle is telling him harshly, then opening the front door.

Back out into the cold night. The metal feels heavy in his pocket. That's the handle, rather than the blade. He's walking slowly along the street. He knows where he needs to go. Taking his phone out and calling Ella. Her phone's switched off.

9

He started tracking him at his office. Parked across the road from it, watching a few people come and go. Little place, doesn't look like much. Peterkinney arrived in his car. Got out looking happy with himself. Little shit. Went into the office and stayed in there for about twenty minutes. He thought about going in then with the knife, but he didn't. Too much chance of being seen. Marty wouldn't want that, so Neil Fraser sat in the car and watched.

See, people are always treating Fraser like he's some idiot. Like he doesn't have the subtlety to do anything important. Young's always treating him that way. Only ever takes him along to look mean and be quiet. Finally someone's giving him a job that matters. That'll let him show people how good he can be. Staking the place. Tracking the target. Waiting for the right moment to strike. This'll show them what a pro he is.

He sat patiently and watched the office. Patiently, you see, patiently. He can do this. And Peterkinney came out, got in his car and drove home. And Neil Fraser followed him. Thought he did a pretty damn good job, too. There was a spell where he was right behind Peterkinney's car, but so what? Even if Peterkinney looked in his mirror, he probably wouldn't have recognized him anyway. So Fraser followed him home, parked a little way along the street from his flat, and waited.

Nice little street it is too. You can see the boy's moving up in the world. Sort of place for the young middle class. People with rich parents. Well, that ain't Peterkinney. But young people with money. Don't need a lot of space, but want to be in a nice area close to the places that matter in the city. Yeah, he's done all right out of screw-ing Marty, Fraser's thinking. Looking at the buildings. Thinking it would be nice to live in a place like this. Maybe he should screw Marty too. But he wouldn't know how. Nah, do this job, and trust Marty to reward him. Marty sees his potential.

Fraser waited there for nearly an hour, which was pretty damn patient. Then got fed up waiting. There's really no need to spend forever waiting for a better opportunity. Take the opportunity that's in front of you. So he got out of the car and started to walk to the door of the flats. Casual, trying to look like he belonged. Then the door of the flats opened and Peterkinney came out. Down the steps, looking relaxed. Didn't look at Fraser. Just walked to his car at the side of the road and got in. Fraser stopped halfway along the pave-ment. Trying to work out what he should do next. Keep on walking to act casual, or turn back to his car and maybe catch the boy's eye. Frozen on the pavement, unsure of himself. Peterkinney's starting his car and pulling away. Fraser, without waiting for Peterkinney to turn the corner at the bottom of the street, has turned and is run-ning back to his car.

Okay, so he handled that badly. He knows it. Doesn't need you ramming it down his throat. But he managed to follow Peterkinney. Caught him up and kept close. Driving into the center, lot of people around. Parked close behind him. Watched Peterkinney stroll along the street and into a cinema. So Fraser hung around outside the cinema, for the best part of two hours.

Two fucking hours, standing in the street like an idiot. Just lurch-ing around, people coming and going. Getting hungry, but nowhere he can go to grab something to eat. Nowhere that he could still see the cinema doors from. People are seeing him, hanging around. Bloody stupid, this is. But he can't go in, he knows that. Got to hang around and wait. Keep watching the door. Keep your dis-tance. Be smart.

He was impatient by the time Peterkinney came out of there. Walk-ing along a busy and well-lit street. Fraser knows better than to attack now. But what if this is the perfect place to attack? This is the last place anyone would expect him to attack. They always say that's the best time. No, not here. Too many people around. Wait until it gets quieter. There'll be a better chance. Back on the street where they're both parked. He can just walk up behind him and stick the knife in him. Keep walking to his car. Yeah, that's the perfect way to do it.

Except Peterkinney isn't going back to his car the way he came. He's taken a turning away off down an adjoining street that takes them further away from their cars. But that's okay, because he's walking to a quieter area. There are fewer people, it's darker. There are more little alleyways down this way. Peterkinney's leading him closer and closer to his chance. Turning again, into what's basically a wide alleyway between shops and a multi-story car park. Fraser keeping close, but not too close. Nobody else down this alleyway.

Must be going to meet someone. Shit, might be going to meet someone tough. Better get a move on. Get this done and get back to the car. That's common sense. If your target is going to meet up with someone else then you get to them before the meeting. Even Fraser knows that. He's turning into the alleyway, wide enough to drive a delivery lorry down, and picking up the pace. Watching the back of Peterkinney as he turns again, out of view. Fuck, must be another alley there. Some little cubbyhole between the shops where Peterkinney can do a deal. Fraser's jogging now.

Down the alleyway. More aware of the darkness. More aware of how isolated he is. But he isn't stopping to think about that. He never stops to think about these things. Some people mistake it for bravery. It isn't. It's a failure of brain to keep up with action. Some dumb people get away with it because instinct takes over. Not for Fraser. Instinct is way in the background. So he's reached the corner. Hardly slowing as he runs round it.

A hand thudding out and into his side. A cold blast running up his side to his head. A flush of adrenaline, causing him to jump backwards. The adrenaline washed away in blood, and he's slumping down to his knees. Now onto his side, clutching at the wound.

"Oh Neil, you are so predictable."

He can hear Peterkinney. Hear him loud and clear. Not fuzzy or distant. He sounds like he's standing over him, which he is. Fraser had dropped to the ground, but he knows better than to stay there. Now turning over, getting back onto his knees. There's blood coming out of a slit in his jacket. He has a hand over it. Got to move. Got to react. Got to do something. Think of something to do next. Come on, hurry up. His mind racing to get there, but always running in the wrong direction. Only a few thoughts entering his head, and most of them come back to dying in this alley.

"You think I didn't know what you were up to? Huh? You think I'm fucking blind?" Peterkinney doesn't sound upset. Not emotional at all. Calm, relaxed, satisfied. Happy with his night's work. "You think I'm as stupid as you are?" Having fun and taking his time. Not intimidated by Fraser. Not intimidated by the thought of being caught behind a shop with a man he's just stabbed.

He had the chance to look around and make sure this place was safe. The car park on one side is lit up, but empty. Nobody moving around in there. The shops behind them are in darkness now. No windows from the shops look out onto this little loading bay anyway. Big doors, covered by corrugated sheeting to deter burglars and encourage graffiti. Silent, dark and perfect for this.

Fraser's not listening anymore. He's trying to get his own knife out of his pocket. He's got his hand on the handle. Taking it out. Struggling for a grip because there's blood on his hand. Peterkinney's seen it and he's laughing. Fraser's trying to get up to get a slice at him. Putting weight on his feet, but as soon as he starts to push up the pain shoots through him. Up his side, through his neck, up behind the ear. It's like being stabbed again. So he's slumping back down. Hand out, trying to prevent him from rolling onto his side.

Peterkinney's laughing again, just a little. You'd have to know him well to know that he's faking it. Good actor. But the laugh has turned hollow; he doesn't find this funny anymore. Time to wrap it up. "You tell Marty that this is what'll happen to anyone who tries to stop me. You understand me, Fraser? You tell him that he can't lay a finger on me. That he better not try again, or he might be next. You got that?"

And Peterkinney's turning and walking away. Back out into the alley from the loading area at the back of the shop. Along the alleyway and out onto the lit street. A bloody knife in his pocket, but that's okay. He'll ditch the knife and the top he's wearing. But this was a good day for him. This message will be enough to deter Marty. Marty isn't a man to risk failing twice. He doesn't care enough. If this was about his core business, women, then he would try again. Keep trying until he succeeded. But he's not going to rock the boat with a second attempt after pissing off Jamieson and Young already this month.

This was in Peterkinney's mind from the moment he saw Fraser parked across the street from the office. Not parked nearly far enough away from the office. They have a large window looking out onto the street, for Christ's sake; easy to see everyone parked on the street. Fraser following him home. Driving right behind him. Right behind him. Unbelievable. Obviously never done something like this before. Marty picked him because he's expendable. Because people don't think of him as being one of Marty's boys. Because he was the only one stupid enough to do it. Stupid enough to carry a grudge from some party months ago. Feels like a lifetime ago. Probably not for Fraser. He hasn't done much of note since then.

Only question was what weapon Fraser was planning to use. You don't bring a knife to a gunfight, that's movie cliché number one. If Fraser had a gun, then this wouldn't have happened. But Peterkinney decided to take the risk that he wouldn't. Let's face it, even Marty wouldn't be stupid enough to arm Fraser with a gun. Fraser is no gunman. Gunmen are a different breed. If Marty used a real gunman, Peterkinney would be dead now. He knows that. So he made the decision that Fraser only had a knife, and he was right. Predictable enough. That made it an even fight. All he had to do was pick the location.

Best thing is, Marty won't make a fuss. Can't. Fraser isn't his employee. Which is a good thing if Fraser does the job properly. Nobody can prove Marty was behind it. It becomes a bad thing if Fraser botches the job. Uh-huh, should have seen that coming. Fraser works for Peter Jamieson. Marty just got a Jamieson employee stabbed. Marty won't admit to being involved. Fraser won't grass him up either. Fraser will use his mobile to call for help. He'll be taken to hospital. One of Jamieson's more intelligent men will go and get him out of the hospital before the police can bamboozle him with anything so fiendish as a question. And nothing more will be said about it.

Peterkinney's back to his car. Looking up and down the street to make sure that Fraser didn't have company. A safety net for the job. Of course he didn't. That would have been the sensible thing to do. Fraser wouldn't organize that. Nor would Marty. It's a two-man job, but he can send one moron instead. It's cheaper. It carries less personal risk to Marty. Those are the things that matter most to him.

By the time Peterkinney's ditched the knife and top and gotten home, it's pitch black. Still, he's feeling good. Into the flat and looking around. His flat. His space. His company. Making money for him. This is what he should have been doing ages ago. Never having to live in someone else's pocket. Bumping into his grandfather every time he opens his bedroom door. Embarrassing himself with crappy jobs for Marty. That's no life. The good life is the life you make yourself, any idiot can see that. This is the life.

10

He's gone back to the flat first. Shouldn't have. Should have gone straight round to the address and gotten the job done. That's what Potty wanted him to do. Get there and do it without thinking about it. You dwell on it, and you're going to think of all the reasons why you shouldn't do it. All the things that can go wrong, and there are plenty of those. But Glass couldn't rush it like that. Had to come home first.

He's called Ella three times and gotten no answer. She's with one of Potty's boys. Maybe Potty's boy is going to keep her there until they know Glass has done the job. Maybe that's the point. He's not experienced enough to know. Never been here before. Hopefully she doesn't know what's going on. He doesn't want to think of her being held against her will. Being scared, or even hurt. Sooner he does the job, less chance there is of that happening.

Walking through the flat. The knife is still in his pocket; he hasn't taken his coat off since he got home. He can feel that knife weighing him down. Walking from room to room. Not looking for anything. Not expecting to find anything. Just wanting to burn off some nerves. He's going to kill a man. He has no choice. If he doesn't, Potty kills him. Maybe Ella too. That was the threat. What choice does he have?

What choice? There could be a way out. There could. He's looking at this from a different angle. There are people out there who would like to know about this job. Who might just want to get involved in this little adventure. Throw a spanner in Potty's works. Except he only knows the phone number of two of them. And neither of them will answer his calls.

He's calling Peterkinney first. They were friends. This was the sort of thing they would have told each other about. That they would have helped each other with. Times have changed. Not thick as thieves anymore. But this matters to Peterkinney. This is something that he needs to know about. He's part of the industry now, after all. But the phone's ringing and ringing and nobody's answering. Typical. Just bloody typical. Thinking he's too good for Glass. Well, he's the one who's going to lose out.

Calling Marty. This is a chance for Marty. Get involved in Potty's business; trip him up in something important. Surely Marty will want that. And a chance for Glass to prove to Marty that he can still be useful. This could be a way in. You deliver information like this, and it can lead to permanent work. Shows Marty how useful he can be, and how much he wants to work for him. Hell, it even involves Ella, and she's one of Marty's girls. He has to take an interest. He has to be willing to help. The phone's ringing. Two rings and it's answered. That has to be a good sign.

"Yes?" An aggressive yes.

"Marty, this is Alex Glass. I want to talk to you about something important. Something that's happening right…"

"Oh, I get it. Yeah. Get his wee bum chum to call up and take the piss. Is he hanging over your shoulder listening to this? Is he? Are we on speaker? You tell him from me, okay. You tell him he can go fuck himself, all right."

"Marty. Marty, it's Alex Glass. Alex Glass." Thinking that Marty doesn't know who this is. That he's got him mixed up with someone else. Must have. What else could explain this outburst? "I used to work for you. I'm Ella's boyfriend."

"I know who you are. And I know what your mate did tonight. You just tell him that this ain't the end of it. One of Jamieson's boys got to the hospital. They won't let this lie. Neither will I. There'll be a price to pay for this. Can he hear me? A price to pay. I'll get that little prick. You tell him that."

Marty was practically spitting into the phone before he hung up.

Not raging and ranting. A cold hatred, hissing out of him. Glass is staring at the phone. Doesn't know what to do now. Marty's up a tree about something. Something's happened and it's pushed him beyond anything as showy as anger. Glass has no idea what this is about. He mentioned Jamieson and a hospital. That has nothing to do with Glass. Nothing to do with tonight. Maybe it has something to do with Potty. That could be it. Marty thinks Glass is working for Potty already.

Still walking round the flat. Trying to make sense of something that doesn't want to be understood. Grasp at any passing straw. Phoning Arnie Peterkinney. He needs help. He needs to get through to Oliver.

"Hi, Arnie, this is Alex Glass." Feels weird calling him Arnie. Not like they're close or anything. "Do you have Oliver's new home number?"

There's just a little pause. "No, I don't. You can get him on his mobile though."

"Uh, yeah. I tried. Never mind."

"Alex, lad, are you okay?"

Didn't realize how emotional he was sounding. That he's close to tears. He knows that if he doesn't get help, he's going to be killing a man in the next couple of hours. Or maybe his target will kill him. Why not? Chances are the target's a damn sight more experienced at this sort of thing. Most people in the business are more experienced than Glass. He's been close to tears since he left Potty's house, but he didn't realize it. Marty was too excitable to notice.

"I'm okay. Just...a few things, you know. Stuff. I was really hoping I might get through to Oliver though. I thought he might be able to help me out. I could use a wee bit of a hand with something tonight, that's all."

"Anything I can help you with?"

It's weird how much it hurts to hear him ask that. Arnie Peterkinney never liked him. Glass knows that. He knows that Arnie always thought he was a bad influence. And he was. Damn right, old man.

Look at where Glass's influence has gotten them. And yet the old man's offering to help. The only person who has offered to help him. The only person who would actually sound like he means it. That's pushing Glass closer to the edge. The only person who wants to help and there's nothing he can do. Shit, even if he could, Glass wouldn't let him get involved. The one person who cares enough to offer, you don't drag him down with you.

"No, no. I can handle it. I just thought it was something Oliver might want to know about. Thought he might benefit from it. Be good, uh, if I could help him out. Listen, it's no big deal." Pulling himself together. Making a show of how small a deal it is. Trying too hard. "I'll sort it out. But thanks for the offer."

"Okay. Well, take care of yourself, kid."

Standing by the front door. Mobile phone tucked back into his pocket. Eyes dried, because you can't go wandering the streets with tears in your eyes. People will see that. They'll spot him and think something's wrong. You have to look like there's nothing happening. Like it's no big deal. Biggest deal of his life.

Out of the flat, into the street and walking. Cold. Bloody freezing. How many things is he doing wrong? How many mistakes is he making that'll get him caught? Hundreds, probably. The sort of mistakes someone like Peterkinney would laugh at now. Ridicule Glass for it. He had a head for this. He could probably do something like this without even batting an eyelid these days. The quiet one. The nice one. Now the one Glass wishes he had at his side to help him.

He's been walking for more than half an hour. Didn't want to take the bus. Didn't want to be seen. Seemed like a smart idea, although he's exhausted now. He's on the right street. Quiet place. Expensive-looking houses, terraced. Not huge, but the area is good. There are trees on the little verge between the houses and the road. Everything clean and well maintained. Tiny little front gardens, an excuse to give the residents a front gate of their own. Good cars parked outside each house. A good place. Sort of good place Glass shouldn't be. Sort of good place this shouldn't happen. It's quiet. It's late enough to be quiet.

Glass is shaking. Not from the cold. That doesn't matter anymore. He's shaking anyway. He can just about hear his heartbeat. He has a strange feeling, like he's disconnected from all this. Not out of body or anything like that. That would make it easier. Still very much there. Just not controlling himself anymore. Watching over his own shoulder, wishing he could take control.

He's walking slowly along the street. Looking at numbers on doors. Nothing could be worse than getting the wrong number. He's found the house. The right number, according to the phone directory. A deep breath. A second deep breath, catching in his throat and almost turning into a sob. Then a moment of panic as he wonders if anyone's watching him. Glancing frantically round, looking for witnesses. Nobody on the street. Looking for lights in windows, people lurking behind curtains. Can't see anyone. Pulling up his hood and walking the three steps from the pavement to the door.

Knocking once. Waiting. Nothing. Knocking again. Come on. Knocking a third time, louder now. Worried that he's drawing attention to himself. But nobody's coming to the door. Nobody's at home. Shit. Potty didn't tell him what to do if this happened. He doesn't know.

Back out onto the street, walking down to the corner. There are no lights on in the house, but that doesn't matter. It's late. Might be asleep in bed. Might be lights on at the other side of the house. Maybe he just doesn't answer the door this late. A man in his position, you wouldn't, would you. You don't rush to answer the door if you know a lot of people are out to get you. If he knows people are out to get him. Shit, of course he does. He knows, and he could be in there, waiting for someone like Glass. Or he could be out at work. These would be his work hours, probably. So Glass is standing at the corner. Trying to work out what he's supposed to do next. Go home. Stay and watch for someone arriving. Or try and force his way into the house.

Not the last one. Doesn't know how to do that without causing a scene. And he won't go home. Potty will want to know why he went home so easily. He'll accuse Glass of chickening out. And he'd be right. There's relief coursing through him right now. The glimmer of hope that this might not happen. But he won't go home. He'll hang around on the street. He knows what the target looks like. Seen him before. He'll keep watching. He has to. He just has to. For Ella. For himself.

11

Bavidge just had another meeting with Patterson. He's narrowed down a list of freelancers he's thinking of using. Has to be careful. Has to be someone with a bit of talent. There aren't that many to choose from. Has to be someone they can trust to do a good job. Won't be someone they trust with the truth. Nobody will get the truth. So it needs to be someone who isn't too inquisitive. Won't go looking for facts they're not supposed to know. Only Patterson and Bavidge will know the truth. They'll try to persuade the gunman that he's working for Marty. Try and make sure word gets out. Drop Marty in it. Maybe drop the gunman in it too. That's the risk of his job.

But it doesn't feel like a safe plan. Feels like there's too much outside of their control. Make or break, probably. Either get rid of Potty or be destroyed by him. The way of the world. The way of the business. But they should have something more solid than this to base the risk on. Bavidge is driving home. Get some sleep. It's the only time he's not working. Right now, his work makes him unhappy, so sleep is a good idea.

Pulling into the street and parking outside the house. Usual spot. This isn't even his car, it belongs to Patterson. Bavidge will use it for the next few days for meetings with the gunman. Using a car that can't be linked directly to him as a precaution. They can't be sure that the gunman won't try and get in contact with Marty. That he won't smell a rat and go looking for answers. So you take the precaution of using a different car so that you can start to deny things. Pretend it wasn't you. Always fucking pretending.

Not looking at the world around him. Trying not to think about it. The holes in the plan. The fact, and Bavidge is convinced it is a fact, that something's bound to go wrong. If something small goes wrong, they'll be okay. Something big and all the little precautions in the world won't help them. Forget it. He just wants to get into bed and try to forget that the world exists. Opening the car door and stepping out onto the pavement without checking.

He can see the movement before he feels it. Someone lurching at him. Coming round the back of the car and getting beside him, their hand reaching out. Something jabs at Bavidge's arm. He knows straight away. It's a knife. This is the end. He doesn't have anything to defend himself with. Some kid with a knife. All he can do is throw himself at the man. Try and fight back. But the man isn't thinking properly. He isn't trying to pick his stabs. He's flailing wildly. The knife comes down across Bavidge's face. Another swing across his stomach. This time a jab that goes deep into his stomach.

Glass has let go of the knife, leaving it in just below the ribcage. Bavidge is still standing. Beginning to slump backwards. Glass is reaching out, grabbing him. Steering him back down into the driver's seat of the car. His legs out on the pavement. Then panic. Nothing but panic. All Glass can think about is leaving the body here. He can't do that. He shouldn't do that. People will see. They'll see him. This is…wrong. He has to do a good job for Potty. This is wrong. Just move it. Get it into the car.

He's lifting up the legs, forcing them into the car. Bavidge is still alive. Groaning a little. But he isn't resisting. Doesn't have the strength. His head is across on the passenger seat now, his body across the center console. He's trying to say something. Something Glass doesn't want to hear. He wants to get out of here. His hands have blood on them. Jesus, he's going to be sick.

Lights. Coming round the corner at the far end of the street. Coming towards them. Glass is frozen. Standing, watching the car approaching. Passing them. The driver looking at him. Looking right at him. Eye contact. And now slowing down. He's gone twenty yards past them, but he's slowing to a stop on the road. Not pulling over. Stopping in the middle of the road. Stopping to intervene.

It's just panic. Crazy, think-of-nothing panic. If that guy comes over and demands to know what's going on, Glass won't have an answer. All he'll have is bloody hands and a body. He's getting into the car. Didn't think about it. Just getting into the car. Sitting in the driver's seat. Bavidge's legs are still in the footwell of the driver's seat. Hardly enough room for him to close the door. Glass is pulling the door shut, forcing himself in.

"Come on," he's growling. Crying. Properly this time. His shoulders rocking. His eyes filled. "Move over," he's pleading to Bavidge.

Bavidge making some sort of response. A low groan, but trying to pull his legs across. Closing his eyes hard and whimpering at the pain of effort. Glass pushing Bavidge's legs across the gearstick and into the footwell on the passenger's side. Bavidge reaching out a hand. The keys. He has the keys in his hand. He's giving them to Glass. And Glass is taking them. Starting the car. Looking in his mirror as the driver's door of that other car opens. A man getting out onto the road and walking slowly towards them. Glass has the car started, and he's pulling out. Racing down the street.

It's taken him three streets to remember to put the lights on. He hasn't stopped at a junction. If this was any other time of the day, he'd have hit something by now. But we're past midnight, and the streets are just quiet enough. Driving. No idea where. Just going straight ahead. Driving to nowhere. Getting distance between himself and the witness. Now looking at Bavidge and realizing that he should have run. Should have left him to die in his car, and run. Now he's with a dying man, driving through the city. This is much worse.

"I don't know where to go," Glass is saying quietly. "I don't know."

Bavidge isn't answering. He's slumped against the passenger door. Bent over, his eyes shut. His mouth is slightly open; he's making groaning noises every now and again, but less and less often. He doesn't seem to be aware. Not hearing or seeing or understanding anymore. So Glass has to make the decision. But he has no idea. He's just driving. Checking his mirror to make sure that other car hasn't tried to follow. Trying to work out where he is now. Trying to drive the car properly. Too nervous to focus on any one thing. The pedals a little too far away with the seat pushed back the way the taller Bavidge likes it. The blood on his hands now on the gearstick, meaning it slips from his hand every time he tries to change gear. And still that disconnected feeling, like this is something he can do nothing about.

It's taken him too long to realize that he's driving into the city center. Now that he has realized, he's also realizing that he has to get out of the car. Get away from Bavidge. Get away from the whole situation. The smell, the silence, the fear of it. Get away. Potty told him. He said to get him on the doorstep. Hit and run. Don't hang around. Get it done and get out of there. But he's still here. Ten minutes after stabbing him and he still has Bavidge sitting beside him, bleeding onto the floor of the car.

Now he's just thinking about stopping. Can't think of anything else. Find somewhere, anywhere, to stop. Anywhere that doesn't have people. That's all you need. Indicating to turn right at a junction. Realizing that it's quieter left and going that way. He hasn't even thought about CCTV. He won't either. This is desperation. The only thing that will save him is luck.

Onto a narrower street, going downhill. Doesn't seem to be anyone around. That's a start. Looking left and right as he drives. Lots of little shops with flats above them. Nondescript. Not the sort of place people hang around late at night. No pubs or clubs, although Glass hasn't picked up on that. He just likes the loneliness of it. There. A gap between two buildings. Leads to the rear of the buildings. Leads out of sight. You can get a car into that gap. Course you can. He's turning. Into the alleyway. But there isn't room for a car behind the buildings. It's just a pathway behind the buildings with a high wall. He has to park in the alleyway. Shaking now, struggling to keep a hold of the steering wheel. Stopping too close to a wall on the passenger side. Now he won't be able to get Bavidge out that side. Reversing back and straightening, to give himself more room.

Switching the engine off. Leaving the keys in the ignition. Surprised by the intimidating brightness in the alleyway. Switching off the lights. Getting out of the car and going round to the passenger side. Just as he's opening the passenger door, a car goes past on the street. It goes past, doesn't sound like it's slowing down. Bavidge is now leaning halfway out of the car. Groaning louder.

"You have to get out," Glass is saying. Reaching down and trying to help him out. Trying to lift him by one arm and giving up. His nerves have exhausted him.

Bavidge is trying. He is. Willing to go wherever he's led. Long past the point of resistance. Long past the point of caring what happens, just hoping it happens soon. He wants this to be over. That's the only thought in his head now. Finish it. But he can't lift himself out of the car. Can't put weight on his legs.

"Please, help me," Glass is saying. Pleading.

Another car goes past as he's dragging Bavidge from the car. Taking Bavidge under the arms and dragging him out onto the concrete. Pushing the passenger door shut to make room. Dragging him round in front of the car and laying him down slowly. Trying to be careful. Trying to be gentle. Looking down at the young man he's killed. Bavidge looking aimlessly past him. Looking at the sky above. Blinking heavily. Breathing short and fast. Too much effort.

"I'm sorry," Glass is saying. "I'm so sorry." He doesn't know if Bavidge even heard him. Doesn't seem like it.

He's three steps past the car when he decides to take it. He needs distance between himself and Bavidge. Doesn't matter if someone sees him in the car. He doesn't care about precautions. He just wants to be away. He's turning back and opening the car door. Bavidge is moving. He just moved. Trying to pull himself somewhere. Groaning. Glass can't watch this. Can't take any more of it.

Into the car, the seat still wet with Bavidge's blood. The passenger seat and footwell are thick with it. Stinking. Turning the key, into reverse. Lurching backwards out of the alley, almost catching the wall. Turning on the road. A screech of brakes behind him and the honking of an angry horn. A glance in his mirrors and he can see that he's pulled out into the path of an oncoming car. Lucky it didn't hit him. It's seen him though. Seen him and will remember him. The idiot rushing out of that alley late at night. But Glass isn't thinking about that. He's just putting it into first and hitting the accelerator. Getting away from Bavidge.

He's driven for the best part of three minutes before he remembers to switch the lights on again. Went past plenty of other cars and pedestrians in that time. All of them will have noticed the car with no lights. Now the panic of getting away from Bavidge has been replaced with the panic of getting rid of the car. Looking for anywhere to park. Doesn't matter where. Just anywhere.

The car park of a supermarket. Pulling in and stopping. Switching off the lights and the engine. Jumping out of the car. Slamming the door shut behind him and taking two steps back, looking back at it with disgust. He's parked as far from the building as he can. Now walking slowly over to the shrubbery at the edge of the car park. Bending over and vomiting. Twice. And then a rush of relief. It's gotten rid of some of the nerves. It's forcing him to realize where he is.

A long way from home. Wearing bloodstained clothes. A knife with his prints still embedded in Alan Bavidge. Fingerprints and DNA all over a blood-drenched car. And he's crying again. Hunching down and crying loud. Shouting between sobs. There's nobody here. He wouldn't care if there were. This is over. Everything's over. He just killed a man. Stabbed him and left him to die. His life is over.

PART FOUR

1

It's only the third time he's seen him since he moved out. Three times in, what, over six months. Didn't expect to see his grandson every bloody day. Glad of a little space, to be honest. The tiny flat has felt more like his home since the boy moved out. Not having to make room for the lad, not having him hear every conversation. The walls have always been paper-thin; a little privacy is worth a lot. But he didn't expect to have to track him down like this. Didn't expect that his grandson would avoid him the way he has.

Everyone says he's changed. They say he's become tough, a little schemer. Everyone who knew him before and knows him now. Aren't many of those. Oliver seems to be doing his damnedest to ditch anyone who knew him before. Arnie isn't so sure about this great change. Oliver was always sharp. Always wanted more for himself than he could get. He wasn't the toughest kid, but he was never what you would call sympathetic. Never emotional. Kept people at a distance. That's probably what makes his work so easy for him. Doesn't think of people as people. Arnie blames his parents. Always did. Ditching the kid like that. Feckless pair of bastards.

Now he's running this business. A business that benefits from his way of thinking. Creating a completely new life for himself. Know what? Arnie would be fine with that if it was the right kind of life. There's something admirable about a young man striding off into the world and building a new life for himself. If he felt he needed to cut old ties to do that, Arnie would respect it. A young man, just gone past his twenty-first birthday, and he already has his own little company. His own flat. His own life. But it's a rotten life. And that's why Arnie's tracking him down.

Arnie knew what Oliver was doing. He knew he was debt collecting. Scraping the bottom of the barrel. Arnie sat in his little flat every day and felt disgusted. Felt ashamed. But he did nothing. Did nothing because he hoped it might not be true. Hoped that maybe it was a short-term thing. That happens. A kid making money. Then the kid finds another way to make some dough. A better way. Maybe a more glamorous one. Less risky. And he moves away from the dirty side of life. But that's six months, and the stories he's hearing keep getting worse.

There's a middle-aged woman who lives in the next block of flats along from Arnie's. He doesn't know her, but he knows of her. Friends of friends, that sort of thing. Anyway, this woman borrowed money. Stupid thing to do, let's be honest. Arnie despairs of people who would borrow in the first place, given what happens. Always ends badly. Mind you, moneylenders can advertise on TV now. See it all the time. It's in danger of becoming acceptable. They're letting the sharks play in the swimming pool.

So this middle-aged woman, Kirsty something or other. She borrowed money and didn't pay it back. Couldn't, at the rates they were charging. The lender sold the debt to a collector. The collector sent someone round to intimidate her. She still couldn't pay. You can intimidate someone as much as you want; fear doesn't make money. So they started taking her stuff. Furniture, that sort of thing. She tried to stop the two thugs who had barged into her flat. So they beat her up. Not life-threatening or anything like that, but they knocked a couple of teeth out of her head. Left her all cut and bruised. Just about scared the life out of the poor woman.

Arnie heard the story and he shook his head. What kind of people would do that to a woman? Two days later he heard the story again, and it had grown a few hideous details. Grown to include the name of the collector who had sent his men round to steal her furniture. Who sent another one round when she was back from hospital the day after the beating to warn her to keep her mouth shut. They were saying it was Oliver Peterkinney.

Shame? He's never felt anything like it. His grandson sending nasty bastards round to beat up women. Never felt so humiliated in all his life. Let's make no mistake about it: he's done some things he's been ashamed of in his time. Things he wouldn't admit to, to you or to anyone else. But they were minor compared to this. The boy he helped raise, doing a thing like this. It's a humiliation. He knows it, and so does everyone else.

Which is what's brought him here. Walking across the road and towards the entrance of Oliver's office. His own little office building. Been here a while. Established, is what they call it. Beyond the point where he's a newbie who might fail at the first hurdle. Nope, he's past that hurdle and halfway down the running track. He's established now. That means people take him seriously. Fear him. Huh.

Arnie didn't want to come here. Would rather have met Oliver anywhere but here. Wanted to meet him at his flat, but he's moved again. Got a new address that he didn't bother to share with his grandfather. Moved again about a month ago. Moved to another flat in a more upscale part of town. Going up in the world, and obviously wants his home to show that. Bringing in a lot of other people's money. Wants the world to see how upwardly mobile he is. Wow the world with his success, like it's something to be proud of. Didn't bother to tell his grandfather where he was going.

Couldn't turn up at his flat. Called the office and got fobbed off by that nasal little lickspittle he employs. So this is the last resort. Turning up at the office and giving the boy no option but to talk. Because, by God, he is going to talk. He is going to explain himself. If he can't explain himself very well indeed then he is going to listen.

Arnie's across the street and opening the door. Stepping into the little office. Small place, but that's all you need when your job is intimidating the vulnerable. That doesn't take much space, does it? But they won't be here long. Arnie would bet on it. They'll stay in the area because people associate them with this area. But they'll get somewhere bigger. Somewhere they don't even need. To look big and clever. Intimidate people with their growth. And to cover their tracks. How much of this money has to be laundered? What other filthy practices do they use to get that done?

The two of them are in the office. Oliver behind his desk, the other fellow taking something out of a filing cabinet. Jesus, they almost look respectable. A pair of office boys. The other one's looking at him without a hint of recognition. Oliver's slumping back in his chair. A look of displeasure on his face. Rolling his eyes to the ceiling and then glaring back towards the door. Doing his best to make his own grandfather feel unwelcome.

"Can I help?" the other one is asking, sliding the drawer of the cabinet shut.

"Not you, son, no," Arnie's saying.

"What do you want?" Oliver's asking him. "You should have phoned. I don't have time for catching up. I'm busy."

"Phoned, that's a laugh. I phone here and all I get is this wee bugger telling me you're not in. You're never in for a phone call. Disappear on the first bloody ring. I figured the only way you were ever going to be in was if I was in with you. No pretending then. So we can talk. Because we need to talk, Oliver. We do." Trying to sound reasonable. Started with an irritated tone, but worked hard to calm it before he stopped talking. He doesn't want this to turn into an argument any earlier than it has to. Inevitable that it will at some point, but he has to try.

"Listen, I need to go out and . . ." But Peterkinney's trailing off, because Arnie's already turned round to look at Kilbanne. He's standing behind his desk on the other side of the room now.

"You can go make yourself scarce. Get lunch. Get lost. I don't care. Just get yourself out. This is a private conversation. Family talk." Not bothered about being polite with him. The amount of times he's been lied to by this sniveling bastard, he hasn't earned politeness.

There's something remarkably intimidating about an angry old man. Arnie's not that big, looks unhealthy and sounds a little wheezy these days. But when he points and barks at you, you pay attention. Kilbanne is looking across at Peterkinney. Waiting for instructions from the boss. Maybe Peterkinney doesn't want to be left alone with this old guy.

"Go. Come back in fifteen," Peterkinney's saying. "This won't take longer than that."

Kilbanne's leaving. Arnie still standing in front of Peterkinney's desk. Looking down at his grandson. Looks a little fuller in the face than he did. A little older. A little more rugged. Like he's lived something of a life now. Yeah. And at whose expense? Arnie's shaking his head.

"Why haven't you been willing to talk to me?" he's asking quietly.

"I've been busy. Working, you know." Said with a hint of sarcasm. Pointing out the fact that Arnie hasn't had a job for some time now.

Oliver still hasn't asked him to sit down. Not that Arnie wants to. He wants to stand over the boy when the argument starts. Feels like a position of strength. But he's noticed Oliver's making no effort at being welcoming. He still doesn't want to talk. Doesn't want his grandfather to be a part of his life anymore. The man who took him in. Gave him a home. Did his best, such as it was, to raise him. Don't throw that at him though. That's not the way to win this argument. Oliver clearly feels no sense of debt.

"I know what work you do."

"Uh-huh. Not a secret."

"No, it isn't, is it? Everyone knows. Everyone's talking about you. Talking about how you had your thugs beat up some woman along the street from me. That you don't give a shit about the law or anything else. Tough little bastard, you are. That's what they say. How tough you are. Hiding behind your thugs. Stealing money from the weakest people you can find. Yeah, everyone's talking about you all right. Tough little nut, uh? Very scary." Damn it. Didn't want to go off on a rant this soon. Wanted to make a persuasive argument, not an aggressive one. Just couldn't control it. Months of knowing what his own flesh and blood was doing. Months of doing nothing about it. His own embarrassment at not doing this sooner was to blame. There was just too much locked away in there that needed to come out.

"You here about her? I heard about that, already reprimanded someone for it. It was a mistake. An accident. Shouldn't have happened. I'm sorry, okay? We done?"

It's a funny thing. Really is. You live with someone for a few years and you get a pretty good handle on the sort of person they are. You lose track of them for six months. Catch up with them again and they're someone else. Completely different person. Oliver was distant, and he could be cold. He wasn't always an easy boy to love. But he was respectful, because he understood that that worked best. He was never a dismissive, arrogant little shit. He understood what it meant to be a good person. He could be morally hazy, sure. Arnie wasn't going to judge him for that. Anyway, he was a kid, a little bit immature. All kids make mistakes. Follow the wrong path once in a while. Didn't make him a bad person, not at heart. He was a decent person, when push came to shove. Now look at him. He's someone else.

"It will kill you, you know," Arnie's saying. Saying it quiet. Saying it with genuine regret. A sadness that catches Oliver out.

He's looking up at his grandfather. A puzzled look. "What?"

"This. All this. The work you're doing. The life you're living. It's going to kill you. You won't be the first one, oh no. It'll destroy anyone innocent first. That's what it does, this life. It kills the good people first, then the bad. This life of yours is poison. That poison will catch up with you. It will. Has to. You mark my words, boy. It will catch up with you and it will kill you. I've seen it. People being murdered. Or getting into drugs. Some stupid thing. And I'll have to go. I'll have to go to your funeral and stand over your grave and know that I didn't stop you. Couldn't stop you from doing it to yourself."

He's stopped talking. He was rambling and he knew it. His voice was quivering with emotion and Arnie isn't the kind of man who likes to hear that in himself. Old school. He came here to be strong. He didn't come here to be emotional.

"I think you should go." Oliver sitting there, looking up at him. There's a look of shock on his face that he's doing a poor job of hiding. Never heard his grandfather talk like this before. Never seen that sort of emotion from him.

Arnie's looking down at him. Scowling to cover the emotion. Shaking his head, because he just can't think of anything else to say. Wishes there was something convincing to say, but there isn't. He's turning and walking to the door. Pulling it open, but stopping. Looking back at Oliver. Just looking at him, because he's scared he might never see him again. And leaving, because he can't help a man who doesn't believe he needs help. Who won't realize until it's too late.

2

Furious. Actually, furious doesn't begin to sum it up. If he had the mobility, he'd be bouncing off the walls. Potty Cruickshank has never been so angry. Never in forty-eight angry years. Six hours ago he was arrested. First time in his life. Some detective and a couple of plods turned up at his house and arrested him. Led him out into the street for all the neighbors to see as they loaded him into the back of a police car. Deliberately embarrassing him. Suspicion of laundering money, they said. Took him away to the station. The thing he was most angry about? They were right.

He's always been so careful with his money. That was hammered into him by Uncle Rolly. The money is the easiest way for the cops to get you. You always hide it away. You take every last precaution to make sure it's well out of view. Someone grassed. Someone who knows about his systems went to the police and spilled their guts. It's the only way. They couldn't have known what they did without inside info. So now he has to find out who.

They haven't charged him yet. Questioned him for a few hours. A lot of questions he genuinely didn't know the answers to. He doesn't know every exact detail about every penny that gets hidden. He hires people to handle that. He has deniability on the details of it. A few questions he did know the answer to. Those he chose not to answer anyway. It did give him a few clues about timing. They only seemed to be asking about money that was moved within a certain period. About a year ago until about six months ago, give or take. That's interesting. That's a place to start investigating.

The cheek of them. Arresting a Cruickshank. Didn't even have enough to charge him with. That's what he thought. Not what his lawyer thought. In the car on the way back to his house the lawyer had a different idea to share. After five hours in the station, Potty wasn't thinking straight. So the lawyer put him right.

"They brought you in to scare you. See if they could trip you up. They'll be arresting other people. Must be, the evidence they have. I think they will arrest you again, Mr. Cruickshank. They're setting you up to arrest you a second time, and this time they'll charge you."

He was right. Potty's been at home for nearly an hour. Taking that time to try to calm down. Not happening. This kind of fury will take days to calm. He needs to find out who grassed him. Find out what damage has been done. There's an easy place to start. The police were asking about money from that period of time. Time to get in touch with the man who was moving his money around at that time.

Potty has two different men who handle the money, but neither of them is young anymore. One of them, Willie Caldwell, has hardly done a hand's turn for a year and a half. The man's seventy and had treatment for cancer. He was Uncle Rolly's moneyman for many years, just carried on working for Potty. He's started doing a bit of work again in the last three months, but nothing as far back as six to twelve months. Which just leaves Steven Wales. Sixty-three, and amongst the most dependable criminals that God ever placed on this earth.

Potty's calling his house. It only rings twice and there's an answer. A woman's voice. That'll be Mrs. Wales then. The often-mentioned, never-seen spouse. Potty's never met the woman, for all that he's heard Wales talk about her over the years.

"Hello, I'm looking for Steven Wales. Is he home?"

"No. No, he isn't. Who's calling, please?"

The woman sounds emotional. Potty doesn't have the patience for emotional. Not in the mood. "This is Ronald Cruickshank."

"Oh, Mr. Cruickshank," she's saying. There's relief in her voice.

Something Potty doesn't like to hear. Usually means someone expects you to do them a favor. "Oh, Mr. Cruickshank, they came to the house this morning. The police came and they took him away. They said they were going to question him and he hasn't been back yet."

Potty's grimacing, but in a sense it's good news. They've arrested Wales, which means Wales isn't the grass. Wales is the one who knows the most. He was the one cleaning the money. So long as he keeps his gob shut, that'll prevent the police knowing the worst of it. So the grass is someone else. Someone a little further away from the center. Someone who knew that Wales did work for Potty. Knew at least roughly what that work entailed. Specifically from that time period.

"Now you listen here, Mrs. Wales. I will do all I can to make sure your husband is well treated. I'll get my lawyers on it right away. Your husband won't be in any trouble if I can help it." He can't say that her husband has done nothing wrong because, well, he has. She must realize it. There may be trouble that Potty can do nothing to stop.

"Thank you, Mr. Cruickshank. It helps to know."

Wasn't Wales. Then who? Sitting down and thinking things through. Considering the options. And there's one there. Lurking in the back of his mind, elbowing its way forwards. Someone who was around a lot back then. Helped him out. Someone who's been drifting away from him for no good reason in the last six months.

He's made three phone calls and come up short. Nobody knows just what exactly PC Paul Greig is up to these days. Conflicting reports. One person saying he's working for Shug Francis. Another person saying he's working for Alex MacArthur. So now Potty's calling Alex MacArthur.

"He isn't doing any work for me," MacArthur's saying. There's an edge to his tone. Their relationship has been good these last few months, since the Bavidge thing. But this call doesn't seem to be welcome. Sounds like the old man's distracted. "I think he's been

doing work for Don though. Call Don if you want to ask about him."
Didn't say Don Park's name with any great love. One of his own
men. Sounds like the old man is finally getting wary of potential
successors. They all do, in the end.

Calling up Don Park. Getting a chuckle at the mention of Greig.
Smooth little operator, this one. One to keep an eye on if
MacArthur's health gets worse. "Working for me? Not exactly.
Working for everyone. You know what he's like. Doing work for me
and doing work for Peter Jamieson. Doing work for you and doing
work for Oliver Peterkinney. That's Greig. A finger in every pie."

That's as much as Potty needs to hear. Greig doing work for
Peterkinney. Of course he fucking is. A new kid turns up and starts
making an impact. Growing untouched. Getting good deals. Knowing where to go. Contacts that others take years to find. Needs experienced people to point him in the right directions. Help him along.
People very much like Greig.

Starting to make a lot more sense now. Peterkinney gets Greig
onside. They strike a deal. Greig helps Peterkinney by removing the
opposition. Good Lord, Potty didn't take the kid seriously enough.
Some little bastard who worked for Marty and set up his own business. Not like he would have learned much from Marty. He did
mean to watch him. Had every intention of doing something about
him sooner. Should have. Would have. Too busy pulling the rug out
from under Billy Patterson. This is what happens when you take
your eye off the ball. Slap on the wrist for Potty, move on.

Move on and work out what he's going to do about Peterkinney.
What he's going to do about Greig. Don't let personal feeling get
in the way of a business decision. Be very careful with Greig. He's
a cop. A lying, cheating bastard, but a cop. You don't pick a fight
with a cop. Not unless you're on solid ground, which Potty isn't. No
way he can make a convincing allegation against Greig without im-
plicating himself. No way he can bring down Greig without Greig
making life even more difficult for him.

But Peterkinney. He's a different business. He can be taken

down. There are things that Potty can and will do to teach that wee boy a few lessons. The first lesson being that you don't pick a fight with a Cruickshank until you're 100 percent certain of victory. So now Potty's plotting. Trying to work out ways of getting at Peterkinney. He tried once before with the Bavidge thing. Didn't work out perfectly, but that didn't matter much at the time. Peterkinney didn't end up getting any of the blame, as Potty intended. But that was always a bonus to the main event. This is different. Now Peterkinney's going to be the main target.

3

Glass didn't leave the flat for days afterwards. Spent the whole time waiting for a knock on the door that didn't come. Only person who came to the flat in that time was Ella, and she has a key. She spent some time with him, trying to work out what was wrong. He wasn't responding to her. Lying in bed, refusing to tell her what had happened. She made an effort. A week of treating him like an invalid. Cooking for him, getting him to shower. Never forcing him to share anything, but trying to coax it out of him. Nothing she did made an impact.

It upset her, seemed like he was deliberately pushing her away. So Ella made a decision. Try and shock him into action. Get him out of his bed and into the world again by giving him no other option. She stopped coming to the flat, and he was completely alone. The idea was that it would compel him to get up. Go out and get some food, get into the world. Didn't work. She waited a week, and no phone call came. Went past the flats a few times and saw no sign of life. When she went back in, he was the same as ever. He'd fed himself, yes, because he had to. But he was eating food way past its sell-by date. Unwilling to leave the flat even for that. She cried over it, and went back to playing nursemaid, fitting it around her work.

One thing Glass made the effort to do was constantly check websites and local TV news. They found Alan Bavidge's body the following morning. Multiple stab wounds, is what was reported. Knife found at the scene. Didn't say that it was still in his body. Said they were hopeful of progress. Glass knew what that meant. Meant his fingerprints were on the knife. Meant they had all the evidence they needed for a conviction; all they had to do was track down the killer. But time passed and they didn't track him down. They had his fingerprints on the knife, but nowhere else.

But there was so much else. The longer he lay in bed thinking about it, the more he remembered what he had done wrong. The people who had seen him. The CCTV cameras that must have picked him up. Leaving the car in a car park. A bloodstained car with the number plates still on it. Would take them all of ten seconds to put two and two together. But nothing. No knock on the door. Nobody coming to tell him that he was being charged with murder.

He'd already decided that if they came for him, he would confess. No point in denying it. He couldn't claim innocence, so he would confess and hope they were gentle with him. He wouldn't tell them why. He'd decided that. If he grassed Potty then Potty would take revenge. Could kill him. No, he would say that he owed money, and that he thought Bavidge was going to collect from him. Something like that. Take all the blame for himself. Looking at a long time inside. Thinking about how he would survive it. Twenty years. Thirty, maybe. But the knock on the door didn't come. It was like they didn't check the CCTV. Like they didn't interview the witnesses. Like they never found the car.

Which they didn't. Not the police's fault. The witnesses never came forward. Not one. Not even the guy who stopped and got out of his car outside Bavidge's house. He went home and decided to forget about it. If he saw the report of the dead body found behind the shops, he either didn't connect the two things or didn't want to get involved. That's the thing. People don't want to get involved. Not if they can avoid it. So the driver of the car that Glass nearly reversed into pulling out of the alleyway said nothing. They must now realize that they saw the killer leave the scene, but he or she is keeping it to themselves. Scared of getting tangled in a gangland dispute.

Without witnesses, the police don't know what they're looking for. Don't know what car. It wasn't Bavidge's own car. That was parked outside his flat. This was a company car belonging to Patterson, but the police don't know that. They're convinced the body was moved, but they think in the killer's car. So they've gone through the CCTV around the scene, but more than half the cameras don't work. They've come up with no reliable image of the car that took Bavidge to the scene.

And they never found the car. Nobody did. A couple of hours after word spread that Bavidge was dead, the car was gone from the car park. Disappeared off the face of the earth. Glass doesn't know that. Didn't know it for those few weeks he spent hiding from the world. Assumed the police had found it. Assumed they would be knocking on his door any minute now. But the car was gone. The evidence they needed, spirited away. Nothing for the police to use. Their investigation undermined. Glass's freedom saved.

After three weeks, he started to reengage with planet Earth. Enough time passed for Ella's pleas to become convincing. She didn't know what he was scared of, but she kept saying that it had been weeks and nothing had happened. Weeks when he thought he was in danger but was safe. Surely it was time to get back to normal. Three weeks was sufficient for his fear to shrink just enough for him to see other people's problems. To see how much he was upsetting Ella. So he made the effort. Out into the big scary world. Afraid of every step. Waiting for a hand on the shoulder. Waiting for someone to say or do something. But nobody did. Nobody cared about him in the slightest.

It was a weird couple of months thereafter. He gradually got used to living again. He knows he was childish about it. Living in fear, needing to be looked after. Even in the month after he started going out again. Ella nursed him through it all. But it hasn't been the same. Hasn't been the same with Ella. Hasn't been the same with anyone. Still living with that fear. Always will. Knowing that he did something he ought to be punished for. Knowing that there are people out there who will seek to punish him. Worse people than the police.

He was waiting for the police, because they were the first fear his mind turned to. Still are. Getting to a point where it would almost be a relief if a copper did come for him. But there are more dangerous people out there than the police. Alan Bavidge worked for Billy Patterson. Everyone knows Billy Patterson is a tough little bastard. Everyone knows he punishes hard. He has to be looking for the person who killed Bavidge. When he finds that person, he's going to kill them. Torture them and kill them. When the police find the killer, Patterson will still try to kill them. You live with that sort of fear, that sort of expectation, and it changes your behavior.

Glass basically stopped caring. If you're going to be arrested or killed tomorrow, it doesn't much matter how you behave today. So he started going out with Ella every night. Even when she didn't want to go, he insisted. She only went because she was worried about him. Thought he needed her there to stop him doing something stupid. Still nursing him, because he was obviously still sick. Living every night like it was his last. Could have been. You never know. So he lived it that way. Drinking a lot. Using a lot more drugs, because that seemed to help. Kill reality.

You know what's funny? He doesn't remember going back to Jefferson for another loan. No recollection at all. Doesn't even remember spending the money. Jefferson happily gave him the money when he asked. He knew that Glass had paid off Potty. Had done something to wriggle off the hook. Potty was happy with Glass, so Glass got another loan. Jefferson working on the assumption that he can sell this one to Potty as well. Glass doesn't remember asking for the money. Doesn't remember spending it. Doesn't remember going back and asking for more.

That's what it's been like. Months of blur. That's the way he wants to keep it. Life doesn't feel real, so life stops being something he needs to care about. His relationship with Ella is suffering for it. She cries a lot, shouts at him. Shouting about things he barely understands. Something about a carpet the other day. He didn't understand that she had been saving up for a new carpet in the living room, and he blew the money on drink. Doesn't understand that she's trying to create a stable home, and that he's destroying it. But that doesn't matter to him. Nothing does.

Jefferson's been calling. Glass is heading round there now. Not thinking about it at all. He doesn't care what Jefferson wants. Doesn't care what he demands or threatens. Jefferson's nothing when you stand him next to Billy Patterson.

Into Jefferson's office. Jefferson actually seems surprised that he's turned up. Raising an eyebrow and slowly nodding his head. Seen this before. Borrowers who just don't care. Don't even try and hide from the problem anymore.

"You came. Good. Sit down." There's a pause while he looks at Glass. Glass has the look of a man who slept for three hours last night. Who didn't shower this morning. Stubble, tousled hair, scruffy clothes. "You look like shit," Jefferson's saying. A hint of concern. Not about Glass. He doesn't care about Glass's well-being any more than Glass does. He's concerned about the debt. If Glass can't look after himself, he can't look after the debt. The boy's really gone downhill in the last few months.

"Thanks a lot. What do you want?"

Jefferson's frowning now. "What do I want? I want my fucking money, is what I want. What did you think I wanted? You owe me money. You owe me four thousand one hundred pounds. You haven't paid back a single penny." That's why he's calling it in. This new debt hasn't been running long, but at least last time Glass showed signs of paying. Not this time. This time, not a damn penny. No money paid, no effort made to pay. So he's calling it in early.

"I don't have any money." Glass saying it like it's no big deal. Like he doesn't care at all. And he doesn't. Last time it worried him sick. This time he has it in perspective. Money is nothing. If he's dead tomorrow, the debt dies with him. If he's locked up tomorrow, the debt gets locked up with him. The debt is a long-term problem in a short-term world.

"You think you're going to get off with this? You think you've bought yourself some sort of credit? Huh, is that it? You think Potty Cruickshank will bail you out a second time? He won't. Let me tell you that now. He won't. Seems like he isn't interested in you anymore. Yeah, I called him. Yesterday morning. Called him up and said I had another debt of yours I was looking to shift. Thought he might be interested. He said no. Not interested at all, thanks for calling. So you're out on your own. You need to come up with that money, because there's nobody in this world that wants to help you."

Glass is laughing. Nobody ever wanted to help him. He never thought for one second that anyone did. Potty? Wanting to help him? That's a laugh. Jefferson's frowning again, and he can frown all he wants. Glass didn't borrow because he thought there was a way out. He borrowed because it doesn't matter to him.

He's out of the office and making his way back home. Pointless meeting. Back to the flat. Maybe get some sleep in the afternoon. Spend a little time with Ella. But she's not there when he gets back. Gone off somewhere without telling him. She does that more now. He hasn't thought about why. She's working more to try and earn more money because he's throwing so much away. She's trying to keep the dream of a good life alive. The dream they used to share.

4

It shocked him, how much it hurt. Billy Patterson is a tough man, make no mistake. He's thirty-nine, and people have come and gone in his life. People he cared about. Didn't slow him down. Always hurts to lose someone you care about, sure, but he coped. Coped well. Shut the emotions away and got on with being his usual hard self. So he didn't expect losing Bavidge to hurt the way it did.

Partly because he blames himself. Never blamed himself before. He's been responsible for people dying before. Two people. Didn't carry out the killings. Didn't order them either. But sent people round to beat these two up. They didn't take the beatings well. Died. Patterson didn't take that hard. That was the job. Some people can take a beating. Some people can't. The risk you run when you're dealing with collectors. This was different. This actually felt like his fault.

Bavidge was a friend. They didn't hang out socially, but that wasn't the point. They were friends in a way that mattered more than socializing. They were on the same wavelength. Patterson sent Bavidge out into the world to do bad things. Bavidge did them, never questioning the role he played. He was honest, and he was reliable. He understood. It was Patterson who sent him out to do those bad things, and one of them caught up with Bavidge. Strange thing is, this is what he expected. He had always viewed Bavidge as a man destined for an early death. He knew that, and it didn't stop him using Bavidge. And that got him killed.

He heard the news from a contact in the police. A civilian, doing office work. They called him up, told him that the police had found

Bavidge's body. Gave all the details. They were confusing. Multiple stab wounds to the arms and stomach. The knife was still in him. He was found behind some shops in the city center. Made no sense. Body had been moved. Probably attacked outside his house: some blood had been found on the pavement by the officers sent round to check the place. The police searching for the car that moved him. Patterson was stunned by it. Took him a few minutes to pull himself together. Then he acted fast.

Sent someone round to Bavidge's house. Wanted to see if the police had found the car Bavidge was using. That car was the link to Patterson. A link Patterson couldn't let the police find. Car wasn't there. Police were. At first he feared the police had found the car and taken it away. Reassurance from the contact. The police still hadn't found anything. Bavidge's own car on the street, but nothing else of interest. So all his people were sent out to look. Find the car. It had to be what the body was moved in. Had to be. It was luck that they found it so soon. The muscle searched car parks and one of them stumbled across the car. Inside soaked in blood. It's been destroyed. Nothing to link the murder victim with the debt collector he was planning crimes with. How could Patterson explain the use of that company car to the police? Admit that they were using it to try and trick a gunman into killing Potty Cruickshank in an attempt to set up Marty Jones? Yeah, good one. The car had to go.

That was the clean-up. The following couple of months were awkward. Just trying to get the tone right. People in the business knew they were vulnerable. Had to know. They knew that Bavidge was an important man and now they know he's dead. So Patterson went into reassurance mode. Making sure all his men knew that they weren't going to be crushed. This was a one-off, not dominoes falling. That meant keeping their heads down. No drawing attention. If people don't look at you, they don't see your vulnerability. Let everything calm down before you launch a counterattack.

Truth is, if he'd been in a strong position, he would have hit back straight away. He wanted to. Would have loved to do something about it. He was burning to punish someone. Two problems. Couldn't be sure who had done it. The hit was a mess, and that pushed him towards thinking it was someone amateur. Someone a bit dumb. Maybe someone Bavidge had collected from. Or a jealous husband. But the main target still had to be Potty Cruickshank. He was the obvious candidate. Would never put it past him to use some amateur to cover his tracks.

But Patterson wasn't strong enough to fight back. Not yet. He needed to regroup without Bavidge. He needed to find answers. He needed to build strength. And he's been doing that. Tough, but not dumb. He's been working silently. Giving people the impression that he's weak. Giving people the impression that he's slowly losing business. Letting them believe what he wants them to believe. Pulling his inner circle closer and getting them to work.

Today is one of the first big steps in his plan. He will take down Potty Cruickshank. He will. He will because he knows. Doesn't know everything, sure, but he knows enough. Suspicion has hardened into certainty. Potty and MacArthur were working together, and MacArthur has a big organization. A lot of people who find stuff out. A lot of people who can talk about it. And they did talk. Conn Griffiths got a lot of good info about the Bavidge killing yesterday. Organized by Potty. No doubt about it. Potty and MacArthur were rather pleased with themselves about it. Jamie Stamford, weirdly, wasn't that happy. Probably didn't like someone else publicly cleaning up his mess. But it was Potty. Everyone in MacArthur's organization is saying so.

Still haven't found out who actually carried it out. Working on that. Won't stop looking until he finds them. And when he finds them, he'll kill them. Potty's the big one. Potty's the one who made it all happen and he's the one who has to pay for it. The person who carried it out has to be seen to be punished. But that takes help. Patterson's been lying low. He's using fewer people now, buying fewer debts. That's deliberate. Self-preservation. If you're too small to win the fight, get so small the opponent thinks they've already won. Potty will think that he's won. Beaten Patterson. But he's got a surprise coming.

Patterson's meeting with Marty Jones. Polite little meeting in an office above a shop. Talk with Marty about helping each other out. Marty will think he's the big half of the meeting. He'll believe Patterson is small now too. So he'll be willing to do a deal because he'll think he can dominate this. That's fine. Let him think that. If Bavidge had lived, Marty would be carrying the can for a hit attempt on Potty right now. Just don't underestimate flashy Marty. Doesn't matter how scatty a shark like him looks, he still has bite. Patterson's increasingly convinced that that's all part of Marty's own self-preservation. The lifestyle. The parties and the women. Profitable, sure, but a smart way to look like a cheeky rogue, rather than a ruthless gangster.

"Good to see you, Billy," Marty's saying. Sticking his hand out and pretending to be a friend. Sitting behind one of the desks in the office.

The office is practically empty. Desks and chairs and very little else to get excited about. Easy to guess what Marty sees in this place. It's on a busy street where he can come and go without standing out. Have meetings like this. Collect things here. Kind of good little office Patterson could do with.

"Good to see you too, Marty." Very disingenuous, but Marty must encounter so many bullshit merchants that he doesn't bat an eyelid. "I think we ought to have a little chat about what we can do for each other."

Marty's smiling and nodding. A guy comes to you and says you should help each other out. A guy who's been under attack. A guy whose business has been shrinking. Of course Marty's going to think that this is a golden opportunity for him. Of course he's going to think that he can take control of this. That's what he's supposed to think.

"Well, I guess maybe we can," Marty's saying. "Although I'll be honest with you here, Billy, I'm not seeing what we're going to be able to do for each other. You and me, we're not exactly the best possible fit."

"See, I think we are," Patterson's saying, getting in there before Marty has the chance to follow that train of thought down the tracks. "I think there's a lot we can do for each other. I think we're as compatible as two men in our business can be. Not a perfect fit, maybe, but you'll never find one of them. You have specific skills and connections that I don't have. I have specific abilities that you don't. And we both have common enemies."

Marty's nodding to that. They sure as hell do. But Marty's been thinking about that bastard Peterkinney a lot, and he's guessing that's not who's on Patterson's mind. He'll be more interested in Potty Cruickshank. Everyone knows he took on Potty and lost. Potty hooked up with Alex MacArthur. Now things are falling into place. Ah, Patterson, you smart little bastard. Potty hooks up with Alex MacArthur. Marty is under Peter Jamieson's protection. That makes it hard for Marty to say no.

But Marty's instincts are telling him to say no. He wants to say no so that he won't get dragged into something big and dangerous. This is a man who's built his career on exploiting the vulnerable, not fighting the strong. He knows what fights to pick. His instincts are razor-sharp on that front. This doesn't look like a good one. But he has to say yes. Jamieson's setting up a run on MacArthur. Everyone in the know knows. Or at least suspects. It's the next natural step. This will help to hurt MacArthur, and Marty still needs to wriggle his way back into the good books. Looking for every opportunity.

"You need to tell me something concrete," Marty's saying. "You give me something concrete, and I can get behind it. I'm not going to throw myself in front of a bus for you, Billy boy, but I could help you."

Billy's turn to smile. Marty's good at this. You have to play him careful. Tempting to believe all the bluster and bullshit, but he's smart. Didn't get where he is by accident. "I want Potty Cruickshank's fat head on a spike. I want the Cruickshank business in ashes. I want that family name to be a distant memory. An old joke. I think that would serve you well. I also wouldn't mind cutting the legs off Oliver Peterkinney. I've watched him grow. He's dangerous. Would be smart to do something to stop that, sooner rather than later. You and me could carve this business up between us. If we're smart. If we're tough. If we use the advantages we have. We could undermine some important people into the bargain. Help bigger players take down bigger rivals. I have the men to go to war with Potty. Don't be dumb enough to believe that my shrinking the business was anything other than preparation."

Marty's looking at his watch. He really does need to hurry this along. "Okay. Listen, Billy. I ain't saying yes. Not certainly. But I'll think about it. Give it some, you know, proper consideration."

"You know that Potty Cruickshank was arrested this morning?" Patterson's asking. Casual tone, making no effort to get up and leave.

Marty looks shocked. He didn't know that.

"The cracks are starting to show," Patterson's saying, getting up from his chair now. "You think about what I said. Give it proper consideration. Potty was arrested because your old employee Peterkinney is moving against him. Dangerous kid, that one. Taking on a man like Potty. Would serve you well to have some extra men around you. Men like my crew." Sticking his hand out to shake. Then turning and walking confidently out of the room.

Down the steps and out through the door onto the street. Marty has to say yes, and he will. He would have anyway, without knowing about Potty's arrest. He would have said yes because he needs to make the moves that make Jamieson happy. But Potty's arrest tips it over the edge. Doesn't matter who you are, an arrest makes you look weak. Once you look weak, you look like a target.

5

His grandfather's still on his mind. Shouldn't bother him at all, but it does. He never exaggerated their relationship. He was already a teenager when he went to live with Arnie. Arnie didn't have any profound effect on making him the man he is today. He didn't mold him. Always seemed to Peterkinney that his grandfather was counting the days to him leaving. Tried to push him in the right direction now and again. Never openly begrudged the expense of having Oliver there. Tried to bring him up with the least possible effort.

Now he's all over him. Giving him an earful. Captain fucking Morality. Where did that come from? Jesus, think back. Who was it that set him up with Roy Bowles in the first place? Bowles the gunrunner. That was his grandfather's grand plan to steer him away from Marty Jones. Get away from that frying pan and into the fire. Please. Coming over all moral now. Gets on his nerves. Really does.

And he's still angry as he pulls up at Jazzy Jefferson's office. Shoving his car door shut and walking briskly inside. Late in the day for a business meeting. It was Jefferson who called him up. Asked him to come round to have a look at the books. Might be a good deal or two in there for him. Sounded a little too pleading. Sounded like Jefferson was having a hard time shifting some debts and wanted the always-generous youngster to help him out. Well, the youngster is more established now. Less need to be generous. And he's not in a helping mood.

"Oliver, good to see you," Jefferson's saying. Smiling so broadly you would almost think he meant it. Smiling so broadly he's beginning to look like he's in pain.

"Sit down, let's see these books." No mood for pleasantries. Not with Jefferson anyway. Like Peterkinney doesn't know what Jefferson's been up to. Like he doesn't keep a keen eye on people like him. Any sensible collector keeps a beady eye on the behavior of lenders. He knows Jefferson's been pawing at Potty's door again. Looking to keep onside with the fat man. They've all heard the stories about Potty teaming up with Alex MacArthur. Squashing Billy Patterson. Big deal, very impressive, whoop-dee-doo. Peterkinney's one of the few who doesn't seem to be impressed by these old farts squabbling. No surprise that Jefferson's gone running back. He really shouldn't be so naive as to think Peterkinney wouldn't realize.

Jefferson's passing the book across the desk. A hardback notebook, very neatly kept. You're always looking at the first page. All previous pages carefully cut out with a razor blade when they've been used. Peterkinney knows the debts Jefferson wants to shift are at the top of the page. There's one up there that's leapt straight out at him. But he's making a deliberate effort to ignore it. Not letting Jefferson see that he's noticed. Making a show of scanning down the page.

"Not a lot of fruit in the garden," Peterkinney's muttering.

"There's a few in there that are as safe as houses. A few where you can't go wrong. Easy profit. Rest of them just need the sort of nudge I can't give them. Nothing there you wouldn't turn a profit on, Oliver, I'll tell you that now. Good list." Selling too hard, realizing and backing off.

Peterkinney looking through them. Looking at the name, the address, the amount, the borrow date, the amount repaid, employed or not employed, known assets. Last one's a key indicator. Do they own a house or a car? If not, and they don't have a job, you're going to have your work cut out. Jefferson's good at detail. Plenty there to read through. Some aren't. Some lenders think you only need a name and an amount. But Peterkinney's eyes keep creeping back up the page. Creeping back to the name Jefferson has put there in the hope of him seeing. The hope of him buying. Alex Glass.

Everyone knows Glass was his best friend. Jefferson only put the name on the list in the hope that friendship would make him buy. No point pretending he doesn't recognize the name, although he has little inclination to purchase. He knows Glass's situation. Still in thrall to that hooker. Pissing his life away, is what he's heard. Heard he was drinking and using heavily these days. No job. No assets. No prospect of paying that debt. Still, Jefferson expects him to ask about it, so he'll ask.

"Alex Glass, what's his condition? Doesn't look good here." Borrowed and didn't pay back a penny. Never a good sign when they don't pay anything at all. The ones who aren't trying are the ones you can't turn a profit on.

"I won't bullshit you, Oliver," says the professional bullshitter. "You'll struggle to get your money back on him. That's if you go the conventional route, anyway. I put him on there for a couple of reasons. First is that I know he's your mate. Won't yank your chain on that one. I thought you might want to know what the situation is. Try and stop him being in debt to someone who might think it's a good idea to get at you through him, you know. Other people might use him to hurt you. Second thing is, he had a debt with me before. Little bigger than this one. Okay, he was in better shape then than he is now, but still. I sold that debt to Potty Cruickshank. This is going back a ways. Few months now. You'd only just set up your own business around then. But he paid Cruickshank off in full. Don't know how. Heard he did some sort of job for him. But he got the debt settled in full. Potty was happy. There might be something there for you. Must have some sort of skill that he used the last time. A chance to get him working for you."

You have to admire Jefferson. You really do. Initially Peterkinney thought Glass had been shoveled onto the list in some desperate attempt by the lender to play on emotions. Try and get him to help out an old mate. That wasn't going to work. Not today of all days, when any part of his old life is a foul reminder of his grandfather. But Jefferson had a backup plan all along.

Jefferson's giving him a route to Potty. Not telling him outright that Glass did something dubious for Potty. Not saying that having Glass under his thumb on the debt could prove useful in attacking Potty. Jefferson would never come out and say something like that. That would look like picking sides. He's too smart for that. But he'll hint at it. He'll talk about Glass doing a single job for Potty that was enough to pay off a large debt. Something that made Potty happy. That's a hint Peterkinney can't ignore.

Potty is a big target. No sniggering, this is serious. He's big. Too big for a young guy like Peterkinney to take on directly. But anytime you get a chance to take a shot at him, you have to. Bring him down a peg. That's what Peterkinney's focusing on. If Glass knows something big. If he was involved in something that Peterkinney can use to keep chipping away at Potty. Well, you don't let a chance like that fly by, do you? He's not in a mood to make people happy though. Doesn't want Jefferson thinking he's done something clever. But he has, the bastard, and this opportunity is too good to miss.

"Okay then," Peterkinney's saying. And saying no more about it, because Jefferson isn't going to give him any more detail than that.

They've talked for another few minutes. Peterkinney's asked a few pertinent questions about a couple of other names on the list. Just going through the motions. In the end, Peterkinney's buying two debts. One that he knows he can turn a quick profit on. The other belongs to Glass. Jefferson does look pleased with himself. That's the downside.

Peterkinney's back in his new flat, feet up. Relaxing in nice surroundings. This is what his grandfather doesn't understand. An old man, spending his life in some shitty little flat. Cramped, damp, dark and hopeless. Thinking that because he spent most of his life on the right side of the law he deserves some fucking medal. Most of his life, not all of it. He strayed from the righteous path as well. Never forget that. Standing in that office and lecturing him. Shit, makes him angry to think.

Walking through to his kitchen. Comparing it to the tiny little kitchen in Arnie's flat. The ancient wall units and the grotty little washing machine that sounded like a struggling helicopter. If that's what your flawed attempts at honest living get you, you can keep it. Peterkinney isn't going to live that sort of life. He knows that if you have the guts, you can have more. You can have the good life. You just need the courage to take it. You need the smarts to take advantage of every opportunity that comes along.

6

It feels like morning. It's morning, right? He's opening his eyes. Still seems dark. And wet. And he's beginning to realize that something's amiss. Slow awareness that he's not where he should be. A few more seconds. Now Glass is coughing loudly. Trying to sit up, but everything hurts. His stomach, his shoulder. Feels like there's something pressing at the back of his head.

Then a few minutes of nothing. Somewhere close to sleep. Now he's suddenly awake. Suddenly very aware of where he is. Lying in the alleyway behind Fourteen. Lying on the wet ground. The pain in the back of his head is from lying on the tarmac. The pain in his shoulder and stomach? They'll take a bit more memory work. First challenge is to get to his feet. Struggling up.

Damn it all, he's soaking. Not just rain, either. They must have dumped him in a puddle. All down his back is wet. Shaking his head, and remembering how he ended up here. Stopping shaking his head, because it makes his shoulder hurt. Coughing hard again. He feels like throwing up. Yeah, that would just about top it off.

Ella wasn't at home when he got back to the flat after meeting Jefferson. That pissed him off a bit. He wanted to be with her. Spend some time with her. So he called her. Didn't get through first couple of times. Got through to her on the third call. Demanded to know where she was. She was oblivious to his tone. Didn't get that he was angry with her for not being there. That he was angry with everything for reasons he couldn't put his finger on. She told him she was at Fourteen. Said she would be home late. He said he would come see her there.

Managed to get into the club. Found Ella. She gave him some attention. She was nervous, and that annoyed him. They had a few drinks. They danced. It was going okay. Then she went off to speak to someone. Some guy, he remembers. Must have been the guy she was there to work. Can't even picture him now. Older than Glass, for sure. Some rich-looking bastard. Glass let it slide. It was her work. What she was there for. He remembered feeling rather mature. Sitting there. Letting her have her conversation with this guy. Not letting his jealousy show.

Can't remember what sparked the argument. Way too far gone at the time to remember it now. They were sitting together. She said something. Something about another guy in the club. That was it. Something about him being a nice guy. It was her way of implying she needed to get back to work. Glass made a snide comment. Ella said something to try and calm him, there was shouting. Then the guy from the earlier conversation came across and intervened. Trying to do the decent thing. Protect a young woman from her scruffy, angry boyfriend.

Punches were thrown. Glass must have thrown some. Can't for the life of him remember connecting with any of them. His knuckles aren't scuffed, which suggests if he hit anything, he didn't hit it hard. More than one person hit him. The guy who was intervening in the fight, and at least one other person. A few hits in the stomach. Then security came and dragged him out through the back. They gave him a few hits as well. Then threw him into the alleyway. He fell over, remembers that. That might be where the shoulder injury came from. Then he passed out.

Glass has spent five minutes just standing in the alley, staring at the ground. Trying to remember. Wishing he still couldn't. The more that comes back, the more upset he gets. It's just humiliating. If the police are going to come and get him then they should hurry up about it. If Billy Patterson wants him killed then he should bloody well do something about it. Living day-to-day, and every day is getting worse. Can't have many more days like today.

No idea what time it is. No watch on. No sound of life from the club. It's still dark though. The sort of quiet dark that suggests everyone else has gone to their bed. Sort of quiet dark that makes him wish he was in his. So he's starting to walk, trying to find a way out of this alley. Never been here before, but you don't need a map to find the end of an alleyway.

One step and he's wincing. The pain in his stomach, mostly. He's cold and stiff and his shoulder doesn't like him much either, but it's the stomach pain that flares the most when he moves. Muscle damage, he's telling himself. Like he knows. Doctor Glass. Another step, and another. Pain doesn't get any weaker. Home. That's a long way away right now.

Out onto the street and looking around. Not a single person on this busy street. Must have been in that alleyway for a few hours. Coughing again, and by God his stomach hurts when he coughs. He's bending over slightly in the hope it'll help, but that's getting him nowhere. Shuffling slowly towards home and stopping. What's the point in trying to walk home when you know you won't make it? He has no hope. Not in this state. Walking just to collapse in the street. Doesn't have his phone on him anymore. Not a penny in his pockets. He needs to find a shorter journey.

Only one place comes to mind. Only one place that he thinks might be welcoming. And a lot closer than his own flat. Shambling along, pathetic and knowing it. Walked past one person on the way. Glass walking hunched, struggling to keep any sort of pace. The person looked at him and walked past. Didn't slow down. Didn't want to engage with him. Didn't want to get involved. They never bloody do.

The walk should have taken ten, fifteen minutes maybe. He doesn't know how long it took, but it was fifty minutes and felt like two hours. Having to stop every hundred yards. A new challenge when he reached the block of flats and had to take the stairs. Every time he pushed up, the pain shot through him. But he's there. Knocking on the door of the flat. Another humiliation. Another desperate act. He's starting to cry. Out of nowhere, he's crying. It's such a weak thing to do. Makes him feel so pathetic. Humiliation piled on top of humiliation. He wants to stop crying before the door is opened. He wants to be able to maintain at least a tiny bit of dignity. But it's gone. Running down his cheeks and out of sight.

A light's come on through the frosted glass. Movement behind the door and it's being pulled open. Arnie looking back at him. He looks so small and old in a T-shirt and pajama bottoms. Unshaven and on alert. Scowling at first, and then looking concerned when he sees who's at the door.

"Bloody hell, lad. What happened to you?"

"I need help. I need somewhere to sleep tonight. Can I?"

Arnie didn't even ask why. Just brought him into the flat. Through to that little kitchen of his. Sat the boy down and told him to get some of his wet clothes off. Got him a towel, made a hot cup of tea. Instructed him to show him the injuries. Bruised shoulder, very bruised stomach. Arnie's no doctor. Has no idea what sort of damage might have been done. But that's one hell of a bruise on the stomach. Two or three bruises holding hands, more like.

"I'm not going to ask for details," Arnie's saying. "Not my place. But if you're in some sort of trouble, you can tell me. I'm no grass. If I can help you, I will."

Glass is shaking his head. Sitting at the kitchen table, an old jumper of Arnie's on, sipping his tea with shaky hands. "There's nothing you can do. Too late for me. Doesn't even matter."

"Now come on," Arnie's saying. Surprisingly aggressive. Talking with the authority of an old man who thinks he's seen it all. "You got no business talking that way. You're a young man. Whatever problems you have, there's always an answer. You got time on your side. Don't piss away the next fifty years just because you had a bad few months."

"It's more than that," Glass is saying. Struggling not to cry again. Thinking about Ella a little. Why didn't she come after him last night? Out into the alleyway to help him. She's spent months helping him, why stop now? Fed up of him, maybe. Or maybe her client wouldn't let her. But it's not her he's thinking about most. It's Alan Bavidge.

"Is it your girlfriend?" Arnie's asking. There's no diplomatic way to ask if her being a prostitute is getting the boy down. He'll leave the question as vague as that. But if it is her, then there's a simple solution that needs to be drummed into the boy.

"Not just her. Not really her at all. She's been so good to me. There's something else." Just about crying now. Crying because he doesn't like to think about what he did. Crying because someone actually cares enough to ask. The first person who has since it happened. Ella kept asking until she realized how big it had to be. Then she avoided it. Didn't want to know something that could ruin their relationship. Another humiliation.

"Tell me, lad. It might do you the world of good." Knowing it almost certainly won't. A problem shared is a problem spread.

Glass is crying properly now. Letting it out. His shoulders rocking, ignoring the pain it causes. "I killed someone. I killed him."

"Tonight?" Real shock in Arnie's voice.

"Months ago. I killed him. They made me. I owed money. I had to do it to get rid of the debt. I did it. I stabbed him. I didn't want to. I really didn't. I only did it because I had to. They would have killed me. They would have hurt Ella." Breaking down now, head on the table.

Arnie's reaching across. Not saying anything. Just putting a hand on the boy's shoulder. If it was months ago, the police aren't likely to be battering down his door tonight. He can take his time with this. Let the boy cry. Let him suffer a little. Do him good to get it out, because he obviously hasn't before. And he is suffering. You can see it. Shoulders bouncing up and down, struggling to catch his breath as he cries. Holding on to his stomach, which is hurting.

Five minutes of silence before Arnie breaks it. "Do you want to tell me about it? You don't have to, but it might help."

Thirty seconds before Glass responds. "I borrowed money. I had to pay it back but I couldn't. They said if I did this thing for them, I'd be off the hook. They said if I didn't, they'd be angry with me. I knew what that meant. They talked about Ella. They were threatening her too. One of their guys was…I don't know. So I did it. Stabbed a man. A gangster or something. He died." Doesn't want to go into any more detail about it. No detail about the night itself.

"Okay," Arnie's nodding. "Okay. Have the police been sniffing around you?"

"No. Nobody has. Nobody seems to know it was me."

Arnie nodding. "Was Oliver involved in this?" A hard edge to his voice. The question he's wanted to ask since the words came out of Glass's mouth.

"No," Glass is saying with honest certainty. "It was nothing to do with him. Nothing at all. It was my fault. It was all my fault. It was so stupid and pathetic. So pathetic."

Wasn't immediately obvious in the end whether he was talking about the killing or about himself. Pathetic seemed to apply to both in his mind. Arnie sent him to bed. Told him to get some sleep in Oliver's old room. Told him it would be a better world with some sleep behind him. Kid didn't seem to realize the time. After four in the morning. Kid doesn't seem to have a keen sense of anything anymore.

Arnie won't sleep again tonight. Might as well get dressed and sit in the kitchen wondering what the world's coming to. Been doing that a lot lately. Now he's got Glass asleep in Oliver's room. Saying that he killed a man. He can't help his grandson, no matter how hard he tries. But he can help someone. Someone who wants to be helped.

7

Marty's been there since half six. Say what you want about him, but the man puts the hours in. He's willing to get up at an ungodly hour to make the money flow. People see the women and the parties and they think of Marty. But Marty's a man of fourteen-hour days, seven days a week. A man of effort. Been in the office now for nearly two hours. Sent out a couple of collectors who won't be back for a while. Took a phone call from a counterfeiter who likes to use this office as a drop-off point for his products. Always helps to keep people like counterfeiters happy. Never know when you might need them. Especially when you run a business like Marty's with a number of foreign employees. Girls who might not be as legally welcome in the country as Marty needs them to be. So you let the counterfeiter use the office, free of charge.

Marty will clear out of the way when the counterfeiter gets here. Before then he has another meeting. One he's actually a little nervous about. He won't show it. He's Marty Jones, he doesn't show nerves. He's always the most relaxed man in the room. He thinks it makes him look cool. Makes him look like a man who can handle any situation. Most other people think it makes him look like the most nervous man in the room, trying to look cool. They don't tell him that though. You don't tell a profitable and dangerous man things he doesn't want to hear.

This meeting brings nerves because it brings Potty Cruickshank. First time they've ever had a meeting. Not the first time they've met, but casual encounters don't count. This is a proper meeting. Potty calling ahead to set terms. Making sure a meeting is a safe thing.

Then agreeing to come to the office. That's a feather in Marty's cap. Potty's coming to him, not the other way round.

Just a question of what he wants. Potty wants whatever's good for Potty. Marty wants whatever's good for Marty. Not impossible that those two things could overlap. Not impossible, but not pleasant either. There's something about Potty that just doesn't sit well with Marty. There's nothing in common there. Nothing that fits between them. Different kinds of people. Different backgrounds. Potty had everything handed to him by his uncle. Marty started with nothing. Fought for everything he's got. Fought hard. But that gives you the image of a scrapper, someone of low rank. New money. People like Potty tend to look down their nose at people like Marty.

Marty's at the window, looking down into the busy street. Quarter past eight in the morning and there are streams of people on either side of the street. Shops on both sides of the street, offices above a lot of them. Always busy this time of day. Marty's on his tiptoes, looking down at the parking spaces in front of the building. There's one beside the door, thank goodness. A large car's pulling up as he looks, stopping in that space. A big fat guy getting out of the back seat. Jesus, what a state. Big expensive car with his own driver. Potty sitting in the back seat like the fucking prime minister. Clambering out and waddling towards the door. He is actually getting fatter. Who would have thought that was possible?

The buzzer goes. Marty across and pressing the button to unlock the door, and waiting. And waiting. And still bloody waiting. It's one flight of stairs. Fourteen of them, Marty knows. Fat bastard must have conked out halfway. Too much effort to reach the top in one go. Making base camp. Jesus, imagine if he fell down the stairs. Imagine if that fat dickhead fell down the stairs in Marty's office and broke his neck. If he died there, nobody would ever believe it was an accident. They would think Marty had planned it. You don't get accidents at meetings like this.

A pang of relief when Potty eventually pushes open the door. A little disappointment as well. The world and the industry would be rather better without this wheezing ball of shit. Marty is too well-mannered to say such a thing. Too well-mannered even to acknowledge that Potty is wheezing.

"Good to see you. Come, sit down," Marty's saying. Almost said take the weight off, but stopped himself. Manners, you see.

Potty's waddling across to the chair in front of Marty's desk. It's not a big chair, not as big as would be ideal for the arse that's about to occupy it. Marty didn't have anything bigger, just office chairs. So Potty will have to make do. Seems relieved just to be sitting.

"So what can I do for you?" Marty's asking, spreading his arms. Making himself seem as available as possible.

"I think, Mr. Jones, that it's time you and I recognized a truth." Potty's voice still has a wheeze in it. Doesn't sound as impressive as he wants it to, which annoys him. "You and I are experienced men. We understand this industry. We both know that to gain strength in this business, you occasionally must consolidate. You understand?"

Ooh, that's not a good start. Marty knows how people see him. They think he's a bit of a clown. Running around with whores and dealers, making money on the side as a collector. They don't take him seriously. Or seriously enough. They don't seem to understand how brutal you sometimes have to be in Marty's other chosen professions. So they think he's a bit dumb. Bit of a soft touch perhaps. Sort of boy who might not understand what consolidate means. They talk down, and that pisses Marty off.

"I understand," Marty's saying. Keeping the always-playful tone in his voice. Don't let a man like Potty see that you're not happy with him. Play him along. Use his ignorance to mask your anger.

"Good, good. You, I'm sure, can see that there are issues we need to resolve. We are competing in the same marketplace, with the same product. We are stepping on each other's toes when we should be helping each other along. There's an opportunity here. I'm sure you can see it. We work together. We work together to remove competition. When we have removed it, we have the place to ourselves. You have your areas, I have mine. Very simple, very effective. Our combined strength could quickly and easily remove the problems we both have."

He speaks so well, does Potty. So comfortable and confident in what he's saying. But he can't be that comfortable, can he? Wouldn't be here if he was. Marty can work that out. Potty doesn't come looking for consolidation unless he has problems. And everyone now knows he has problems. He was in a police station yesterday. That's a pretty big problem. There's a whiff of desperation in the air, and Potty's trying to cover it with his self-confidence.

Marty's leaning back in his chair. "Of course I'd love to help you," he's saying, looking to pick his words carefully. "There could be a problem, though. I mean, word on the street is that you're a good friend of Alex MacArthur." Letting that hang. That should be enough.

That's Marty's get-out clause. You're with MacArthur, I'm with Jamieson. Even if those two are playing at being on good terms, doesn't change how we behave. They're just playing. We keep our distance from each other, because common sense says that they will fall out. That's the business. They have to fall out so that they can try to take market share from each other. And they have to take market share from each other. Have to be seen to be growing, otherwise they stagnate. Stagnate, and you become a target. The industry turns on rivalry. Everyone knows this.

Neither of them will mention the arrest because Potty doesn't want to talk about it. It's a sign of weakness, and neither man will acknowledge it. It's another very good reason why Marty doesn't want to be anywhere near Potty. But he can't publicly use it. Needs the MacArthur excuse instead.

Potty's nodding. "I can see why you might view that as an issue. I do understand. I think you and I need to rise above that sort of thing. I think you and I should be able to seek our own advantages without having to worry so much about the reactions of others. Essentially, this is nothing to do with them. I shouldn't imagine anyone outside of the collecting business would be at all concerned with it." A little smile on his face, trying to make it seem so obvious. Trying to make Marty feel small.

Easy for Potty to say that other people can be ignored. He doesn't need MacArthur for protection. MacArthur was just a useful friend to attack an enemy with. Marty depends on Jamieson. He needs the strength of the Jamieson organization to keep him safe. Potty wouldn't be risking anything with an association. The risk would all be Marty's.

"I'm not going to sit here and say no," Marty's saying with a smile. "But I am going to ask for a little time. There are things I would need to check out first. You know how it is. I mean, I need to take a few more precautions before I do anything, my business being smaller." Saying it with a self-deprecating shrug, and knowing that his businesses combined make nearly the same money as Potty's. The collection business is smaller, sure, but collecting is all Potty does.

"Of course, of course. I'm not going to bounce you into anything, Marty," Potty's saying. Trying to sound generous, something he's never been. "But I will need a quick decision. You know this business. You know how fast the swings and roundabouts move."

Marty's nodding. This is Potty pushing him into a corner. A corner he doesn't want to be in. Looking at his watch. Making a show of it, but he does need the office cleared. Grateful for the excuse to get rid of Potty, before he's forced into making a decision. Making a commitment.

"Damn it. Listen, I have a fellow coming to use the office. Good guy, doesn't like to have other people here when he's having his wee meetings. It'll scare him."

"Of course," Potty's saying, struggling to his feet. No arms on the chair for him to use as leverage. Might be an excuse, might be genuine. Sort of thing he can understand, people looking for a good office to use. Hard in this business to find a reasonable place. "But you let me know when you've made a decision."

Marty nodding. Trying to seem all enthusiastic. Walking Potty to the door and opening it for him. Not going to walk him down the stairs. Doesn't have the time for that. Besides, Potty won't want someone like Marty treating him like he's disabled. He's not, he's just fat. Marty's back across to the desk and sitting in the chair. Both hands on the top of his head, leaning back in the chair. Potty coming to him for a union. Talking about what they could do together, like it's that easy. They wouldn't be a great fit. And why go looking for any help at all? MacArthur's his buddy. Why not use MacArthur for protection? Must be because MacArthur isn't willing. Must be. Potty's under attack and he doesn't have cover. So he's desperate.

A desperate Potty Cruickshank. He could use that. He could. It would be fantastic, if the best-case scenario played out. He could have Potty under his thumb. He could use Jamieson's influence to force Potty under control. He could make a killing. But he won't. Won't because he doesn't trust Potty. Won't because Jamieson would never trust Potty. Wouldn't want him anywhere near his business. Won't because he has a better offer. A tough bastard like Billy Patterson is an excellent weapon to use against Potty. A man with no other baggage, a man with reason to try and make this work. Marty and Potty would be a bad fit. Marty and Patterson? That could work.

8

He's early. And now he's complaining about where they're meeting. This isn't like Paul Greig. Making a big play of the house they're meeting in, like it's the worst option he's ever seen. Like he's used to so much better. He seems tense. Peterkinney isn't saying anything. This is a routine meeting, nothing more. Routine for Peterkinney, anyway. Whatever's crawled up Greig's arse is Greig's business. He should be professional enough to leave it at the door.

"You need to start thinking bigger," Greig is saying, slumping onto the couch.

Little bit over a year ago Peterkinney had no job. Now he has a business of his own. An established, credible collector. And he's still only twenty-one. Now Greig's shouting at him to think bigger. Doesn't make any sense at all, but you have to let people rant.

"I'm thinking big," is all Peterkinney's saying. Saying it calm, a little disinterested, wanting Greig to get down to business.

"Thinking big. Aye right. You don't know what big is." Saying it with a mutter and looking down at the floor. Making no effort to hide the fact that there's something very wrong in his life.

"Problems?" Peterkinney's asking. Not concerned at all. Sounding a little smug. A man with no problems of his own. Sounding like a man who disapproves of Greig bringing his problems to work with him.

Peterkinney hasn't earned the right to talk in that tone to Paul Greig. Not yet, anyway. Boy has potential, but you don't act superior to a guy like Paul Greig this early in your career.

"Problems?" Greig's saying. "Yeah, I got problems. I got problems all over the fucking place. I'm under pressure and I need a little support. Am I getting it? Am I fuck. You help people your whole life, soon as the going gets tough they disappear. You're no different. Don't you go pretending that you are. Don't you go pretending with me. Would you go into battle for me?"

"Do you need me to?" Peterkinney's interrupting. Fed up of hearing this, wanting an end to it.

Greig's laughing at that. "You couldn't if you wanted to, kid, couldn't if you wanted to. Forget about it. Let's just focus on what we're here to talk about. Just so you know, there are things going on. I'm under pressure. I might need to lower my profile for a while if I get through this at all. Don't get all shocked if I go off the radar for a while. A long while, maybe."

Peterkinney's nodding. Making an effort to look concerned, but he couldn't care less. He's long past the point of thinking someone like Paul Greig is important. Greig is helpful, but he's nothing more than that. Most of what Greig will ever do for him, he's already done. Peterkinney remembers that first meeting. The pick-up with Howie Lawson. Lord knows what's happened to him since. Meeting Greig and being so impressed with him. Not anymore. It was good to have his guidance in the early days. Still good to have a police contact. But let's not pretend Peterkinney still sees Greig as important. Certainly not as important as Greig sees himself. And would he go into battle for him? No. No, he wouldn't.

"Okay, well, anything I can do, let me know," Peterkinney's saying.

Greig's waving a hand. "Forget it. I'll let you know if there's anything you need to know." A dismissive hand for a man who can easily be dismissed. Wouldn't have dismissed Potty Cruickshank that way. Might have tried to use Cruickshank's help. Cruickshank is connected enough to make a difference. Not this kid. Not yet. Greig's own fault. Wanted someone younger that he could better control. The price of that is that he hasn't built enough strength to use yet.

"So what's the news?" Peterkinney's asking.

"They arrested Potty yesterday morning. You probably heard. Let him go yesterday afternoon. Plan is to try and gather more evidence and arrest him again. Seems like the accountant isn't as feeble and talkative as I thought he'd be. He's keeping his trap shut, for now. That could change. The way things are stacked, the info we already have, there should be a second arrest on Potty. Should be charges against him."

Peterkinney nodding. That's the news he wanted to hear. He wants Potty weak. He wants to make some serious moves. Getting an itchy trigger finger. You start fast, and things inevitably slow. This is the challenge now. The need for patience. The earlier in the process, the faster you grow. The more you grow, the harder it is to grow much further. Peterkinney can feel it slowing down. Not that it's going badly. Just that that breakneck sense is waning. He wants it back. The sense of momentum. You get it back by taking on opponents. Taking their business. You lurch forwards by swallowing them. That's what Peterkinney wants. That's why he wants to bring down Potty. More business, more money, more success.

"You have to be careful," Greig's warning him. There's a depressed tone. Like he's about to say something he learned from painful experience. "Doesn't much matter who brings Potty down. I mean, good that someone does, but that's not the pay-off. Him out of the business isn't the prize. The prize is taking his share of the market. You won't be the only one aiming for it. There'll be a queue."

"And I'll be at the front of it."

Greig's shaking his head. The boy's getting a little bit too confident now. "You won't be at the front. It won't be some orderly line. Never bloody is. It'll be a mad scramble. And it won't just be the usual suspects either. It'll be people who worked for Potty, wanting to start on their own. Thinking their inside info will serve them well. It'll be every opportunist little shit in this city. It'll be big people like Alex MacArthur thinking they might as well take a slice of the business if it's going free. No bigger opportunists than the big organizations."

Peterkinney's shaking his head. This isn't the conversation he wanted to have. "So you're saying I take Potty Cruickshank and in return I get fuck-all. Actually, less than fuck-all. In return I get a bunch of other people who might try to take me down?"

Greig's shaking his head. Not the boy taking Potty down, it's Greig. But he'll let that slide. "If you wait, yeah, that's what you get. What you want to do is take advantage now. Start pulling business away from Potty now. He'll know you're doing it, but that's the gamble. He'll come after you, but when the second arrest comes, he's finished anyway. If you're willing to take the risk, then you move now. He's weak, but he'll try and hit back. Try and damage you. You just have to hold out until he gets arrested."

"Hold out?" Peterkinney's saying with a confident smile. "I can do more than that."

"No," Greig's saying loudly. "Don't be some fucking idiot about this. He attacks you once so you attack him twice. That's all bullshit. You don't fight back. You don't do anything. You get into a war with that fat bastard while the police are investigating him and you get swept up in the arrests. Us cops aren't fucking blind, you know. A guy we're investigating is being attacked and we'll see it. We'll do something about it. You hold out. You take his business while everyone knows he's weak. You make him look even weaker. Then you sit back and let the police take him down for you. You get rid of him without breaking sweat."

There's a pause while Peterkinney considers this. The idea of getting rid of Cruickshank without even having to attack him is nice. But there's a problem. The problem of PR. "People see me taking shit from him without hitting back. People think I get lucky when the police put him away. That doesn't help my image."

"No, people in the business will think you were playing it this way from the start. They'll know it. They'll respect it. It's not about winning. It's about winning with as few losses as possible. That's what people respect. Don't…" Pausing as he lets his frustration with Peterkinney slide. The boy's still young. You have to be patient with him. Ambitious and determined, but a little naive. Trying again now that his tone will be calmer, less aggressive. "Look, you're smart. You get it. A lot of people will tell you that you have to look strong. How the way other people see you is important. That's true, but not at any price. See, the people that really matter are the people you do business with. The people you do business with know the business. They know that someone who takes advantage of a guy getting arrested before he gets arrested is well connected and smart. They will like that. They'll be impressed and they'll be intimidated. See what I mean? That's the PR you want."

Now he's got Peterkinney nodding. This is something he can get behind. You might sacrifice a little of your image with the muscle, but you gain more from the moneymen. He can handle that. He's agreeing with Greig. He'll work to take business from Potty. He won't strike back if Potty moves against him. Which he might not, because he knows he's being watched by the plod. Although he might try one or two sneaky maneuvers. Take it. Survive it. Then profit.

Greig's up and walking to the door. "Listen, this stuff about me going off the radar. It's not a maybe, it's a definite. There's a lot of stuff going on. But I'll still be around, sort of. I'll keep in touch, now and again." He can see that Peterkinney isn't bothered by that. He can see the boy doesn't think he's important anymore. Which is fine. Happens with all of them eventually. They think a cop as a contact is a great thing at first. Then they get blasé about it. Finally they start to resent you because you don't do everything they want. So be it. Important thing to Greig is getting someone like Potty Cruickshank off the streets. That fat scumbag and his family have done so much damage in this city. Potty won't survive a year in prison, and he'll get at least that. The collection industry will be better in the hands of someone more controllable, like Peterkinney.

Greig's gone. Peterkinney sitting and waiting a decent amount of time before he leaves. Doesn't matter what his grandfather thinks. Doesn't matter what any of them think. He has a plan. He's going to take down Potty, and then all the rest of them. He'll have the whole collection business under his control by the time he's twenty-five. Then what? Ha. Easy. Then he goes looking for other challenges. Shit, he could have the city under his thumb by the time he's thirty. See what his grandfather thinks of that.

9

He knew Glass would sleep late. Physically and emotionally drained. Arnie had been to the shops and back and started making lunch by the time he showed his face. Not a great face to show. Tired and haggard. If you said he was thirty-five, Arnie would believe you. Kid looks a mess. A mess of his own creation. Walking gingerly, still clutching that stomach.

"How are the wounds?" Arnie's asking.

Glass dropping slowly down into the chair at the kitchen table. "Shoulder's a bit sore but not as bad as it was. Stomach still hurts when I move around."

"You hungry?"

"Yeah, really hungry." Trying to remember the last time he ate something, rather than drank or snorted it. Can't. Yesterday, probably. Might have been the day before. No, yesterday morning. Before he went to see Jefferson. Hell, was that only yesterday. Time slows down when you're waiting for it to stop.

Arnie's pottering about in the kitchen. Working silently between frying pan and fridge. Getting the lad something wonderfully unhealthy. Looks like he needs it. Looks skinny, which he didn't before. Never fat or chubby, but used to be healthy-looking. Now he looks thin, weary and beaten.

Arnie's putting the plate down in front of him. Watching silently as the boy eats. One of them has to bring it up. One of them has to mention the fact that last night Glass admitted killing a man. Someone certainly has to mention the fact that he turned up in the middle of the night with lumps kicked into him.

"Do you remember who gave you the beating?" Arnie's asking.

Ask the safe questions first. A beating is an easy conversation opener compared to murder.

"I do," Glass is saying, slurping tea before he goes on. "Bouncers at a club. Ella was there. We had an argument. Some guy got between us and there was a scuffle. I think him and his mate landed a few blows. I think the bouncers probably did too. Threw me out the back of the club. I passed out. Couldn't make it home after that." Said quietly and apologetically.

Arnie's actually relieved. This sounds like no big deal. A few punches thrown in a nightclub. Bouncers chucked him out. Chances are nobody even called the cops. As soon as the door was shut behind him, they all forgot him and got back to their partying. The odds are slim that last night's incident will draw the police to Glass, which is good. This boy wouldn't cope with a police interrogation. If he burst out crying and confessed to Arnie, what would he be like with some rough detective barking at him? He'd crumble. He'd tell them everything. He'd end up looking at fifteen years, minimum. Worse than that, he would grass the people that made him do it. Then he'd be a walking target.

Let him finish eating in peace. Let him sit back in the chair, a little uncomfortable at having a full stomach for the first time in a long time. A boy making no effort to look after himself. Holding those bruises on his stomach. They did look bad last night. In normal circumstances, Arnie would insist on him going to see a doctor. These are not normal circumstances. Glass won't go to a doctor. Won't go near anything that looks like authority.

It's Glass who breaks the silence while Arnie washes the dishes. "About what I said last night," Glass is saying. You can tell he's thought about how to bring it up. Tried to work out the best tone to use with Arnie. "About, you know, killing that guy. I don't...I would appreciate it if you didn't tell anyone."

Arnie's looking at him with a raised eyebrow. "Of course I'm not going to tell anyone. It never occurred to me for one second to tell anyone. But you have to do me a favor in exchange."

Glass is looking at him. A little bit crestfallen. Didn't expect Arnie to be demanding favors from him. "Okay."

"You have to promise me that you're going to get your life in order, okay? I mean, come on, look at you. You're in a bad place right now, and I don't like to see that. I want you to sort yourself out. I want you to get your life back under control. I'm willing to help you, lad. I am. But you have to be willing to help yourself. You have to want to change this life of yours."

Glass is crying again. This time it came from nowhere. He had no intention of crying. Wasn't emotional. Just suddenly came bursting out of him. Someone offering to help. Someone who cares enough to help. Not wanting anything in exchange. Just wanting to help.

Arnie's no social worker. He's no good at the old give-us-a-hug stuff. He's standing back at the sink and letting the boy cry it out at the table. When he's quite finished with the emotional stuff, Arnie will start talking again. They'll try and come up with something. A plan that'll direct Glass back onto the right path.

Strange to see him this way, young Alex Glass. He was a strong and independent kid. Always in trouble, which is why Arnie didn't like Oliver hanging out with him. But he was independent. Went and got a place of his own when he was eighteen. Always seemed to earn enough money to keep him going. Not sure how, but he always did. He seemed like a kid who knew how to point forwards. But now? Now is different. Now he's stuck in the spiral.

They spend nearly an hour talking round in circles. They both want the same thing. Neither has any clear idea on how they're going to get it. Glass is walking home now. His stomach still hurts, but he can walk without bending over. He's not the wreck he was last night. Back to the flat. Not expecting to find anyone there. Surprised to find Ella sitting on the couch in the living room, her phone in her hand.

"Hello," he's saying. Uncertain.

"Where have you been?" she's saying, getting up from the couch and walking to him. She said it louder than she intended, more emotional than she realized. "I didn't know where you were. I went back to the club. I looked around for you. I was going to call the hospitals, or the police, I don't…Where have you been?"

"I stayed at a friend's," he's saying, nodding slowly. "Didn't want to, uh, walk all the way home last night. I was pretty out of it. His place was closer."

There's an awkward silence. Each filling the silence with thoughts of what the other's just said. Ella said she went back to the club looking for him. Back to it. So she went with the guy. Left him there and went with the guy. Has to do her work. Has to earn money. She's thinking about Glass, not being able to make it home.

"How are you now?" she's asking quietly.

Glass is nodding. "I'll be okay. Little bruised, nothing more than that."

"Okay."

More of that silence. Both building up to a big conversation. Just a question of who gets there first. It's Glass.

"Can we sit down, and talk?"

"Yes," Ella's nodding. She's not sure if this is promising or ominous. They're both on the couch now.

"Listen, Ella. Thing is, last night. I…well, thing is, it was like, a wake-up call. That's what I'm trying to say. Last night, it was a wake-up call for me. We need to look at, uh, the way we're living."

"Yes," she's saying, and nodding her head enthusiastically. This is what she wants to hear. Glass accepting that he's been behaving poorly for the last few months. Committing to changing that behavior.

"Yes," he's saying, and smiling. "Good, yes. And I think we can. We might need a bit of help, but we can get that. And we're both young, we can do what we want to do. I'll go find something serious. Something proper. Make some real money. And you can find something as well. It'll be so much better."

She's not nodding now. She's frowning a little, because she thinks she can see what this is. This is Glass trying to come up with some conniving way to get her to change her job. Stop her doing what she's been doing. If that's what the last few months have been about…

"How do you think I'm going to change my job?" she's asking quietly. "What am I going to do? We have no money. You're not earning anything. You haven't been able to find anything for ages. And I won't be able to find anything else. Not for a while, anyway. So what are we going to use for money in the meantime? Alex, you're not thinking."

"But we need to change."

"I know that," she's saying, voice rising. "I know that. And I want to. But we have no money, and we need to have money. I have to work. If you're not working then I have to, and this is the only thing I know how to do."

"I will find something," Glass is shouting. "I will. I will find something, okay."

This shouldn't have turned into an argument. Glass is sighing. Ella's getting up from the couch, going through to the bedroom. Her relief at his return has been wrecked. Felt like he was blaming her. Glass is sitting on the couch, wishing he was better at explaining the things he wants. The things he's sure they can get. He has Arnie to help him now. They have the chance at a life they can be proud to live. A life that isn't lived under a ticking clock. Waiting for time to run out.

10

You make sacrifices. That's how you do it. That's how you help people. Especially people who are in real trouble. They need help. You give it. You lose a little something along the way. Dignity, for one thing. Something you spent sixty years clinging on to. Believing it's the one thing of value you have left. The one thing you have to protect ahead of everything else. Arnold Peterkinney has clung on to his dignity long past the point anyone else noticed he still had it. Now he's going to let a little go.

He's telling himself that he's doing it for the right reasons. That's supposed to make it easier, isn't it? When you're doing it for someone else. Doing it to help them. Your sacrifice becomes something noble, rather than something pathetic. Doesn't help. Not a damn bit. It's humiliating, and that's all it is.

He's been standing across the road from Oliver's office for more than ten minutes. Making sure his grandson's in there. Hoping that other fellow in the office will leave. Oliver's there. So is the other one. Some poor-looking bastard went in a few minutes ago. Arnie's waiting for him to leave. Doesn't want anyone else in there. Not unless it's unavoidable. He'll tell the other one to leave as well. Just him and Oliver. But then, it's only Oliver's opinion he cares about.

There was a day that boy wouldn't have sneered at him. Wouldn't have dared. Wouldn't have wanted to. Today he'll be in his element. Reveling in what Arnie's going to ask. He'll be one snide remark away from a punch in the mouth. Arnie might be older than him and smaller than him. He might love the boy. But he will punch him in the bloody mouth if he pushes his luck.

The fellow who went in looking sorry is coming out looking sorrier. Actually looks scared. Went in looking for a favor and didn't find any waiting. Poor sod. Another one like Glass. Another one who couldn't see another way. Ah, the hell is he standing here thinking this for? Get in there, get this done. The sooner it's over, the sooner he can go home and punch a wall.

Across the street and pulling open the office door. Oliver and the other one are in the same seats they had yesterday. They're both looking at him as he comes in. There's a glare from Oliver. Not welcome. Did the other one roll his eyes? Looked a bit like it to Arnie. Probably fed up of being sent out of the office. Well, he's going to take another walk today. Either he walks, or Oliver doesn't get to hear what he wants to hear.

"Get rid of him," Arnie's saying quietly to his grandson.

Oliver's sighing. This is tricky for him. He sends Kilbanne away every time his grandfather shows up and it looks like he's under the old man's thumb. It also makes him look like a childish amateur. Papa's turned up to tell him what to do. But he'll do it this one last time. Not because he owes it to his grandfather. He doesn't. He'll do it because he's intrigued by the old man's tone. Because he's intrigued about him coming back so soon. Yesterday's conversation seemed like a goodbye.

Oliver's looking across at Kilbanne. Nodding just a little. There's an audible sigh and very clear shake of the head from the older man. Not happy at his young boss's behavior. This is not how you run a business. Not the successful sort of business they both keep saying they want. But he's getting up because the young guy making the error is still his boss. Getting up and walking out of the office. Going for a ten-minute walk from which he will gain absolutely nothing. He'll negate the health benefits of walking with a couple of cigarettes along the way.

"So what do you want today?" Oliver's asking as soon as the door shuts behind Kilbanne. Little bit of sarcasm. Oliver wants this over fast. Another awkward goodbye.

"I want to talk to you about something, and it's a little awkward." Arnie sitting down this time. Didn't do this yesterday. Suggests this is going to be a long conversation, which isn't what Oliver wants.

"Go on." Hurrying him up.

"I need to ask you a favor. It's just come up. It's not for me. It's for your little friend, Alex Glass. You remember him? You two were like two peas in a pod. Now he says he never sees you."

"Uh-huh." A cautious response. Now he is intrigued. How the hell could he know that Oliver bought the debt yesterday? How could he have found out this fast? How could this old fart have found out at all? He's never shown any interest in Glass before. Always hated him, it seemed to Oliver.

"Well, Glass showed up on my doorstep last night. I won't go into detail. It's none of your business. Let's just say he was in no good condition. Me and him had a good long chat. The boy's in all sorts of a mess. He needs someone to help him. I want to help him. So that's why I'm here."

"Uh-huh."

"The boy's in debt. It's the second time he has been, and it's pulling him down. See, anything he does is ruined by the debt now. We get him back clean and sober and working, and that debt is going to drag him down."

"But you can't expect the debt to just be written off," Oliver's saying. "He borrowed the money. He has to pay it back. You can't just wipe out a debt like that." His tone is incredulous. A little confrontational.

"I know, I know," Arnie's saying. Getting tetchy himself. "I'm not saying he shouldn't pay it off. I'm saying that he needs to be given time and space to pay it off. Let the boy have a fair chance. That's why I'm here. The debt is with a guy called Gary Jefferson. I want you to buy it from him. I know how these things work, and I want you to do this as a favor to me and to Alex. You buy the debt, and he'll pay it back. Not with that bullshit interest you people put on it. But you can work something out. Something that gives him the time he needs to rebuild his life."

He managed to stifle the smile. Wasn't easy, but he did it. He almost wants to tell his grandfather the truth. Wants him to see that with enough hard work, everything falls into your lap. The old man wouldn't like hearing it, but Oliver would sure love telling it. But he won't say it. Works out better if he doesn't. Think about it. The one thing that's been playing on his mind is his grandfather. That part of his past. This gets that under his control as well. Jesus, everything falling into place.

"You want me to buy Alex's debt? Despite the fact that he doesn't have a job and probably couldn't pay it off?"

A little sigh. "He doesn't have a job just now, but that's going to change. He's going to get his life together. He is. He's committed to it."

"Please, he hasn't had work in months. Not qualified for anything either. And he's got that wee girlfriend of his. A hooker, working for Marty Jones. Come off it. I'm telling you, if you want to help him, you need to get him away from her. He's obsessed with her and she'll drag him down. Been that way from the start." That sounded surprisingly personal. Sounded like he actually cared. He was there at the start of Glass's relationship with the girl. Saw it for himself. Maybe he knows better than Arnie on this subject. Arnie hasn't even met the girl, so he'll accept Oliver's word on this one.

Arnie's nodding. "Sure. I know it's not going to be easy. I'm not naive about this. But the boy needs help and he has nobody else to help him. I know you're not a charity, but this is a chance…to do some good." Looking around him at the office. Thinking of the sorry sap who sauntered out of here while Arnie was watching.

Oliver's shaking his head a little. "I need to know that he can pay it off. If I take it on and get saddled with however many thousands he owes, it kills my profit. I can't put myself out on the street just to help you out."

"He had a debt before," Arnie's saying. "Bigger than this, and he paid off the whole thing. He can do it again." Desperate now. Trying to use the old debt as a persuading factor in the purchase of the new one. Arnie knows what Glass did to pay off that old debt. But he won't tell. He'd rather walk out of here with no deal.

Oliver's nodding. Now we're getting to what matters. All the hints Jefferson dropped about Potty. "Managed to pay it off. Pay it off or work it off?"

"Paid it off, I think," Arnie's saying with a shrug. Such a terrible liar.

"All right, then. I'll buy the debt. But you have to keep him honest. You got to make sure he pays me back; otherwise I look like I'm doing favors for friends. I look weak. That gets me into all sorts of trouble."

You can see Arnie fighting to keep his temper in check. Oliver can see it and he loves it. That's basically why he said it. Wanted to get the old man's hackles up. See how he reacted to the suggestion that he was the one getting Oliver in trouble. That someone else needed to be kept honest. After all the moralizing yesterday, today Oliver has the chance to accuse his grandfather of causing trouble.

"I'll keep him straight," Arnie's saying. "You'll buy the debt?"

"I'll try."

A nod. "Okay then. You can be in touch about paying it off. I'll, uh, hear from you, then."

"You will."

Peterkinney's leaning back in the chair as his grandfather disappears out the door. This time with his tail between his legs. Ah, good old Alex Glass. You always had a head full of nonsense. Fancy turning up on his grandfather's doorstep looking for help. What a tool. Now Peterkinney has the debt under his control. He has his grandfather's permission to use it. His grandfather, for Christ's sake. And he has something to use against Potty Cruickshank. Don't know what it is yet, but it's something. Yep, today is a good day for Oliver Peterkinney. Know what? It isn't over yet.

11

Patience is an uncommon virtue. Patience is often profitable. In this business, people like to rush things. They worry that if they play a long game, someone else will blow the final whistle before their pay-off arrives. Peterkinney's been smart. Playing the long game whenever that was his best chance of profit. Won't always work. A long-play failure is the worst kind. You put money and effort into something over the course of months, even years, and it yields nothing. That's infuriating. But not this time.

When he bought Collette Duffy's debt, he was playing the long game. Looking to make the right connections. Profitable connections. For a few months, nothing happened. Just Collette being a hapless liability. A tenuous grasp of real life, that one. Didn't seem to realize that she still had to pay off the debt, just because he was being nice to her. But he was patient, and kept being nice, kept letting her off the hook.

It was about three weeks ago that her brother got in touch. Told Peterkinney that he knew about the debt. Told him he was doing the right thing by playing soft with Collette. Didn't exactly sound thankful because that's not Liam Duffy's way. Gratitude is a form of weakness. But he made it clear that he was aware of Peterkinney's behavior. That he was happy with it. Peterkinney was making the right impression with the right people.

Week after that, Liam Duffy suggests a meeting. Something casual. No big deal. The two of them met in a pub. Liam was a little less frosty this time. Talked about his sister. Actually paid up a little of her debt. Made it very clear indeed that if Peterkinney kept behaving to this high standard, there could be a profit in it for him. Duffy didn't say it was his boss he was talking about, but he said the right people were taking notice. People who could put good work Peterkinney's way. That was an easily deciphered code.

Couple more brief meetings with Duffy after that. They were obviously attempts by Duffy to make sure Peterkinney was a serious guy. Scouting him out. Scouting out his business. Asking a few pertinent questions about a man his boss might want to work with. Surprising that Duffy was as smart as he was. Surprising that Chris Argyle gave him so much responsibility. But there you go. People talking about a shakeup in the import side of the market. Big dealers falling out with each other and putting pressure on suppliers. Maybe Argyle is making changes as well.

Peterkinney hopes so, because he has his first meeting with the man tonight. Going round to his house. Going to have a nice polite chat about the kind of people Argyle would want pressured. This won't be as straightforward as a normal collecting agreement. Argyle doesn't have the usual supply of dimwits and suckers owing him money. Anyone in debt to Argyle is likely to be a serious person. They're the only sorts of people Argyle does business with in the first place.

It's a gamble. If Peterkinney suffered from self-doubt these days, he might worry that he's not ready. This won't be conventional collection. He won't be buying the debt from Argyle and going after the target for himself. He'll have a business agreement with Argyle to collect money on his behalf. He'll get the protection that someone like Argyle can offer, but he will have to deliver. He will have to go and collect money from some real tough bastards. He will have to get that money, because most of it will go directly back to Argyle. He'll need to collect every penny owed. Drop the ball, and Argyle gets angry with him. A failure here could be the last mistake he makes. But he's ready. He's sure his business is ready.

Going to Chris Argyle's house. Shit, imagine. A year ago going to Marty Jones's house would have seemed like a big deal. How small does that look now? Argyle has a big place north of the city. A rich bastard surrounded by a lot of other rich bastards. The very sort of place Peterkinney intends to land in one day. Big front garden and a wide driveway. Parking in front of the double garage. He's never had a meeting of this scale before. Of this importance. He ought to be shitting his pants right about now, but he isn't. He's ringing the doorbell and taking a step back, looking back at the manicured front garden. Dressed for the occasion, shirt but no tie. Smart casual. He feels important. He feels good.

It's Duffy who opens the door and welcomes him in. Seems in good spirits. Better than his usual grumpy self, anyway. Leading him through to a living room. Looks like a room that doesn't get used much. For guests and business meetings, probably. Couple of couches, a big TV and a coffee table in the middle of the room. Big window looking out on the side garden. But no personal touches. No photos, no magazines or newspapers left lying around. A useful but little-used room. Argyle's there. Sitting on one couch, staring idly towards the door. Looks like a man who's just sat down after waiting in another, more entertaining room for the doorbell to ring.

Peterkinney doesn't know a lot about Argyle. Knows what he does for his money. Knows the basics about his business and how he runs it. Doesn't know any of the personal stuff. Middle height, thin on top, thicker around the middle. Not fat, just slack in the gut. He looks like a guy in his early fifties, which he is. Looks like any normal kind of guy. Could be a lawyer or a doctor. Some git working in a bank. Looks perfectly ordinary, which is probably the point.

"Oliver, good to meet you, take a seat." Sounds like a bank manager too. Doesn't have the thick accent that Peterkinney's used to dealing with on a daily basis. Sounds like a well-educated, well-spoken sort of chap. A good egg. "Let's talk business, shall we."

The first few questions are all very normal. A few repetitions of things Duffy already asked. Just making sure he gives the same answers second time around. They want him to be consistent. Which he is being. Answering every question accurately. Answering them all with confidence. Displaying the fact that he is a man who knows his business. Which is exactly what they want to see.

"If you and I have a business agreement," Argyle is saying, "then it will be different from anything you have now. You'll be collecting from people who are willing to fight back. From some people who are determined to fight back. There are people who simply choose not to pay what they owe because they'd rather try a fight. People will rip you off on a deal, and believe they can handle the consequences. These will be people who have been preparing to fight for a while. It will take more than grunt to overcome them."

"I understand that," Peterkinney's saying. "I've always employed on that basis. Make the assumption that people will fight back. Make the assumption that you need the best people around you. A good collection business isn't about muscle, it's about smarts. I have good people. People who can be subtle and use their judgment, as well as being tough." Saying it because it's true. Saying it also because it's what Argyle wants to hear.

Argyle does seem happy with that. He likes a lot of what he's hearing from Peterkinney. The more they talk, the more Argyle understands that Peterkinney is ready. Duffy was right. This boy can go and fight battles for them. The business he has, the people he has around him, are good. Solid. He's not some five-minute wonder. His age was a worry, but not now. Now his age is a strength. Gives him greater potential for longevity and growth.

After an hour or so of conversation, Argyle is convinced. He'll give Peterkinney a couple of jobs. People he's given supplies to who haven't lived up to their end of the bargain. They were going to pay him back with money made from sales, but they didn't get the sales they were looking for. Too bad. This is business. They still have to pay. They haven't, and someone needs to persuade them. A simple enough job to start with. If Peterkinney does well with that, there could be more for him. Big jobs, big responsibility, big profit.

A cordial shake of the hand before Peterkinney leaves. As soon as Duffy has closed the front door behind him, Peterkinney is grinning. Wants to punch the air, but someone might be watching. There are a lot of windows in the house for someone to look out of. Probably cameras as well, although they're not immediately visible. Argyle keeping his security low-key, so as not to alarm his neighbors.

He has music on in the car as he drives back south. Heading home, tapping the steering wheel happily as he does. Another leap forwards. Two in a day, when you think about it. Well, two in two days, but that's being pedantic. This thing with Alex could give him a shot at Potty Cruickshank. With Greig doing his business and the second arrest coming, Potty's looking nice and vulnerable. Now a deal with Chris Argyle. Yep, today was indeed a good day.

PART FIVE

1

Everything changed. It's amazing to look back four months and think about it now. One ordinary day, the news started to filter around the city. People began to hear all about it. Made the news. Charges were brought. More arrests expected to follow. Peter Jamieson. John Young. Hugh "Shug" Francis. David "Fizzy" Waters. Shaun Hutton. All important men in their own right. Either important for what they'd done or for what they knew. A major player like Jamieson, with a string of charges against him. None of the really big charges. Not yet. But he'll get time inside, everyone knows it. In one afternoon, without any warning, the industry in this city changed.

People had to change with it. Things you'd planned for months went out the window. Everything was different. Everyone was paranoid, for a start. If it could happen to those guys...Other organizations started to look weak. Alex MacArthur, arrested. Unbelievable. Un-be-fucking-lievable. They let him out, but he was weak. Straight away, people were talking. Don Park is moving to take control of the organization. That was the rumor then. Still the rumor now, months later. Park hasn't taken over, but the stench of weakness from that organization is sharp. Jamieson and MacArthur in trouble. That unnerved everyone.

Of course, some people thought it would be all change. Those guys would fall and there would be a new order. Bright young things would step up and fill their shoes. That's despite the fact that Jamieson was the bright young thing right up until he got arrested. But that wasn't what happened. Never is. You don't build something as big as they had without putting some safeguards in place. MacArthur was back on the streets and acting the boss. Even if Park was still trying to take control, he wasn't doing it publicly. That would damage the very thing he was trying to take control of. So MacArthur's organization kept on operating as it had, and pretended the rumors weren't whirling around its head. And Jamieson's organization. That was the most interesting.

Most interesting to Billy Patterson, anyway. Jamieson, the boss, was inside. His right-hand man, John Young, who should have stepped into his shoes, was inside too. That was the clincher. That was why everyone thought his business would fragment and disappear. Everyone would look for a different boss without Jamieson or Young to hold them together. But it didn't happen. Didn't happen because a group of senior men in the organization got together and did something nobody thought they would. They worked together effectively, loyally and intelligently. Most remarkable of all, to those on the outside, was that Marty Jones was one of those men.

He would have been a junior player at that first meeting. People are already talking about that meeting like it was something legendary. Was only three months ago. People love to mythologize these things. The meeting in the office above the nightclub. A big table brought into the office for the occasion. Extra security put on. All very Hollywood, to hear the story. Wasn't actually like that at all. No big table to sit around, looking menacing. Just the chairs that were already there. No extra security, just the drivers and sidekicks of the men at the meeting. That lot all stayed outside the office, playing snooker. So not dramatic in presentation, but still vital.

Jamieson and Young had been inside a month, things were starting to settle and the organization needed a plan. It needed organizing. Marty got an invite. But he can't have been an important part of it. Angus Lafferty, he was there. He would have been a big part. Kevin Currie was there too. He would have helped lead the way. Two or three other senior guys. But Marty was in the office, and that's what mattered.

The last three months, Marty's seemed like a new person. Seemed like it, but he doesn't think he's changed at all. Treating the world the same way he always did, it's just that now these things matter more to others. People are paying more attention to him. In a way, this is what Marty always wanted. To be taken seriously. To be given responsibility. Didn't want his bosses being arrested. Didn't want to lose the protection they provided him. But it put him in a position where he had the chance to step up and perform, and he has done just that. You can bet the big players are treating him more like an equal now. You can also bet that he loves that, so he'll keep performing.

He's been working like a Trojan. No more messing around. The parties still happen; the women are still a part of his business. That's not going to change, because they're still profitable. Profit is what makes Marty a big player at a time like this. But Marty isn't at the parties anymore. He has minions to run those things for him now. Marty's making a serious effort to look serious.

Patterson's got a meeting with him this lunchtime. Marty might be the same guy he always was, but the changed circumstances mean you have to treat him differently. He's given up any hope of manipulating Marty. Treating him as the junior party. Thought he could at the start of this alliance, but that's not going to happen now. Even if he could manipulate Marty, the other senior men in the organization wouldn't let it happen. Hurt Marty, and they'll hurt Patterson. They're all protecting each other, because they have nobody above to protect them.

Marty's taking the collection business seriously now. He's taking everything seriously. No more short-term money-grabbing. Everything is long-term now, for the good of the organization. He's also gotten ruthless. Much more willing to strike against the competition. Not petty beatings using people like Neil Fraser. Marty's willing to do the real dirty work to protect the organization, because there's no protection above him now. Everyone's gotten a little more brutal, because of the uncertainty. Twitchy, ready to fight.

Patterson's pressing the buzzer up to the office. Marty doesn't use this place often now. He's got a few other offices he uses. Not particularly impressive places themselves, but he needs more of them. Needs to move around more. Needs to take his own security more seriously than ever. He's a senior man in an organization some still see as vulnerable. Also has more money to hide, which means more legit places as fronts. But this is where he always meets Patterson. This is where he'll keep meeting him. Not letting Patterson get a taste of Marty's other businesses. Keeping Patterson in his place.

Patterson's up the stairs and through the door. Into the office to find two other men leaving. One of them he doesn't recognize. The other one is Ray Buller. He'd bet his right arm on it, and he's right-handed. Ray Buller, slouching out of a meeting with Marty Jones. A senior man for Alex MacArthur. One of his best friends for decades. Meeting in Marty's office. Bloody hell, Marty is moving up. Working this old bastard as a contact. Buller's giving Patterson a brief glance. Poisonous, angry that Marty's allowed someone to see him here. That's deliberate. Marty wants him to be seen. Wants a witness to the meeting.

Patterson's furiously putting two and two together as the door closes behind him. This must be an early meeting between them. Marty organizing a witness to make sure Buller can't back out of whatever corner Marty's boxed him into. Killing Marty won't now be enough to hide the betrayal. He'd have to kill Patterson too. And then kill anyone Patterson told. An ever-growing list that makes compliance so much easier than killing. Clever little Marty.

"How are you, Martin?" Patterson's asking, shaking his hand. Started calling him Martin as a joke, like he's too serious for a nick-name these days. Suits him though.

"Good enough," Marty's saying. No small talk about parties or women. No bullshit. Just get on with business. No time for dicking around. "We need to talk about Potty Cruickshank. He's going on the offensive. Shame the police dropped their interest in him, but that's how it goes. Lot of good opportunities fell off the table back then. Means we have to do the job instead. If we leave him doing what he's doing, he's going to take serious market share from us. Time to deal with him."

"Agreed," Patterson's saying. Past time to deal with him, in fact, but that couldn't be helped. Marty had other things to deal with. Bigger games to play. Patterson doesn't begrudge that.

"I know for a fact that Potty is going to Alex MacArthur tonight. Going to look for a deal with his old chum, but he won't get it." Not mentioning Buller, not going to mention him. Patterson already knows and these things don't need to be spoken about. Marty no longer needs to brag about how clever he is. "MacArthur doesn't want to get involved in other people's squabbles. He's got plenty shit on his own doorstep. That's going to leave Potty isolated. Now is a really bad time to be isolated. Then, tomorrow, I'm going to visit Potty. I'm going to arrange a big meeting."

Patterson's nodding, but not with enthusiasm. It's the slow-motion nod of a man who doesn't like where this is going. "A meeting. Okay."

"You, me and Potty. We're going to sit down and come up with something that makes me happy. A private meeting, away from prying eyes. We'll have an agreement."

Patterson's fuming. Trying to keep it under control. He knows what happened to Alan Bavidge. Still doesn't know exactly who carried it out, but he knows exactly who organized it. He will make Potty suffer for one. One day, come hell or high water, he'll make sure Alan Bavidge gets payback. "And if we don't get a deal that makes you happy?" Spoken through gritted teeth.

Now Marty's smiling a little. Just a little, but it means a lot. It means Marty's already thought that far ahead. It means Marty already has a plan for that. "You know what? I have a funny little feeling that we won't come to an agreement. Too much distance between you and Potty. I have a feeling we may have to settle the issue there and then. Goes without saying, you and I will be the ones making the demands. I think you and I are very close in what we want. You might want to bring a couple of your best with you, just in case there's tension."

Patterson's not fuming anymore. He likes the sound of this meeting now. Sounds like it's going to be the meeting he's wanted to have with Potty for a long time. Agreement is made. The meeting place. The people they'll bring with them. The timing, which means so much. By the time he leaves the office, Patterson's a very happy man. Happy with Marty. Happy to be led by him.

2

It's just not good enough. Not anymore. Not for Peterkinney. Not for the business he has now. You just can't have these little debts getting in the way of the bigger work that needs to be done. Makes you look small-time, something he no longer is. His contract with Chris Argyle has been successful. He's making more money than he thought he would at this point. Well ahead of schedule. He's becoming influential within Argyle's business. Handling all of his awkward muscle work. And throughout it all, that debt is still there.

He's arranged a few meetings with his grandfather and Alex to talk about it. The first one went well. Glass said he would do whatever it took. Said he'd work the debt off, whatever. Made it seem like there was nothing he wouldn't do. Except there was something. Just one thing. The thing Peterkinney wanted from him. The truth about how he paid off his first debt to Potty. There's nothing else Glass has to offer. Doesn't have any skills. Sure as hell doesn't have the money. Only thing he has is information he won't share.

A few meetings since, and Glass has come up with nothing. It's stopped feeling awkward to Peterkinney, organizing a meeting with a former best friend. Used to be he dreaded it. Calling him up, having the meeting. Trying to make polite chat. Make it seem like they still had any sort of relationship. Not awkward anymore. Now he doesn't feel like he knows Glass. Doesn't feel like he wants to know him. So it's a formal meeting. The kind he has every day. But no more. Glass has run out of chances.

All he had to do was tell Peterkinney what he'd done for Potty. Tell a little story. Simple as that. Every time they met, he refused to talk about it. Got angry whenever Peterkinney brought up the sub-ject. No point pushing it. He won't talk. And he won't pay either. No matter how many times Arnie tries to cover for him. He's paid off some of the debt. But it's slow going. Glass can't get a permanent job. He's getting odd jobs here and there. Putting some money to-wards the debt, but it's slow. Never going to be fast enough.

And that hooker's still around. He warned his grandfather about her. Girls like that, they're always a drain. Always going to keep Glass trapped in a world of parties. But Arnie didn't get rid of her. Now, Peterkinney would have been good enough to turn a blind eye to that, if Glass had been smart about it. But no, he had to do the usual idiot act. One of Peterkinney's boys saw it. Glass out at a nightclub, with his expensive little girlfriend. Ex-pensive nightclub to be hanging around. She was there to work, and Glass wasn't actually spending money, but Peterkinney's boy didn't know that. Just saw Glass in a place a poor man shouldn't be. Told Peterkinney about it. Peterkinney arranged a meeting with Glass. Glass told him he was skint. Didn't have a penny to his name. No, because he spent it all in some shitty club the night before. Idiot. Thinking he can play Peterkinney for a fool. Nuh-uh, doesn't work that way, old pal.

Makes Peterkinney look bad. Makes him look like he'll let a debt slide if you happen to be a mate of his. Can't have people thinking you're soft. All of his people knowing about it. If your own staff think you're a bit soft, they'll try to take advantage of it. They all know he's doing good work for Argyle, but even a small debt can undermine that. It can be the chink in the gleaming armor. So he's going to do something about it.

He's called in one of his more junior muscle. New fellow they hired a couple of weeks ago. James Holmes, his name is. So many names come across Peterkinney's desk. His world is full of new faces. Doesn't remember this one. Looks rough as all hell. Got a scraggly beard and bags under his eyes. Thick dark hair that could seriously do with a wash. Doesn't seem to play well with others.

Quiet and miserable. Looks like a boozer. Tough bastard though. He'll do for a job this simple.

"Here's the address," Peterkinney's saying. Passing a slip of paper across the table. Not bothering to say hello. "Name's Alex Glass. Lives there with his girlfriend. She works, he doesn't, so most likely he'll be there and she won't. He owes about three and a half grand now, but the debt's gone on too long. I want you to make it clear that it's time for him to take this debt seriously. He's been spending money elsewhere, and I want him to know that that just won't do. You understand?"

"I understand," Holmes is nodding. He knows exactly how it works. Go round there and kick some sense into the boy. What could be simpler?

Holmes remembers Peterkinney. Remembers being kicked down the fucking stairs by him. Oh yeah, he remembers. All too well. Remembers his life plummeting down the toilet after that. Needed work. Needed something he could do that would pay fast. Weren't many places left he could go looking for work. Not many places where he hadn't burnt his bridges. This was one of the very few. And everyone knows that Peterkinney's expanding. Everyone knows he's taking on new people. If you're tough and willing to do dirty work. If you're willing to put your life on the line. Some of his collections are from very dangerous people these days.

He thought Peterkinney would remember him. Probably a sign of how well the kid's doing that he didn't. Holmes doesn't look the same. Lost a bit of weight, grew the beard to cover the scar. Peterkinney gave Holmes a couple of jobs to do. Holmes did them well. He's past caring about his security these days. In debt. Drinking heavily. Shifting from place to place, waiting for the council to find him a flat. Was in sheltered housing for a few weeks. Slept in a car park for three nights. Now he's willing to risk the last thing he has left, his life. Do it for some money. Enough money to drink himself to death, hopefully.

"Get it done later this afternoon, let me know how it goes,"

Peterkinney's saying. "I want detail on this one." He knows he's going to get a call from his grandfather. Or a visit. Those are always fun. Talking awkwardly. Arguing. Each pretending he doesn't owe the other anything. Arnie will be furious, and Oliver will have to defend himself. For that, he needs detail.

Holmes has left. Scruffy-looking bugger, Peterkinney's thinking. Might have to tell him to tidy himself up. Not yet. Not while he's doing garbage jobs at the low end of the business. The people he's collecting from look even worse than he does. But he'll have to clean himself up if he wants to work the bigger jobs. Presentation matters. You need to look professional and decent. If you're collecting from a rich man, you need to look rich in his presence. At least look respectable.

Kilbanne is back from his lunch. Seemingly happier in his work these days. He knows what he's doing is still fundamentally crooked, but now it's on a big scale. There's something exciting about that. Peterkinney's starting to talk seriously about legitimate businesses. That's what it is. That's what gets Kilbanne excited. The thought that they're making so much money, they can start to look at buying legit concerns to hide it all behind. Then Kilbanne can hide his guilt behind the legitimacy.

"I know pubs, clubs and bookies are clichéd," Kilbanne's saying, "but they're a great place to start. Easy to manipulate the figures coming in. But there are other things we can do. Things that will raise less concern. They are more complicated, though. Probably more expensive to get off the ground, as well. Worth it, though, long term."

"Right now we need something that's going to work fast," Peterkinney's saying. They've had this conversation before. Often. Peterkinney wanting to go the obvious route, Kilbanne wanting to do something unnecessarily clever. Right now they need to come up with ways of cleaning up their cut of the Argyle money. Doesn't matter how clever it is, it just needs to work. Sooner the better. Money's starting to pile up and it needs to be cleaned and put somewhere safe.

"I'm going to start moving some money," Kilbanne is saying. "Need to have it to purchase with. I mean, you're right; we should go for the simple stuff first. I'll start looking around. There's always pubs shutting down. Should be easy pickings."

Easy pickings. Two best words in the criminal lexicon. Often the two most misleading, as well. These things are almost never easy. Peterkinney isn't naive about that. The economic situation will make it easier for them to find struggling places willing to sell. They'll either buy the whole place or a share. More likely the whole thing. Only buy a share if you can rely on the other shareholder to keep their mouth shut. Peterkinney isn't willing to trust people he doesn't know. Not big enough to scare people into silence yet. Kilbanne will take control of the books. Filter dirty money through them.

By the end of the afternoon, Peterkinney's in rather good cheer. He knows to expect his grandfather. It'll be a call now, because they're going to lock up the office. His grandfather's never been to his flat. Might not even know where it is. So he'll telephone and bitch and moan, and Peterkinney will have to explain the way the world works. And he'll rather enjoy it. It's about time Arnie Peterkinney found out that his Good Samaritan routine is a shambles. Worthless and ineffective.

3

He's nervous. Potty's actually nervous about this. It's because things are so different. Until a few months ago, this would have been routine. And even if this didn't go his way, he'd still have other options. But not now. The whole industry is changing. You can't take anything for granted now. Even he's trying to find a foothold in the shifting sands.

It started out looking like good news. Potty thought he was going to be one of the big beneficiaries of this turmoil. Some gunman belonging to Peter Jamieson blabbed to the cops. Dropped a lot of people in the shit. Somehow or other, that involved Paul Greig. PC Paul Greig wasn't a PC anymore. He was quietly shunted out of the force. Police didn't want the embarrassment of it going to trial. His superiors would have had to admit that they knew some of what he was doing. But all the evidence he'd provided them with was suddenly useless. The cases that hinged on his evidence were quietly dropped. Including Potty's.

Throw in the fact that Jamieson and his organization looked like they were finished, and it seemed like a good day to be Potty Cruickshank. For a start, that would be the end of Marty Jones. Marty was never a major concern, too much of a playboy, but this would get rid of that nuisance. Without Jamieson's protection, he couldn't possibly survive. And Jamieson's fall would make Alex MacArthur stronger. Potty had been cultivating his relationship with the MacArthur organization. So good news all round. Three cheers for the gunman who talked.

But it didn't turn out that way. MacArthur was arrested a couple of days later. It didn't go anywhere, but that doesn't matter. He was weak. That was the opening the ambitious younger ones had been looking for. People like Don Park, looking to take control. For the last few months, it feels like it's been silent civil war in the MacArthur camp. People trying to slice each other, without the outside world hearing about it. Potty hasn't been able to get a meeting. Hasn't been able to get anyone to pay him any damn attention. To top it all off, that bastard Marty Jones seems to be going from strength to strength.

He's finally got himself a meeting with Alex MacArthur. Was offered a meeting with some junior a couple of weeks ago. Turned that right down. Don't they remember who he is? Don't they remember the respect the Cruickshank name commands? Whatever their internal problems are, they're no excuse for disrespect. Maybe they remember him now, because MacArthur's agreed to see him.

He's sitting in the back of the car. Sweating, which isn't good. He needs to look relaxed when he goes into MacArthur's office. It's a small office they're going to. That's a bad sign. Might be more to do with MacArthur's recent struggles than Potty's. The old man moving around more to stay safe. Not using his preferred meeting places so often. Maybe it's not another sign that he doesn't take Potty seriously. Maybe. Still, it's a negative to focus on and make him sweat a bit more.

He needs this. Needs an alliance that can protect him through the storm. With Marty growing and seemingly pairing with that shit Patterson, Potty's feeling the pressure. Peterkinney's growing, becoming a serious player and a serious threat. Potty seems to be the only one standing still. The only loser in this little game. He needs support. Cut MacArthur in. Give him the chance to open up a new avenue of revenue, something he ought to want to do. Should want it even in good times. He should be bloody grateful for this chance now. Someone of Potty's stature coming to him and making him a generous offer. He has no right to turn it down.

Pulling to a stop in the sort of area a car like Potty's doesn't stop in often or for long. The driver will stay with the car. Potty's getting out and waddling slowly towards the door. It's a small building in an industrial area. The parking's tucked in just off the road. Up a step and pulling open the glass door. There's a small reception desk inside and the young woman behind it is asking if she can help him. She doesn't even know who he is. Bloody cheek. He's telling her, and now he's having to stand there waiting while she makes a call.

He'll put this down to MacArthur's increased need for security. He'll forgive it, which is generous. They should not be making a man like him stand in some waiting area like this. She's hanging up the phone and smiling at him.

"If you'd like to go through, the office is second on your right."

Not even going to show him the way. Nobody coming to meet him. This really isn't the way to treat a person. Treatment like this is remembered. Alex MacArthur should know that. He wouldn't accept it, and he shouldn't hand it out. Potty's pushing open the door at the side of the woman's desk and walking slowly along the corridor. Finding the appropriate door. Two knocks and then opening, not waiting for an answer. Potty Cruickshank doesn't need to wait for answers.

MacArthur's sitting behind his desk. Ray Buller is sitting in a chair in the far corner of the room from MacArthur, and there's a chair in front of the desk. It's a small office. Not the sort of place you would expect to find a man with the business concerns of Alex MacArthur. Yeah, that would be the point, smart guy. MacArthur's hiding himself away.

No wonder he looks miserable. Looks even older and frailer than the last time they met, and that was only a few months ago. A man of his stature should not be hiding away in wee places like this. It's embarrassing for him. It makes him look weak, and he did not get where he is by looking weak. Does beg the question, just who is he hiding from? No stories about people outside the organization targeting him. Bloody hell, is he in here hiding from his own people? Bang goes any chance of a deal worth having.

"Mr. MacArthur, how are you, sir?" Potty's asking, and regretting it. You don't ask an obviously sick man how he feels. That's the last thing MacArthur will want to dwell on.

"Good enough. Sit down, Ronald. What do you want?" Said with obvious impatience. An implication that Potty couldn't possibly have anything useful to talk about. This is all a waste of an important man's time.

It's an insulting way to speak to a man like Potty. This whole visit has been one long insult. Longer it goes on, the more Potty thinks he shouldn't be here. Thinks MacArthur might not be capable of helping him. Might have been wiser to try and start a relationship with Don Park instead. Too late. He's in the chair in front of MacArthur's desk, so he might as well play to the end.

"I have a business proposition for you, if you care to hear it." That was a slightly snide way to end a sentence. Potty's struggling to hide his impatience. Should always maintain your manners around people like MacArthur. Doesn't matter what you feel or think about someone, you stay polite. Then, if you need to move against them, they're less likely to see it coming. Good manners cost nothing. Bad manners can be very expensive indeed.

"I care to hear it," MacArthur's saying. His voice is weak, almost whispery. Makes his tone seem even more dismissive.

"We both know that the city is changing. Things have happened..." Potty's saying, and trailing off. Hardly needs explaining. Few people know better than the man in front of him. "I'm offering a chance to open up a new revenue stream. I know you're not involved in the collection business in a big way. It's a potential new source of revenue for you. It offers me an opportunity of growth that will protect my business through this time of upheaval. It's good for both of us."

MacArthur's making a good effort at looking unimpressed. He's about to say something when he starts coughing instead. A long-drawn-out wheeze of a cough. If Potty had heard that cough before he came here, he wouldn't have come. Everyone knew MacArthur was ill, but he's been ill for so bloody long, people assumed it was no big deal. One of those things that last long enough for something else to kill him. Now it looks and sounds like a big deal. Now he seems like the wrong horse to back. Truth is, if he was a horse they would shoot him. Someone still might.

"I'd be looking at providing you a cut of 25 percent," Potty's saying. As he'd come in the front door of the building, he had been committed to offering forty. Now he's not sure he wants MacArthur to accept his offer. Forty might have been enough to win him over. Twenty-five shouldn't be.

MacArthur's looking at him. Then looking past him at Ray Buller. Then back at Potty before he answers. And that look tells Potty a lot. The old man struggling. Not sure who he can trust. Pulling his friends close. Looking to people like Buller for more advice. Because he's not sure of himself anymore. Giving them more power because they're the ones he would like to hand over to. Because they're not Don Park.

"I don't think so," MacArthur is saying. "Timing isn't right. I'm not saying never, but not now." Said with finality.

A finality Potty has no interest in arguing with. "If that's your thinking," Potty's saying, and getting slowly to his feet. "Hopefully times will change," he's saying, a sentence that could mean just about anything. He's reaching out a hand to MacArthur. His fat hand swallowing the bony hand offered. Feels cold. Feels like good-bye.

Potty's nodding to Buller as he leaves. No handshake there. Buller was the one who said no. He was the one who made the decision. Maybe he should shake his hand. Thank him for killing the deal with a shake of his head. But Potty's already out the door and making his way along the corridor. Feeling the effort by the time he ignores the receptionist and pushes his way out the front door. Relieved to drop into the back of the car and be driven away.

Dodged a bullet, sure, but for how long? The deal with

MacArthur could have been a bad deal, given how weak the old man looks. But what's the alternative? Stand alone? No, that won't do. No deal is worse than a bad deal. He needs support. He needs to be able to survive these changes. By any means necessary. Dear God, he just needs to survive.

4

Peterkinney told him to do it this afternoon. And he meant to. He really did. But he got sidetracked. Happens to Holmes a lot these days. Life is a pursuit of the bottle. Everything else is a means to that end. Working to make money to drink. And he has some money. Not a lot. Money never lasts long for Holmes these days.

He wandered into a supermarket, is the short version of why he's late. Bought a half-bottle and six cans. Took it back to the flat he's in now. Blotted out the world for a little while. Blotted out what he's on his way to do now. The memory of that night when those two little bastards smashed their way into his house. His house. Man, if you could turn back the clock. He had his own house. Wasn't much to look at, but what does that matter? He had Norah. She wasn't much to look at either, but she was his. All gone now.

His things. Didn't realize that he cared about them until it was all gone. Until he had nothing. Stupid cliché, but that's all that's left. Into the bathroom to splash a little water on his face before he goes out. That straggly beard. Hair's too long as well. Needs a haircut, but that's money he could spend on something wet. Could trim the beard himself. Hates it. Only has it to cover the scar. The scar's ugly, but he stopped caring about that a long time ago. The long, thin red line is a reminder. That was the real punishment. Lets the world see his failure.

Can't hide the bags under his eyes. The sag of his chin. Jesus, he looks like his grandfather. Bloodshot eyes and loose skin. Same bad teeth the old man had. Same reason. It was booze that eventually killed Grandpa Holmes. Took its time though. Holmes can't wait that long. Won't wait. All those dreams of the good life. A better life than the one he had. Skimming money because he thought he could have a better house. A better woman. He'd give everything he has to get back the home and woman he lost, but he has nothing to offer. Fuck it: staring in the mirror is only a guarantee of misery. A splash of cold water and he's leaving. Little bit drunk, little bit angry. Nothing new.

He threw away the slip of paper with the address on it. Doesn't need it. Born and raised round here. Knows the place like the back of his hand. Spent his working life pounding the streets, finding and punishing people. If it's a shitty part of town, you can bet Jim Holmes knows it well. It's starting to get dark. Damn, must be pretty late. Doesn't have a watch to check. Never mind. Peterkinney won't care too much about the timing. He'll just want to know that it's been done.

It's a small block of flats, four stories high. Not the best exit when the target's on the third floor, but Holmes doesn't care. This is going to be simple. One target. Only other person likely to be there is the girlfriend. And the boy isn't expecting him. That's always the difference-maker. If you don't expect it. If you aren't ready. If Holmes gets the first punch in, he'll have no problem here.

Up the stairs and along to the front door. A quick knock on the door. Then, thirty seconds later, another one. He's not patient. He doesn't want to have to come back a second time. Too much like hard work. Also, being seen repeatedly in the location of your crime is a dumb move. Holmes knows that. The old instincts are still there.

He has to wait another twenty seconds before the door slowly opens. It's a young woman looking back at him. She looks scruffy but pretty. Didn't someone say she was a hooker for Marty Jones? Wearing a T-shirt and jogging bottoms. Greasy dark hair tied back. She has a cloth or duster in her hand. Looks like she's been cleaning up. A woman taking care of her home. Quaint. A reminder of Norah. Not quaint. Hard to take.

Disappointing that the girl's here. Always easier without some squawking woman thinking she has to defend her man. That's the problem with them. They always defend their man, even when he's wrong. And even if they don't get physically involved, they can raise the dead with their shouting. Certainly raise the alarm. That's Holmes's experience of them, anyway, but his experience with women has made him sad. Not bitter. He knows it was his own fault.

"I'm looking for Alex Glass," he's saying. You wouldn't know he was drunk to hear him. Maybe if you knew him well, but otherwise he would sound strong and in control. Takes a lot of practice to be able to control yourself that well whilst brimming with alcohol.

"He's not in," she's saying, and moving to close the door.

You don't take them at their word. That's not instinct, that's just common sense. People who owe money become good at hiding. Practice makes perfect there too. They know when to shut the door and when not to. They have instincts of their own. Holmes is sticking his boot in the door and shoving into it shoulder first. He's not as big as he used to be. Lost a bit of weight. Not eating properly. Still a lot bigger than Ella, doesn't take much force to push her backwards.

"Hey. Bastard." She's stepping back and letting him in. She can complain, but there's no point fighting back.

Holmes is inside the flat, looking around. Not much of a flat. Door opens into the living room, and you can see the door through to the small kitchen. No hiding places. There's a little corridor off to the side that he'll have to check. No sign of Glass at first glimpse.

"Where is he?"

"I told you, not here. He has a job. Something or other, I don't know what. Just for tonight. I don't know where."

Holmes is ignoring her. If the answer isn't within the flat, then he doesn't want to hear it. He's going into the kitchen. Dishes in the sink, but no Glass. Out into the living room again. Along the corridor and pushing open a door. A bedroom. Small, with only a single bed in it. Doesn't look like it's used. Pushing open another door.

Bathroom. Nobody hiding there. Into the final room. Second bedroom. Bigger, more furniture, a bed with a disheveled look about it.

If he's hiding in the flat, then it's in this room. No room under the bed. Lifting up the quilt and looking under. Nope. Last-chance saloon is the wardrobe. Otherwise he's not here and Holmes is going to have to make a return visit. Opening the wardrobe doors and finding nothing but clothes inside. Damn it all. Shit. They can never just make it simple. Now he'll have to come back and go through this again. He'll get the job done late. Might not even get it done tonight. Then Peterkinney will be pissed off with him, and he'll be struggling to hang on to another job.

He's slamming the wardrobe door shut. It's not a door designed to be slammed. The wardrobe is shaking and doing its level best not to fall apart under the assault. Holmes is marching out of the bedroom, along the corridor and into the living room. Looking furious. Ready to pick a fight with anyone over anything. Just a good old-fashioned fight. It would make him feel better.

"Where is he?"

"I told you. I don't know." She's getting fed up of this now. She doesn't know, and even if she did, it's obvious she wouldn't tell this gorilla.

"When's he going to be back, huh?" Almost shouting now.

A sigh. "I don't know. Don't know where he is, don't know what he's doing, don't know when he'll be back. He's doing a job. Trying to make some money, okay. So that he can pay some back. But it was all rushed, and I don't know what it was." Trying to be persuasive, but running out of patience. "He shouldn't be long. You can come back in an hour. There's no need to be so angry about it. I don't know what your problem is."

That's it. That's just enough to spark a rage. "You don't know what my problem is? Do you want to know? Eh? Will I tell you what my fucking problem is? It's people like you and your wee guy. Your Alex Glass. Borrowing money you can't afford to pay. And then I have to come and collect it 'cause you're all so fucking daft. And your fellow ain't here to pay. Big fucking surprise there, eh. Always hiding. Always hiding." He was shouting at the end, spitting as he did.

Ella's just glaring at him. "He's trying to earn money to pay you back. And you don't need to be shouting at me, I don't owe you anything."

Defiance. Not much, but enough for Holmes. "Oh, you don't? Well, your man does. He's yours and so is his debt. You owe." He's moved towards her, pushed her shoulder. Not violent, but looking to provoke violence.

"Stop that. Just leave. Please, just get out."

"What did you say to me? You telling me to get out? That what you said?" Lashing out with a slap, catching her hard on the side of the head.

She didn't see it coming. Holmes was always a fighter, since he was a little kid. Always had a quick hand. It's the surprise as much as the force that's knocked her sideways. Knocked her off her feet and onto the floor. Lying on her side. Shaken, sore, but no permanent damage. But she's staying down. Convinced that if she gets up, she'll get hit again. She's been hit before. She knows how this works. Let them see they've won. Let them see that they're more powerful than you. When they see they've won their power game, they can back off. So she's staying down and hoping that'll be enough for him.

But it won't. Not for Holmes. He's not like her clients. Not trying to make himself feel big. Feel like a winner. He already knows he's lost. He's drunk and angry and remembering that time Glass smashed his way into his house. He's remembering all the failure that followed. Remembering Glass and Peterkinney at the bottom of the stairs in the old house. Standing there and kicking him while he lay on the floor. Now he can make one of them suffer.

He's lashing out with his boot. Not holding anything back. Hitting her in the stomach, his boot scuffing along her side. Didn't catch her square, but it felt good to him. Good to be kicking out. Good that he can make Glass suffer.

"You feel that?" he's shouting. "You ask your boyfriend if he re-members. You ask him. I remember. You ask him if he does."

Kicking her again. Hard as he can, all his weight behind it. Square in the stomach this time. Knocking her onto her back. She's rolled onto her other side and stopped moving. He's making to kick her in the back this time, but stopping. Instinct. Walking round to the other side of her. Looking at her face. Her eyes are half shut, her mouth half open. There's no movement. Her arms are down on the floor, not raised to defend herself.

"Come on. Come on, get up. Come on." Holmes is bending down, grabbing her by the hair. Lifting her head half an inch and letting it drop onto the floor. There's a faint groan. Her eyelids flicker. But that's it. "Shit, come on. I didn't...you're not that badly hurt. Come on." Getting angry with her now.

Taking a step back and looking around. A deep breath. What do you do? Instinct says run and right now instinct is all he's got. He's out the front door, just aware enough to pull it shut behind him. Down the stairs and out into the night. Breathing heavily, in real need of a drink. This need isn't just pesky old alcoholism. This is fear that needs to be drowned before it hurts him. That girl was in trouble. He went too far.

5

Arnie's sitting in his living room, watching TV. Skimming through the newspaper for reasons of habit. A boring quiet night, until the phone starts ringing. He's looking at it with suspicion. Nobody phones him in an evening. There aren't many who phone him at all. This is going to be something annoying, he's sure of it.

"Hello, Arnold Peterkinney."

"Arnie? Arnie."

He knows already that it's Glass. Young voice, emotional. Sounds like he's looking for help.

"Alex, is that you? What's wrong?"

There's a pause and heavy breathing. "It's Ella. She's not moving. She's just lying on the floor and she's not moving."

He instantly assumes drugs, and then stops himself. She's a good girl. Didn't think she would be. Thought she would be the biggest problem in Glass's life. Nope, not her. She was helping Glass. She was the one with sense in the relationship. Okay, she does a job she shouldn't. Arnie doesn't like that. Doesn't like to think about it. Knows what it does to Glass to think about it. He tried to talk her into changing career, but she wouldn't. Stubborn wee thing. Only way she knows to make money. But she wasn't a waster. Not a boozer. Not a druggie. Oliver was wrong about her. She wasn't the problem. So not drugs. Must have been a client.

"Listen to me now, Alex, listen carefully. What happened? How did she end up on the floor?" Worried now that Glass might have been involved. Worried that something bad could be about to turn into something horrendous.

"I don't know. I don't know. I just came home. I did that job for Mr. Currie that you got me. I parked the van where he told me to and walked back. I came into the flat and she was just lying there. Lying on the living-room floor. She's not moving. She won't wake up. She's not...She won't move for me, Arnie."

"Okay. Steady on, now. Listen to me. You have to hang up and call an ambulance. Dial 999 and tell them what you told me. You got that now, Alex. Call an ambulance. I'll come round to the flat, okay. I'm on my way now."

"Okay. Okay."

Arnie's hanging up the phone. Running to the hall, grabbing a coat. Out of the flat and along to his neighbor's front door. Knocking loudly, making sure they can't possibly ignore him. The door's opening, a confused neighbor looking back at him.

"Arnie?"

"I need to borrow your car. It's an emergency, really, or I wouldn't ask."

The neighbor's nodding. Arnie's a reliable guy. He's not going to go off and trash the car. And he doesn't ask for much. Doesn't ask for anything, actually. If he was the sort of neighbor who borrowed a lot, Arnie might not get what he wants right now. But the neighbor's fishing in his pocket, pulling out a set of keys.

"I won't keep it long, I promise," Arnie's saying. He was going to say something about filling up the tank before he takes it back, but he hasn't. Too much of a hurry. Also, it's a nice thing to do, and nice things cost money. He's not sure he has any of that on him.

He's down to the front of the building and into the car. Driving quickly through the streets, hoping he can get to the flat before the ambulance does. He wants to see Glass. Wants to see the situation. It's a terrible thing, but he's hardly thinking about Ella at all. He's only thinking about what this might do to Glass. How he might react to this. Worried that he might get into all kinds of trouble if this is serious.

Little traffic, and he's there quickly, but he's not there first.

There's an ambulance outside the building. Arnie's parking out of the way and running up the stairs. Struggling a bit. Wheezing as he gets to the door. The two paramedics are down on the floor, on their knees beside Ella. One of them is talking to her. The other one is fiddling around her mouth and neck. Glass is standing behind them, hands at his sides, just staring.

Arnie's walked past the paramedics, over to Glass. Putting an arm on his shoulder. Glass is noticing him for the first time. Just looking at him and looking back at Ella. He doesn't look emotional. Doesn't look like this has hurt him. But that's what worries Arnie. This kid was emotionally all over the place after getting beaten up in that nightclub and turning up on his doorstep. Now he's not reacting at all. Before he was damaged. Now he's broken.

The girl looks bad. Can't see what's wrong with her. The medics are still working on her. One of them is lifting her T-shirt. Arnie assumes they're looking for puncture wounds, but they're not. They're looking for a larger injury and they've found one. Her stomach and side are red, heading for purple. The medics are talking in whispers to each other. One of them getting up and running down to the ambulance.

"We need to get her to hospital now. Have you a car to follow in?" the remaining one is asking Glass. Doesn't have a friendly tone in his voice. He knows what caused this injury. He suspects he knows who. Usually domestic. That's why he wants the boy in a car, not in the back of the ambulance with the girl.

Glass is nodding. Unsure.

"I do, I'll take him," Arnie's saying. He wants to stay near Glass. Wants to make sure he doesn't react badly to this. Start talking and get himself in trouble.

The medics are moving her down on a small stretcher. Going fast. There's a new sense of urgency about them now. Glass staying close, Arnie close to Glass. Arnie's watching them put her in the back of the ambulance, Glass standing beside him. Watching his girlfriend. Watching them close the ambulance door.

"Come on. Alex, let's go," Arnie's saying. Needing to provoke him into action. Glass is following him to the car. They're driving behind the ambulance, through the quiet streets of the city.

The next hour is a disquieting blur to Arnie. They rushed her in and about ten minutes later a doctor came out to talk to them. Came out to tell them that Ella had died. That she had suffered internal injuries after a blunt trauma. There was silence for a long time. Arnie and Glass sitting together in a private room in the hospital. Arnie didn't know what to say. What do you say?

"Someone killed her," Glass is saying eventually. Talking in a whisper.

He's right, but Arnie doesn't want this conversation to go any further in that direction. He knows where the road goes. Someone went round to the flat and killed her. Not like there are many obvious candidates. There's an obvious candidate that Arnie doesn't want to think about. He wants to move Glass in another direction.

"Would she have had someone back to the flat?" he's asking quietly. Trying to put the thought in Glass's head. Try and persuade him that it might be a client of Ella's. Try and persuade him that the dead girl introduced her own murderer into the situation. Anything to convince him that it's not the obvious option.

Glass is shaking his head. "No. She never would have. Never did. Home was separate. Home was home."

Ella never took men back to the flat. Not once. It was the place of safety that she clung to. Meant so much to her. She put so much into that flat. Little poky place, didn't deserve someone like her to take so much care of it. Mattered to her though. Proof that she could have normality. Safety. Something nice and neat that she was responsible for. Something grown up.

There's another period of silence. Arnie has to change this. Ella is dead. The girl is gone. They both know who's responsible. Who's almost certainly responsible. They need to get out of here. The hospital is just a reminder of death. Even this private room, that tries to be so nice. That tries to be so reassuring. It isn't. It's just death in nicer packaging.

"Come on. Let's go back to my flat. It's late, you need to get some sleep," Arnie is saying. "There's nothing we can do here." Get him home. Get him sleeping. Emotions will be less bloody and raw in the morning. There will be a better chance to sort this out.

Arnie's given his address to the girl at the accident and emergency reception desk. If the police want to get in touch, they'll know where to find them. Arnie's driving them home. Going in silence. Glass doesn't want to talk. Arnie doesn't know what to say. Leading Glass up to the flat. Patting him on the shoulder and saying goodnight. That's all they've said. Goodnight. Glass disappearing into Peterkinney's old bedroom to try and sleep.

Arnie still has the car keys in his hand. Bouncing them up and down in his palm. Thinking about giving them back to his neighbor. He's spent ten minutes standing in the corridor. Listening at Glass's bedroom door. No sound from in there. He might be sleeping. Hopefully. A glance at his watch. Half an hour. That's all it would take. Get there, ask a few questions, get back before Glass realizes he's gone. Take the chance. He has to know. That's why he's sneaking out of his own flat. Pulling the front door shut behind him as softly as possible and jogging to the car.

6

Marty still hasn't left the office. Third office he's been in today, mind you, so technically he's left two already. But he's still there. Still working. Trying to figure out how the hell the Allen brothers, who are still just cousins, incidentally, managed to pull off some major deal that has them selling all over the city now. Marty knows a little about the brothers. Used to know Charlie Allen a little bit. Charlie came to a few parties.

They were small. They were smart and tough, but they stuck to their own patch and they knew how to avoid pissing off big people. Marty heard stories about them looking for new suppliers back in the past. That was a legit story. They had a falling-out with Alex MacArthur over one of his muscle owing them money, something like that. So it makes sense to Marty that they would have changed supplier.

What doesn't make sense is them suddenly having enough gear and enough backing to expand rapidly. Angus Lafferty is pissed off about it. You can bet the hair on your head, if you have any to gamble, that in a jail cell somewhere Peter Jamieson is pissed off about it too. Someone thinks they can force their way in, and they're using Ian and Charlie Allen to do it. That's got Angus worked up. Got him looking for answers. Got everyone in the group that runs the organization trying to find out the truth behind it. And they will. Marty's sure of it, because this group is good. By spreading their talent like this, they're getting results. And he loves being a part of it. Loves it. Loves what he's going to do next.

Out of the office, at last. Standing on the street for a few seconds, breathing in some sort of fresh air. Into his car and driving. Doesn't have a driver of his own. Not permanently. Uses one now and again, when he needs it. Doesn't need it tonight. Doesn't want it. This is going to be a private meeting, and he doesn't want anyone knowing about it. Not even a driver.

Nice street, nice area. Better than Marty's living in right now. He could afford to move up in the world. Not a question of cash. Question of time. Hasn't had the opportunity to look around at new houses, pick a bigger place. He should. All part of the image. Lets people see that he's more successful, moving up in the world. Also lets the other guys running the organization see that he's moving up. That's important too. Always that need to prove that he's one of them. To prove that he's a senior man. And when he does move up, it'll be to somewhere like this. The sort of street that Potty Cruickshank lives on.

He's parked outside, getting casually out. Looking up at Potty's house. Potty will be back from his meeting with MacArthur. Will have had a few hours to think about it. Potty's a thinker. He'll have worked out every angle of his position. He must know that he needs protection. He must know that he needs to make a deal with someone. He must know that he's fast running out of options. His own men will be getting nervy about how exposed he is amongst the turmoil.

MacArthur probably wouldn't have taken the deal anyway. He's not in a position to do anything that might lead to trouble externally. He has way too much going on trying to keep possession of his throne from his own young pretenders. But there was a risk he would have seen this as flexing whatever muscles he has left. That's why it was reassuring to see Buller turn up and spill the beans. Reassuring that all the work he did setting up the meeting with Buller paid off. More reassuring still that Marty's judgment on MacArthur's situation turned out to be correct.

Up the front path and ringing the doorbell. He knows what the initial reaction is going to be. He knows that Potty won't be happy to see him. Might be nervous, scared about it. But Marty's very de-liberately on his own. Unarmed. Coming to Potty's house, so it's a location Potty can feel comfortable with.

Takes a little while before the hall light comes on and the door opens. Potty looking back at him, frowning. Glaring at him for a few seconds before he recognizes Marty. The look moves from frustra-tion to worry. His eyebrows are raised. He's opened his mouth, but nothing's come out. Too busy looking past Marty, trying to see if there's anyone with him.

"Hello, Ronald," Marty's saying to him. "Can I come in? I think you and I need to have a grown-up, man-to-man chat about the way things are going."

You can almost see the wheels turning. Potty standing there, thinking it through. Nodding his head slowly. Doesn't matter where this goes, but he can't leave Marty standing outside. Has to invite him in.

They're in the living room now. Potty in his usual seat, Marty sit-ting opposite him. Potty offered a cup of tea or something stronger. Marty made a point of refusing any alcohol, pointing out that he has to drive himself home. Letting Potty know that there's nobody outside. Just the two of them. Marty's making a point of not looking around at the living room. A feminine room. Must have been his ex-wife who picked out everything in here. Just seems ludicrous with Potty living here alone now.

"I want to talk about you and me getting together. Working out a little deal that I think can make life easier for both of us."

"Well, of course I'm interested in anything that may benefit us, Marty," Potty's saying, "but you'll have to furnish me with more detail than that." Sounding like he's humoring Marty. Going for a superior tone he wouldn't have dared use to Alex MacArthur.

"Well, of course," Marty is saying. Not saying it in a sarcastic tone, but it might just be sarcastic. "You and I have common enemies," Marty's saying. "We have common solutions. You're a smart man. You know how things are changing right now. You and I together could be strong. That's what you need. It's what I need. It's what my organization wants. We want strong people on board with us."

"On board?" Potty's saying. Letting his enthusiasm for that suggestion get the better of his silence.

"On board," Marty's saying. Knowing now that he has the fat fish halfway into the boat. Only has to clobber him over the head to seal the deal. "See, my role has changed. I need to bring as much money to the table as possible. I have other ways of doing that. Collection is tough work, better suited to a specialist. I'm spread too thin. I can bring more money into the organization if I get you on board. You take over my books. I step out, and the organization takes a third of your profits. I'll be working on other things that you don't need to concern yourself with. There won't be overlap. You can expand your business, make more money than you are now and have the protection of the organization."

It's a good offer. It's as good an offer as Potty could possibly hope for. A third of his profits is a little more than he'd like, but, Jesus, he'd have given a strong MacArthur 40 percent. It's not unreasonable for Marty to demand it. The upper end of reasonable, given that profits will surely increase. With Marty's books merged into his, that covers much of the 30 percent. Marty's books are smaller than Potty's but they're not thin. And with the backing of the Jamieson organization. Now, there's the risk. It's not the Jamieson organization as long as Jamieson's rotting in a cell. He'll be sitting in that cell for another year and a half, minimum. The leadership is ragtag. Only takes one falling-out and all the protection his 30 percent is supposed to buy him falls apart. So there is a gamble. But the gamble of no deal is bigger.

"I would be open to the suggestion," Potty is saying. "I'll want to see the small print, obviously, but I'm certainly willing to discuss this further. One question, Marty: these common enemies. I presume you have a solution in mind?"

Not hard to understand why Potty's concerned. It's easy for people to promise solutions to your problems when they're trying to get you to do a deal. You do the deal, and suddenly the promises are forgotten. Happened to other people before. Marty promises that the big organization he's a part of will take care of these problems. Once Potty's on board, they're Potty's problems. Marty's off dealing with other things.

"Oh, I do. Billy Patterson is the first one I'm going to deal with. I think that would benefit us both. I'm actually going to deal with him tomorrow night. You know what, might be a good idea for you to be there. The first step of bringing you in. You interested?"

"Absolutely," Potty's saying, because he can't say no. Wishes he could, but he can't. Marty wants him to be there for good reasons. If they're going to do something serious with Patterson, Marty wants Potty to see it. Wants the commitment that being there shows. Make Potty as culpable as Marty. It's a reasonable thing to demand. Besides, much as Potty is repulsed by the idea of watching Marty do dirty work, it might be nice to bear witness to Patterson's ending.

"Good," Marty's saying. "I've got Patterson to agree to come meet me in an old pub Kevin Currie just bought. I'll send you some details in the morning. Agreements, that sort of thing. The pub's on the south side, I'll send you the address. Come alone, of course."

"Of course."

A few minutes of small talk. Now Marty's leaving the house. A shake of hands on the doorstep. Potty seemed happy, seemed enthusiastic about the agreement. Marty's into the car, got another visit to make. A long-arranged meeting with Kevin Currie. Chance to kill a few birds with one stone here. Needs to get a set of keys for that old pub Currie bought. Going to tart it up and run money through it. But Marty has a little plan for it first. Going to need a few people to come help him make that plan work, as well. Lots of calls to make.

They'll be fun calls to make, though. Nobody ignores his calls anymore. Nobody ever sounds reluctant when he puts an idea to them. It's a funny thing. He's pretty sure that most of his ideas are no better now than they were six months ago. How could they be? He's learned a lot in the last six months, but not so much that he's suddenly a strategic genius. No, people just respect him now.

He's pulling up outside one of Kevin Currie's offices. Currie's a senior man. Always brought a lot of money into the organization through booze and fags. Rips off the taxman no end, and the organization makes a good profit on it. Not just booze and fags though. That's the thing. People think that's all he does because in the old days that's how he started. That was all he needed back then. It made him rich. But now he has a good grip of every aspect of the counterfeit industry.

Into the office; Currie and a couple of others already in there. Marty the last to arrive, but not late. Nodding hellos, and stepping to the side of the room to talk to Currie with a little privacy. The other two guys work for Currie, and if he wants to share these details with them then he can go right ahead. But you don't risk blurting out details in front of people who may not be very important.

Currie is quite happy for Marty to use the pub. Telling him where he can get the keys whenever he wants them. One of Currie's men has a duplicate set he can use. Asking hardly any questions about it. That's another big change. Used to be a man like Currie would have swamped Marty with his suspicions. Not now. Now there's trust.

"I'll be using it for a job, Kevin. What we discussed at the last meeting. Cleaning up the collection business."

"Ah," is the response. A slight pause, but only slight. "You have the men you need to get it done?" And that's all he's asking. Not demanding more detail. Not suggesting that Marty isn't senior enough to pull this job without one of them there to oversee. Just offering his own men to help.

"I'm fine. It's all set up, ready for tomorrow night. Should be clean. Should be simple."

The two of them rejoining the group, and going through the business of the week that needs to be discussed. This is just a small meeting. Currie and Marty the only two senior men. There's a business opportunity Currie wants to pursue that he thinks Marty can help him with. That's why it's just the two of them, and Currie's men. Talk of money. Talk of putting pressure on people. The talk of senior men.

7

Arnie knows the address, but doesn't know the area. He's driving round for the best part of twenty minutes before he finds the right street. A nice little area. Sort of place Arnie's never lived a day of his life. And it hurts a little. His own grandson. He should be proud of this, not ashamed. Driving into this area that was always above him. Going to see his own grandson, his own flesh and blood. That's a thing that decent people get to be proud of. Maybe Arnie isn't a decent person. Maybe this is his punishment for never being quite good enough.

He's on the street, stopping about ten yards from the front door of Oliver's building. A nice street. Three-story buildings, all made into large flats. Coming to live here doesn't come cheap. This battered old car doesn't belong here any more than the battered old man driving it. Ninety-nine percent of him wants to drive away. Forget it. Take the coward's way out. There's nothing to gain from being here anyway. This is going to go badly, and there's no way around that.

Sitting in the car for nearly an hour. A couple of people have walked past. Arnie still sitting there, still trying to persuade himself that he shouldn't be here. But that 1 percent just won't be won over. The 1 percent that says it doesn't matter how fruitless this is. Doesn't matter if it only confirms your worst fears. You have to know.

He's gotten out of the car. Walking up to the front door of the building. There are doorbells at the side, names of the owners beside them. Closing his eyes and pressing the buzzer. Hoping to God that nobody answers. Then he won't have to find out.

"Yes," comes the voice.

"Oliver?"

"Yes," is the reply through the intercom. One word of annoyed recognition.

"Can I come up? We need to talk."

There's a pause of a few seconds. Arnie not sure if Oliver heard him or not. "Fine, come up."

There's a buzz and Arnie is pushing open the front door. Stepping into the building and taking a look around. A tiled floor, a large staircase in front of him. So this is what that sort of life pays for. Yes, it sure is nice to look at. Up the stairs into the corridor. A nice carpet on the corridor, which would last about a day in Arnie's building. Finding himself in front of Oliver's front door. Is a pretty home worth it? Does it matter that much?

The door's opening just as Arnie is raising a hand to knock. His grandson staring back at him. There's an angry look there. Peterkinney wasn't expecting his grandfather to turn up at the flat. Thought he would phone to complain. Whinge about the warning given to Glass. The fact he's here means it's been delivered. The fact he's here rather than phoning probably means he's very angry.

"What's up?" Oliver's asking. Standing in the doorway. He'd like to get through this without having to let his grandfather inside. Let the old man vent on the doorstep and then piss off home.

"Can I come in, please?" Arnie's asking.

There's something disconcerting about a man who should be angry and isn't. Peterkinney was waiting to hear venom in the old man's voice. An angry tremble. Thought he'd start shouting straight away. But he hasn't. He just sounds weary. Sounds like he's gone beyond the point where angry would do any good. That could be a good thing or a bad thing.

Peterkinney's stepping aside, pulling open the door. Letting his grandfather in for the first time. Arnie's stepping inside and stopping. Doesn't know where to go. Oliver's shutting the door and walking past him, leading him through to the kitchen. Large kitchen, wide-open space and everything in white. Seems appropriate, somehow. When he thinks of conversations with his grandfather, it's always in the kitchen of the flat.

"You're up and about late," Oliver's saying. Polite conversation. Try and keep the tone civil for as long as possible.

"I have reason to be," Arnie's saying.

Oliver's sitting down at the unnecessarily long kitchen table. Gesturing for his grandfather to take a seat opposite, but Arnie's shaking his head.

"I won't sit. What I have to ask won't take long. I don't think you'll want me to stay long anyway. I need to know something, Oliver. I want you to be honest with me. Did you send someone to Alex's flat today? Someone to collect money, or give a warning?"

Seems like Arnie is going for the old "I'm so disappointed in you" routine. Fair enough. Oliver will counter with a well-practiced "I had no choice, what could I do?" performance. Hopefully they can keep the conversation calm and it'll all be over in a few minutes.

Oliver's starting with a sigh. "Look. I have a business to run. I made that very clear from the start. I needed to know that Alex was making an effort. That he wasn't messing me around. Playing on our old friendship. And I found out he was," Oliver's saying with a shrug. "I found out that he was out partying with his girlfriend. Spending all kinds of money to keep a smile on her face. Not spending any to put a smile on mine. He went out and spent bucketloads the night before he came to me and said he was skint. What am I supposed to do, huh? Makes my business look weak, and makes me look like I don't know how to run it. I had to act. What other choice did I have?"

"You sent someone round to beat him up. Deliver a warning." Not a question. Just a sad acceptance that his worst fears are correct.

"I had no choice," Oliver's saying. Saying it quiet. Less and less sure of his position.

"Your fellow went round to the flat and Alex wasn't there. Did you know that?"

Oliver's shaking his head. "I haven't heard from my man." A shrug. "Lucky for Alex then."

Arnie's looking at him and there's disgust on his face. This is closer to the anger Oliver expected, although its reason remains unknown to him. "Lucky? Lucky, you think? Lucky for Alex maybe, not so lucky for Ella. She was there. She was there on her own."

Oliver's looking down at the table and shaking his head. "Shit, well, that was unlucky." Some muscle will take advantage of women in these situations. Treat them in ways they shouldn't. If the scruffy bastard he sent did something inappropriate, then he'll ditch him. Doesn't want his company having a reputation for things like that. Would make him look grubby in the eyes of men like Chris Argyle. "Shame for the girl," he's saying, "but it was Alex who put her in that position. Borrowing money he couldn't pay. If she wasn't badly hurt, then I don't know, she might consider herself lucky as well."

Arnie's just staring at him. Looking down at the seated Oliver. His grandson, but it doesn't feel like that anymore. The words coming out of his mouth would never have come from the boy he knew. The boy he helped raise. This little bastard is someone else entirely. Someone he can no longer bring himself to care about.

It comes without warning. Arnie looking at his grandson. Not intending to react. And then lurching at him, throwing a wild punch. Arnie's knuckles brush through Oliver's hair. Doesn't catch him. Doesn't do any damage. But Oliver's dipped sideways to avoid the shot, and is now on his knees on the floor. Looking up at his grandfather. A shocked expression. In a normal situation, he would fight back. Start throwing punches, aim to hurt. He's done collection work, he knows how to fight. But not this time. This is still his grandfather. The same old man he always was.

"She's dead, you silly little bastard," Arnie's saying. Saying and not shouting. Keeping it quiet. Fighting so hard to resist the urge to punch again, because what good is that going to do? "The thug you sent beat her to pieces. Killed her. The girl's dead and you ordered it. It was you, Oliver. You did it. You killed her."

Know what? It's not the suggestion that he killed her that annoys Oliver. It's the suggestion that he made a mistake. He didn't kill her, the muscle he sent did. The muscle blundered, obviously. Last thing you ever do is draw police attention towards your boss. Oliver knew that back when he was working for Marty. Knew it as sure as he knew anything when he worked for Roy Bowles. The man his grandfather got him a job with. The moralist standing over him and the gunrunner he got Oliver a job with, now in jail after the Jamieson shitstorm.

"I didn't mean for her to be harmed. That was never my intention," he's saying. He wants to sound sorry, but he doesn't. Can't quite control his tone. He sounds annoyed and he sounds a little dismissive, but he doesn't sound sorry.

Arnie's looking down at him, Oliver still on his knees. It would be so easy for the boy to look sorry. So easy for him to sound like he knows what regret is. Just fake it. Just this once. But he can't even be bothered. On his knees, and he can't make the effort to be sorry. A shake of the head.

"I don't know you anymore," Arnie's saying. Turning and walking out of the kitchen. Along the corridor and opening the front door. He knows his disapproval means nothing to Oliver. Doesn't care. Oliver just stopped meaning anything to him.

8

Arnie was sitting in the kitchen with a cup of coffee when Glass got out of bed. Had a shower, put on last night's clothes. Went into the kitchen and started making a cup for himself without saying anything. Doesn't feel like talking. Not to Arnie. Not to anyone. If the world stayed silent forever, Glass would be happy with that. Talking will remind him.

He heard Arnie leaving last night. Heard him coming back. He was gone a while, longer than Glass expected. When he heard Arnie leaving, he guessed where he was going. Going to see his grandson. Going to confront him with the news of Ella's death. That's what Glass would have done. Makes sense. Oliver's family. Go and warn him about the inevitable police investigation. Go and warn him that he crossed a line, perhaps. But that would have been a short visit, and Arnie was gone for a long time. Doesn't occur to Glass that he spent an hour sitting outside Oliver's flat before he plucked up the courage to go in. But Glass won't ask. Doesn't want to know.

"You sleep?" Arnie's asking him. Painfully obvious that Arnie didn't. Would be obvious to Arnie that Glass didn't either if he was alert enough to see it. It's been too long a night to be alert now.

"Little bit," Glass is saying. "On and off." Stirring his mug and sitting opposite Arnie. Not looking him in the eye.

A few moments of silence. "The police will want to talk to you," Arnie's saying. No doubt they won't be far away.

Glass is sighing. Taking another sip of coffee. Doesn't want to speak to the police. Doesn't want to have to tell them the truth. For so many reasons. The fact that Ella dying was his fault. He borrowed money he couldn't pay back. She ended up paying for it. Doesn't want to be a coward either. They'll ask him if he knows who was behind the beating. He'll say no. Has to. If he says yes he's a grass. He'll be punished severely. Doesn't want that. He's afraid of that. And he doesn't want to talk to the police anyway. They might ask about Alan Bavidge. So that's plenty of reasons. Add the fact that he doesn't want to hurt Arnie by having Oliver arrested. All adds up to a justified silence.

"I don't want to talk to anyone," Glass is saying.

"You'll have to, eventually," Arnie's saying. His tone serious. "You need to think about what you're going to say."

Fishing for a clue. Wanting to know what Glass plans to tell the police when he speaks to them. Wanting to know out of concern for Oliver, Glass assumes. Assumes wrong. Wanting to know out of concern for Glass. Arnie's terrified that Glass will say something stupid. That he'll confess all about the man he murdered and get himself put away. He's prone to emotion. He might blurt something out during a difficult interview. There's no need for him to throw his own life away over this.

It's a horrible thing to think. Arnie knows it, doesn't need to be told. But he has been thinking that this is an opportunity for Glass, if he's smart enough to take it. This is a chance to separate himself fully from his old life. Didn't want it to be this way. Didn't want to see the girl dead. She was a nice girl, and she was desperate to help Glass. But she lived in the criminal world, and didn't seem to know how to live any other way. Being separated from that is a chance. Arnie won't say that, obviously. He's not that crass. But this is an opportunity that he won't let Glass squander.

"I don't know what I'll say," Glass is saying quietly. "I think I want to go out for a walk. Clear my head, you know."

"Sure," Arnie's saying. "Take your phone. If I hear anything, I'll call you."

Glass is just happy to be out of the flat. Thinking about Ella. She's gone. She was what it was all about for him. The life, the thrill, the money, the danger. It was all encapsulated in her. She was the life. Worth every risk, every sacrifice. He destroyed that. Destroyed her and destroyed the life. He knows it's his fault. His and Peterkinney's. Can't get away from that. Peterkinney sent someone to collect the money and they killed Ella. Glass doesn't need to be told to know. There was nobody else who would have done it.

And he'll get away with it. Like he always does. People like him always fucking do. They get away with it. They live their lives getting away with the sort of things that people like Glass have to pay the price for. How is that fair? A man like Peterkinney can get away with this. A man like Glass never would. People like Peterkinney have protection. Connections which keep them safe. Other people willing to shield them for the right price. There's always a price they can afford to pay. Not Glass. He can't pay any price at all.

He was walking aimlessly, but now that he's found himself in the vicinity of a pub he knows, he might as well go in. Getting a drink, sitting down. Alone in the corner. Nobody will bother him here. The background murmur of other people's conversations doesn't bother him. This is as close to silence as you get in the city. Close enough to silence for Glass to think about his position.

He has enough money in his pocket to sit in that pub for a few hours. So he does. Sits there nursing his drinks. Tells himself that he's thinking about his position. Thinking through all of his options, but he isn't. He doesn't have a lot of options. If he was sober and smart, he would realize that he's always known what he's going to do. Known it since he left the flat.

Instinct. Everyone has it. Some instincts are better than others. Some people are a lot better at listening to their instincts than others. If this was Peterkinney, he would have spotted what he was going to do within seconds. Acted on it within minutes. Not Glass. He's been trying to drown his instinct in booze. Trying to pretend that he isn't going to do what he knows he's going to do.

He's just drunk enough. Not so drunk that he can't walk from A to B. Not so sober that he'll be able to talk himself out of this.

He's out of the pub and realizing how much time has passed. It's gloomy now. Afternoon long since killed morning. Afternoon falling to evening. And he's starting to walk. Knowing exactly where he's going. Knowing exactly what risk he's taking.

Back to his flat. Convinced there should still be cops there. There aren't. They've been and gone. Not a lot of flat for them to look around. They'll have done everything there is to do before looking for people to interview. That'll be the last part of their investigation. Interviewing people like Glass. That's where their good information will come from. Glass doesn't know it, but they found fingerprints in the flat that have got them excited. Known violent offender James Holmes. They're now trying to find him. Find out who he works for. They're going to look for Glass as well, but Holmes is the current priority.

There's nobody to stop him unlocking the front door. Nobody inside the flat. He's standing inside the door, looking at the spot on the floor where she was lying. Last time he came in this door, he found her lying there. Panicked. Didn't know what to do. Maybe if he'd acted faster...No. Don't start thinking like that. You know what you're here for. Get it and get out.

Through the living room, down the corridor and into the bedroom. Their bedroom. Turning to the wardrobe. There's something on the door. Markings that weren't there. Some police thing, he figures. Why on the wardrobe, he doesn't know. Then he's stopping. Damn it all. They'll have gone through the wardrobe and taken the money. The little money Ella had set aside. She kept that money to cover emergencies. The ones she knew about, anyway. They'll have taken it when they searched the wardrobe.

But they haven't. They found it. The two shoeboxes on the floor have been opened and emptied. The shoes put back in both. The little bundle of money taken out of one. Placed back on top of the shoebox. Obviously not enough that they would consider it significant. It's not suspicious. There isn't enough of it to be evidence.

Glass is picking it up. Looking through it. There isn't much there.

He never counted it before. Knew it was there, but it was hers and not his. He respected that. She didn't talk about it to him. Didn't hide it from him, as such. He saw her putting money in there, she let him see. It was for a rainy day. Pay bills that crept up on them, maybe. Or maybe it was for a treat. Saving up to get something nice, something she could be proud of.

One hundred and eighty quid. He thought there would be more. Seemed like the bundle was bigger in the past. Enough for them to live off for a little while. Maybe there was more. Maybe someone took it. One of the cops? No. If there was ever more, Ella spent it. Something came along and she had to dip into her savings.

So it's a hundred and eighty quid. There's another twenty in the biscuit tin in the kitchen. Two hundred quid. Not enough. Not even halfway to being enough. But he has to try. His instinct has been trying to tell him for hours now. He's come to realize it eventually. No matter how much or how little money he has, he has to try this. Won't ever forgive himself if he doesn't. Won't ever stop regretting it. He's stuffing the money into his pocket and making his way out of the flat.

9

Marty told him to bring a couple of his men with him. Patterson's taking him at his word. Called up Conn Griffiths and Mikey Summers. His two best. Griffiths has become his senior man since Bavidge's death. Not as sharp as Bavidge, and there isn't the same bond there, but it's a good relationship. A man he trusts. Smart, tough and always willing to put the business first. Summers is tough. Properly tough. One of the best muscle in the city. You could have a conversation about who stands as the best muscle in this city. Nate Colgan would get a lot of mentions. Jamie Stamford has profile. Patterson rates Summers as high as either of them.

He feels he needs them both. Would be more comfortable with more than just these two. It's late afternoon and he's meeting Griffiths and Summers. They'll travel to the pub together. Ex-pub. Future pub. At the moment it's just a convenient empty location, in a quiet area. Businesses around it, all of which will be closing right about now. They'll be perfectly silent by the time the meeting starts. A good choice of location by Marty.

And that's what makes Patterson nervous. This has all been organized by Marty. Patterson's been tied to Marty for months now, but it takes more than that to erase years of mistrust. He would feel better if he'd seen the location beforehand. Would feel better if he'd sat in on Marty's conversation with Potty. All Patterson knows is that the conversation happened, and Potty is going to be there.

They're in the car together. Griffiths driving, Patterson in the passenger seat, Summers in the back. The usual silence that comes before a big job. They're all familiar with it. They've all done big jobs in their lives. They've all learned that the time to ask questions has passed. If there was something you wanted to say, you've missed your chance. Summers wanted to suggest taking guns, even though he knew it would be refused by the other two. Griffiths wanted to know more about who Potty would take with him. He always has someone with him, even if it's only his driver. Doesn't want to walk into an ambush. This could be a good chance for Potty to decapitate Patterson's business. But they didn't ask before the journey began, and now they never will.

Griffiths knows the area, says he knows where the pub is. These moments, you start to doubt everyone. The last couple of minutes before you reach the destination. Can you trust Marty? Can you even trust Griffiths and Summers? People who have given you no reason not to trust them. That's the nature of the business. People give you no reason to doubt them, and then promptly let you down. It's what a good set-up looks like.

"That's it, up there on the left," Griffiths is saying. Slowing down the car before he needs to. Buying Patterson a few seconds to take in the scene.

Not much to look at. A lot of small buildings seemingly scattered at random. Less a street than an accident of bad planning with a road through it. The pub is a small, flat, single-story building. Even by the standards of this street, its architect was one lazy, talentless bastard. Patterson's shaking his head. What a terrible place to build a pub. Who the hell would drink there? Nobody, and it doesn't matter a jot. Currie's bought it to pretend that people are drinking there. Helps him explain his earnings.

There are three cars parked out on the street. One will belong to Marty. One will belong to Potty. The plan was that Potty should get there first. Get him into the building before he knows Patterson's going to be there. Stop him getting spooked. That's what Marty said.

The third car? Marty said he was going to bring some people of his own, but surely not two carfuls of them.

"Pull up behind them," Patterson's saying. They've come this far. Spent months cultivating the relationship with Marty. He's put his eggs in this basket. Has to go for it now.

They're getting out of the car. Griffiths making a little noise and then nodding to the car in front when Patterson looks across. There's someone inside. Patterson's on the pavement now, ducking slightly to look into the car. Summers is doing the same thing, neither of them acting with the kind of subtlety they ought to pride themselves on. The driver is sitting in the car. Looking straight ahead. Looking bored. Making every effort not to look at the people who have just turned up. He knows better than that. Potty's driver. Has to be. A man experienced enough to know that you don't stare back at men like Billy Patterson and Mikey Summers.

The three of them are stopping outside the front door of the pub. No reason. Just seems like a smart idea to stop for a second, gather breath, and prepare yourself. Patterson's turning and nodding to the two men behind him, and pulling open the door. The three of them disappearing inside.

It's not a big place. And it's not glamorous. Dingy, cold and unwelcoming. To be fair, it's been shut for six months, although it doesn't look much worse than it did when it was open. The bar directly in front of you. Tables to the left of the room. Stained benches under the stained window opposite the bar and beside the door. The kind of benches a hygienic person steers clear of.

Not that the layout or the decor matters to Patterson. It's the people. Two large men sitting on stools at the bar. Both staring at the door, obviously waiting for the new arrivals. Another large man standing in front of the benches. Patterson doesn't recognize any of them. Sitting at a table, off to the left, are the two men he does recognize. Marty Jones and Potty Cruickshank. Sitting side by side behind a table, their chairs facing the door. Both waiting for Patterson. Both looking rather pleased with themselves.

"Billy," Marty is saying loudly, "come over and join the conversation."

The invitation was to Patterson alone. Implied, an order for Griffiths and Summers to stay where they are. Show no hesitation. This was always supposed to be part of the plan. There's nothing here he ought to be concerned about. Unless some of these men belong to Potty. Then he has a lot to be worried about. That smile on Potty's flushed face is worthy of concern.

Patterson's across and pulling up a chair at the table. Sitting facing both men. Potty looks smug, as per usual. The biggest man in the collection business, pun intended, who didn't have to earn any of it. Was handed to him on a plate by his uncle. He looks comfortable where he is right now. Sitting next to Marty and opposite Patterson. Marty, he looks a little different. He has the ebullient, playful look of the young playboy. The look he used to have a lot. The look of a man playing a game he wrote the rules to. The look that had disappeared these last few months.

"Well, this is a good opportunity, wouldn't you both say?" Marty's saying. All the enthusiasm he can muster. "Let's talk business. Billy, why don't you start?"

That got a glance from Potty. Wasn't expecting Patterson to get the first go at this, but that's okay. Marty's been the perfect host since Potty arrived. Made it very clear that tonight they will wipe Patterson and his best boys from the equation. Let him have his little moment first.

"You killed Alan Bavidge," Patterson's saying to Potty. Got caught on the hop by Marty. Wasn't expecting to be thrown in quite like this. Should have had something smarter to say.

"Perhaps I did," Potty's saying. The fat man's sweating, but he still looks relaxed. "You understand the nature of this business, Billy. Sometimes these things have to be." Smiling, like he knows the words coming out of his mouth are bullshit. Like he knows it doesn't matter.

"The only thing that will pay for that is a 100 percent cut of your business," Patterson's saying. No idea if he's on solid ground here or not. Glanced briefly at Marty before he said it, but Marty was looking happily at Potty. Marty might be about to chuck him under a bus. Cut a better deal with Potty. That's what it feels like. If those guys behind him belong to Potty. Jesus, this could be it. His last words could be idiot bluster.

Potty's laughing. "A 100 percent cut, is it? That is terrific. Is that all you're looking for? Well, you should have asked sooner. Ha, that's terrific. Why don't I give you my firstborn as well, eh? Young man, you are in for one nasty surprise."

Potty's turning to look at Marty. Looking into the smiling face of Marty Jones. Marty raising his eyebrows slightly as he realizes both men are looking at him. Marty turning his head and looking at Patterson, still smiling happily.

"Surprises. Yeah. Thing is, Potty...You don't mind if I call you Potty, do you? Thing is, you did have his man killed. A good man, by all accounts. Did you no harm. That's what I heard, anyway."

Potty's laughing again, but he can't hide the nerves this time. The mood with Marty was so positive when he arrived. They chatted, they joked around. Marty still has that smile on his face. But there's something more sinister there now. He isn't laughing with Potty. He's laughing at him.

"Well, now, hold on," Potty's saying, trying to meet Marty's smile with one of his own. This might be some sort of game of Marty's. Lulling Patterson in. "The business is the business. These things have to be done." Turning now to face Patterson. "I apologize for your loss." Said with such sarcasm. Then looking back to Marty, who isn't smiling now at all.

Marty's shaking his head. A quick glance over Patterson's shoulder at the men there, then looking back at Potty. "I don't think sorry is going to be enough," Marty's saying. "See, we have a problem here. Three people. That's one too many. We need to reduce the numbers. Better for the industry as a whole if we do. I need someone who can take over my books while I focus on other things.

Someone I can trust." Trailing off and looking back and forth between Patterson and Potty.

Now Marty's laughing. Laughing enough to unsettle both Potty and Patterson. Both are looking at him, waiting for some explanation. Marty's getting serious now. This is fun for him. This position of power. He worked so long and so hard to get here. These two will never appreciate that. They both think he played his way to power. They'll never appreciate the shit he had to wade through. The bodies he had to climb over. Done a lot of things he's working hard to forget, and they'll never respect that. Oh well.

"There's a problem, Potty. A serious one. A lot of people don't like you. See, it's not just Billy here. He has every reason not to like you. Getting someone to kill his mate like that. That was too much. But other people don't like you either. Other people see you as part of the old guard. They don't like the old guard. Complacent old men who held everyone else back. Our organization has to show that it's still fresh. We got to make people see that we're the future. Sorry, big man, but you don't belong in the future."

Marty's getting up from his seat. Nodding to Patterson to follow him. They're both walking across the floor of the pub towards the door. Neither man looking back at Potty. The large man sitting on the small chair at the table. Not moving an inch. Watching them go. Watching as the two men who had been sitting at the bar move to block the exit. Potty watching them. Knowing this is the end for him.

Marty's politely holding the door open for Patterson, Griffiths, Summers and the guy who had been standing at the benches. Out onto the pavement. The guy from the benches is getting into the passenger seat of Potty's car.

"Don't worry about the driver," Marty's saying to Patterson. "He's bought and paid for."

Two men are getting out of a car that wasn't here when Patterson went in. One he doesn't immediately recognize. Late thirties, maybe early forties. That's a guess. That fellow's looking at the ground as he walks silently past them and into the pub. That's when the penny drops. Russell Conrad, freelance gunman. The bigger one behind him Patterson recognized instantly. That was Nate Colgan. Patterson's watching him go in. A few seconds after the door closes behind them, it opens again. The two men from the bar make their way out and over to the extra car. Colgan and Conrad must be the kill squad. No one else required.

"You could have warned me about the performance," Patterson's saying quietly.

Griffiths and Summers are making their way back to the car, mumbling to each other. If you listen carefully, you can just hear Griffiths use the words "fucking heart attack," but you'd have to be listening carefully. Doesn't want Marty to hear him complain.

"Yeah," Marty's saying. "I guess. But you didn't really think I would ditch you for him, did you? That reptile? The one who just went to Alex MacArthur for support?"

Patterson's shrugging. "It's an unpredictable business."

Marty's laughing. "It is that. We need to get together and discuss you taking control of my books. Not like they're all that huge, but still, best to be prepared. You might want to take one or two staff of mine on board as well. Although there's a few you can ditch. Good opportunity to clear out the shit. Have to move fast to grab some of Potty's business as well."

He's about to say more when his phone starts to ring. Taking it out of his pocket and looking at it. Frowning as he sees the name on the screen. "I better take this. I'll call you tomorrow morning, set a time for the meeting." Taking a few steps the other way up the street and answering the phone. A private conversation.

Patterson's made his way back to the car. Dropping into the passenger seat. Griffiths is starting the car, pulling out. Potty's car has gone, Marty's muscle are pulling away. Three men exhale at once, and then laugh a little. Tension making its happy departure.

"That was a bit more drama than it needed to be," Griffiths is saying.

"It was," Patterson's agreeing. But they got what they wanted. A deal with Marty that makes them the only collection business in the Jamieson organization. With Potty gone, they're very close to being the biggest in the city. But it's more than that. It's revenge for Alan. "It was worth it though," Patterson's saying quietly.

10

Instinct has carried Glass this far. No reason to rely on anything else now. There are a few places he could go, but he's settled on Mark Garvey. Nobody likes Garvey. A complete bastard and an absolute show-off, but he's the one Glass is going to. Not sure why, but instinct tells him that Garvey will take two hundred quid. Can't think of anyone else who would sell to him at low price.

It's not as though Glass knows a lot of places he could go for help. Spikey Tokely for one. But Spikey wouldn't help him for two hundred quid. Might not help him at all. You go to the person you're sure is willing to give you a hand. Someone who won't apply any standards to their sales, so long as the money is paid.

He's been walking for longer than he thought. Feels like hours, but it probably isn't. Lost track of time ages ago. Sitting in that pub. It's getting dark now. Must be early evening, he figures. Time doesn't matter. Just distance that matters. He's got a lot more walking to do, and the backs of his legs are already beginning to hurt. He's not used to this much effort. He'd rather be back at the flat, warm under the covers in bed. But that's not an option now.

That life, it's gone. All of it. You can't just take Ella out of his life and expect him to keep living the rest of it as normal. Doesn't work that way. In Glass's mind, all of it was tied together. One part of it falls, it all falls. Ella, the flat, the life. He'll never go back to any of it. Couldn't bring himself to. It's all gone now, and he has to move on. Has to move on by cutting all those ties to that life.

That's what he's doing now. Yeah, he's a bit drunk, so it sounds much nobler to him. But he knows it has to happen. What he's going to do tonight has to be done. Otherwise this follows him for the rest of his life, however long that happens to be.

He's nearly there now, which is a relief. He's feeling the tiredness of too little sleep and too much effort. He won't rest though. If he stops to rest, he won't start again. He knows that. Knows he's too much of a coward to motivate himself a second time. Now or never, as they say. So he's pushing on. Onto the right street. Knowing which house it is. Everyone knows where Mark Garvey lives, and what he sells from that house. As long as Garvey hasn't moved, he'll be okay. Now he remembers who pointed out Garvey's house to him. Told him it might be useful one day. Oliver Peterkinney. One of the last times they hung out together. That wasn't long after Peterkinney started working for Roy Bowles. Man, that feels like a long time ago now.

Glass is walking up to the door. Knocking twice and stepping back. He doesn't know how Garvey will react to this. Instinct said this was the guy to try. No better option. But it's late and he might not react well to a drunk young man turning up on his doorstep. But then, how else does a man like him make a living?

The door's opening. Garvey looking back at him. A deep frown because he doesn't immediately recognize the young man before him. Then a creeping recognition, although he's still not quite sure.

"I need to buy a gun from you," Glass is saying.

Garvey's leaning his head out the door and looking up and down the street. Letting Glass know that that's not the sort of sentence you blurt out on a man's doorstep. "That right?" he's saying.

"Yeah, but I don't have much money. But I need it. I really do. I have two hundred quid."

Garvey's snorting. "I think you came to the wrong house, kid," he's saying, and moving to close the door.

"Please. They killed my girlfriend last night. I need that gun. They killed her and I need the gun."

Garvey's looking down at him. Pausing. Thinking this through. Some dumb emotional kid running round with one of his guns is usually bad news. Sort of thing he's careful to avoid. Only sell to people you trust. People who know how to use and then safely get rid of a gun. Only sell to people you're sure won't be caught and blab about where they got the gun they were caught with. But chances come along. The opportunity to ingratiate. You don't pass that up.

"Hold on there. I'll be back in a couple of minutes," Garvey's saying. Closing the front door and bounding upstairs to the spare room. Getting one of his mobiles out from the drawer in his desk and ringing the only number stored on it.

Takes a while for Marty to answer it. Must be busy. Always busy these days. Answering the phone with a curt hello. Sounds like he's outside; there's a car driving past.

"Marty, Mark Garvey. Listen, I got a kid at the door you might be interested in. The Glass kid. Remember him? Wasn't he pally with that Peterkinney boy you were after?" Marty told Garvey the story at a party. How Peterkinney screwed him over. His way of making sure Garvey knew that Peterkinney was persona non grata. That any man who sold him weapons would be an enemy of Marty's.

"He was. What does he want?"

"Says someone killed his girlfriend last night. Looking for a gun he can't afford. Revenge, probably."

There's a pause while Marty thinks about it. Garvey allowing him the time to work it out. If it was one of Marty's boys that killed the girl then this is a warning. Letting him know that Glass is on the prowl. If it wasn't one of Marty's then this might be an opportunity for him. Let Glass cause problems for someone else.

"Sell him the piece. I'll make up the difference."

"You don't need to do that, Marty. Just thought I'd clear it with you first. I'll catch up with you sometime," he's saying. His way of saying that he's doing Marty a favor here and that he expects something in return.

"Sure," Marty's saying, and hanging up. Obviously it's not one of Marty's boys that did the deed then.

Garvey's out into the corridor and pulling open a cupboard door. Opening a suitcase on the floor and taking a small handgun from the inside lining. He doesn't make a fantastic effort to hide his stock. If the police come calling, they'll turn the place upside down anyway. No such thing as a good hiding place. You make a little bit of effort to hide the stuff, but you're just inconveniencing yourself to do more.

He's wrapped his hand in a cloth before he handles the gun. Now he's stuffing it into one of the large Jiffy bags he keeps in the cupboard. Making his way quickly downstairs. Opening the front door. Glass is still there. Looks like he hasn't moved an inch. Perfectly still and perfectly miserable.

"Let's see your money," Garvey's saying quietly.

Glass is reaching into his pocket and pulling out a bundle of notes. Some twenty-pound notes, some ten, some five. Always a sign that the person wasn't prepared for the purchase. That this is a rush job, bringing together any note they can lay their hands on. Garvey's reaching out and taking it, handing the Jiffy bag to Glass.

"It's loaded," Garvey is telling him. "If you get caught with it, you do not tell anyone where you got it from. You got that?"

But Glass has already turned away and is walking down the front path to the gate. No desire to stay and chat. No desire to stay and hear a rule book he already knows. He'll never talk to anyone about the gun. Never would. He's not even thinking about it. Just walking along the street with the Jiffy bag in his hand for all to see. He knows exactly where he's going now.

11

Arnie's waited and waited. Hoping that Glass will come back to the flat of his own free will. He wasn't emotional when he left. Just worried about the police coming to talk to him. Something they will eventually do and something Glass will have to face. Needs time to get used to that idea. Just wait and the boy will come back.

Sitting in the flat, waiting for the phone to ring. Waiting for the police to demand some answers. They should have called by now. Maybe they didn't think to ask the receptionist at the hospital. Well, if they're that desperate they'll put out some sort of appeal. Arnie worried about what Glass will tell them. What moronic act of self-sabotage he might be drawn into. But that's not the only worry.

What will Arnie tell them? They'll question him too. They're not stupid. Well, the ones that ask the important questions aren't. They'll spot the connection to Oliver. They'll begin to piece it together. Sitting in his armchair, wishing there were other people in his life. Sixty-four years old and he has so few people to care for. Even fewer who care about him. It would help if there was someone else he could talk to. Tell them about this. A different perspective. But there's nobody. There's Arnie, there's Glass and there's Oliver, and that's the end of it.

It's well past teatime. Getting dark out there. A silent day. No Glass. No police. He wants to do something. Needs to do something. Needs to go and find Glass. He could be sitting in a police station right now. Might have gone straight there in the morning and started talking. Arnie's phoning Glass's mobile. It's ringing, but there's no answer. Calling again and being ignored a second time.

It would be switched off if he was in a police station. A deep breath. Think about it. Where would he have gone? An emotional boy, who just lost his wee girlfriend. He would have gone back to their flat. That's an obvious answer. He wanted to be away from everyone. Away from the world, and living in silence. His own flat would be a good place to do that. Time of crisis, flee for home. The right place to check first.

Going to his neighbor's flat first. He could take the bus, but there's a feeling of urgency settling in his guts. Wherever Glass is, Arnie wants to be there fast. If the kid doesn't know what he's doing, then he has to be stopped from doing it. His neighbor is still willing to lend the car. The more Arnie asks, the less willing he is, but Arnie's built up a decent store of goodwill.

Driving through the city, but the going is slow. End of the working day. Everyone eager to get away from whatever place they call work. Not all so eager to get to whatever place they call home. Arnie's struggling to get through the traffic. Not getting impatient though. Glass has had hours of a head start. Could be anywhere he wants to be at this point.

Parking outside the block and going inside. Up the stairs and along to the front door. The door of the next flat is wide open, although there's nobody there. Arnie's knocking on Glass's door. Standing back and waiting.

"Not in," a voice is saying gruffly to him.

Arnie's looking to his right. A man of roughly his own age is now standing in the open doorway of the neighboring flat. Stocky, wearing a T-shirt and tracksuit bottoms. Lighting a cigarette, which is presumably the reason he's standing in the corridor.

"Has he been here today, do you know?"

"Uh-huh. Here a while ago. Came and went... The girl died."

"I know," Arnie's nodding. Not sure whether this man has any idea who he is, or whether he's just making bad conversation. "You don't know where he was going?"

"No. Came and went. Didn't have anything with him when he left…He do it?"

Arnie's looking at the man. Angrier than he should be. Hardly a surprise that people are speculating on who killed Ella. Hardly a surprise that people want to point the finger at Glass. He's an obvious target. A young man with no job and known connections to criminals. Too easy a target to miss.

"No, he did not," Arnie's saying. Letting the anger rumble out. Turning and walking back along the corridor, leaving the neighbor to raise his eyebrows in barely bothered response.

Down the stairs and back out to the car. Glass came to the flat and then left. Why would he come to the flat? Maybe to collect something. Well, that doesn't take a lot of working out. What would he have in the flat? A weapon? No. Any weapon in the flat the police would have taken. Money, maybe. Money to drink. Money for drugs. Or money for a weapon, if you want to wake up and get real here.

Arnie's standing beside the car, hands on the roof. Take a deep breath. Think clearly. Would Glass do it? He's come to think of him as such a likable boy. Always thought he was a loser when he was pals with Oliver. Thought he was a bad influence and a waster. Got to know him and decided that he was a waster, but one that could be saved. A goof with a good heart. And he's tricked himself into thinking of Glass that way ever since.

But he's thinking back to that night when Glass turned up at the flat. Thinking of that conversation. He can be as likable as he wants, but Alex Glass has killed before. Killed because he was in debt and that was his way of getting out. Essentially, killed for money. This isn't money. This is something more powerful. He could do it again. Don't kid yourself, he could do it again.

Arnie's getting into the car. Heading for Peterkinney's flat, cursing himself for not going there first. Because he's a coward. That's what he's telling himself. He's a coward, and if he wasn't, he would have gone to Oliver's flat first. Even just to warn him. But he warned him last night. Told him what had happened. That was a warning. Ah, stop trying to persuade yourself that you've done enough. Stop hoping that the worst-case scenario won't play out. You're going to get what you deserve, and you deserve the worst.

He's turning onto the street where Oliver lives. No sign of drama at first, but as he pulls to a stop outside the building he can see something. People on the street. The front door to the building wide open. Arnie's jumping out of the car, leaving the keys in the ignition. Running to the steps at the front of the building. There are four or five respectable-looking people standing nervously around, some in their nightclothes. Not the sort of people to be seen in public in their nightclothes unless they had a very serious reason.

"You shouldn't go in there," one of them is shouting at Arnie as he bounds past. Which is when Arnie knows he should go in. Knows he should have been here hours ago.

He's at the top of the stairs, struggling to catch his breath. He can see the door of Oliver's flat, ajar. Something lying on the floor outside the door. Looks like a big envelope. He's walking slowly towards the door when he hears the bang. A single gunshot, muffled and shocking. Arnie's stopped. Standing in the corridor, waiting for something else to happen. Taking baby steps towards the front door. Pushing it open. Nothing in the corridor before him. Walking slowly forwards. Pushing open the door to the kitchen, praying that his instincts are wrong.

12

Glass's legs are aching now. Walking through the streets with the Jiffy bag in his hand. Nobody cares. Nobody paying him attention. Just some young guy wandering the streets with a large padded envelope. Why should anyone care about that? There are stranger things to see in this city at this hour. Glass can walk without raising an eyebrow, even if he's walking unsteadily. Weaving a little, on autopilot.

He bumped into a woman. She said something to him, shoved him sideways. He said nothing. Kept on walking. Doesn't want to be stopped by her or by anyone. It has to be tonight. There won't be a second chance. If he gets into an argument with someone, they'll stop him. Maybe call the police, and then it'll never happen. He'll never be able to finish this. Never be able to give this the ending it needs.

Onto the right street. He knows it. Ewan Drummond told him where the building was, one night in a pub. Ewan seemed impressed. Been along here a few times in the last few months, just to see. See where his mate ended up. See what he left the rest of them behind for. Nice street. Nice buildings. Seems like it would have been worth leaving a lot behind for. The sort of place he always saw himself being in the future. Him and Ella. Maybe with kids. Both making good money in jobs they didn't have to be ashamed of. With loads of friends. This was where he saw it ending up. It started with the fun lifestyle they had in the beginning. It ended with the sort of life you live on a street like this. It was the bit in the middle that he never figured out. How do you get from one to the other?

Walking up the steps to the front door. Names next to numbers next to buttons. O. Peterkinney. Pressing the buzzer and waiting. It's dark now. Must be nighttime. Wait a little longer than you usually would before you press the buzzer again.

A crackle. A voice. "Yes?"

Doesn't know what to say. Hadn't thought this far ahead. "It's Alex," he's saying in response.

There's a long pause before Peterkinney's voice comes back at him. "It's late."

"I know. But…but we need to talk. We do, don't we?"

There's a pause. Another long one. Peterkinney is getting a lot of practice at these. "Come up," he's saying, and the buzzer on the door goes.

Glass is pushing his way inside. Out of the cold and into the building. He doesn't know where in the building the flat is. Walking along the short corridor and looking at the numbers on the doors. Neither of these. Turning back and going up the stairs. Slowly. By the time he's reached the top of the stairs, Peterkinney has opened his front door. Standing in the corridor waiting for him, wondering what's taking so long. The conversation with his grandfather was tough. This will be worse. Hurry it up, get it over.

Watching Glass walking the few steps from the top of the stairs and resisting the urge to shake his head. He looks a mess. Not just rough, but like he's aged a decade. Okay, sure, he's had a tough day or two. But there's something else. He looks wasted. Like he's staring just off-center. He's got a big padded envelope in his hand. Carrying something around. Probably something belonging to Ella. Pictures, Peterkinney's betting. This is going to be one of those tearful look-at-what-you've-destroyed conversations. Glass has had a breakdown, Peterkinney's sure.

"Alex. You want to come in?" Better to have this conversation away from the neighbors. There might be shouting. There'll almost certainly be crying on Glass's part. He looks halfway to tears already, and they haven't started yet.

"I didn't want to do this, Oliver," Glass is saying and shaking his head.

Pitiful. "All right, okay. It's been tough, I know. Why don't you come in, we'll talk about it." Doesn't really want this wreck in his flat, but it's the only option. He can talk to him. Maybe win him round. Make sure he leaves here with the right message to tell the police next time they're talking to him. He's smarter than Glass. He can get him under control.

But Glass isn't moving to come into the flat. He's still standing there, looking at Peterkinney. Then, like he's just realized he still has it, looking down at the Jiffy bag. Holding it in front of him and stuffing his free hand inside. Great, here come the photos or some other trinket of the past. Something that's supposed to provoke guilt and regret. Something that's supposed to drag Peterkinney down to Glass's emotional level.

Glass is pulling out the gun, holding it in front of himself for a second. Then dropping the Jiffy bag on the floor and pointing the gun at Peterkinney. Weird thing is, as soon as Peterkinney sees the gun, he's thinking about the Jiffy bag. He knows that the gun must have come from Mark Garvey. He's the one who uses those padded envelopes rather than a carrier bag. Takes him a few more seconds to realize that an emotional Glass is pointing a gun at him. He just doesn't associate Glass with danger.

"Come off it, Alex. Look, come in, we'll talk, okay. This? This isn't the right way to do this. Come in, okay. We can talk."

Glass taking a step towards him, but not lowering the gun. He's not following Peterkinney's instructions; he's pushing him backwards with the point of the gun. Trying to take control of the situation. Neither of them spotting the neighbor who's emerged at the top of the stairs. He's seen the gun. The Good Samaritan who'll get everyone out of the building. Peterkinney's stepping back, leaving the door open for Glass to follow him in. Still doesn't feel dangerous. After all, it's Alex Glass. His old mate. He's harmless. He can be talked round.

"Inside. Go on," Glass is saying, nodding in the direction of the first door he sees. The kitchen. Peterkinney's going slowly. Glass trying to shove the front door shut behind him, but not closing it all the way. Draft excluder at the bottom always catches on the carpet. You have to give it a good shove, which Glass hasn't. Doesn't seem to care. Walking along the corridor, gun still raised.

Peterkinney's walked backwards into the kitchen. Trying to work out how to get the gun away from Glass. Glass might be harmless, but the gun isn't. Only takes one slip and this goes south fast. He's obviously emotional. Went and got a gun and wants to show it off. Wants to scare Peterkinney. Fine, scare away. That's a reasonable punishment for the suffering Glass is going through. But let's get that gun out of emotional hands as quickly as possible.

"I heard what happened to Ella," Peterkinney's saying. "I really am sorry, Alex; I know how much she meant to you."

That was supposed to calm things down, but it hasn't. It's gotten an angry reaction. A frown from Glass and the gun raised to point at Peterkinney's head. Peterkinney's taking an extra backward step. Raising both hands.

"Okay, look, why don't you tell me what you want to say. You have something to say, right? Well, you go ahead and say it."

Glass hadn't thought this far ahead. There was no plan to say something. Just to shoot. But he does want to talk. Suddenly, for no good reason, he wants to talk. He wants to get it out before it's too late.

"You don't care what I have to say," Glass is saying. "You just want to delay me. You want to sucker me into giving up the gun. I'm not stupid, Oliver. I'm not one of your dumb muscle. You remember when we met? I was the one that led the way. You were all quiet. Riding along on my coattails. I was the one got you into this business. My own fault. But I got you in, because you didn't have the guts to get yourself in. Have the guts to make money from other people's effort, yeah. Never the guts to do it yourself. I did it. I was always the one with the guts."

"Okay. Yeah, you're right. You are. Nobody's saying you don't have guts, Alex, you do."

"Shut up!" Shouted this time. Fed up of hearing that smug voice coming back at him. Telling him what he wants to hear without any genuine meaning. "You lost it, Oliver. You got so far away from that guy you used to be. You ended up killing Ella."

"I didn't kill her, Alex. Honestly, I didn't."

"You did," Glass is saying sadly. Lowering the gun half an inch. "You killed her. I killed someone too. Yeah. Know what? It's horrible. Worst thing you can do. It is. It's horrible. And when you do it, you have to pay a price. That's how it should be."

He hasn't lowered the gun much, but it's enough to be a temptation. Enough that an impatient man would make a grab. Peterkinney's taking two steps forwards. Looking to grab the gun, pull it away. Thinking that Glass is just too emotional to stop him. But he isn't.

Glass was waiting for it. Knew that Peterkinney would be arrogant enough to try something like this. Thinking he could take the gun from Glass. Peterkinney's made two steps, but not a third. One shot, and he's falling backwards. It was loud. The shock of it has knocked Glass back a step. A tingling pain in his hands. Watching Peterkinney tumble to the kitchen floor. Holding his hands up to his chest. Breathing so loudly, trying to catch his breath.

Glass is walking towards him. You can see the blood spread out on his shirt, through his fingers. Glass is standing over him, looking down. Waiting for Peterkinney to look at him. Waiting to catch his eye. This matters. It matters because he can't stop thinking of what was going through Ella's mind when she died. The confusion and the fear. Knowing she couldn't defend herself. Peterkinney has to feel that.

Takes the better part of ten seconds for Peterkinney to look up. To look him in the eye. Glass is pointing the gun again. This time at Peterkinney's head. This time he pulls the trigger twice. There's no movement from Peterkinney. No reaction. Silence and stillness.

Glass is ignoring the sound of the neighbors shouting in the street. Ignoring everything. He isn't finished here. If he leaves this flat, he'll never finish this. Not the way it ought to finish. He won't move another step.

The horrible thing, what really gets to him now, is that this didn't feel bad. Didn't feel good either, but it didn't feel as bad as killing Bavidge. This should be worse. His friend. But it isn't. It's nothing. Maybe because he knows the ending. Ella gone. Peterkinney gone. The end of the life he thought he would have. The only life he wanted to live. Raising the gun and awkwardly putting the end of the barrel in his mouth. A little fumble. Pulling the trigger.

ABOUT THE AUTHOR

Malcolm Mackay was born and grew up in Stornoway, where he still lives. His much-lauded Glasgow-set novels have won the Crime Thriller Book Club Best Read award and the Deanston Scottish Crime Book of the Year Award, and have been short-listed for the CWA John Creasey (New Blood) Dagger and the Scottish First Book of the Year Award. *The Night the Rich Men Burned* is Malcolm Mackay's fourth novel.

MULHOLLAND BOOKS

You won't be able to put down these Mulholland Books.

CLOSE YOUR EYES *by Michael Robotham*

THE EXILED *by Christopher Charles*

UNDERGROUND AIRLINES *by Ben H. Winters*

SEAL TEAM SIX: HUNT THE DRAGON *by Don Mann and Ralph Pezzullo*

THE SECOND GIRL *by David Swinson*

WE WERE KINGS *by Thomas O'Malley, Douglas Graham Purdy*

THE AMATEUR'S HOUR *by Christopher Reich*

REVOLVER *by Duane Swierczynski*

SERPENTS IN THE COLD *by Thomas O'Malley, Douglas Graham Purdy*

WHEN WE WERE ANIMALS *by Joshua Gaylord*

THE INSECT FARM *by Stuart Prebble*

CROOKED *by Austin Grossman*

ZOO CITY *by Lauren Beukes*

MOXYLAND *by Lauren Beukes*

Visit mulhollandbooks.com for
your daily suspense fix.

Download the FREE Mulholland Books app.